MW00947741

We the Women Series

My Independence

BEVERLY JANE

Copyright © 2021 Beverly Jane
All rights reserved
First Edition

Fulton Books, Inc.
Meadville, PA

Published by Fulton Books 2021

ISBN 978-1-63860-360-3 (paperback)
ISBN 978-1-63860-361-0 (digital)

Printed in the United States of America

This book is dedicated to the most important and strongest woman I have ever known, my mother, Joyce Gutekunst. Her love for her family provided her with the courage to move heaven and earth for their happiness. Though she was in pain for over twenty years from cancer, she didn't allow it to show, and her priorities were first and foremost on the needs of those around her. Even in the end, she was fighting to stay with us.

Although she started to read my book, she never did see the finished product.

May everyone who decides to pick up this book find the strength and courage to keep their heads held high and moving forward to the next good thing. You will find it if you keep looking.

I love and miss you with all my heart.

Until we meet again!

Chapter 1

A New Begining

Life in December 1776 for the Continental Army was easy to explain when they made camp in Morrisville, Pennsylvania. HARDSHIP. There was nothing else to say about it. Congress did not believe the army was out of supplies so refused to send the provisions so desperately needed. However, in this once quiet town, Dr. Jonathan and Margaret Madder saw the plight of the army firsthand. Men starved so severely you can see their bones under their tattered uniforms. The men lucky enough to be wearing a coat kept pulling up the shoulders as it would fall right off their bodies. They saw the blood trails from the feet of the men without boots trying to walk in the snow with only cloth wrappings. It looked like the walking dead, and the war was already over, but someone forgot to tell these men. Both Dr. Jonathan and Margaret started to assist the army's medical team and help the sick and wounded pouring in from New Jersey.

A few nights later, Dr. Madder was looking over the notes of the day while Margaret was quietly knitting socks for the troops. They were startled by a soft knock at the door followed by a thud. Dr. Madder whispered to his wife to stay put, reached for the handgun on the table next to him, and made for the door. In a rough voice, he barked, "Who goes there?"

A small mouse-like whispered plea came from the other side of the door. "Please, sir, help…" At this last word, her voice faded into silence. Obviously, a young lady in distress was calling at this late hour.

Margaret came to her husband's side as he opened the door to reveal a dark-haired figure in a ball in their entranceway. The far too small quilt wrapped tightly around her body, trying to protect her from the snow and chill of the evening. She only had an evening gown on beneath her quilt. She didn't even have shoes to protect her feet from the frozen ground.

Dr. Madder quickly picked her up and brought her into the house. They had a small room with a fireplace and bed for emergencies such as these. They placed the girl on the bed to warm up and assess what happened. At this point, they were able to tell that she was around eighteen to nineteen years of age with a fair complexion. Margaret retreated from the room to get more suitable clothing and warm water for the girl. When she returned, Dr. Madder went to gather blankets while Margaret helped the girl get cleaned up and changed. Overcome by the cold, the girl was making small incoherent noises as she swayed side to side. The doctor came back and started to examine her to see the extent of the damage.

"Luckily, it doesn't look like frostbite took hold," he said. "Her feet need to be wrapped and heal, but I believe all she needs right now is to warm up and rest. God was definitely with her tonight."

The following morning Margaret went to check in on the young woman. At the sound of the door opening, the girl sat straight up and looked around, fear overwhelming her. "Where am I? Who are you? Leave me alone." This sound was much more assertive than the voice she called with the prior evening.

The first thing Margaret noticed, however, was her piercing blue eyes. Then Margaret, trying to calm her down, said, "Good morning, dear! You are safe in Dr. Madder's home. I am his wife, Margaret." She moved closer to the new patient and asked, "What is your name, dear?"

In a defiant manner, the girl replied much more militarily than she should, "I pray the only name I can provide is Sara." Since General Washington was now in town and had a price on his head, any newcomer was looked upon with caution.

"Well then, Sara, how are you feeling? Are you in need of anything, breakfast or more blankets maybe?" Margaret replied with some caution in her voice.

Sara folded her hands on her lap and replied, "No, thank you, I am well."

Feeling a little put off, Margaret answered, "Well, when you finally come around to the hunger I am sure you are feeling, I will not be making a second meal, so yours shall be cold." She turned to go in a bit of a huff; she finished with "Dr. Madder will be in to see you shortly" and left, closing the door a little harder then she should have.

"Ungrateful little wench," Margaret snapped as she entered the dining room. Her husband was at the table, drinking coffee and coughed at her entrance. "Calling on us late in the evening, then having the gall to act as I am intruding on her!"

"Ah, dear," Jonathan quietly stated, "you were up far too late and haven't had breakfast yet. I am sure once she realizes where she is and remembers what happened last night, she will be more agreeable."

With a deep sigh, Margaret replied, ashamed, "Yes, she must have gone through something horrible to end up here in that state last night. I will remember myself, my dear!"

Their servant, June, had finished cooking the eggs she picked fresh that morning from the henhouse, but that was the extent of the meal. The food shortage was being felt at all levels. Jonathan, however, said, "*Ah*, what a feast you again created out of the meagerness of nothing, June. How do you do it?"

With a sideways glance and smile, June replied, "You jest me, sir. I needs to beg your pardon for the smallness of your breakfast with the fullness of your day."

At that, the doctor finished his eggs, got up to see his patient, and started to walk out.

Martha called to him, "Oh yeah, she said her name is Sara."

When Margaret left her side, Sara looked around and tried to recall the events of the last twenty-four hours. Her belly growled in defiance to her answer to Margaret. Quietly she said to the noise, "*Shh*, we mustn't allow these people to know we need sustenance.

I do not know yet who took us in, and if they are the enemy, my head is worth much more than your emptiness." A knock at the door startled her, but she did not respond. Her mind challenged herself. "Name only, no information…Name only, no information…Father, I will not disappoint you."

"Hello there," called Dr. Madder, "are you decent?" Sara kept quiet. "Sara, I will enter either way. I just want to give you the opportunity to cover yourself."

"I am covered," Sara finally gave a quiet response.

The doctor entered the room and smiled. "Oh, there you are. I thought you left us already," he said, trying comedy. With a stoic face, Sara just looked at the doctor in another moment of silence. "At some point, I will need a response if I am going to treat you, my dear," Jonathan stated. "But for now, I believe some courtesy is in order." Jonathan checked Sara's fingertips to make sure his first diagnosis of no frostbite still was true this morning. Then he turned to her feet that were slashed. He applied a salve of his own creation to her feet and wrapped them with a cloth. "Well, if you have nothing to say, I will attend the soldiers. I will look in on you again this evening."

As the doctor left the room, Sara's eyes turned toward the window. *What camp am I in?* she thought to herself. She couldn't see anything from her vantage point on the bed, so slowly she set her feet upon the ground. At once she winced! *I can do this*, she kept telling herself, *I must do this!* She stood for a moment and fell to the floor with a crashing noise.

Jonathan reentered the room, followed by Margaret. Sara was facedown on the floor with fresh blood showing on her newly bandaged feet. The doctor moved toward her, saying, "Walking is not the best-prescribed medicine in your condition, madam!" As he reached her, she looked up to him, her blue eyes tearing up from the pain but did not make a noise. "What is it you wish to see?" he said patiently. "How can I help you? All you need to do is ask, my dear."

"The window, I want to look outside," she said quietly.

With ease, he picked her up and allowed her to look. She saw a snow- and mud-covered street with the river on the other side. There were soldiers walking up and down the street, all wearing blue uniforms. She turned to Jonathan and asked, "Sir, please, where am I?"

"You don't know, little lady? You are in Morrisville," he said with a smile, walking her back to bed.

"And this army camp, it is for the cause, am I correct?" she asked, a little timid.

"Why, yes, it is," he answered her.

"Are you helping these soldiers?" she questioned.

"Seems you have found your tongue. Well, here in town, you will find division about this war, but we are Patriots," Jonathan answered.

"I made it, thank God, I made it," she said graciously. She took one last look at him, then closed her eyes in peace.

"I think you will find her a bit more agreeable now, my love," Jonathan said to Margaret as she moved from the doorway, letting him pass. "I have a feeling she thought we were Tories!" He picked up his coat, put it on, grabbed his medical bag, and kissed her goodbye. "I shall be back this evening," he said sadly as he started toward the door. He opened the door and, with a pause, took a deep breath to prepare for the day and stepped outside.

During the next three hours, Margaret and June took turns looking in on Sara. "I do believe him right again," Margaret said to June. "I do think when she wakes, as long as she remembers where she is, she will be more agreeable."

"Yes, ma'am, and I got her evening gown all cleaned up," June replied as she handed Margaret the outfit.

Looking at the gown, Margaret squealed, "My God, this is from Paris. I haven't seen one of these in years."

"Ya think she's from a wealthy family?" June questioned.

"Must be with this item," Margaret said as she drifted into a long-past memory. With a jolt, she came back to the present and returned the item to Sara's room. Seeing Sara awake, Margaret said, "Well, hello, my dear, feeling better now?"

Feeling a little safer with Margaret, Sara said, "Madam, I must beg your pardon and offer my sincerest apologies for my behavior this morning. I didn't realize I was with Patriots and provided you with a lack of respect you deserve."

Margaret smiled and said, "With the evening you had, don't pay it any mind, my dear." Trying to keep this line of questioning going, she then asked Sara what happened.

Sara looked down into her hands, trying very hard to keep herself composed. She took a deep breath and said quietly, "I wish to go over my story only once and would very much like General Washington to be here when I do, as it pertains to him and his army."

Margaret was taken aback by this. "As much as I wish I could walk up to the general and invite him to dinner, he is a very busy man. I couldn't get close enough to invite him!"

"Please, madam, if you send him a letter that Sara Weinstein, daughter of General George Weinstein, is here injured and wishes to speak with him," Sara said in a heartbroken voice.

Margaret gave a small gasp when Sara told her who she was. "So that is who you are! I understand the secrecy now," she said.

General Weinstein was an important member of the British army during the French and Indian War and even helped train militia for the colonies. However, when the Revolutionary War began, he became a general for the Continental Army and considered a traitor. The price on his head was close to General Washington's.

"I will send a message to him at once, but I can't promise a response," Margaret replied a bit in awe. "As for now, do you wish for a stew? I can have June start something right away."

Sara looked down, a bit ashamed of the offer, as she knew all too well the state of the men not far off. "I am a bit hungry, but please do not go out of your way for me. Anything you have would be sufficient, thank you."

As Margaret suspected, two days went by before receiving a return response from General Washington.

To Mrs. Margaret Madder,

I regret to inform you that I did not receive your letter of request in a sufficient time frame.

*However, I do wish to call upon your family
and Sara at my earliest convenience. To this, my
wife and I shall be there tomorrow afternoon if that
is sufficient with you? Please advise my aid-de-camp
of your answer.*

Thank you,
G. Washington

Reading the note twice to make sure she read it correctly, she told the young soldier in front of her that she will be happy to receive the general and his wife for the afternoon meal.

June became very busy cleaning up the house and doing whatever Margaret wanted. Sara would slowly leave her room and try to help since she requested the presence of the general. However, Margaret would not allow her to. She just said that she and June had everything under control. The two ladies decided on what meal to make that was both enough food and worthy of the general. The doctor was able to kill a couple of rabbits while June worked her magic to procure carrots, potatoes, celery, and everything else she needed to put on a stew with a loaf of bread. They were only able to get one bottle of mediocre wine and hoped it would be sufficient.

The house started to get the aroma of the meal when a knock came on the door. Dr. Madder hurried to and opened it up and revealed the aide-de-camp. "The general wishes to convey his apologies for his lateness. Pressing matters came up, but he will be along as soon as possible," the aide said in a cracked voice showing his young age. He then tipped his hat, turned around, and walked away.

"Well then, let's not waste this meal, letting it go cold," Margaret replied unapprovingly.

"You know the general is a busy man right now, Margaret. Let's give him a bit of time, we owe him that much," Dr. Madder pleaded.

"I will see to Sara," she continued as she turned to the closed door to Sara's room. She knocked and entered the room, where she found Sara knitting and mending socks. "Well, you have been busy," Margaret said, looking at the sight of the pile next to the bed.

"Well, you wouldn't let me help with the house. Besides, it is nothing compared to what these men must endure," Sara stated, wiggling her feet in acknowledgment.

"Speaking of that, my dear, do you feel well enough to join us at the table?" Margaret asked rather motherly. It seemed her mood toward Sara changed as she had been caring for her.

"Wait, is General Washington here? I thought he was going to join us?" asked Sara.

"He will be along as soon as his business is taken care of," Margaret answered. "But as your walking is still a bit staggered, I figured we could get started!" she answered. At this point, Sara felt Margaret wanted to help more than she needed but allowed the guidance. "Slowly, my dear," Margaret protested as Sara started walking faster than she would have liked. Sara sighed but obliged and slowed her pace. Finally, they made their way to the table, and Sara sat down in the chair Margaret steered her to.

"Please, may I help tonight?" Sara questioned a little impatiently.

"You just sit there and heal, little one, we can set the table," Margaret replied.

Sara did not like the idea of slavery and grumbled at seeing June doing everything once again. She, however, was a guest in this house, so she kept quiet.

When everything was out, another knock came on the door. "Ah, General Washington, and you must be Mrs. Washington," the ladies heard Jonathan say from the other room.

"Oh dear, I hope I remember how to do this," Margaret mumbled under her breath as she stood up and went to greet the guests. "General and Mrs. Washington, welcome to our home," Margaret said in an aristocratic manner, and Sara knew it would be followed by a proper curtsey.

"I guess she remembered," Sara giggled to June, getting her to join. They were still smiling as Dr. Johnathan and Margaret showed their guest into the dining room.

Even though it was midday when General Washington entered the room, it seemed to become even brighter. This man's presence just commands a room. However, his gaze and attention were on

Sara. As she started to rise to greet him, he protested, "Please do not injure yourself further, my child," he said, concerned, looking at her. "I am sorry I was not able to join you earlier. I dare say, where is your father? I sent a request for him."

At that, Sara's eyes dropped to the floor, and a tear started to well up within them. Seeing this response, Martha Washington spoke up, "Ah, dear, we can speak of these things after the meal. It smells wonderful here, Mrs. Madder."

Sara wiped the tears away, and everyone took a seat. Dr. Madder said grace, and they all started to eat. June was the only one not at the table and made sure everything remained just right as she ate in the next room.

"I hear you have been helping the doctors with my men, thank you, sir," Mr. Washington said.

"It is you and your men who deserve our thanks, General," Dr. Madder replied.

As Dr. Madder talked to General Washington about the medical needs of the men, the ladies were talking about who they knew in society and how to influence help for the men. Sara decided to just sit back and listen to what everyone else had to say.

At the end of the meal, they started getting up, but General Washington refused to allow Sara to rise. He picked her up and carried her to the sitting room. She did not protest and put her arms around him in a warm embrace. They all filed in behind him, taking a seat. Even June sat in the corner with no objections. They were all very eager to hear the story Sara was about to tell!

As everyone waited quietly, Sara took a deep breath and began her tale. "I was again traveling with my father as I did during the Seven Years' War, this time old enough to help with the sick and wounded men while he commended. He received your orders to head to Fort Mifflin to help recruit and train more men, General. We decided to rendezvous with our family in Princeton for a night, not realizing the British were no longer in New York and moving south. We had the misfortune of not having you pass through Princeton and get word that we were about to be attacked. That evening, as they stormed through town, they went after anyone they thought was a Patriot. My parents were out on the street when the redcoats came. He was recognized at once and shot, followed by my stepmother. Then they rounded up the rest of the family and had them shot as well. Finally, those lobsterbacks torched our home. I was able to conceal my location and scrambled out the back window and into the shadows before the house was engulfed. I could hear them laughing while families screamed and scattered."

She paused and took a deep breath before continuing. "I kept to the darkness, making my way through the forest. I knew from the letter about Fort Mifflin that you would have allies there, so I decided to head there. When I was on the outskirts of Trenton, I noticed General Howe leading his British army back north. He decided to leave Trenton to the Hessians. I was able to tie some logs together with my dress and started to cross the Delaware. My boots became stuck in the shoreline, and I needed to abandon them, hearing the guards walking my way. When I came ashore, I was so cold. I went to the first house I saw. I remember knocking, and then it all went dark."

At this point, hot tears were running down Sara's face. Martha moved next to Sara and just held her with tears in her eyes as well. This was the first time Sara allowed herself to feel the events, and her heart felt like it was being ripped from her chest.

There were two to three minutes of quiet before anyone made a noise. Dr. Madder was the first to talk. "I do believe the angels were walking with you. To get here from Princeton in these temperatures plus crossing the river on a makeshift raft without getting frostbit. It is just remarkable."

General Washington was the next to talk. "My courageous girl, I am so sorry to hear what happened. Had I only known you were in Princeton when we marched to the river, I could have—"

At that, Sara interrupted him, looking directly into his eyes. "I do not hold you to blame, sir. We all knew the risks when joining this fight. I just pray when I am well enough you will allow me to continue my service to the men."

With the closeness felt in the room, it was easy to tell Sara and the Washingtons have known each other for a while.

"And you're sure about General Howe going north?" General Washington asked.

"Yes, sir! Very sure!" Sara replied sternly.

Then General Washington changed the conversation. "Ever since I met your father, you were there—inseparable! I remember you two visiting Martha and myself at Mt. Vernon. Your father talking about training the militia and you would pick up the gun and fire away," Washington said with a smile. "The men just adored you, and the ladies couldn't get enough of you. There was always a special place in your heart for the men," Washington said, looking upon her longingly. "When you are in better standings, we will discuss your service." Then he paused and finally said, "Maybe I will take you in as my aide-de-camp as I have no one I trust by my side," he said sternly.

"I shall think not, sir," Margaret countered. "A lady such as this does not belong as an aide-de-camp."

"I find you do not yet know this lady," Washington replied. "She was always the best marksman with the best horsemanship on the fort, though I do believe your calling is to care for the ailing men," he said.

"Marksmanship," gasps Margaret.

"Yes," Sara interjected. "After seeing what the French and Indians did to women and children during that war, my father made it a point that I knew how to take care of myself!" Sara said proudly, then continued, "The ladies at the fort, however, made sure I knew how to be a typical lady and provided me with my sampler. Finally, I was even given the schooling of the young boys so I can read, write, and calculate complex numbers. I barely had time to sleep, but it was the best time of my life." Sara finished.

"And if you don't mind me asking, what about your mother?" Margaret questioned.

"My birth mother died giving me life. Donna was my step-mother, whom I met when I was ten years old," Sara answered sadly. "She finished my education, making sure I could live in high society, as she called it," she said while rolling her eyes.

"My word," squeaked June from the corner. "Is there anythin' you haven't done in your short years?" This at least broke the tension and allowed everyone to laugh.

Sara covered her mouth as an unsuspecting yawn came upon her. "Oh my, please excuse me!" she said, surprised at herself.

"It is I who needs to be excused, my dear," Washington said. "As I would love to remain with you the rest of the day, I have stayed away too long already." At that, General and Mrs. Washington rose and said their farewells.

"No, no, I can manage," Sara said as Washington tried to help her to her bed. "There is too much waiting for you back at headquarters." She then turned to Mrs. Washington. "Would you mind if I called upon you to help with the mending?"

"Always the outspoken one." General Washington laughed.

"I will call upon you when the time is right, dear," Mrs. Washington said, looking at Sara, and followed in a whisper, "but you know you are always welcome!" At that, the Washingtons took their leave.

Closing the door, Margaret turned around and said, "Well, that was too much excitement. Let me get you back to bed, dear." She walked up to Sara and guided her into the bedroom. Margaret left the room, returning to Dr. Madder, thinking Sara fell asleep. However, the door remained open enough for her to hear the Madders' conversation. "I can't believe what that girl went through!" she said.

"She does seem to have quite the constitution," Jonathan replied.

"And knowing the Washingtons like that," Margaret added in awl.

Dr. Madder gave her a whimsical look and said, "June can take care of Sara today. I need your help with the soldiers." The suggestion was made, so his wife didn't pepper Sara with questions.

"I will get my shawl!" Margaret answered, completely unaware of the plot behind her husband's words.

After sleeping for about an hour, Sara called for Margaret, knowing she would not answer. June entered the room and explained where Margaret was.

"Well, that is wonderful news," Sara said, tossing the blanket off her and putting her feet on the floor.

"I don't think you should be doin' that, miss, the doctor won't like it," June said nervously.

Sara was never one to stay in bed for long. "I am fine June, I need to use my feet so I can get back on them," she said. Then Sara looked out the window and saw the sun was still up and it was a beautiful day. "Well then, I prescribe myself some fresh air. Wish to join me?"

June stood, shocked, looking at Sara, "But, miss, you don't have any shoes."

"I suppose I also need a dress as well," Sara added as she looked down at herself.

A knock came at the door, and when June answered it, another soldier handed her a sealed envelope addressed to Sara. As Sara opened the letter, some coins fell onto the floor. "What the...?" she questioned as she started to read the letter. "It's from Martha," she said, then began to read aloud.

My dearest Sara,

George and I want to tell you again how sorry we were to hear what happened. Here is some money to get yourself a new dress and shoes when you are up to it. I am sorry it is not more. When the good doctor says you are fit to leave, please come join me as I can use your help. With so many men and not too many ladies on this run, I feel outnumbered.

M. Washington

Sara picked up the blanket off the bed and wrapped it around herself. "Well, I guess this will have to do to get me to the general store."

"I can give you my Sunday dress to go to the store," June offered. "But I'm not sure about shoes that will fit." She finished looking down at Sara's feet, which were much larger than her own.

"Thank you, June, I greatly appreciate it. As for shoes, maybe the good doctor may have something. Otherwise, I will just wrap them up tight," Sara decided.

June went to gather the items and brought them back to Sara. She had a straight white dress but no shoes. "Let's see how this does," June said, starting to help Sara. Sara tried to protest, but June just jumped right in and started dressing her. She then gently put a pair of socks Sara had been sewing over the wrappings on her feet. "Is that okay, miss, does it hurt?" June questioned. The dress was a bit tight and the socks a bit large, but since she was just wearing them to the general store, she said it would do.

When they were ready, the two headed out into the crisp air. Sara took a deep breath in and smiled. "I just love the outdoors, don't you?" she asked June.

"Well, I much better likes the warm air," June said, shivering, and the two began to walk. "Do you want to do your own sewing?" June asked.

"Seeing as I do not have a stitch of fabric that I can call my own, I do hope they have some ready-made dresses."

The general store was not that far from the Madders' house.

Upon entry, the owner said, "Well, good evening, June, and this must be Miss Sara."

"That it is on both," answered June.

Sara extended her hand with a small curtsey as the clerk took it and gave a small kiss on the back of it. "How do you do, sir?" Sara said.

"I am Mr. Tom Johnson. I own this piece of the world. How can I help you today?" he answered, puffing himself up a bit.

"It is very nice to meet you, Mr. Johnson. As you can see, I am very much in need of some proper clothing. Do you have anything already made?" she asked politely.

"Well, with this war, we don't have much, but you can find some things in the back here. Feel free to look around and let me know if you need anything."

There were only three ready-made dresses in the store and about four wrapped bundles of fabric. One of the dresses was black but entirely too small for Sara. The next dress was the right size but a little too bold for Sara's taste. The last one was a navy-blue dress with a button-down top, long sleeves, and a separate pleated skirt. This was a bit too big, but she figured it is easier to take a dress in, then make a new one and settled on that dress. She also ordered two yards of black fabric to make a shawl since she was mourning her family. To June's surprise, Sara then picked up a pair of trousers.

"What do you need them for, ma'am?" she questioned.

"Well," Sara began, "I have always found trousers to be more comfortable and much warmer than petticoats. Besides, it makes the ride more comfortable if you need to mount a horse quickly." June just about fell over at the explanation. Now for some shoes," Sara said, not paying any attention, turned on her heels, and headed toward Mr. Johnson.

"Did you find what you were looking for, miss?" he asked when she strode up to him.

"I am in need of stockings and shoes if you have them," she replied. "Do you have a woman's shoe in a size eight?"

Mr. Johnson took a hard gulp. "I am not sure, ma'am, that is a rare size, and in these times, shoes are hard to come by." He then lowered his voice to a whisper, "With all the rabble out there, I had to lock the shoes up lest a raid would come upon me," he said as he nodded out front. "Let me check what I have," he said.

As Mr. Johnson was searching in the back, Sara questioned June about him. "Is he a Patriot or a Tory?"

June laughed and answered, "Neither, he doesn't care which side wins, as long as your money's good."

He came back with one pair of boots that were one size too big for Sara. "I will take them," Sara said. "Nothing a few extra socks can't fix."

Mr. Johnson calculated everything and provided Sara with the total. She was looking at the change and, with a sad expression on her face, looked up. "Sorry, sir, I don't have that. What can I get—"

Mr. Johnson cut her off. He whispered to her, "I heard what happened and how you got here. I can't just give it away, but I will allow you to have it for what you got there."

"You heard?" Sara questioned indignantly, not even paying attention to the offer.

"Yesum, how those evil redcoats grabbed you at gunpoint in Trenton and tried to tear everything off. But you showed them even our women can fight those intruders off. I believe they said you gave one of them a black eye and cut another's ear off and crossed the river. You should be very proud of yourself, miss," he said with a smile. "We will keep you safe until we can get you back to your family, don't you worry none about it."

Sara didn't know what to say to this story. She just thanked the man and walked out the door. When they got about two houses down, they both began to laugh. "Interesting stories get told in your town, June," Sara said, still not able to stop laughing.

"And quickly too, I might add," answered June.

They were still laughing when June and Sara opened the door to the house. "*Where have you been?*" shouted Margaret.

June jumped back, scared, but Sara stood her ground. "Since I did not have a stitch of cloth or shoes, I needed to go to the general store. I asked June to accompany me as you would not like it if I went there alone," Sara grilled back. Margaret tried to fire back, but Sara would have none of it, "My feet are fine, my body is fine, my mind and spirit, however, are not, and lying in bed is not going to cure that. I appreciate everything you have done for me, but I do know how to take care of myself." She did not blink or quiver or draw back. She stood her ground firmly, almost edging Margaret on. As they stood there, Margaret could not fathom what just happened.

Hearing the commotion, Dr. Madder came out, put his hands on Margaret's shoulders, and spoke to June. "Please warm up the evening meal." He turned Margaret into the sitting room. He looked back at Sara, "You have some things to put away."

Sara felt bad about talking to Margaret that way and gathered up as much composure as she could. Regaining control of her anger, she walked toward the sitting room. There she found Margaret crying in Jonathan's arms and this sight made her feel awful. She looked toward them and asked, "Please accept my sincere apologies…again. I had no right to speak to either of you that way after everything you have done for me. I thought you were going to take things out harshly on June because of me. She is your…pro-pro-property…and I shouldn't have acted that way."

Margaret looked up at Sara, still very angry. "June is our servant, and she is very well paid for her service," she said, indignant, now on top of being angry.

"Oh shit!" Sara spat out, covering her mouth, trying to put the words back in.

At this, Jonathan became angry and said, "I will not have that language in my house, especially by a young lady."

"Yes, sir," Sara squeaked out.

"The meal is on the table," June said from around the corner.

Shaking his head, Jonathan then said, "Let's go my, dear," pulling his wife up by the shoulders. They both walked past Sara, Jonathan in between them, and left her standing there.

Sara took another deep breath, paused for a moment, then continued into the dining room. Jonathan and Margaret were at opposite ends of the table, and June was sitting between them. Wanting to try and make amends, Sara quietly asked, "May I sit down?" A few moments passed, and she was about to turn around when Jonathan showed his hand to the seat opposite June.

The meal was a repeat of dinner without the wine. Apparently, sometime that afternoon before they went out, June had started making cider, which was still warm. Jonathan said grace and acknowledged everyone to eat. Margaret just stared at her plate and wasn't moving.

"Please, Mrs. Madder, I am so very sorry. After telling my story this afternoon and feeling so lost, when we stepped into the house I heard…I heard Donna, my stepmother, and I just got so angry with the loss I…" Her voice faded away.

"Your mother," Margaret said quietly. "You heard your mother?"

"My stepmother never seemed to like my boldness. 'It is just not proper for a lady to act that way,' she would say to me and father. 'How will she ever find a suitable husband?' My father would only reply, 'I hope I taught her well enough to never have to,' and he would always finish with a wink in my direction."

Tears started down Margaret's face as she looked to Jonathan. "A mother," she said again. Confused, Sara looked toward Jonathan as well.

"We were never able to have children," he told Sara.

"I didn't mean to upset you again…I should just go."

As she was about to depart the table, Margaret stopped her. "Please stay. Actually, I wish to talk to you. *We* wish to talk to you about something." She looked at Jonathan when she said *we*. "We know you lost everything, and it would mean so much to us if you would stay here with us. As our daughter." The question took Sara's breath away, and no sound would come to her. "Don't answer right away, take your time, but know you are always welcome here," finished Margaret.

"You have done so much already," Sara finally said.

"I can't even repay you for helping me this far. I am truly honored by your request and will say that no matter where life takes me, I will be happy to call this house home."

The fight seemed years ago as the evening progressed. After the evening meal, Sara showed Margaret what she bought, and they started right away on alterations taking two days to finish.

She was still embroidering the shawl when she decided to take Martha up on her invitation. She walked up to the Thomas Barclay's house, where Washington had his headquarters. The closer she got, the more soldiers she saw, and the more soldiers saw her. Two sentries stood out front.

"Who goes there?" one of them shouted at her.

"Please tell Mrs. Washington that Sara Weinstein is here to thank her properly," Sara told them.

One officer knocked on the door, relaying the message, while the other was trying not to smile at her. She was looking around the grounds when the door opened up again. A young man called Sara forth, and she entered the building. He took her upstairs to a door at the end of the hall and let Sara inside.

"The missus will be with you shortly," he said, tipping his hat and closing the door on himself.

A few moments later, Mrs. Washington entered and since it was now just the two of them, they embraced. "Oh, you look lovely, my dear," she told Sara, holding her out to look upon the dress.

"How can I ever thank you, Aunt Martha? You really shouldn't have," Sara said back.

"Oh, please, those rags you were in, I couldn't stand it," Mrs. Washington said back as they both took seats. "Are you in need of anything, Sara?" she asked, picking up her needles and started knitting. There was a basket next to Sara as well, and she did the same.

"The only thing I am in need of right now is to be a part of this army. It's this only thing I know!" Sara said.

"You hold yourself way too short," Mrs. Washington said back.

"But I lost everything. I cannot support myself as is and couldn't find a suitable husband even if I wanted one," Sara almost barked back.

"You have not lost everything. You know you are like family to George and me. Plus we will write to Governor Livingston. You are the only heir to your father's property. You are not destitute," Martha snapped back, trying to get Sara to control herself.

Calming her voice before she spoke again, Sara said, "I know you will not just walk away from me, but you know my uncle is going to try to take control of Father's property. I just don't want to be a burden on anyone," Sara said.

"You are grieving but were never a burden to us, Sara, never!" Martha said plainly. "I know, but you also know I have to stand on my own two feet, battered as they may be."

She tried to laugh but only got a sideways glance from Martha. "Please talk to Uncle George and see if I can help with the sick men, please?"

After a few moments, Martha responded with a nod and said, "Now on to more pleasant things."

The two talked and knitted the remainder of the afternoon before they realized it was getting dark. "I must get someone to walk you home, and don't look at me like that, my dear. You're getting an escort," Martha said, not even looking at Sara but already knowing the look on her face.

After Sara placed down her knitting and rising to Martha, they hugged again before opening the door and together walked downstairs. At the foot of the stairs, they met up with General Washington.

"Well, isn't that a sight for sore eyes," he said with a bit of a smile. "How are you feeling today, Sara?" he asked.

"Very well, thank you, I just came to—"

She was cut off by General Washington. "No need, my dear, you are worth it," he answered, already knowing what she wanted to say. "It is late. I will have my aide, Richard Cary, walk you home."

At that, a young man walked up to her tipping his hat, saying, "It will be my pleasure to get you home safely."

Richard bowed to the general and his wife as Sara made her farewells, and they were off. It didn't start off well because his first words were "So you the famous young lady who fought off all those British men by herself?"

"No, sir, I am not. Whatever you may have heard about me, I assure you, it is not true," she said in a huff.

"I beg your pardon, my lady. I didn't mean to distress you."

She just glared at him, wishing the Washingtons would have let her walk by myself as she was perfectly capable. However, just then, she tripped over a rock she was too mad to see and fell down.

"Are you hurt? Here let me help you up!" Mr. Cary stated.

"I'm fine, I just bruised my pride," she said.

"Well, I didn't know that is where ladies kept their pride, but okay!" he said back.

They both started to laugh and continued on their way.

"This is me," she said, looking at the house.

"Well, whatever story you have, I can tell you have a strong constitution to have come through it so well."

She said thank you for both the compliment and the walk home and entered the house.

"Glad to see you made it home okay," Margaret said, trying not to restart the fight from the night before.

"Yes, Mr. Cary, one of Washingtons' aides, made sure of it," Sara replied.

"Alone!" Margaret said, rolling her eyes.

"Trust me." She smiled at that statement.

"General Washington was watching us the entire way. We are not that far." Sara knew this because she could hear him laugh when she fell. "It was a long evening, and I wish to retire," she said, kissing them both. "Good night!"

Chapter 2

The Freedom Fight

S ara woke up early the next morning, ready for the day, got dressed, and went to the cooking house, hoping to help June with breakfast. "Good morning, June, what can I do to help you this morning?" Startled, June jumped and dropped an egg onto the floor. "Oh, I am so sorry. I didn't mean to scare you. let me get that" Sara tried not to laugh.

"Miss, whatcha doing here?" questioned June, pushing Sara away and cleaning up the egg herself.

"I just wanted to help, that's all," Sara said sadly.

"Well then, take this to the table and wait there," June said in a huff, handing Sara a bowl of hard-boiled eggs.

Sara did as she was told, and upon entering the dining room, she found Dr. Madder entering from the other direction. "Good morning," Sara said with a smile.

"Well, good morning, dear. You are looking well today," Jonathan replied.

"I am doing well, thank you," she said, then continued a bit nervously.

"I was wondering, sir, may I join you today when you help those army men?" she asked. Jonathan cocked his head with a questioning look.

So Sara continued, "I have been helping the doctors look after the men in my father's battalions. I assure you, I know what I am getting into by asking. I have seen amputations, have taken care of dysentery and malaria, and have been vaccinated for smallpox. I can help, sir, please?" she asked again.

"Well, I repeat my June when I say, what haven't you done in your short years? How are you feeling?" Jonathan asked.

"My feet are a little tender but nothing I can't handle," she said, not wanting him to think she was trying to hide something. "And it would do my heart good to help the sick since I was unable to help my..." That last part trailed off.

Jonathan looked at her with a touch of sorrow in his eyes. "I think it will do you good, but please stay with Margaret and do as she asks, all right?"

"Anything," she said excitedly, giving him a hug as Margaret entered the room.

"Well, what have we here?" she said with a smile.

"Oh, ma'am, I am just so happy!" Sara said, hugging her as well.

When Margaret looked at Jonathan with a questioning glance, he said as if it were his idea, "I invited Sara to join us today on our rounds. I believe it would be good for her." Margaret was about to question it when Jonathan lifted his hand, which told her no more talk on the subject would be tolerated.

June entered a few minutes later with the pot of coffee and started to complain that no one was eating her food. At that, they all took their places and ate.

After breakfast, Jonathan, Margaret, and Sara left for the army camp. The smell upon entering the house turned hospital holding the sick was so strong it made your eyes water. Sara was sad to see that most of the men were on a blanket on the floor as their only source of comfort. Dr. Madder went directly to the army doctors (Benjamin Rush and John Cochran, physicians, and Nathaniel Bond and John Riker, surgeons) to see what they needed help with today while Margaret and Sara went up to the first patient they saw. His name was Captain James Moore of the New York artillery under

Captain Hamilton. Captain Moore, like most of the men here, had a fever and was writhing in pain.

"Sara, go get me a bucket of cool water," Margaret asked, not looking away from Captain Moore.

As Sara started to walk out of the hospital to get a bucket, she looked up to see Dr. Madder and the other two physicians in a heated argument. Taking a quick look at the other men and seeing some of them being bled, Sara could only guess that was the nature of the argument. Dr. Madder wished to do away with the practice and use herbs and teas to help the men while the army doctors would have none of it.

Sara left the hospital, and she spotted a young man with red hair and violet-blue eyes walking toward her. There was no mistaking this man who stole the cannons from the British in New York. The stories and description reached her father quickly after that happened.

"Sir, may I ask where you are going?" she asked as he started up the stairs to the hospital.

Captain Hamilton was almost indignant being asked his destination, looked at her in a bit of shock, but tipped his hat, bowed to her, and said, "I have a man sick in here. I just wanted to check in on him."

"I really wouldn't recommend it, sir. These men are very contagious, and there are too few able body men to go around for you to risk yourself."

"I know what I am doing," he said sternly and entered the building, now even more put back on her boldness.

Shaking her head, Sara picked up a bucket and crossed the road to the river. When she returned, Captain Hamilton was still with Captain Moore, shaking his hand, and asked, very concerned, "How are you feeling today?" He was not bothered in the least at Margaret protesting his being there.

The doctors came running over with Dr. Benjamin Rush talking very sternly. "What is going on here?" he questioned. "Even though this was a house last week, it is a hospital now, and my patients need quiet and rest." He then turned to Captain Hamilton and politely asked, "Please, sir, I must ask you to leave as I have another matter to attend to." He gave a not-so-small nod to Margaret.

A little put off but willing to oblige the doctor, Hamilton turned back to James. "Get well, and I will return at my earliest convenience." He stared at Margaret, then turned and noticed Sara. Again he tipped his hat, bade his farewell, and left.

"Oh, that man!" Margaret hissed. "You mind me, my dear, and stay away from that one. He likes to run after young ladies such as yourself."

Sara almost dropped the bucket at that statement and replied, "Margaret, it is not nice to gossip!"

Margaret replied, "It is not gossip when it is true."

"Now, now, ladies, these men need rest," Dr. Rush said but was cut off by Margaret.

"And a change of sheets," she countered.

Dr. Rush didn't know what he wanted more, for Margaret to leave or clean the sheets. He huffed and turned to Sara, realizing introduction had not yet been made. "Good morning, miss. My name is Dr. Benjamin Rush. This is Dr. John Cochran, as well as Dr. Nathaniel Bond and Dr. John Riker." He pointed out. "There is a brush for the floor in the back," he continued after seeing her with the bucket. "That is for the fever."

Margaret huffed, moving around the doctor and taking the bucket from Sara and kneeling next to Captain Moore. She then ripped off a piece of her dress and dipped it into the cool water and placed it upon his head. Trying to calm himself as much as possible, Dr. Rush then said, "Please change the men. Leave the medical decisions to me and my team."

Without waiting for anything further, they all turned and went back to what they were previously taking care of. It seemed most of the men did not want to be in a hospital setting, so the ones with minor injuries waited outside for a doctor to come and provide them with materials (if they had any) for their individual issue. Margaret turned to Sara and, in a much calmer voice, said, "Please help me with this."

As she started to take the sweat- and sour-stained sheets off the floor, Sara walked over and slowly lifted Captain Moore up to remove the sheet to his waist. With the stained sheet down and the captain seated up, Margaret started to put a fresh sheet down and finally laid him back on top of it. Then they lifted his legs to remove and replace the bottom half. Finally, they put another clean blanket on top of him and tried to make him as comfortable as possible.

"Thank you," he said quietly and fell off to sleep.

Sara took the fabric from his head, dipped it into cold water again, and wiped down his face and neck.

"Come along, Sara. There are far too many men to just stay with this one," Margaret said as she picked up the bucket and moved to the next patient leaving the dirty sheets on the floor by Captain Moore's feet.

They spent the next several hours continuing to wash the faces of the men. Unfortunately, there were not enough blankets, so they only changed the direst cases. There were thirty men in all, most having the same fever and symptoms. Some of the others just had an amputation for frostbite or infection.

"Seems illness will be the death of this army and not the red-coats!" Sara said wearily.

"Ay, I think you are correct, dear," Margaret said in response.

Looking up at Sara, she continued, "Maybe you should return home and rest."

"No, I will help with the blankets. I want to…I need to," Sara replied.

They gathered up all the dirty blankets and walked back to the Madder house. There was a room in the back of the kitchen for laundry with two large buckets. June had started heating water for the sheets they were bringing. Margaret and Sara put the sheets in the tubs and placed cheesecloth on top. Ashes from the cooking fire were already in a bucket and placed on top of the cloth. Hot water was then poured onto the ashes, the lye was collected, and the process was repeated. When the soaking was finished, they would then hand scrubbed every sheet with soap and hung them on the boards for drying near the fire. June was in the next room cooking the evening meal as they had missed dinner. It seemed like she somehow got a hold of two small quails during the day. Margaret and Sara finished the sheets, then helped June bring the meal to the table. That was when Jonathan finally came into the house.

"Those barbarians!" he shouted as he entered.

"They will not take me seriously and believe bleeding is the only way to help those men," he grumbled.

Margaret gave him a hug and walked him to his seat at the table. "Well, maybe they will allow your herbs while they are bleeding to get the best of both," she said to him with a smile.

Jonathan took a deep breath and looked upon the table, then at June. "What have you done, my dear!" he said happily.

"Where did you find quail at this time of year!" Pleasingly he looked at her.

"I must keep my secrets, or no one will have it" June smiled back.

After the meal, Sara went to the sitting room to start on some more socks for the men going barefoot. "Aren't you tired, dear?" Margaret asked.

"I am, but those men need something on their feet, so this must be done," Sara answered.

A short time later, they heard a knock at the door. "Who would be calling at this time?" Jonathan said, picking up his pistol again.

"Not another Sara, I hope," he said mockingly, looking at her.

He answered the door to find another aide to Washington providing another letter. The aide then tipped his hat without saying a word and walked away. Jonathan walked into the sitting room and handed the letter to Sara.

"Looks like it is for you," he said.

Sara opened the letter, read it quietly, then began to read aloud.

My dear Sara,

Martha passed along your request to join her while we travel and possibly help with the injured men. We feel it is our honor and duty to your father to make sure of your safety, so please join us tomorrow as we march out of Morrisville.

Martha will be very pleased with your company, and I must say, so will I.

G. Washington

"Leaving tomorrow," Margaret gasped.

"You're leaving us?" Sara looked up at Margaret and said, "I must honor my father, please understand that. But I will not leave you forever. Like I said the other night, no matter where I go, I will be happy to call this house home."

She stood up and gave both Margaret and Jonathan a hug. "I can never repay your kindness, but I will try," she said when they finally let go. Margaret was trying to find words, but none would come.

Jonathan, however, said, "I am so glad we had this time with you. Please take care and come back to us sometime!" They all hugged again, and Sara excused herself for bed.

Early the next morning, Sara got dressed and found the Madders and June in the dining room. Margaret and June were both crying, and Jonathan looked a bit sully.

"I must get going, so I can join the Washingtons before they leave," Sara said.

Jonathan stood up and said, "I will walk you there, dear."

Margaret and June gave Sara more hugs and almost didn't let go until Sara pushed herself away. "Please send letters when you can?" croaked Margaret. Then she turned and walked away, not able to stand it another minute.

"June," Sara said. "I miss you already," June said and followed Margaret out.

"Well, let's begin," Jonathan said, guiding Sara out the door.

They walked along quietly for a bit when Sara said, "I am so glad your light was still on."

"What's that, my dear?" Jonathan said, not really hearing Sara.

"I said I am glad your light was on and it was your door I knocked on that night."

"I am too, Sara, I am too."

There was a lot of activity as the military was starting to pack up for their march. When they arrived at the headquarters, Sara saw the same two sentries out front.

"I am here to meet up with Mrs. Washington again," she said before they asked anything.

"I am sorry, but no one is allowed entry today," the first soldier said.

"Excuse me, sir, but Mrs. Washington is waiting for Sara here," Jonathan said.

"We have our orders, sir. No entry," the soldier repeated himself.

Just then, the door opened, and the aide that delivered the letter last night was standing there. "Oh, so happy to see you, Miss Sara," he said. "I was just about to come get your answer for the general."

Sara and Jonathan looked at each other and gave each other a hug. Sara kissed him on the cheek and turned to go inside. "Thank you, Sara," he said. "You brought us so much joy in this little bit of time." All she could do was give him a small nod and go inside.

Most of the items were already packed up when Sara arrived. Martha was upstairs, putting the last few things of hers in a box when Sara heard shouting outside. It seemed the army had finished packing up and was marching past the building. Sara went to the window to see the men go by. There was General Washington mounted on his white horse, riding up and down the road next to his army. The soldiers were marching along, still looking disheartened and worn. They were followed by the artillery division pulling the cannons. Captain Hamilton was calling out orders to his men as he walked beside one of the cannons. Just then, the aide asked Sara to join Mrs. Washington upstairs.

"Good morning, Sara," she said as she continued telling the servants what needed to be done.

Sara tried to hide the fact that she was rolling her eyes. Since the Washingtons had a plantation in Virginia, they were accustomed to having slaves and didn't think twice about it. No matter how much

Sara protested about owning a person, George told her, "People sold themselves into slavery all the time in the Bible. Jesus even talked about how slaves should treat their masters and how their masters should treat their slaves."

"But these people did not sell themselves to pay off a debt. They were stolen, and their children automatically put into bondage," she would protest.

"It is just the way of it," he would say to end the conversation.

She would bring it up every now and then, however, just to plant a seed. Once he even said he would release them when he passed. *Not the best but at least I am getting to him*, she thought. Sara knew everyone they took with them. There were William (Billy) Lee and Ona Judge, George and Martha's personal servants, and Frank Lee, who was William's brother and the butler. The cooks were Doll, Hercules, Nathan, and Lucy, the laboring servants were Fanny and Betty, and finally the postilions (carriage drivers and house servants) were Giles and Paris.

"You're going to ride with me today, so just take a seat and I will be with you shortly."

Not wishing to cause a problem, Sara did as Martha asked. Sara definitely knew her well enough that when she starts giving orders like this, it is best to just stay out of her way. Once everything but the chair Sara was on was taken downstairs, Martha came to her and said, "Let's go!" and turned and started downstairs with Sara just behind her.

They both stepped out into the cool air and walked down to the makeshift hospital. Martha wanted to make sure the sick and injured were taken care of before departing. Only when the last man was on the wagon and ready for the transfer did she step into her coach. Sara followed her in and sat down across from her.

"You would think with how many times I have moved with this army, I would be used to it, but I would just prefer to be at Mt. Vernon for the rest of my days."

"I think you married the wrong man for that," Sara said as they both started to laugh.

"One thing George will not do is walk away when his country needs him, and since I love him, I can do it too," Martha said.

"I just hope the tide will turn, and we can end the war with a victory soon."

The carriage jerked into motion, and we were on our way. "Do you know where we are headed?" Sara asked.

Martha looked up, a bit surprised at the question. "You know my answer to that, dear," she said sternly.

Sara understood the secrets of the army very well from her father. Even if Martha knew the answer, she would say she had no clue. "Yes, ma'am," Sara said, looking down. "I shouldn't have asked. I am sorry," she said apologetically.

She did notice that some of the men would turn off the road where the ferries would cross the Delaware. Sara guessed George was stationing the men all along the Delaware to make sure the redcoats could not cross. It seemed other battalions started to join up with Washington as well as the ranks were starting to swell. The destination wasn't that far away, though, as the coach came to a stop.

"Oh, here already, well, let's get to it," Martha said.

Then Giles opened the door and helped the two women out. They were staring at William Keith's house in Upper Makefield Township in Bucks County, Pennsylvania. The enlisted men were busy building their makeshift housing. The ones without tents were using fencing or whatever they could find on the vast fields to protect themselves from the elements. The servants were busy taking the medical supplies into the house for the new hospital. The family that owned this house stood in the corner together, watching their home being rearranged to suit the needs of the army. William Keith was out hunting when the army arrived to take over their property. Most families in Bucks County were not fond of the idea of fighting with the British but refused to say anything. You really couldn't tell which side a family was for here the way you could in other locations like New York. When Mr. Keith came home to find all the commotion going on, he became angry.

"What is going on here, what are you doing on my property?" he shouted.

A different aide walked up to him and told him that General Washington was in need of his property for the Continental Army. He then explained that General Washington would allow them to stay in the house as long as they do not interfere. "General...Well then, if it is for the Continental Army, I would be happy to oblige."

He then called to his family and they all went into the second part of the house grumbly. The cannons were being lined up, the animals were put in the pasture or in the barn, and the men were either trying to build shelter or hunt for food.

"Oh my," Martha said in Sara's ear. "Looks like we got a tent at this camp."

They looked to the right, and sure enough, General Washington's two marquee tents were going up with a smaller one right next to them. They made their way over, and Martha continued, "You're new home, my dear," pointing to the smaller tent.

Since Sara didn't have anything, she just looked in and saw a wooden framed cot with a wire base and a blanket on top of the wire. Sara then went to Washingtons' tents. The one on the right was for dining and hosting the officers. The second tent, however, had another smaller tent inside of it, making multiple rooms. The first room was his office, and the second was the bedroom. Martha was already talking to the servants about which chest to put where.

"All settled Sara?" she questioned.

"Well, I just have to walk into my tent and I am unpacked," Sara replied with a smirk and then added, "With so many men without shelter, shouldn't this one go to some of them?"

Martha turned around and said, "You are a young lady, and in my care, this is how it is going to be, so let's have a look, then, shall we." Martha went to Sara's tent and said, "This just will not do. Oh, Fanny," she called to her house slave. "Please see to it that some straw makes its way to this bed, as well as a lantern, thank you." Then Fanny went off to take care of Martha's orders as Martha returned to her own tent.

Being so close to General Washington, Sara was able to hear that troops up and down the Delaware swelled to about 7,400 men as other battalions joined Washington at this location. She also overheard that General Lee was captured, and his men of nine hundred troops crossed the Delaware and joined up. For a group this size, it looks like this army will stretch all the way down to the Madder's house, she thought. By her estimation, only about five hundred men took residence at this particular location.

Of the group of men who were ordered to find food, some had gone to the Delaware River and caught fish for the camp. Another such group went to look for deer, but by the looks of things, they came back with two stolen, or as they put it, *commandeered*, sheep. General Washington stopped by the tent to make sure the women were all right. He told Martha that not only did some of the generals' wives join them, but the camp followers (wives of enlisted men) had arrived.

He then looked at the camp and the food and said, "We need God to bless this as he did the loaves and fishes." When they went to the dining tent to sit down for dinner, they found only some bread and dried meat.

After they ate, Sara was asked to go see Dr. Rush in the hospital. When she arrived, the inside of the house was just as busy as outside. The doctors were trying to get their patients and supplies settled. Not all the men made it to this site, however, and she hoped they were just in other housing along the way. Then she noticed Dr. Rush at the far end of the building.

"General Washington asked me to join you, sir, how can I help?" Sara asked.

He looked a bit bothered by the interruption when he remembered why she was supposed to come. "Ah yes, I have heard from the general your background, and I have seen you work with the men personally. Since we are growing in ranks with the inclusion of women, I would like you to consider a position of matron here and keep any nurses in line. Can you do that?"

Joy overcame Sara, and the smile that appeared on her face seemed to provide the answer, but she did finish it with "Thank you, sir, I would be honored!"

"We will also need just your help back here when there is an operation or injury. You have worked with doctors before, am I correct?"

"Yes, sir, I have seen it all," she answered.

"Good, so if you don't mind then, tomorrow gather all the new ladies and young men arriving and recruit some help out front. Now be off with you." He finished with a wave of his hand.

"I will do that, sir, thank you again," she said as she left to head back to her tent.

When she arrived back, she found some straw wrapped in a blanket on the wire base of her bed and a second blanket on top. Finally, a lit lantern was hanging, giving a light glow all about.

"Sara, is that you?" Martha questioned from her tent.

"Yes, ma'am," Sara responded as she walked over.

"Can you please find out what Ona did with my dress brush? I don't have it here." When the brush was finally located, Frank was setting the table for the evening meal. "Well, sit down then." Martha pointed to the table.

There was bread, cheese, and milk served to Martha and Sara. George was still too busy to stop and eat, so Billy brought him something. After the meal, Sara excused herself and went to bed. She was still able to hear some stirring around the camp, but it was beginning to quiet down. The last thing she remembers was hearing George enter his tent and say good night to Martha.

Early the next morning, Sara got up and dressed and stepped outside. The tent to the dining area was open as Frank was setting everything up for breakfast. "Morning, miss, food will be out shortly," he said.

"Thank you, Frank, I really appreciate it," Sara said back.

Martha and George came in shortly after as Frank was bringing out hoecakes and goat's milk. George said the prayer, and they all began to eat. Not much was said to each other at this time as much of what was on their minds could not be discussed.

Toward the end of the meal, Sara did speak up and say, "Thank you for talking to Dr. Rush about me, Uncle. I really appreciate it."

"Think nothing of it, dear, you can do a lot of good with those men," he replied.

"Don't forget I still need help with the mending, though." Margaret voiced.

"I won't forget," Sara said as she started to get up. Frank picked up her dish and removed it from the tent. "I will see both of you later." Sara finished as she departed.

She could hear George and Martha begin talking now that she had left but didn't pay any attention to what was being said. Instead, she went looking for Richard to ask for some paper and a quill. I guess he figured it was for the general because he raised his eyebrows when he looked at her but passed over a sheet, quill, and ink. Once supplied with the materials, she started walking around the camp and talking to the women who were there with their husbands. She found three women and two younger boys who said they would be willing to help at the hospital. After taking down their names, she had them follow her to the hospital.

Upon entry, she introduced all the nurses to the doctors. There was Elizabeth Price, Mary Jones, Charlotte Cook, Amiel Morgan, and John Miller. As Sara started going over the procedures of changing the dirty linens and cooling off the men, Charlotte said that she knows how to put blankets on the floor with an arrogant tone. Apparently, she didn't like someone younger than her telling her what to do.

Sara, not willing to take that type of attitude from anyone, said, "I don't care what you think you know. Here, you do things one way—*my* way. You do not talk to the doctors, you talk to me. You do not provide any other care than that which you have been entrusted in doing. You don't like it, go pick out another job because you will not be staying in this camp without helping! Do you understand me?" she said very firmly.

Charlotte did not like being talked to this way and was about to yell back. However, Sara stopped her. "No, you don't get to talk. I am in charge of taking care of these patients. You are here to help. It will not happen any other way. You do not talk back, you do not get a say, this is how it is." Apparently, she inherited her father's general skills and knew how to take command. "You don't like it, leave the camp!" Charlotte didn't really know what to do and just stood there. "Good, I am glad we got that settled," Sara finished.

Sara restarted going over exactly how she wanted the bedding changed, how she wanted patients taken care of based on their needs, and how they were to report any changes in conditions to her directly. She then sent everyone to work while she went to talk with Dr. Rush. "Well, know you seem to be living up to the general's thoughts of you."

"He knows what I can do, sir," she replied.

"Is there anything you need addressed today?" she asked.

"I know what I am doing," he snapped back.

"Very well, sir," she said as she turned around.

Dr. Cochran walked over and requested that Sara help him with a patient.

"I would be happy to, sir," Sara responded, and they both walked off to a patient in the back.

"Just a broken leg that needs to be stabilized. Can you get some wood please?" he asked firmly, then continued.

"Don't mind him," John said. "He believes his version of bleeding is the only way to cure these men and will not listen to whatever anyone else has to say about it."

"I didn't think you really needed my help with a broken leg." She laughed.

Dr. Cochran started talking about different treatments he was working on to try and help. He was very interested in what Dr. Madder had to say on the subject. "I would like to know if you were interested in helping me on a small project."

"I would be happy to, sir, what is it you would like me to do?"

"Well, for one thing, can you keep a secret?" he asked.

"Yes, sir," Sara quickly replied.

"Okay, the general told me I could trust you. He also told me you can read and write as well as calculate. Am I correct?"

"Yes, sir!" she replied, again a bit excited.

"I would like to provide some of these men with different medicines and record their progress," he began. "It must be done without Benjamin knowing. Think you can do that for me?"

"I would be happy to, sir," she acknowledged.

Dr. Cochran and Sara then went to a small corner where a desk for the doctors was. He found a small piece of paper on his desk and handed it to her. "These are the directions for the men with fevers. This is only between us. Whatever happens, Rush is not to know, understood!"

"I understand the need for discretion in this matter. You can depend on me," Sara confidently confirmed.

"We will begin tomorrow!" he finished.

When everything in the hospital was finished, Sara walked back to the generals' tent. "Mrs. Washington, it's Sara. Can I enter?" she asked at the door.

"Yes, Sara, we were just talking about you," Martha said.

Upon entry, Sara found three women sitting with Martha, all mending uniforms, knitting hats and socks, or stitching. *Oh good, a sewing circle*, thought Sara. "Good afternoon, ladies," she said.

"Good afternoon. Ladies, this is Sara." Martha introduced her, then continued, "Sara, this is Lucy Knox, wife of General Henry Knox; Kitty Green, wife of General Nathaniel Greene; and Gertrude Cochran, wife of Dr. John Cochran."

"It is very nice to meet everyone," Sara said as she sat down and started mending some pants.

"How are the men feeling today?" Martha asked, and before waiting for an answer, she added, "Sara is our new matron."

"They are still responding poorly to treatment, I'm afraid. We can't seem to get their fevers down."

"Matron, that's exciting," Gertrude said.

"It's not yellow fever, is it?" asked Kitty.

"No, the symptoms are not correct for yellow fever. I believe it is camp fever," Sara said sadly.

The ladies continued sewing and talking about the men, the challenges, the accommodations, and whatever else came to mind until the evening meal was starting to be served.

All the ladies retired to the dining tent, where they were joined by their husbands. Apparently, someone was able to find and shoot a deer as venison was the meat for the evening. There was also cheese, bread, rice, and rum placed around the table. The woman continued their prior conversations while the men talked in code about military matters. Sara ate quietly, reminiscing about the times she would be sitting at a table like this with her father.

"Are you all right, my dear?" Martha asked.

"Yes, ma'am, I am just a bit worn out. I think I am going to retire early, if it is all right with you?" Sara asked.

"Go ahead, I will check on you in a bit," Martha said.

The men got up as Sara did. "Good night, Sara," said George.

"Good night," the rest of the men echoed.

"Good night, everyone," Sara said as she left the tent. She prepared for bed and said evening prayers, then climbed into bed. She could still hear the talking of the guests next door, but after thinking about her father, she was happy to just be alone in the dark. After about an hour or so, the guests bade their farewells, and Martha came into Sara's tent.

"Sara?" she said quietly. Sara didn't say anything and just pretended to be asleep. "Well, good night, dear," Martha added as she went back to her tent.

"Good night," Sara said quietly to herself. Tears started to roll down her cheeks, and she drifted off to sleep.

The next morning when she awoke, Sara still felt sad. However, she got up and got dressed and went to the dining table. The Washingtons were already seated when she arrived.

"Are you all right?" Martha asked when Sara entered.

"I just miss my family," Sara answered. "I will be all right." She finished.

"You know you can always talk to me if you need to." Martha wanted to make sure Sara understood that.

"I know, thank you so much," Sara replied, taking her seat.

George finished and got up quickly and moved to the office in the first tent. His officers and aides started arriving, and they were going over new information. Sara could hear someone confirming her information regarding General Howe moving out of Trenton. The thought of her story being of some help made her feel a little bit better. Martha moved around the table to Sara and gave her a small hug.

"I know it's hard, but it will get better, I promise." She hoped her words could provide some comfort.

"I know, Aunt Martha, thank you," Sara quietly responded and reached up to hold onto Martha's arms. "I should get to the hospital," she finally said.

Martha released her embrace and allowed Sara to stand up. They both looked at each other both with smiles on their faces. A conversation took place between them without a word being said. Sara then stepped aside and started out the door.

After leaving the tent, Sara pulled out the directions for the medicine that Dr. Cochran gave her the night before. She needed to collect herbs to put into a hot liquid for the men to drink. Doll was walking by, so Sara asked her to help find the herbs needed. Luckily most of the herbs were used for cooking, and the general's cooks were sure to have dried herbs somewhere. They both went and found the supplies that were needed. "Thank you so much, Doll. I never seem to know my parsley from my sage," Sara said with a giggle. Sara boiled some mead with the herbs based on the instructions. When they were done, she poured the drink into a wineskin and picked up a cup to take with her to the hospital.

The other nurses were already there as she entered. Dr. Rush stormed over, asking where she had been. With a quick response and thinking, Sara said, "General Washington needed my help before I came over, sir."

"General…" Dr. Rush stuttered. "Well, I guess that's fine. What do you have in the wineskin?"

Again using quick thinking, Sara answered, "Just something for me for the day. Are you going to bleed some of the men today again? Do you want me to sit with them?" Sara asked, trying to change the subject.

"Yes, that would be a good idea. For now, just get to work and check on the patients." He snorted and walked away.

She then walked over to the first patient, who was sleeping and unresponsive. Most of the men here were that way by now. She felt his head and found it to be quite warm and full of perspiration. She had some paper where she could keep track of the findings. She marked him down as *patient 1, fever, cool compress and herb mixture.* Then she proceeded to wipe the man down with cool water and held him up to provide as much of the solution as she felt safe before he choked. She went to the next patient and felt his head which again felt very hot. This time she marked *patient 2, fever, cool compress.* She continued this way down the line of patients until she had marked down five with the solution and five without. After all, ten men were taken care of, Dr. Rush came in with a pot of leeches. He began applying them to different patients and marking down who got them today. Sara would sit by these men to help them in any way as bleeding made them even more uncomfortable.

The next week went by the same way. The healthy men in camp were continually doing drills while the generals were planning for the winter and military strategies. The aides were running in and out of camp, taking messages to other encampments and to Congress in Philadelphia. Sara and Dr. Cochran were going over the results of the mead every evening. At this point, two of the men on the solution were improving while the other three stayed the same. The other five men without the drink were getting worse. It was now December 22, and the temperature and snow were falling hard. This made the morale of the men grow as cold as the day. Finding and distributing meat became more difficult with the increased numbers and decreased game in the area. Bitter herbs, bread, and goat's milk became the normal one and only meal for most of the camp. Sara could hear the generals talking late into the evening regarding something that might help lift the spirit of the men. She hoped whatever it was could happen soon as she drifted off to sleep.

The next day Sara went to the kitchen to brew up more mead and headed to the hospital. She came upon the first man and started cooling him down when she heard a noise outside. Just then, the door opened, showing the silhouette of one soldier trying to carry another through the door. The second man was slumped over, barely able to stand on his feet. The doctors rushed over and took the weak man from the first and got him onto a bedroll on the floor. Now that she could see his face, Sara could tell it was Captain Hamilton. "Oh no!" she whispered to herself as the doctors started to check him over. It seemed he had the same fever and body aces as the other men here.

Dr. Rush removed his coat and placed a blanket over him. "Get me the leeches, Sara," he said as he had intended on bleeding Hamilton. After he placed six leeches on Hamilton, Sara asked Dr. Rush if he wanted her to sit with the new patient as she usually did. Without looking at her, he nodded and continued onto another patient.

Sara picked up a bucket of cool water and placed it down next to Captain Hamilton. He was very weary but able to look at her. "I told you James was too sick and contagious to be near!" Sara said sadly.

"He wasn't too sick for you to be next to him," Hamilton quietly whispered back. Everything he said was in a whisper.

As Sara picked up a rag from the bucket and started dabbing cool water on his head, she said, "I am not nearly as important as you are, sir."

"I know you jest, miss," he said back. "You're the girl that stirred up trouble for the British," he continued.

Sara sighed. "Please do not believe everything you hear, sir," she murmured.

"Well then, the truth." He grumbled a little more groan in his voice this time.

"Only if you stop talking. You need to rest, sir," she protested.

"I will keep talking until I get a story," he said back.

"You, sir, are incorrigible." She smiled back.

"And you, miss, are intolerable," he came back once again.

"Okay, okay, I will tell you just to get you to be quiet. Do you always get your way?" she said in jest.

"I do," he responded as he closed his eyes.

Sara told Captain Hamilton her story as she kept dabbing cool water on his face and neck. By the end of the story, Captain Hamilton was staring at her with weary eyes. "I thought my story so boring compared to the rumors it would put you right to sleep, sir," she said in jest.

"On the contrary, your story is much more impressive than any of the tails being told," he said even more wearily than before.

"You need your rest, sir," she insisted.

"How can I in such company," he replied.

"Well then, I have to take my leave of you for your own good," she answered and rose to depart.

"Please stay," he said, finally starting to close his eyes, The fever began to overcome him.

"I will return, I promise," she said and walked away toward Dr. Rush. "Are you in any more need of me?" Sara questioned.

This time Dr. Rush looked around and said, "It looks like we are okay." He started to say as he then faced her. Sara, after telling the story, once again had tears in her eyes. "Are you all right, dear? I know seeing all this can be overwhelming!" he said.

"It's not the men, sir. I just need to take a breath today, if that is all right." She calmed her voice.

"You may take your leave." He watched her walk out the door.

She went straight to General Washington, who was standing a few yards off, surveying the men and land with his leaders. "General, sir," Sara said very boldly, having interrupted these men. All of them were stunned as they turned to look at her. "I am in dire need of a horse for an hour, would that be all right?"

General Washington stared at her for a moment, cocked his head, and said, "Excuse me one minute, gentlemen." He stepped forward and grabbed Sara's arm harshly and walked her away from the men a few yards. "I don't know who you think you are, but do not ever interrupt me and my men again," he said sternly and loud enough for the others to hear. Then quietly, he whispered, "If it is necessary, take one."

"I assure you, it is." Sara nodded and then a bit louder. "I am so sorry, General, I forgot my manners. It will not happen again."

"Make sure of it," the general said with a wink and turned back to his waiting officers.

Sara walked off in the other direction where the horses were.

There was a guard there, making sure no one was stealing a horse and deserting the army. "Good afternoon, sir, I am in need of a horse, and General Washington has approved it," Sara said confidently.

"I can't release a horse without direct orders. I am sorry," he replied.

"But General Washington is discussing urgent matters with his officers and cannot come," Sara pleaded.

Just then, Richard Cary walked up to the two of them and said, "I am in need of two horses." Then he looked at Sara and said to her, "One is for you, the other is to make sure you don't fall again." He laughed. Sara was able to smile at herself, knowing she was about to get the horse she needed. "By the way," he continued, "where is it we are going?"

"I need to talk to Jonathan," Sara replied.

"You miss him already," he said with a smirk.

"No, actually, it is a matter of life and death," Sara pleaded.

"Well then, we should be on our way," Richard stated as the Sergeant brought the saddled horses. Richard was about to help Sara up, but by the time he got close to her, she was already mounted.

"I am guessing you know how to ride," he said, looking up at her. "You'll find out," she said as she nudged the horse on.

"Wait!" Richard yelled and mounted his own steed and nudged it on. They were both at a gallop within seconds and riding down the road.

Richard didn't catch up to Sara until she was stopped out front of the Madders' house. She was already dismounted when he rode up next to her. "What was that all about? You couldn't wait for me?" he questioned.

"I told you it was a matter of life and death, every minute counts," she said, walking up to the house. She knocked on the door and heard movement behind it.

June answered and smiled. "Miss Sara, welcome back!" she said happily.

"I am not here to stay June. I need to see Dr. Madder. Is he home?" she asked hurriedly.

"He is not at home, miss," June said.

"Mrs. Smith fell and broke her leg, he went to help her."

"And where does Mrs. Smith live?" questioned Sara. Though it was small, she was not here long enough to get to know the entire town.

"Go down there past Mr. Johnson's store and make a right. Three houses to the left is the Smiths'," explained June.

"Thank you so much!" Sara called as she ran back to her horse and, in one quick motion, was mounted and riding again. Richard had just turned around as Sara was turning the corner.

"She is quick," he said as he mounted his horse and started after her.

Sara was already at the door talking with Dr. Madder by the time Richard arrived. "I believe your herbs will help some of these men. Please, what were you going to give them?" Sara was asking the doctor.

"I am almost done here. Please wait outside, and I will be right with you," he told Sara.

"Thank you so much!" she squealed, returning to her horse.

"And did you have to run off again!" Richard scolded.

"You just have to keep up." She laughed back.

"What is it you need so badly from the doctor?" he questioned.

"Well, he created something that he put on my feet, which helped them heal. I thought it was worth it to show the doctors and see if we can help the men," she lied.

"A foot cream is life and death?" he said, questioning her answer.

"Well, yes, if the men can't walk, they can't fight, and that will be the death of America," she provided back. Then Sara noticed that Dr. Madder didn't have a mount to ride back, so he must have walked.

"Can I ask a favor of you, Mr. Cary?" Sara asked.

"I don't believe I am willing to do a favor with you running off all day," he replied back.

"Okay, if I promise to not run off again, will you please ride with me back to the Madders' and take my horse back here for the doctor to ride back?"

"Only if you promise," he said with a smirk.

They turned their horses and, with a canter, rode back to the Madder house.

"Thank you, I will wait here for both of you," Sara said when they arrived.

She then knocked on the door and entered when June answered. Richard took off for Dr. Madder as the door closed behind Sara. She looked to the left and found Margaret mending some pants for Dr. Madder.

"Hello," Sara said, walking into the sitting room. Margaret didn't say anything and just kept stitching.

"She has been so sad since you left, miss," June stated.

Sara knelt down in front of Margaret, taking her hands off her work. Margaret looked up with tears welling up in her eyes. "I did not leave you completely, and I will always return here."

The tears started rolling down Margaret's face. "I know my departure was quicker than either of us wanted, but I need to do this," she said, trying to help.

"I know," Margaret said quietly. "I was just enjoying taking care of…someone."

"I get it, but don't worry. First of all, my stepmom and her family never accepted me. Second, since my birth mother died without leaving me any memories, you are the closest thing I have to a mother." Sara decided not to tell Margaret about her relationship with Martha. "I will just be moving with the army in the winter. They don't usually allow women to follow in the spring and summer when battles are more likely," she said with a smile, knowing that since she was now the matron, she would most likely stay with the army. "I will come back here then, all right?"

Margaret smiled and hugged Sara as the door opened, revealing Richard and Jonathan.

"Well, hello, ladies," they said.

"This way, Sara," Jonathan said, leading to the room that she had stayed in.

First, he wrote down the directions for the medicine, then put some together for her. "Oh, I also need some more salve if you have it?" she asked.

"Are your feet splitting open again?" he asked as he started to get some for her.

"I am all right, this is for the men," she said.

"I hope you have better luck than I did with that," he said sarcastically. "That so-called doctor wouldn't even let me come in the door with it," he finished.

She gave him a hug, "Thank you, sir, this means so much to me."

"I find a hot cider to be the best drink for that, but anything they can get down is fine," Dr. Jonathan added. "I need to get this back, but I will stop by to see you when I can," Sara said.

After another hug from Dr. Madder, Margaret, and June, Richard and Sara rode back to the camp, this time side by side.

When they got back, Sara quickly dismounted, thanked Richard, and ran to Nathaniel so he could brew a cider. She added the mix Dr. Madder provided and put it into a different wineskin. When it was complete, she went back to the hospital.

"Feeling better, Miss Weinstein?" asked Dr. Rush.

"Yes, sir, thank you so much," she answered and went up to Captain Hamilton. Feeling Dr. Rush's eyes on her; she just sat there, looking at the leeches.

"Is that my nurse back again?" Captain Hamilton whispered.

"Yes, sir," she answered with a smile. "I gave you a promise!"

"Well then, an honorable young woman as well," he said back.

"Please don't talk, you have to save all your strength," she pleaded.

"Do you have another story?" He smiled.

"No, but as soon as Dr. Rush gets back to work, I do have a drink for you," she explained.

"Oh, well, that's intriguing." He winced.

Just then, Dr. Rush came over, looking at the leeches.

"I think we can take those off now," he grumbled.

"Go get the jar, Sara," he ordered.

Sara pushed the wineskin under Hamilton's blanket with her foot as she stood up. "Yes, sir," she said as she rushed off. She came back with the jar and tweezers and handed them over to the doctor.

She also had a piece of fabric to dab at the wounds the leeches left behind.

"I will leave you in her care for now," Dr. Rush said, then walked off.

Sara looked around and made sure he was with another patient before picking up the wineskin and gave it to Hamilton. "Ugh, this is awful." He coughed.

"I never said it was good, just that I had it." She laughed. "Now drink up," she finished as she lifted the drink, making him take it. When it was empty, Hamilton coughed again and asked Sara if she always got what she wanted. "I do," she jested, tossing his words back at him. She reached down into the bucket and wiped away the sweat from his brow. "I better go to the other patients before they become jealous," she said.

"None of them can open their eyes to see you. I am the only one around here who can be jealous," he responded.

"If you promise to rest, I will stop by before I leave for the day," she offered.

"That I will accept," he answered, closing his eyes.

She went around to the rest of the men, giving the five who have been taking the mead their drinks. The two that were getting better were still improving and finally opened their eyes when she was there. It sounded like the first one, patient 1, was named John, and the second one, patient 5, was named James. They were still weak so that was all they were able to say, but it was music to her ears. She was happy to report that the other three men taking the drink seemed to be improving as well. She finished her rounds and told Dr. Cochran what was going on. However, she neglected to tell him she provided Dr. Madder's brew to Hamilton. She wasn't sure if it was because it was a different product or if it was because she did it without asking. She decided to just keep this one to herself.

When everything was finished, she went back to Captain Hamilton. He stirred awake again as she came closer to him. "Captain Hamilton, you do not need to force yourself awake just for me," Sara said.

"I didn't wish to miss you," he answered.

"Plus all my friends just keep it to Hamilton, so please do so."

"I will if that is your wish," she replied. "How are you feeling? Any better?" she asked while cooling his head again.

"Not really," he said, trying to shake his head, which quickly turned into a cry of pain. She jumped back, thinking she caused the pain at first but realized what happened.

"You mustn't more, you're just making it worse," she pleaded.

Dr. Rush came over to see what happened and why he yelled. He began to question another round of bleeding when Sara suggested the foot salve to him. "I can show you my feet if it would help," she offered.

"No need for that as we will not be using any garbage remedy to treat our army," he said and stormed away.

Relieved he forgot about the leeches, she sarcastically said, "Let's not do that again, shall we?"

"Don't worry, I don't intend to," he coughed back.

"You should rest, and I need to go," Sara said quietly.

"Wait, can I trust you?" Hamilton asked.

"Sure you can, but make sure what you want to say is not because of the fever," she answered.

"No, but you told me your story. I just wanted to say, I am also an orphan. Please help me get better so I can die with honor on the battlefield."

With that, he drifted off, and Sara was left just staring at him. She was not expecting that but totally understood where he was coming from. She grew up in the army and saw men do that exact same thing. To find honor in death when life refused it to you. To die here and now with a fever would take that from him. In the short time she knew him, she could not let that happen. Then she left for the Washingtons' tent to sew and for the evening meal.

The next morning, she decided to skip breakfast and went right to Doll for two more wineskins, one with Cochran's mix and one with Madder's. As she started walking to the hospital, she prayed over both that they would help. When she got close, she could hear Mr. Keith discussing military matters that he should not be privileged to. She turned around and went back to the dining tent, where she found the Washingtons finishing up their breakfast.

"I was about to come check on you. We thought there was a problem," Martha said. "I wasn't hungry this morning and started for the hospital when I overheard Mr. Keith talking. How much do you trust him, Uncle?" she asked.

"Why?" He looked up, startled.

"It seems he was discussing military matters." Sara started to say when George stood up in a huff.

"I thought so." He then directed Sara to move closer and whispered, "It is good you have eyes and ears on us, Sara. I felt the same way and have already put in motion plans to rectify the situation." He provided as he put his hand on her shoulder. "Keep up the good work." He smiled.

"I will, Uncle, thank you."

Sara walked to the hospital and found the other nurses arriving. "How has everything been going?" she questioned. "Any changes with the men?"

This was the same question she asked every morning but dreaded the answer. Charlotte spoke up, sadly saying, "It looks like five of the men are improving, but the rest are starting to look like death itself. I don't think we are going to have a Christmas miracle this year."

Sara took a deep breath looking at the door handle she was holding and said, "Thank you, Charlotte. Thank you, everyone. Just try to keep everyone as comfortable as possible today. I fear that is all we can do now." She opened the door and entered.

Not wanting to be called out for having favorites, she walked to the left across from Hamilton but did take notice of him writhing in pain. She felt the first man's forehead, and if it was even possible, he felt even hotter than before. Amiel and John picked up the buckets to fill with water, and Sara stopped them.

"We have to cool these men down. After filling the buckets with water, add some ice and snow. Maybe that will help," she said, looking for answers.

The two boys did as she asked, and she looked around at all the men. Most of them were gray and moaning with discomfort. It was a sorry sight to see and left a very helpless feeling in the pit of one's stomach. She walked over to Dr. Cochran and asked if he knew of anything else they could do for these men.

"If there was, we would be doing it," he said with anger and despair in his voice. "We will start with John today."

Just then, the boys came back with the water and ice. She had them wipe down the men from forehead to waist, followed by the women to change the sheets. Finally, she walked over to Dr. Cochran, who was talking with John. John was sitting up and doing a lot better. His voice was a bit harsh, but at least he looked and acted alive.

The doctor looked over to her and said, "I think we should send these five back to their tents to fully recover. I don't want to risk them becoming ill again being in here."

"I am so glad you are feeling better, John," Sara said, putting her hand over his. "I will go get a horse and travois to take them back." She finished as she turned to the doctor. Then she whispered, "I am glad it helped some of the men." Feeling a bit discouraged, Dr. Cochran just shook his head and walked away. Sara's eyes followed him, and he went to another patient, then turned to leave.

She walked the short distance to where the horses were and told the guard what was needed. This time he did as she asked without question. Sara wondered if General Washington gave orders regarding her requests but didn't take the matter any further. Once the horse and travois were ready, she thanked the man and walked it back to the hospital. She reentered the hospital, and Hamilton called to her softly. She walked over to him and asked what was wrong and what he needed.

"I thought you didn't want to see me today," Hamilton half complained, half joked wearily.

"I didn't want the other men to think I had favorites," she joked back with a smile.

"So I'm your favorite now!" he said, followed by a moan.

"I didn't say that either Hamilton." This time followed by a small laugh.

"Once I can sit with you, I will be back," she said as she placed her hand on his forehead.

He was still warm but not as much as before. I hope Jonathan's herbs are helping you, she thought. Then she went to Amiel and John, who were both on their last patients.

"Can you please take the five improving patients to their tents when you are finished? There is a horse and travois out front for you."

"Yes, ma'am, they both said in unison."

Sara was gathering her papers when Dr. Rush walked over to her. "Two wine sacks?" he questioned. "Don't you think that a bit much for a young lady such as yourself."

Always quick to answer, Sara replied, "Well, after dealing with the leeches and wounds, my hands are so grimy. I wash them, so this one is filled with water," she finished as she pointed to one of the sacks on her side. With everything that happened this morning, she forgot she was still wearing them and didn't try to hide them.

"Well, that's the craziest thing I ever heard. You will give yourself frostbit and be useless to us," he snapped.

"I will be careful, sir, I promise."

He looked down the tip of his nose at her, then grunted and walked away.

She turned to the ten men plus Hamilton she was experimenting on and decided today to start with the tenth patient on her list. "Hello, sir," she said, not expecting a response, but talked to the men anyway. "It looks like you're not feeling the best today," she continued as she wiped down his head again. "It's Christmas Eve, so you may want to start feeling better to celebrate the day with us, all right?" She started pouring the solution into his mouth, and it just ran out the sides. A tear began to burn in her eyes and drip down her face. "You take care, sir, and I will return to check on you." She walked up the line and had this same interaction with all the men, so by the time she got to Hamilton, her face was wet stained with tears.

"I didn't take you as someone who cried," he said.

She wiped her face and took a deep breath. "There is that better," she huffed. "I just don't know how to save these men." Gaining more composure as time passed.

"I saw men being helped out. Was James one of them?" he questioned.

She looked Hamilton directly in the eyes and said, "I am sorry, but I don't know. He wasn't taken to this camp." She then pulled out the second wine sack with the second mix and gave it to Hamilton to drink. "Every last bit please," she asked.

"This is not nearly as bitter as the news you just provided me," he said sadly.

They both sat in silence as Hamilton finished the drink and handed the wine sack back to Sara.

"You're looking better," she heard a grumpy voice say behind her. She turned to see Dr. Rush walking toward and hoped he didn't see the exchange of the bag. "How are you feeling, Captain?" he questioned.

"About the same, sir," Hamilton replied.

"My head is still swimming, and it's painful to move right now."

"Is that the fever or the nurse?" Dr. Rush said with a smirk.

The two men grinned as Sara blushed and rolled her eyes. "We are going to need your help in the back today, Sara, so please don't stay too long out here." Then he walked away laughing at his joke.

"I am sorry about that," Sara begrudgingly said to Hamilton. "Why do people always turn the innocent into something more and wrong?"

"Why is it wrong?" Hamilton questioned.

"Your eyes alone can make a man's head spin."

"Please, sir, don't say that," she pleaded.

"You do not like compliments, Sara?"

She smiled at hearing her name but did answer with "It has a lot to do with what you said last night." Seeing the questioning look on his face, she ended with "That is a story for another time, but for now, I need to go see what Rush wants," she said as she stood and walked away.

She walked into the back where Dr. Rush was looking through the remaining medical supplies. "If you think I don't know what's going on here, you are out of your mind," he said, still counting the number of fabric strips they had.

"I'm sorry?" she questioned yet prepared to be fired.

"You and Hamilton, I have seen you sitting there for hours while neglecting the other," he said, then continued, "I think you are doing a good job here, and I have come to like you, so I wish to say, do not chase after that one. He is a bit of a ladies' man, if you know what I mean." Finally, he looked up at her as she began to chuckle.

"It's not like that, sir, I have seen enough men in the army to know about the men that walk the streets at night. Besides that difference, we actually have a lot in common. Anyway, he is about the only one out there now who is able to talk," she explained.

"Okay, I just want to make sure you don't get hurt," he said. "Now I need for you to go find someone who can arrange a transfer for me as I need to move the fevered men to the next encampment. There are more men there with the same illness, and I would like to stay at that one spot instead of traveling back and forth."

"I hope I didn't say anything embarrassing," Hamilton murmured as Sara walked back to him.

"On the contrary, what you said made a lot of sense," she replied.

"How so?" Hamilton questioned.

"You asked me to make sure you didn't die here of some fever to be placed in an unmarked grave and forgotten about." She paused a second, thinking of the seriously ill men in need of graves soon.

"You want to die on the field of battle where your life would have some meaning."

"And you don't think that arrogant of me?" he asked.

"Actually, I completely understand. At least you have a choice," she said. This really confused him, and he asked her to explain.

"Well, if you die on the field of battle, you would be remembered probably as a hero, especially if you are as reckless as I hear." She smiled, then went on. "However, I do not have that option. When I die, I will be nameless and meaningless no matter what I do in life. Being a woman and now an orphan, I have no hope of ever being important to anyone," she said sadly.

"Well, there is no reason you can't marry someone who will give you importance and take care of you," he said boldly.

"You have got to be kidding me," she scoffed. "When a woman gets married, she is no longer a person and is just as much a slave as…" She stopped there, not knowing how he felt about that subject. "She has no say over what she does or even has a say about what happens to her own children. Everything is the husband's property. If he dies and doesn't leave the finances just right, she has no hope to fix the issue. If he beats her, oh well, he has every right to do so. And for the rest of her life, she is just his wife like she is no longer a person."

"Well, that is just the way of it. You can't expect a woman to be able to…" He stopped talking at that point as she glared at him.

"And that is what I expect from a man," she said arrogantly. "So with that, I repeat myself, you can die in battle and be remembered for all time as a hero, and I can be the wife of a king, and no one would remember me all because you have an extra appendage and I do not."

At that, she walked away. Something about her boldness intrigued and shocked Hamilton. He always had a soft spot for women who have been wronged and wanted to help. She fit that persona; however, she didn't need or ask for help. She actually reminded him a bit of himself when his mother passed away. He had to choose to change his story or stay put and die. That is precisely where Sara was in her life now, and he admired the choices she was making. He decided the next time he saw her. He would tell her that and closed his eyes.

Sara stormed off back to the tents and found Martha with Kitty, Lucy, and Gertrude knitting again. Sara found out from Martha that General Washington was no longer at the site. He and the other generals went to a different location. Sara figured this is what George meant when he said he had a plan in place and thought nothing else of it.

"I need to go find a captain then and will be right back," Sara said.

"From the sounds of it, you already found a captain," Gertrude said with a chuckle, and the other ladies joined in. Still, in a huff from leaving Captain Hamilton, this did not sit well with Sara.

"I am pleased to inform you that whatever you think is going on, it is not. *And* I would be extremely happy if you would stay out of my life." All the women, even Martha, gasped and looked up at Sara, watching her back as she departed. At this point, Sara didn't care. She was so full of emotions between the dying men, all the rumors about her, and needing to start moving the sick men, she couldn't help herself. Luckily walking in the cold and snow did help her cool off, and she told herself she would fix everything when she got back. She found a captain and asked him to set up transportation as requested by Dr. Rush.

"It looks like both camps are going to have a lot of men die, and the doctor wants to be in one area. You should start on some graves as well," she added. The captain took a deep breath and assured her it would be taken care of, turned around, and started recruiting some men for the job. Now Sara had to face the woman she just angered again and like the captain took a deep breath and returned to the tent.

When she got close to the tent, she could hear the ladies talking, but all went silent when she entered. "I am sorry for my earlier outburst. It was impolite and undeserved. It is just I had to go tell the captain we are going to be in need of some graves." The other ladies seem to have taken this as a reasonable excuse for the outburst; however, Martha did not.

"You know men die every day, Sara, but you need to keep your composure at all times. It is not worth working anyone up for something that can't be helped or changed. Now sit down and help mend those pants over there."

"Yes, ma'am." Sara graciously accepted the scolding she knew was coming.

After that, the talk became whimsical again, and Gertrude turned to Sara. "Now, dear, are you interested in our Captain Hamilton?" she questioned.

"I hope not," Martha answered. "I plan to call that ginger tomcat Alexander Hamilton if he returns again tonight."

Everyone, except Sara, laughed. She just looked up at everyone. "I am not interested in Captain Hamilton as anything other than a friend."

"He is not any more or less important than the other male friends I found on base growing up as Martha very well knows." At that comment, an orange tomcat walked in and up to Martha. "However, that Hamilton is adorable," Sara finished as everyone, including Sara, laughed even harder.

Chapter 3

Back to Princeton

December 25, 1776, had to be one of the worst days of Sara's life. When she got to the hospital, she found several of the beds empty, including Captain Hamilton's. Dr. Cochran told her that one surgeon and the nurses would stay here with the injured men, but the two of them would be going to the Thompson-Neeley house, where all the fever patients went. Upon their arrival, Dr. Rush and the woman of the house were moving from bed to bed, checking for breath signs. She heard Dr. Rush say, "This one is gone, take him away," and walked onto the next patient. Two privates come over to get the patient Dr. Rush was talking about and removed the body. "They are dying one right after another!" Dr. Rush said, exasperated as another called for help to remove yet another dead body rang out. Sara looked at the next patient who passed and saw it was Captain James Moore.

At this point, there were only about ten patients left, and Captain Hamilton was nowhere to be seen. One by one, they departed this world as well, with the last man dying as the sun started to go down. All in all, twenty-five men lost their lives that day due to illness, and since they were not able to talk when they arrived, no one knew who they were. All the doctors and nurses sat down on the floor, listening to the piercing silence of the now-empty hospital.

They were startled when the front door busted open, and General Knox came in. He stopped for a moment, shocked at the sight of only the doctors and nurses there. He regained his composure, then said, "Tonight we fight, be prepared." He walked out the door, leaving everyone weary.

"Well, merry Christmas," said Dr. Cochran indignantly as he pushed himself up and walked out the door.

"I should help him ready the surgery supplies," said Dr. Rush pushing himself up as well.

"Do you think you are going to need another surgeon?" Sara questioned. "Dr. Madder has performed them and could help if you want me to go get him."

"If you don't mind, just ask him to be ready in case we do. Thank you, Sara," Dr. Rush said sadly.

"I will leave at once," Sara said, then left the hospital.

General Knox started to march his army off the property and down the road. Sara started walking behind these men, a bit numb from the experience of the day as well as feeling warm from the walk. It took about two hours to get back to Morrisville. The army kept walking as Sara walked up to the door for Dr. Madder's house, where June answered the door and let Sara in. Dr. Jonathan and Margaret came out of the sitting room happy to see Sara but became very concerned when they did.

"Are you all right, my dear?" Jonathan questioned, taking hold of her. "It was just a long walk, and I needed to see you. The army may need your help with surgeries after this battle they are to partake in."

Jonathan felt her head and explained that she was burning up with fever. They quickly took her into the exam room and laid her down on the bed. Quickly Margaret went to get a bucket of cold water as Jonathan started putting together the herbs for her to drink. Her clothes were cold and wet from the walk, so Margaret again washed her down and changed her clothes to just a nightshirt. Sara was so weary by this time she excused herself and fell asleep.

The next morning, Dr. Madder came in, bringing in another cup of hot cider and herbs. "He was right," Sara started. "These are bitter."

"Who was?" Jonathan asked.

"Hamilton," she answered. "He was the one I gave the medicine to."

"Oh really, and how is Captain Hamilton doing?" he wondered.

"Not so good, he died yesterday morning," she said.

"I am so sorry to hear that, Sara," Jonathan said as he finished up wiping off Sara's forehead.

At that moment, a loud cannon fire was heard from across the river. She jumped up, and Jonathan pushed her back onto the bed. "That must be the battle starting, it sounds like it is in Trenton."

"They must be going after the Hessians I saw on my way over," Sara said.

"I just never heard of fighting in winter, but I guess General Washington knows what he is doing," Jonathan added. "Are you hungry? Do you need anything?" he continued as the gunfire picked up the pace.

"No, thank you, I just want to rest," Sara lied.

"Okay, I will check in on you later," he said as he left to check in on Margaret and June.

Sara walked over to the window, opened it, and crawled out. She ran to the shoreline of the Delaware to look at the battle taking place across the way. The snow and ice from the storm that accompanied them were getting worse. Sara knelt down in the snow and began to pray for everyone involved. Then close to an hour in, she heard the cannons sound off again. She started thinking about Hamilton and all the loss she had encountered within the last month. At this point, Jonathan and Margaret had realized she was missing and was out trying to find her. Finally, he saw her at the bottom of an embankment on the river shore. He ran down to her, picking her up and bringing her back into the house.

"What were you thinking?" he said angrily when they got back inside. "You're going to get yourself killed." The gunfire stopped, and the sounds went to people gathering in the streets to try to see what happened.

Sara's adventure made her illness much worse, and she fell asleep for the next two days.

During that time, Dr. Madder found out that only two soldiers from the Continental Army passed away, and that was during the march to Trenton from the weather. The surprise attack on Trenton worked, and it was a one-sided victory. General Washington ordered his army back across the Delaware to celebrate and regroup. The win caused the joyous reaction the officers were hoping for. During the celebration, Jonathan was talking with some soldiers and found out that not only was Captain Hamilton still alive, but he was the one firing the cannons and helped secure victory. The army did not return to the Keith house due to security concerns and recamped from the Thompson Neely house to the south of Morrisville as they were deciding their next move.

On the third day of taking care of Sara, a knock came on the door. June opened the door to find Captain Hamilton looking woebegone. "Excuse me, miss, is Sara Weinstein here?" he asked, very concerned.

Dr. Madder saw who was at the door and answered for June. "Captain Hamilton, please come in, come in, she's here."

Hamilton took off his hat and entered the house. "I have heard about what you did. Congratulations!" Jonathan said, shaking his hand.

"Thank you, sir, but I don't really feel like celebrating today. I just heard that Sara came here and never returned. Is she all right?" Hamilton questioned.

"Unfortunately not. She has a fever and has not woken up since the battle."

Panic came across Hamilton's face. "Can I see her please?" he begged softly.

The visit both was improper and had no resolution to the argument between him and Margaret. Captain Hamilton felt he was going to be kicked out. Instead, Dr. Madder showed him into the room with Sara. She was still asleep and not responding to the visitors. Hamilton looked down at Sara and began talking softly, "Sara, can you please wake up? I need to talk with you, Sara, things can't be left that way!" Hamilton pleaded.

Dr. Madder looked at him sideways and was about to ask what that meant when Sara opened her eyes. "I died and went to heaven," she stuttered.

Hamilton laughed, and Jonathan went down on his knees. "If you died, heaven would not be where you would find me," he joked.

Then Jonathan spoke up, "Captain Hamilton didn't die. He went to fight and won the battle," he said with tears in his eyes.

Upon hearing the commotion, Margaret entered the room, completely ignored Hamilton, and kneeled at the other side of the bed. "Oh, my dear girl, you terrified us!" She then picked up Sara's hand, kissed it, and started crying into it. It took a couple of minutes for Sara to figure out what happened since her arrival.

"I guess I shouldn't have gone out in the snow like that," she said.

"That also would not have been what I would have proscribed, my dear." Dr. Madder laughed. Then he felt her head and noted that the temperature was coming down. "You need more cider mix. Please help me, Margaret."

"You can do it by yourself. Besides I don't want—"

Jonathan cut her off. "Margaret, he is the reason she is awake. It will be all right."

Margaret got up in a huff and put a chair on the door so it would not close. "We will not be far away, and I will have my broom if I need it, sir. You best be a gentleman." They walked out of the room as she kept grumbling.

Hamilton took another chair and sat down next to Sara taking her hand. "Hamilton, I thought you were dead," she whimpered.

"Even if I did, I would have returned to rectify our last conversation. The improper legalities when it comes to marriage. Well, let's just say that I understand why you oppose the institution. I don't like talking about this, but I feel you need to hear it. My mother's marriage to her legal husband was arranged by her family. He was older, did not love her, and abused and mistreated her, so she left. But only after he forced her to give him a son, then took the child away from her. It was after her escape from that awful man that she met my father. They loved each other and wanted to marry but couldn't afford a divorce. The scum she was married to, however, could afford it and proclaimed her a whore. A rich person can escape a bad marriage and marry again but not a poor person. Their new relationship is considered adultery, and any children conceived are bastards.

"After that, my father decided it was best to depart and left my mother alone. She struggled, trying to do everything herself until we both became ill with a fever. That time I was the only one to make it through. Sometimes I wonder if she pleaded with death to take her and leave me. Then because of the laws, we lost our home to the boy she had with her legal husband. My brother and I were bastards, left destitute. I had to fight or die myself. I understand. I think that is why we get along so well," Hamilton said, taking over the conversation and not allowing her to talk.

"I have to admit that when I talk with you, I feel like I am talking to my brother," Sara managed to squeeze in.

"And I would very much like to call you my little sister!" he agreed.

"Alexander, I need to tell you about Captain Moore," Sara started to say, but he stopped her.

"I know I heard what happened to all of them," he said mournfully. Then Jonathan and Margaret came back in with the cider.

"Oh wait," Hamilton said excitedly. "There are paybacks to be had here." His eyes widened, and a smile came across his face. "Now all of it must go down," he said.

Sara rolled her eyes and tried to take the cup. "Oh no, you poured it down my throat, I get to do the same!"

The next day, when he had a chance, Hamilton went to see Sara. She was improving, but the Madders were still very cautious with her. He provided some military news he normally wouldn't share with another person; however, Washington knew of his visit and asked him to relay a message. The army would be moving back to Trenton the next day if she was fit enough to rejoin them. If not, they would send a letter with their whereabouts to the Madders.

"I must rejoin them tomorrow as sending locations in the mail is very dangerous," she complained to Hamilton.

"You most certainly will not," protested Margaret. "You are too sick to be running around the countryside."

"I am fine and will make up my own mind," Sara firmly stated.

"Not this time." Margaret jumped up.

"Mrs. Madder, if Miss Sara wants to travel tomorrow, it is my job to see to it that she has a safe passage by orders of General Washington. You will not be able to stop it," he said firmly.

Dr. Madder entered the room to check on things when he started hearing commotion. After hearing what the argument was about, Johnathan said to Margaret that Sara had the right to make the decision. He, as a doctor, would release her to the military if she wanted to go. Margaret stormed off without another word.

"You're going to have a very fun next few days, Jonathan," Sara said.

"I know, but no matter what, I need to do what is best for my patient, and in this case, it is for you to follow your father's wishes," Dr. Madder said.

"Besides, your fever is gone, and your strength is coming back."

"I will leave you to rest and collect you in the morning," Hamilton said, bowed his head, and left.

"Thank you, Jonathan. I am glad you understand," Sara said.

"All too well, Sara," Jonathan finished.

"Get some rest, and I will have June bring in some soup later." He left the room and closed the door, leaving Sara to close her eyes and rest.

The next morning, Sara got dressed and left the room she became all too familiar with. Only Jonathan and June were there as Margaret was too upset to join them. As Sara hugged them, a knock came on the door. June answered it to reveal Dr. Cochran and Martha.

"Do you mind if we come in?" he asked.

"Please do!" June said, moving aside, allowing entry.

"Hello there, I thought I was supposed to come and meet you," Sara asked.

"Well, there has been a change of plans," Martha explained. "It seems the redcoats are marching on Trenton, so us ladies are going to stay on this side of the river for now. We just came to check in on you, Sara."

Margaret heard the sound of Martha downstairs and entered the room as she was explaining the situation. "Do you need a place to stay, Mrs. Washington?" Margaret asked.

"Thank you, but the other ladies and I will be staying at the Summerseat House until further notice," Martha replied graciously.

"And I believe you need more rest before traveling, Sara," Dr. Cochran said, looking at her.

She wanted to protest, but she decided not to do so. Martha and Margaret walked Sara back to bed, much to Margaret's delight. "Well, I guess you have me for a little bit longer," Sara said to Margaret as she closed the door on the way out.

Things became quiet outside as the army made its way back across the river. Sara wondered if she would ever see George, Alexander, or Richard again. However, this was normal for her as the woman in the camps took care of her while her father went off to battle. Sometimes the army was so far off you couldn't hear anything, and other times, they were so close they could watch the fighting. Sara much preferred being close enough to know what was going on. Since she was supposed to be helping with the wounded men, staying here just didn't feel right. There wasn't much she could do about it, however, as she was still a bit weak. Just going to get something to eat and back to her room tired her out. She wondered how Hamilton crawled out of bed like this and went to fire the cannons.

She got stronger over the next couple days and even sat with everyone to celebrate the New Year coming in. The ladies even came by and toasted that the war would be over by the end of the year. However, on January 2, they were awakened by the sound of guns and cannons across the river. The noise continued throughout the day and into the evening. It didn't settle down until darkness came over the cities. However, another bit of noise started up around town. Jonathan went out to find out what was happening. When he came back, he told them that the Philadelphia militia was marching and going to cross the river a bit further down to join up with Washington. He then said good night and escorted everyone back to bed. Sara, however, had a different idea.

She got dressed and went outside to the militia marching past. She found someone in charge and told him that she was the matron with General Washington's army and was separated when she was taking care of a man who sadly passed away. He agreed to take her across and help her rejoin the doctors there, but they had to move swiftly. If she couldn't keep up, she would be left behind again. She agreed and started marching down the Delaware with the men. Taking notice of everyone around her, she saw fit men, fully clothed and fed, looking every bit ready for battle. However, she knew this was militia and started asking "womanly" type questions such as "How many battles have you been in?" and "Have you been away from home long?" Things a typical young lady would ask. By their answers, she could tell they were lying, trying to impress her. With that, she decided to press a bit harder with the questions.

"Did you see a man get his leg blown off yet?" One younger boy, maybe sixteen, turned green and almost lost his last meal. Someone else spoke up and said that a young lady like Sara should not be bothered by such things. At this point, she knew they were more fit, then the experienced army under Washington, but the only thing they ever shot at was a rabbit. She decided not to ask any more questions as they were at least helping her get back to the doctors.

When they were far enough out of Trenton, they examined the river. It was completely frozen over, so they were able to just walk across. Since he sent the request for more troops before he left for Trenton, Washington was hoping these men would be coming and had his aides waiting for them. The first men to cross got the news from the battle and started passing it along to the other men.

"Washington's held them off!" someone was shouting.

"Cowards stopped as soon as it got dark," someone else called.

Sara knew the British were not cowards and were just stopping tonight to finish the job in the morning. She also knew Washington wouldn't wait around for that to happen and would try to outflank the British. She began to run across the river, pushing the men out of her way.

"Slow down, miss, the battle will still be there when we arrive!" one man shouted to her.

"Oh no, it will not, it will be a long way off!" she called back and kept running.

When she reached the shoreline, she saw Richard helping the men off the ice and pointing them toward the rest of their unit.

"Miss Weinstein?" he questioned. "What are you doing here?"

"I have to get back," she said, her voice shaking partly from the cold and partly from being nervous she would be left behind again.

"Wait here," he pointed. "A relief with new orders will be arriving shortly, and I will bring you to the camp."

"Thank You!" she exclaimed as she started rubbing her hands together.

A few minutes later, another aide rode in and told the commander that the militia was to move toward Trenton, leave a few men there with Washington's men to set a trap, and continue quietly toward Princeton using the newly created road. This road was not on any map, and the aide would guide them through.

"Princeton," Sara said, her eyes doubled in size.

"He's going after Princeton?"

"Sara," the aide said, "I thought you were a goner."

"I am stronger than I look," she replied and turned toward Richard. "Can we please go?" she asked.

"Safe passage," the aide said to Richard.

"Safe passage," Richard returned and mounted the horse. He then reached down for Sara's hand as she mounted the horse behind him. When she put her arms around him to stay on, he set the horse in motion.

They were a few miles outside Trenton and found the back end of Washington's army slowly moving away. Richard needed to get back to the general with the news that the militia was shortly behind with 1,600 men. Sara, however, knew she would be in trouble and sent back to the Madders if he saw her. She asked Richard to let her down back here. Richard agreed that being in the back of the army would be the safest place for her and let her down.

"That was the best ride I had all war," Richard said to Sara.

"Don't even try it, Richard," she snapped back.

They smiled at each other, and he rode off toward Washington. Some of the men recognized Sara from the hospital and moved her toward the center of the lineup to be safer and hopefully warmer. She enjoyed the spot because Washington usually rode up and down the line, and this would conceal her from him. They walked all night, and by daybreak, a group of men was ordered to turn west and head toward Trenton to hold Howe's men from returning. The rest continued straight ahead and found an orchard right outside Princeton to hide in. As the group split, General Washington was close enough for Sara to see now, but it was too late for her to be sent back.

A heavy mist covered the ground that morning, concealing the position of the army as they saw a group of redcoats marching out of Princeton. The British commander saw the militia group marching up behind the hidden army. When he realized they were not Hessians, he tried to take cover in the orchard that was already occupied by Washington and his men. Cannons shot off, and guns started to fire from the waiting Continental Army. Then it was the British army's turn to fire back. Since they were in an orchard, most of the men hid behind the trees waiting for the shots. Sara was able to duck under a tree that had fallen down already. It wasn't the best cover as a cannonball went right through the tree just to her left, tossing bark into her face. When it was time for the Continental Army to fire again, she moved her position and found a dead soldier who was hit by a cannonball. She quickly removed his coat, powder, and shot and put them on. She also removed her skirt, revealing the breeches so it would be easier to maneuver the terrain. Another round of cannon fire and gunfire came from the British, and the call to attack rang out. Since most of the men around did not have bayonets, the Continental Army fell back, Sara with them.

Across the field, the part of the army that was blocking Howe's retreat from Trenton joined in this fight. General Washington rode his horse in front of both battalions, trying to rally the men to no avail.

Then gunfire came from behind as another group of Continentals made their way to the fight. General Washington had his men attacking from three directions. Some of the redcoats charged with their bayonets but most retreated back to Princeton. Sara was seated next to a captain she didn't recognize as he started calling orders. She was not sure if he thought she was a man or just didn't care if she wasn't. All she knew was now she was in the midst of the fighting. At that moment, one of the charging British soldiers jumped over the fallen tree in front of them with his gun and bayonet pointed at the captain. Sara quickly raised her rifle and shot him in the head. His lifeless body came crashing down between them, and the captain looked at her and gave a nod of thanks.

There was gunfire, cannon fire, and screaming all around. Some were shouts of orders from commanders, some shouts of pain, and even some shouts of fear. It seemed to Sara that some men were pushing forward while others were pulling back. Her troop would push forward a few yards and take cover by trees, rocks, or whatever they could find. They would take aim and fire on the captain's orders, reload, then push forward again, chasing the British further into the city. Even though she spent most of her time with the military, this was where her father's family home was located. She knew the streets very well and helped guide the captain down alleyways to gain better strategic vantage points. They were able to encircle some of the retreating men and fire on them before they got away.

As the Continental Army pushed into the city, the British army split up, with some men heading north, while most of them took refuge in Nassau Hall at the college. The troop Sara was with covered the north side as the cannons were moved into place. There was a loud blast followed by the whistle of a cannonball traveling through the air and the explosion of impact. This cannon shot a hole right through the wall and apparently removed the head of King George III's from his picture. This caused the men inside to surrender. The battle was over, and Sara felt pride as she avenged her family by helping take back Princeton. She looked up and saw the doctors trying to help the wounded men and started off toward them. The captain she helped called out to her and asked her name. She yelled back, "George Weinstein."

Realizing she could not go back in just trousers, she went back to the orchard to find her skirt. While looking, she also found an injured man shot in the leg and helped him to Princeton. They were not there long, however, because Washington got word that the British army who had started the day in Trenton were heading back. They gathered whatever materials they could find quickly and loaded both that and the injured men onto wagons. Sara made her way onto a wagon that was trying to perform surgery on men while moving. Dr. Riker was the surgeon on this wagon with Dr. Cochran there to help. Dr. Cochran looked at Sara, disgusted but just went about their business. The first man they were working on had his arm severed from the elbow down. Sara put a stick into his mouth to bite on as the doctor started sawing away at the exposed bone. Dr. Cochran tried to hold him steady as the cutting started. The screaming was intense until the patient passed out. Dr. Riker tossed the unneeded bone out the back of the wagon. Once the wound was closed, the two doctors moved him to the front of the wagon for Sara to bandage up while they started on the next patient. It seemed each wagon had at least ten wounded men in it that needed to be operated on. Some needed to have limbs removed, others needed to be stitched from bayonet wounds, and still others needed a bullet taken out of their bodies. By the time they got to the next destination of Morristown, New Jersey, some of the men had passed on.

Chapter 4

The First Winter

There were men riding in and out reporting on the battles and the progress of the British. Word came that the British had moved to New Brunswick to lick their wounds and rest for the winter, so General Washington decided this was the best place for his forces to take refuge. The people in town started packing up and moving on away from the fighting but agreed to allow higher ranking soldiers to rent their homes while they were away. Dr. Cochran was able to rent one of these homes and allowed Sara to take a room so he could keep a closer eye on her. After getting the wounded settled and getting her own cuts attended to, she and the doctor went to the house and fell asleep.

"WHAT THE HELL WERE YOU THINKING!" Sara awoke to this thundering noise as her bedroom door was being kicked in. Even though he was a southern gentleman and normally very quiet, George Washington had a bad temper.

"What happened? What did I do?" Sara questioned, trying to figure out what was going on.

"WHAT DID YOU DO, REALLY! WHEN A CERTAIN OFFICER TRIED TO GET RECOGNITION FOR A PRIVATE'S HEROISM FOR SAVING HIS LIFE AND PROVIDED THE NAME GEORGE WEINSTEIN, I KNEW EXACTLY WHO IT WAS!" His temper did not subside with any words. "WHY THE HELL

WOULD YOU PICK UP A MUSKET AND RUN INTO BATTLE LIKE THAT? YOU COULD HAVE DIED!"

Now Sara was just as upset as General Washington and yelled back, "THEN I WOULD HAVE DIED ON THE SAME LAND AS MY FATHER!"

This must have hit a nerve with the general because he started to get his voice under control. "Get dressed and we will continue this discussion." He then turned around and saw Dr. Cochran.

"Did you know about this?" he asked as he started getting angry again.

"No, sir, the first I saw her was on the wagon here. I figured I better keep an eye on her from that point on," the doctor replied.

"Oh well, then thank you very much, sir," Washington said as he left the house.

"That was fun," the doctor said to Sara, then closed the door.

After she composed herself and got dressed, Sara left the house searching for General Washington. However, the first angry person she came across was Captain Hamilton. "If it wouldn't get me court-martialed, I would put you over my knee and beat you!" he said as he approached.

Still angry with Washington, Sara turned and said, "Don't even start with me today!" Her face got very red with anger and wind.

"What on earth..." Hamilton tried to say, but Sara cut him off.

"Not on earth!" She let loose again. "I did it for my father," she yelled but not as much now.

"Remember, I told you that a man can go out and die on the battlefield, but a woman is not allowed to. Well, I changed the rules. And if I did die, it would have been for my father. I don't need any other reason."

She turned to walk away, but Hamilton took her arm. "No, you don't get to play the 'my father' card and walk away just like that," he said.

Her eyes widened, and she sternly said, "Get off of me."

"I am not letting go till we talk about this," Hamilton said back.

"You really don't want to do this!" she said, the emotions growing even more inside her.

"Yes, I really do. I care about you, sister, remember? I don't want to see you just throw your life away."

Now she was yelling again. "WHY DO YOU GET TO DO IT, BUT I CAN'T?" With that, she twisted in such a way that her father taught her to break free of the grasp. She then started backing up, leaving him in a state of shock. Finally, she turned around and walked toward the general's new headquarters.

"I am of a mind to send you home right now!" General Washington said as she arrived.

"And where exactly is that home," Sara snapped back.

He looked up right into her eyes and said, "Mt. Vernon!"

"THAT'S NOT MY HOME!" she yelled back.

"You better get yourself under control and sit down right now, miss," he said. She took the seat in front of him and waited, just staring at him. "Look, you wanted to stay with the army, and I allowed it. You wanted to help the men, and I got you a job with my doctors, but you *cannot* go running into battle because you feel like it. Do I make myself clear?" There was a long pause that caused a lot of tension. "DO I MAKE MYSELF CLEAR?" he said again and louder.

"Yes, sir," she finally said back, still with a lot of attitude.

"Martha and the other ladies will be here tomorrow. If she wants to send you off after what you did..." He paused, then continued, "Well, when she arrives, I want you to stay with her at all times now. No going to the hospital."

"So what, you're grounding me?" she complained.

"I can have you locked in a house under military arrest for impersonating a soldier, would that be better?"

Her fists tightened and her face contorted, but she finally replied, "No, sir."

Finally he said, "Now I appreciate the doctor taking you in, but I want you here with us so you will be taking a room upstairs. That is all." His eyes followed her out the door as she left. Then he thought to himself, *Oh, Sara, I hope you know I am only trying to help you.*

Sara was confined to her room for a century until Martha arrived the next day. When she finally did arrive, it was a few hours before she even went to see Sara as she was getting all her things put away. A knock finally came to Sara's door, and Martha walked in, not waiting for an answer. They just stared at each other in silence for a long while. "I can't believe you ran away like that," Martha finally said.

"I didn't run away, I ran to," Sara snapped back, knowing it wouldn't make any difference.

Martha was much better at staying calm than both George or Sara. "You could have cost the general the battle. Would it have been worth it?" she said sternly.

"But I—" Sara began but was cut off.

"The point is, dear, you could have. If he found out you were there, he would have been thinking about you and not the fight." Martha looked at Sara with piercing eyes as she talked. "He loves you very much and would do anything to save you, just as your own father would have." She continued, "What would he have to say right now?" That did it. Martha used the one thing against Sara that she couldn't fight back with. And since Martha knew him so very well, she knew exactly what he would have said. "He would have sent you to Donna for the remainder of the war, and you know that." Sara tried to look away, but Martha's eyes made it impossible. "I am going back to my room to sew, come along." And that is how she ended the conversation. There were no more words spoken between them the rest of the afternoon. They just sat in Martha's sitting room sewing. The only amusing part of the afternoon was the arrival of Martha's favorite tomcat, Hamilton. "I guess he found home," Martha said as she scratched his head.

A few days passed, and the tensions of the battle at Princeton started to disappear. Even the rules of staying by Martha diminished, though she required an apology letter sent to the Madders. Sara was able to go to the hospital to tend to the injured men that survived. Unfortunately, forty men fell at the Battle of Princeton for the Continental Army, but it was still considered a victory. With three victories in ten days, there was news of help from France that started to circle within the camp. Sara even found Hamilton, and they were able to calm the tension between them from their heated argument.

Even though her freedom was restored, Sara still stayed closed to the headquarters with Martha as the weather continued to decline. All the ladies would gather there around midafternoon to discuss the unimportant details of the day. They were happy to still have their husbands but knew that in the spring, the fighting would start up again. Such was the life of a soldier's wife. More often than not, Sara remained quiet as the discussions among the other ladies grew into laughter. Sometimes she would even leave the sewing room and just walked the halls listening to the gossip among the men. There was one story she was particularly fond of hearing: "A young officer walking along the trail toward Princeton with his thoughts far off in the distance and patting a cannon like it was his favorite pet." It was believed that this same officer was the one who fired the shot that took off King George's head and persuaded the British to surrender. Sara giggled as they tried to figure out who the skinny young officer was. Though she knew it was Hamilton, she said nothing and did not want them to know she was listening in.

At every afternoon meal, generals, officers, wives, and Sara would sit in the dining room of the headquarters. The men would then retire to his office to discuss new matters. One afternoon, General Greene (after finding out Hamilton was the captain firing the cannon at both battles) invited Hamilton to join the officers at that meal. When the ladies arrived, Sara was surprised to see him across the room talking with General Greene. They all sat down at their designated seats, and General Washington provided the prayer. Then he lifted his glass and toasted the young office for his heroics on the battlefield. Sara lifted her glass toward the other end of the table where Hamilton was and smiled. She was sitting with the ladies at the other end of the table, allowing the men to discuss strategies among themselves. Martha was so pleased with the recent events and concerned about the morale of the men that she suggested a winter ball be held for the officers. Sara wasn't sure how a ball for the officers would help the men but decided it best to keep her mouth shut.

The ladies, however, all chimed in excited for the event and started matchmaking the unmarried young ladies in their lives with the eligible officers in the camp. This conversation had Sara staring at the food on her plate and trying to be invisible. This did not last long as Lucy Knox turned the uncomfortable question to Sara.

"Aren't you excited for the ball, Sara?" she asked. "I am sure by now you found some suitable man to turn his head," she questioned.

Is this all a woman had to live for? Sara asked herself. *Primp yourself up like a bird to find a man and become his property for the rest of your life.* She knew all too well this was not her dream but also knew how to please the ladies and keep herself out of trouble. "There are a few heads I would like to turn, but I only have this one dress which is not suitable for a ball." She hoped that would help stop the questions. However, Gertrude spoke up this time.

"My niece Eliza is about your age and size. I will write to her to come and have her bring an extra dress for you," she said, settling the matter.

At the end of the meal, as they were starting to take their leave, Sara heard George ask Hamilton a question that made her heart jump. "I need someone like you who has been in battle and has your vision and I can trust as my aide. I pray, what do I have to do to have you by my side?" he questioned. From talking with Hamilton, she knew he had already declined this same position from other generals but hoped he would join Washington. Hopefully, he could find the acceptance and self-worth he long been looking for.

"I accept," she heard him say as her heart jumped for joy for him. A smile crossed her face as she walked out of the room with the ladies.

As the winter took its toll on the army, all talk about a ball died down to Sara's relief. By mid-March, Hamilton surrendered his post in the artillery and joined Washington's men of aides-de-camp. This also meant that his lodgings moved inside the headquarters with the rest of Washington's "family," as he liked to call them. One day when it was just Sara and Martha doing the needlework, they were talking about Washington's new help.

"Hamilton sure has proved himself an incredible help to George," Martha said. "I just wish he would stop his nightly escapades."

"Most women would, Aunt Martha," Sara said, not looking up from her work. "George even tried to keep him so busy he would be too tired, but that didn't work either."

Martha laughed. "Ah, the joys of youth." She continued. Sara shook her head and laughed with her.

"George says he has a promising future ahead of him."

"That remains to be seen," chimed Sara.

"You don't think so?" questioned Martha.

"I think he has potential that buds right up against arrogance," Sara added. "If he can keep his head and listen to what others have to say, I think he will do great things for this country. However, death has been chasing him for so long, I don't know if he can put his past behind him," Sara finished.

"You know of his past, he never talks about it?" Martha questioned.

"If you want to know, you will have to ask him. I will not break his confidence," Sara pointed out, looking right at Martha.

Then trying to change the subject, Martha asked, "Do you like him?"

Sara just stopped her needlework and looked up. "That depends on what you mean," Sara said back. "If you mean 'Do I care about him and his well-being?' then yes, very much so. However, if you mean 'Do I want to marry him?' no, I have not changed my mind on that situation," she stated defiantly.

"I just don't understand why you are so against the proposition of marriage," Martha questioned, putting her own sewing down.

"The men are fighting for independence against England, but we ladies will not see an ounce of that freedom. Not if we marry, that is," Sara said plainly.

"I will not watch these men fight and die for this cause and then so willingly hand over my own freedom. If the laws change after the revolution allowing women to keep their assets and make decisions, then I may consider it but not till then," Sara concluded.

"You know that will not happen because it will be the men making the decisions regarding the laws in this country," Martha added.

"What you can do is learn how to manipulate the conversation. Your husband has to think what you want is his idea. It is the burden of being a woman!" Martha countered.

"Then it is a good thing my father raised me to live off the land and not out of the pocket of a husband trying to own me," Sara retorted.

"You know there are benefits to marriage, dear?" Martha asked.

"Well, what some people call benefits, I call ownership. I could never be happy living like that."

At that, Martha gave up, not wanting to risk pushing against the happiness of her children. They continued the afternoon talking about much more pleasant notions. What the country might look like after the war and how long they think it will last before being called to the meal.

The next month went by pretty much the same. Sara helped at the hospital when there was needed and sewed with the ladies when there was not. General Washington kept up the heavy pace for Hamilton, trying to keep him busy and out of trouble though that didn't work too well. Every now and then, Sara and Hamilton were able to say more than two words while passing in the hallways. One day Sara noticed Hamilton was carrying a large package that was addressed to him. She became curious and asked him what he received.

"Come with me, Sara," Hamilton responded. They walked into the aide's office, where he excitedly opened the packages.

"Books!" Sara said happily.

"Yes, once we win this thing, we must put a financial system into place so we can stand on our own. These are examples of how to do just that," he said excitedly. "After the finances are taken care of, we then need to unify the country and not be individual states. Otherwise, someone else can attack, and we would easily be defeated," he continued.

"Where did you get so many ideas for a brand-new country, Hamilton?" she questioned as she picked up one of the books.

"I saw what can happen without it in the Caribbean and what can happen with it in England," he said. "We have the opportunity to build a brand-new nation, the strongest ever made if we piece it together right."

"Do you mean to create another monarchy?" she questioned indignantly.

"No, but if we take the best of the strong nations and remove the issues with laws in place to hold it together, can you imagine?" He was so excited about building this new nation it became intoxicating.

Sara finally ended with "Would you mind if I read one of the books you are not working on?"

Hamilton looked up, questioning her. "Well, if you plan on creating the new financial structure from these books, then I best learn them to know how to survive in our new nation." He smiled at her and handed over a book.

"Thank you," she replied and walked out the door.

Sara's ability to comprehend the books was as good as any boy about to start college. Hamilton, however, was something else. He was able to keep up with the general, ride out on errands, log the supplies, keep his evening rituals, and read and understand two books to Sara's one.

When Sara returned one more book for another, she questioned him. "Still have the reaper right behind you, don't you?"

"What?" Hamilton asked back, his mind somewhere else.

"You're still trying to get as much done in one day before death takes you. You have been running from it for so long. You don't know how to slow down," she explained. The understanding she had of his innermost demons never ceased to amaze him.

"The depth of your understanding of another person is nothing short of otherworldly."

"I just understand trying to decide if you want to outrun death or let it take you," Sara answered back. They both stared at each other, understanding what was not being said between them.

"I didn't think women felt that way," Hamilton questioned.

"How many times do I need to tell you? Women have the same feelings as men. Most, however, don't act on them. I am the exception," she answered.

He gave a small huff and said, "Would you like to talk tonight? Taking an evening off, so to speak?"

"I think that would be good for both of us," she replied.

Just then, Washington walked in, looking at a piece of paper and grunting about something. He started to yell at Hamilton before he noticed Sara there as well. "What are you doing here?" he said, agitated. "Are you interfering again?" he barked.

Hamilton was about to say something when Sara cut him off. She was used to her uncle's rages at this point. "I was not asking anything regarding the army. I was getting something for Aunt Martha when I walked by and saw Hamilton and asked for a book. That is all. No time wasting, no chatting, I was just leaving." She then turned to Hamilton and said, "Thank you for the book." Raising the new one, he just handed her. She turned back to George and finished with "Uncle, I will see you later" and walked out the door.

The two men just looked at each other, dumbfounded. Sara believed she heard George say, "Sometimes I just don't know what to do with her."

Sara walked back to Martha to talk about that evening. "Aunt Martha," she began, "is there any way you will allow me to talk with Alexander tonight?" Martha looked up deeply in thought about the question. Sara then continued, "Our relationship is that of siblings, and we just want to clear our heads a bit."

Martha finally replied, "In here with me only. Even if you don't want to get married, I will still protect your reputation."

Sara knew this was not a point to press on and was why she asked in the first place. Then she added, "That is as long as Uncle George gives him the night off."

"You know those tricks of making one think it was his idea only works with men, right?" Martha said, looking at Sara.

"But you are so good at it, Aunt Martha!" Sara said, admiring her.

"Note taken, and I will get George to back off tonight."

"Thank you, Aunt Martha," Sara said, rising and giving her a hug. Joy overwhelmed Sara until she heard Washington becoming angry at some military detail. Sara started to get up when Martha had her take her seat.

"You will not help this situation, dear. It is best to leave it for right now," Martha said, shaking her head, frustrated at her husband. Soon after that, she heard men running through the halls trying to rectify the situation to Washington's satisfaction.

At the afternoon meal, Sara took notice that Hamilton and a few of the other aides were missing. Worried, she looked up at Martha, who understood her concern. "It will be all right, dear, don't worry," Martha said, trying to comfort her. The women began talking among themselves about needing sewing supplies when Washington addressed the table.

"If we have another outbreak of smallpox, this war will be lost. Because of that, I have ordered the men, women, children, and civilians who stayed behind to be vaccinated in shifts." A quiet hush overcame the table, then Washington continued. "Sara, I know you have already been vaccinated, so please help with the men as they become ill." She nodded in agreement.

"But won't that just kill the men?" questioned Lucy.

"Dr. Cochran assured me that even though the men will become ill, it will not be as bad as getting smallpox, then the army would be safe from the disease." Some more people started to complain when Washington held up his hand, and Martha spoke up.

"I will get it first," she volunteered.

"Thank you, dear," George said, knowing very well Martha already got vaccinated prior to joining up with the army.

Sara knew she said it just to calm down the woman and make it hard for the men to oppose if she was willing to do it. "Hamilton and Richard rode out to get some more doctors to help. We will start tomorrow. After the meal, please go to the hospital and help the doctors, Sara."

"Yes, sir," she answered.

When she was finished, Sara excused herself and left the table for the hospital. She stepped out into the cold air and started walking down the road. The sun was high and bright, giving Sara a small bounce in her step. She believed in this vaccination and it was a good decision for Washington to make.

When she arrived at the hospital, they were already trying to get enough clean blankets on the available beds and hay on the floor with coverings. Dr. Cochran noticed Sara and walked over to her, asking how she was doing. He then pointed out what the plan was for the patients as well as for the people they would be bringing in with smallpox. Apparently, the enlisted men were building a small shed in the back with some trees they cut down to help stop the spread of the actual disease. There were four rooms in the house turned hospital, and the doctors wanted ten patients per doctor and one doctor per room. The rest of the afternoon they all made sure the beds were set up, a desk was set in each room for the doctors, and each nurse was assigned to a different doctor. Dr. Cochran wanted Sara to be able to move between each room and pass information as she was already protected.

The moon was high by the time Hamilton, Richard, and the new doctor and his patient road into camp. That doctor was going to stay with the sick man in the shed in the back. He would then cut off some of the sick person's skin that included the bumps with the puss and put it on a piece of glass. Sara was then to bring the glass with the pustule matter to the doctors in each room. Finally, the doctor would make a small cut into the healthy person's arm and put a small piece of string in the matter then into the cut. This will cause the healthy person to contract the disease mildly and hopefully create antibodies without dying. There was still a risk of dying from this form of inoculation but less likely than if it ran through the camp.

When the sick patient and doctor were settled, Sara, Hamilton, and Richard walked back to headquarters. Both men looked dusty and woebegone as Sara asked if it was a rough ride. They both looked at her sarcastically, and all three began to laugh.

As they arrived, Richard needed to complete one more task before going off to bed and said his farewells to Hamilton and Sara. Even though Hamilton wanted to make good on his offer to talk, he realized it was late and told Sara she could say good night if she wished to.

"Martha said we can talk in her room with her, and I am keeping her to that promise," Sara protested.

"I don't wish to get you into any more trouble, Sara. Besides, tomorrow is going to be a very long day," Hamilton offered again. Sara just turned around and walked to Martha's room.

"One minute, Sara," he called to her again. "I have one question to ask first." Sara stopped, turned around, and cocked her head. "Aunt Marth and Uncle George?" Hamilton questioned, raising his eyebrows.

At that, Sara realized the mistake she made earlier in the day. She usually never called them by that name in someone else's presence but was so worried about George getting mad at Hamilton she completely forgot. "Ummm!" she stuttered. "No one is to know that *please*!" she begged Hamilton.

"If they are your relations, then how are you orphaned?" he questioned.

"They are not blood. General Washington and my father were very good friends, and I spent a lot of time at Mt. Vernon. They are as close to me as any aunt and uncle could be, but they also know my need for independence," she explained. "We try very hard not to let it be known. I have a feeling you will learn what I mean in time."

He smiled and said her secret was safe with him, then they both walked into the sitting room where Martha was sewing.

"I wasn't sure if you two were going to make it," she said, not looking up.

"It is getting late, you two should sit down while I am still in the mood to sew." Her eyes looked at them before looking back to her sewing.

"Thank you, Martha, I really appreciate it," Sara said as she took a seat across the room.

Hamilton removed his hat and bowed to Martha and thanked her as well.

"Have you ever had smallpox, Hamilton?" Sara questioned.

"No, I am going to need the treatment," he said, looking worried.

"It's not nearly as bad as it could be. I think that poor guy they brought in to vaccinate everyone may die before all the men get treated."

"I hope not," Hamilton said. "I don't want to have to go get someone else."

"What do you want to do after the war?" Sara asked.

"Well, I was studying law before I joined. I think I will go back into that. But I really want to help make this the best country possible," he answered.

"We have a blank canvas and can create anything we want. It has never happened before. To build a unified country, each state beholden to each other, backing each other and supporting each other. Somewhere the poorest orphan can have the same chances as the purest-bred noble if he is willing to work for it. Where someone whose only crime is being born can be washed clean and have his voice heard and accepted."

Sara could feel Hamilton's heart ripping open as he talked. "How far does that go, sir?" she asked. Caught a bit off guard, he just looked at her. "Can this country be available for everyone or just white men?" she asked. "Well, we definitely need educated white men to guide everyone else in the right direction, but that doesn't mean there shouldn't be a place for everyone," he said.

Martha knew this conversation was not going to end well and gave a little cough. Sara ignored that sign and asked her next question. "So white men only allow white men into college to be educated so that only white men can lead everyone else, am I correct?" Hamilton looked at Sara and gave a bit of a smile. "Oh, this is funny, is it?" Sara asked, starting to get a little heated.

"Umm, excuse me!" Martha called out.

However, Hamilton spoke up. "I am saying right now the laws say only white men can attend college, so yes, someone with exceeded knowledge of the law and practices needs to be in charge. However, I hope to see that slavery would come to an end so people of color can have rights as well as women," he said, looking at Sara.

"But the first thing we must do is get a financial structure in place to be able to challenge the rest of the world and hold ourselves up. Then we need to put a constitution of sorts into place, where every state will agree so we are united. Finally, once our democracy is set up, we can challenge the laws that don't work for everyone who lives here!" Hamilton concluded.

"You want to do away with slavery?" Martha, now curious in the conversation, asked.

"I do not agree with the practice after seeing the slave trade in St. Croix, ma'am," Hamilton answered.

Martha continued, "You will never convince someone to give up their property and livelihood to live as a pauper!"

"Just hear yourself, though," Hamilton replied back.

"You're saying owning someone else is acceptable, beating them into submission and killing them is fine," he questioned.

"No, I don't feel mistreating another person is all right, but these people don't know any better and are happy doing their work," Martha countered.

Knowing where this conversation would be going all too well, Sara changed the subject. "But what can we do if the people making the decisions and laws are not providing the rights to all the people?" Sara asked.

"Then we vote those people out?" Hamilton said.

"I see different parts of Congress being elected by different classes of people, so everyone is represented. Then each elected office is responsible for a certain area of government. Finally, each area of government is held accountable to each other. That way, one class cannot be ignored or misrepresented by another." Washington had entered the room at this point, and the four of them discussed the dream of the nation.

The next three months went by at a crazy pace with the vaccinations, illness that followed, and deaths that still happened. Sara, Hamilton, George, and Martha, however, made time every night to get together and discuss the possible future of the country after the war.

"Do you understand what I mean now about, Aunt and Uncle?" Sara asked Hamilton one night, walking to the sitting room.

"It feels like a family, but I have lost that before," he said cautiously. "I like and respect the Washingtons very much, and our nightly talks are amazing but..." Then he paused. "It's just, sometimes, the general can be..." Another pause.

Sara chimed in. "Uptight and mean?" she answered frankly. Hamilton looked at her again in wonder as if she was able to right into his soul. "I have been around him a *lot* longer than you have," she said, answering his expression. "He displays a certain amount of discretion and softness, the typical Southern gentleman, but then the other side of the man shows through." She stopped and looked at him. "Take it from someone who knows. If you see that side of him, he likes you."

"Oh, great!" Hamilton scoffed. "He must *really* like me then."

"You may even say he considers you a son." She laughed.

"I already have a father!" he added a little harsher than Sara expected. "Look, Sara, I thought you would have guessed by now, but I am very cautious of my innermost thoughts. I know I talk *a lot* when I am excited about a topic, but I don't have many friends who challenge me, like Lawrence and even..." He paused again. "You."

"Me?" she questioned.

"Yes, your thoughts intrigue and challenge some of my positions. It's mentally exciting," he expressed.

"Well then," she said, "I am happy to be a challenge!"

"As am I, but the general seems to want something from me that I can't give," Hamilton finished.

"I know!" said Sara quietly. Then they entered the room for another night of discussion.

It was spring by the time all the people were vaccinated. There were a few issues, but most of the people came through it fine. Sara was sitting with Martha when George came in to tell them the army would be moving soon. This time, however, he was sending Martha and Sara to Mt. Vernon as he predicted to be constantly on the move. The two women looked at each other for a moment before Martha asked when they would be leaving.

"In two days' time," George answered then left the room.

"If you don't mind, Aunt Martha," Sara began, "I would like to stay with the Madders. I did promise them I would."

"That sounds very acceptable to me," Martha answered. "Well, I guess I should start packing," Martha said to Sara.

Sara walked away to her room, picked up the last book Hamilton gave her and went to find him to return it. She found him at his desk writing away when she handed the book over.

"Sara, did you finish it yet?" Hamilton asked.

"Not yet," she said, worried. Hamilton stood up and asked her what was wrong. "Look after him for me please," she asked. This, to her, was twofold. If Hamilton was making sure Washington was safe, he wasn't running into danger himself.

"I will make sure he returns to both of you safely," Hamilton assured her then gave her a hug.

"Make sure you both return safely, will ya," she said into his shoulder.

During the next two days, the other ladies were deciding if they would travel with their husbands or head back home as well. Most of the enlisted men's wives decided to stay with their husbands. The officers' wives all decided to return home and were departing sporadically. Two days later, Martha's son Jack arrived to escort her home. They all gathered for dinner before she departed. It was a bit melancholy, and the conversation was kept low-key. At the end of the meal, only Martha and George remained in the dining room as everyone else gave them space to say goodbye.

As she exited the building, she hugged Sara and Hamilton, asking them both to keep in touch. Finally, Martha and George walked hand in hand to the carriage, and she entered. Paris picked up the reins and started the horses with Jack riding beside. Martha waved out the window, and she was gone. Billy was the only slave of the Washingtons to remain. He was never far from George, be it in the headquarters or in battle.

Sara walked into the hospital to finish putting away the supplies. Dr. Rush had already departed for the newly built hospital Mount Independence. Dr. Bond and Dr. Riker will be joining him shortly, while Dr. Cochran will be staying with Washington's army.

Once everything from the hospital was put on the wagon for travel, Sara gave Dr. Cochran a hug and bid him farewell.

"I will rejoin you when I am allowed," she said.

"That will be a welcome reunion, my dear," he replied. Sara departed the hospital and headed for headquarters. As she arrived, she found two horses out front saddled and ready to go. George and Hamilton were talking just inside the door when she entered.

"Hamilton will see you safely home," George said to Sara.

"Then please accept the horse as a gift. Besides, if I need to call you back early, you need a way to join us."

"Thank you, Uncle. Be safe," Sara said, giving him a hug.

Then George shook Hamilton's hand and said, "Be safe!"

Sara walked up to her new light brown bay horse and slowly put her hand on the horse's neck. "Hello, beautiful," she said, looking her over. "We need to find the perfect name for you." There was a white blaze from her forehead to her nose, and she had three white socks on her legs. Sara went back to Washington and gave him another hug.

"I can't thank you enough for her."

He smiled and nodded back, extending his hand forward, telling her it was time to leave.

Hamilton, having heard the stories from Richard, was already mounted and holding the reins for Sara. "You're not gonna run away from me the way you did, Richard," he joked. She took the reins and mounted herself, and they were off.

It was a gorgeous spring day with the birds chirping, flowers starting to grow, and the sun shining down on them. "If I wasn't parting the army, I would be so happy right now!" Sara said.

Trying to change the subject, Hamilton challenged Sara, "Race to the tree at the end of the field?"

She looked at him then kicked her horse into a gallop, shouting, "Go!" Her horse was as quick as lightning in a storm. She easily won the race. "Storm," she said, leaning down and patting her horse on the neck.

"You are a scoundrel but a damn good rider!" shouted Hamilton as he came up beside her.

She looked back at him and said, "Scoundrel?" sounding undignified. "Oh really, well, at least she now has a name—Storm!"

"It suits her," he replied as they went back to a walk.

"Are you going to be all right with the Madders?" Hamilton questioned.

"Of course I am, why would you ask?" Sara questioned.

"Just be careful with them, Sara, all right?" Hamilton said in a low voice as she gave him a questioning look.

"I know you are not fond of Margaret, but they are really nice people," Sara said.

"Like I said, I don't trust a lot of people, and something about them just concerns me," he finally said.

"Well, I guess I should count myself lucky that you consider me someone to trust," Sara answered.

The rest of the day, they talked and laughed without a care in the world until they made it to the barge to Morrisville, Pennsylvania. They both dismounted and waited for the barge to arrive.

"We almost lost everything right there," Hamilton said, looking across the river.

"But you gave us hope right over here," Sara said, pointing toward Trenton.

"And somehow I truly believe you will be a defining point in all of this."

"You think way too much for an orphan from the islands," he said.

She hugged him and gave him a kiss on the cheek as the barge was tied up. She led Storm aboard and watched Hamilton as she crossed the river.

Chapter 5

A Long Summer

The Madders were excited to have Sara back, and daily life quickly fell into a routine. Sara offered her services as a nurse to Dr. Madder for room and board. "Margaret and I really could use your help as a nurse but not for room and board. We will pay you for that. The room is yours whenever you want," he said.

"However, would you allow Dr. Madder the use of Storm to get around better?" asked Margaret.

"That will be acceptable to me," Sara agreed.

There was enough land around the house for Jonathan to start building a small stable and tack room for Storm. Sara tried to help him as best she could, but building was one area she didn't have much knowledge in. The only time her father would work like this was when they were home at Princeton. Once remarried, Donna would never allow Sara to partake in an endeavor like this one. She had a basic understanding of the tools used from the surgeries she witnessed. As he would explain the nuisances of building, she remembered similar conversations with her father, and she felt safe.

Then there was Margaret; she was so excited to have someone to mother that she was happy to supply Sara with anything she felt Sara needed, even if Sara didn't exactly want it. She also had the tendency to want to tell Sara what to do. This had Jonathan mediating between the two to keep the peace. He had to remind Margaret that

Sara was raised with a free spirit and would not tolerate confinement. He also reminded Sara that having someone like her to keep safe was new and exciting for Margaret, and she needed some learning space. One evening, the ladies were arguing over what was proper in society. Jonathan just laughed, causing both ladies to look at him angrily.

"You think this to be funny?" Margaret asked.

"Yes, both of you are so stubborn and opinionated that you can't see you are exactly alike." He chuckled.

This caused both ladies to storm off in either direction.

On the days when there were no patients, Sara would ride Storm up and down the river and try to imagine where the army was now. There was little news about anyone's whereabouts. Just a lot of gossip saying that the British were going to attack Mt. Vernon, Philadelphia, and Richmond at the same time. Occasionally Sara received a letter from Hamilton or Washington, but she never expected to hear about their location or well-being. They did say that since it was summer, they were able to increase supplies, and the army was doing better. Remembering the army in the summer, she knew there was more game for food, but the pains of the military did not subside. There was a longing to know if they were saying this to shield her from the truth. She longed for the days her father would write in code to her. She would at least have some piece of information or location about where he had been. Not knowing anything created a new loneliness within her. Martha tried to ease her mood by taking her to Philadelphia and getting new clothes.

They rented a horse and buggy to ride into town when Sara asked, "I know Jonathan likes to live moderately, but he is really in the need of a horse and buggy?"

"Well, he will rent a horse when he goes out of town and doesn't mind the walking distance in town. However, I agree with you and have been asking him for years to get a horse and buggy. Why do you think I wanted him to use Storm? He has been enjoying the ease of getting around so much I think he may just break down and get one!" Margaret said.

It was a beautiful day at the beginning of September, and the ride into town was uneventful. "There are a few really good places just past Congress Hall, if my memory is correct," Margaret said to Sara.

Sara, however, shouted back, "STOP!" as she saw Hamilton coming out of Congress Hall, having just delivered a message. She jumped out of the buggy and ran over to him, giving him a hug.

"SARA, STOP THAT!" yelled Margaret.

Sara pulled away but was still paying attention to Hamilton, saying, "Is everything all right? You don't look right. What happened, what's wrong?"

Hamilton was smiling back and said, "We are doing all right, just trying to stay one step ahead, you know."

Then he turned to Margaret, tipping his hat. "Good morning, Mrs. Madder."

"Good morning, Mr. Hamilton. Please excuse the indiscretion of this young lady, though I don't know why I call her that."

Hamilton laughed, but Margaret was still appalled. Sara, however, recognized that Hamilton was not being honest with her.

"What are you ladies doing here?" he questioned.

"Well, I felt it time to take Sara into the city for shopping."

"Please make your day short and don't come back for a while," Hamilton said.

"So it's to be Philadelphia," Sara stated. Hamilton knew lying to Sara wasn't working, so in a whisper, "They are already here. We lost at Brandywine. I just advised the Congress to leave. I believe they will take over Philadelphia in a week or two." Sara never saw this amount of concern on Hamilton's face.

"I must head back. Please leave as soon as possible." He then mounted his horse and rode off.

"Let's get this done and get home," Margaret said in a huff back to the buggy.

"You still want to shop after what you just heard?" Sara questioned.

"Well, I certainly don't want those redcoats to have it, do you?" Margaret said.

Sara laughed and returned to the buggy.

They only went to one shop to keep things short. They purchased three more dresses, two pairs of shoes, and a petticoat (to Sara's protest). They also bought as many blankets, shoes, and dried meat as they could before heading home.

"I have an old chest you can put your new things in, my dear," Margaret said.

Sara just looked at her, knowing she was having the best day of her life. "Can we stop at the Miller farm on the way home please?" Sara asked.

"Miller farm, isn't that where you and Jonathan were last week? Is everything all right?" Margaret questioned.

"Yes, the young boy Tommy cut his knee so bad, he needed stitches. I just want to check in on him, if you don't mind," Sara lied. Tommy did cut his knee, but when they were there, Sara made a deal with Mr. Miller for his two-year-old black filly with a white star to give to Dr. Madder.

Margaret cried the rest of the way home after picking up the filly. "I just can't believe it," she kept saying. "I told you I would repay your kindness one day. Well, today is that day!" Sara repeated. She tried to quietly bring the new filly back to the stables, but Jonathan heard them arrive and came out the front door.

"What is this?" he questioned, looking at Sara.

"Isn't it wonderful, Jonathan!" Margaret said, crying again.

"I wanted to thank you for everything you have done for me, so when I saw her last week, I just had to get her for you," Sara said, handing over the lead line to Jonathan. "She is saddle- and harness-trained, so you will not need to rent a wagon anymore."

Jonathan scratched the horse in amazement and decided to call her Shadow.

"There is another reason I wanted to get her for you today," Sara said sadly. "The British are making a run on Philadelphia. You may be needed again soon."

"Well then, I best go buy tack and a cart."

All correspondence stopped coming in, but Sara did get word that the British took over Philadelphia on September 11. At this point, no one knew exactly where the Continental Army fled to after

Brandywine. Something more upsetting to Sara, however, were the stories that Washington was incompetent and should be removed if the army still existed. There were also stories of an army moving down from Canada, either trying to split the country around Saratoga or keeping Washington from escaping west. Sara didn't know what to believe in anymore and almost wished she was with Martha. She could at least read Martha's body language and tell if there was something to worry about. All she could do here was wait for some sort of factual news and continue day-to-day operations around Morrisville.

The leaves started changing color and falling down as time moved into October. A soft, crisp chill started creeping in as Sara waited for the letter for her to rejoin the army for winter encampment. There were many occasions where a rider would come through town to cross the river using the barge, but Sara didn't recognize any of them. She could only wonder what happened to Richard or Hamilton. One afternoon Jonathan came running in the house waving a newspaper from up north.

"We won at Saratoga!" he was shouting. "General Gates and General Arnold took Saratoga! And there is news in here of the French sending help!"

This news would be amazing if it were true, Sara thought. She just didn't want to get her hopes up if it was more gossip. She hugged Jonathan pretending she was happy with the news. "I need to go for a ride," she said. "I will be back shortly." As she was saddling Storm, Jonathan walked up behind her.

"Are you all right, dear?" he questioned.

"Yeah, I just need to clear my head a bit," she said as she started walking out front.

She was riding along the river when she noticed another barge with a message rider onboard. Again it was not someone she recognized. However, as they got close, he started calling out to her. "Miss, miss, Can I talk with you for a moment please?" She turned around and stopped where the barge would dock, and the gentleman would get off. "Please miss, can you help me find a Miss"—he pulled a note from his pocket—"Sara Weinstein?"

"Well, that's an interesting name for around here. Do you have any other information to help?" Sara tried to probe.

"I know she is with the doctor, Dr. Madder?" He looked up at her with his piecing gray-blue eyes. He was a handsome young man with a long face, but Sara was very cautious about him.

"Well, it sounds like you know about this Sara, but what about you, who may I ask is calling for her?" she asked.

"So you do know her!" he said, looking at her questioning her motives.

"Most around here know her and are willing to die for her, so I ask again, who are you?" She dropped all pretense of playing nice.

"I have a message for her and her only." He also stopped the game. She pulled out a gun and pointed it right at the young man. "You should be careful with that, young lady, it may go off," he said.

"I know exactly how to use this, and my shot is straight. If it goes off, it is because I wanted it to," she said back.

"Sara, I presume. Hamilton said you are very bold and courageous, he was right!" he started to say. "It is a pleasure to meet you. My name is John Laurens, another aide to General Washington." He bowed as he introduced himself to her formally.

"Prove it!" she said, still not dropping her weapon. He took out a letter from Washington and handed it over. She recognized his seal, put her gun away, and took the letter.

To my Sara,

> *I hope this letter finds you well. Dr. Cochran is in need of your services, if you are able to get away from your duties with the Madders. This young man, John Laurens, will be able to safely escort you to our camp. If you can not get away at this time, I understand and pray for your continued happiness.*

> *G. Washington*

Sara looked up and said, "Thank you, Mr. Laurens. I am sorry about that, but one can't be too cautious these days. Please ride with me to the Madders so I can gather some things."

"I would be happy to. Actually, I also have a letter for the doctor," John replied and mounted his horse.

Once they were on their way, John began to say, "You are as bold as Hamilton said you were!"

"Is he all right?" Sara asked, unprepared for the answer.

"He is fine. We are all busy following the general's commands, but he seems to put extra on Hamilton," John said.

"He sees something in Hamilton, something he loves and something he despises," she answered.

"He is trying to control the uncontrollable again."

The letter John gave to Jonathan also asked for his assistance and to join up with the army. Margaret questioned his leaving because of the needs of the town.

"You can handle whatever happens here, Margaret. The men need me more than the town does," he explained.

They packed the extra blanket, shoes, and dried meat they purchased to give to the soldiers. Sara only took a small chest with a few things Margaret had gotten her. Dr. Madder also had a small chest for clothes and a larger one for his medical supplies. Everything was tied down onto the cart, and Shadow hooked up. Margaret was sad to see them leave but was better about it this time. Sara wasn't sure if it was because Jonathan was also going and could protect Sara or because she left a lot of her new items behind. Either way, the parting was pleasant, and the three were on their way.

"So where are you from, John?" Sara asked.

"I am from South Carolina, Charleston."

"Charleston, that was an interesting town," Sara replied.

"You've had the pleasure of visiting our city?" he asked.

"I traveled the South with my father when I was younger," she answered.

"You don't sound like you enjoyed your travels," he questioned.

"It is not that I didn't enjoy the town, but some of the Southern cultures and styles are different from my own," she tried to explain.

"These states are close in distance but far apart in beliefs. It makes me question whose independence are we fighting for, the North, the South, or both? I had hoped that question would be answered in the Declaration of Independence, but it is still confusing. Do you agree?" she asked.

"I hope we as a nation can make the words become reality, that all men are created equal," Laurens answered.

"The only change would be they need to include women as well as slaves. That idea is neither North or South," Sara said in response. That began a long conversation regarding women's rights, the ills of slavery, John wanting to form the first black battalion, and allowing the men who fought to go free.

When they arrived in Upper Dublin Township, they could tell the army was in very poor shape. The cold of winter hasn't even started yet, but the men look worse than they were last year.

John saw them looking at the depleted army and said, "It has been difficult since the Battle of Germantown, and now we are getting more recruits but not enough supplies for everyone."

"That seems to be the challenge, having enough men or having enough supplies," Jonathan murmured.

They arrived at the James Morris House, where General Washington had his headquarters. Hanging out front, they saw a new flag posted. It had thirteen stripes of red and white, just like the British colonial flag. However, instead of the British flag in the upper left corner, there was a circle of thirteen stars.

"Impressive," Sara said, looking up at it.

"General Washington said the red is for hardiness and valor, the white is purity and innocence, and the blue is vigilance, perseverance, and justice. The stars are us, the thirteen colonies fighting for independence," John said. All three looked at it for a bit before John continued, "You both will be staying in here. There are two rooms set aside for you upstairs. The hospital is right over there," he continued as he pointed to another building. "Sam here will take care of the horses, your belongings, and supplies you brought for the men."

Sara and Jonathan thanked Laurens and walked to the hospital. They found rows of men with battle wounds from Brandywine and

Germantown. Dr. Cochran was pleased to see the reinforcements and put them quickly to work. This is where Sara first set eyes on Marquis de Lafayette, the young French officer who joined up with the Continental Army. She was unwrapping the bandages on his calf to clean the wound with alcohol as he woke up.

"Bonjour, mademoiselle!" he said with a very heavy French accent. "Je m'appelle Marquis de Lafayette. Comment vous appelez vous?"

"Je m'appelle Sara," she said back, learning French as a child in the army camps with her father. However, she didn't speak the language very often and forgot most of it.

Lafayette was excited about her response and tried to start a conversation in French, but she stopped him. "Je parle un petit peu de français," she added to let him know she only spoke a little French.

Luckily, he was able to switch to English better than she could speak French. Again, in a very heavy accent, he said, "It is very nice to meet you, Sara."

"It is nice to meet you, Marquis de Lafayette."

"Ah, Lafayette will do nicely no!" he said. "How does my leg look today?" he asked.

"Actually, it is not that bad, Lafayette. You were very lucky," she said, smiling back. "I do believe you should be going back to your unit very soon."

"General Washington would be very pleased to hear that, mademoiselle," he answered.

"I am sure he will be," she said while applying another bandage to his leg. "Have you tried walking?" she asked.

"When the doctor is not looking." He smiled back.

"Well, let's see what you can do," Sara said as she started to help him up.

He was able to take some steps using her as a crutch when Dr. Cochran came by. "Doing well, I see, Lafayette. Do you feel up to heading back to the headquarters?" he asked.

"I would very much like that," Lafayette answered back.

"I will have Dr. Madder and Sara here take you back when they are finished. They are staying in the headquarters as well so they can keep an eye on you there," he said.

Lafayette looked at Sara. "You will be staying with General Washington?" he questioned. He knew Washington wasn't fond of the young unmarried ladies who followed the army, and this surprised him.

"She has a special place when it comes to the Washingtons," Dr. Cochran said, giving her a wink.

Sara just glared at him and turned her question to Lafayette. "Are you familiar with the general's 'family'?"

"Oui, I am an aide myself," Lafayette answered.

"Then you may know some of my friends there, Richard Cary and Alexander Hamilton?"

"Oui, I know Monsieur Hamilton. However, I am not recognizing Richard Cary," Lafayette said.

"He was transferred to another unit," Dr. Cochran told Sara. "Come on, there are more patients to attend to," he finished.

Dr. Cochran asset the patients first while Sara followed from bed to bed, cleaning and redressing the various battle wounds that required surgery. Dr. Madder was caring for the men who were walking up to the hospital for supplies. These were men with minor wounds or just didn't want to be in the hospital. He would check the wound, making sure it was not infected, then tried to provide supplies from the limited amount they had remaining. Most of the time, old bandages were reused to cover something. When Sara asked where the other nurses were, she was told there were other hospitals Dr. Cochran would go check on throughout the camp. With so many men away from this hospital, they were able to finish quickly.

Dr. Madder and Sara helped Lafayette return to the headquarters. He directed him to the room for the general's aides and helped him to his bunk. Sara quickly looked around and noticed it didn't seem like Hamilton had been here for some time. It was lacking the mounds of books and crumpled pile of papers that would usually surround his area.

"The general sent him upstate and he has not returned," Lafayette said.

"Who was sent?" Sara questioned.

"Monsieur Hamilton, that is who you are looking for, is it not?" he answered.

"I was…I just…What?" she stammered.

"Monsieur Hamilton, you are looking for something, and I assumed it was a sign of him?"

That was when General Washington entered the room, and hearing the conversation, he said, "His return has been delayed for now." Then he smiled and added, "Sara, Dr. Madder, it warms my heart to see you both."

Sara jumped up to greet him but caught herself curtsied and said, "General Washington, how do you do?"

"How do you do, sir," Dr. Madder said, shaking his hand.

"I am about to go for an evening meal, will you join me?" General Washington offered.

"Thank you, sir," they both answered.

Then turning to Lafayette, he said, "Son, how are you feeling, are you up to walking to the dining hall or should I have something taken to you?" he questioned.

"Ay, General, I am feeling well enough to sit at your table again, sir," Lafayette answered.

They gathered around the table, where they were greeted with fire cake and rum. "My cooks are still in Mt. Vernon," Washington said with a smile.

The conversation over dinner was mixed. The news of Saratoga and the French army helping were true, but so was the devastation after the battle of Germantown. They talked about how Lafayette bravely organized the retreat at the battle of Brandywine, saving the army even though he was shot in the leg. They also explained how they thought Hamilton was dead based on Captain Lee's report of him being shot off his horse in the Schuylkill River only to show up hours later.

"Death just can't catch him," Sara joked.

Finally, they discussed how the people were no longer accepting the currency, so obtaining supplies for the growing army has become increasingly difficult. The conversation lasted a lot longer than the meal itself when the general decided it was time to retire for the evening. Dr. Madder and Sara were shown to their rooms while the general guided Lafayette back to his.

Chapter *6*

Battle of White Marsh

General Washington and Sara were eating breakfast when an aide interrupted them. He provided a message from a Quaker housewife named Lydia Darragh explaining General Howe was planning a surprise attack. This allowed the army to prepare a defense to stop Howe's advancing army. "Sara, please let the doctors know they need to prepare."

As Sara ran over to the hospital, the generals were entering headquarters to plan their strategy. Sara told Dr. Cochran and Dr. Madder about the upcoming battle. Both doctors believed the sooner they started treating an injured man, the better that man would be. They decided they would be on the field to try to get to the wounded as soon as possible.

On December 5, the shooting started with the Pennsylvania militia advancing forward just enough to cause damage. Dr. Madder and Dr. Cochran had their medical supplies on Dr. Madder's cart and were waiting far behind the lines. Sara rode up behind them and surprised both of them.

"What are you doing?" Dr. Cochran called.

"I am gonna help pull the men from the field for you," she called back as she rode toward the shooting.

This battle turned into a military dance, as Howe moved his army forward and the Continental Army moved deeper into the woods. Then the British would retreat back, and the Continental Army would advance to the edge of the woods. Washington already learned not to fight the British in open battle. To Sara, it seemed each side was trying to "poke" at each other and cause them to make a mistake and weaken their defenses. As the army would move forward, she would search for injured men behind the lines to bring them to the doctors. Sara was pulling a private with a stomach wound when she fell over and got a sharp pain in her shoulder. She wasn't sure what she tripped on but went back to the wounded man and continued pulling him out of the way. Dr. Cochran came over to help her when she fell over again, a bit weak. That is when Dr. Cochran noticed she was bleeding from her shoulder and tried to attend to her. Sara looked down and noticed the wound herself.

"Oh my," she said, the adrenaline of the situation taking over. As the doctor tried to look at her, she said, "No, he is worse than I am, him first."

"Only if you pull back now," Dr. Cochran insisted. Sara nodded and retreated on her horse back to headquarters.

Elizabeth Price and Mary Jones saw Sara riding up injured and quickly rushed into headquarters to attend her. They applied pressure to the wound and poured alcohol into it to clean it out.

Sara was starting to feel the pain of the injury now and let out a moan in protest. "Is there an exit wound?" she asked the ladies. They turned her over and found the bullet went right through to the other side. "That's good news. Apply more alcohol and bandages until the doctor returns," Sara said, losing her voice.

Dr. Madder showed up shortly after, saying he had been told what happened. "Elizabeth, please go help Dr. Cochran on the field." Then he picked up his bag, took out his scalpel and tweezers, and started cleaning the wound of any material that entered with the bullet. Mary placed a leather strap into Sara's mouth the same way Sara did so many times to others. As the doctor was probing around in the hole, Sara couldn't help but scream out in pain even though she tried not to. He finished with pouring more alcohol down into the wound and stitched her up. They used bandages to wrap her wound and secure her arm to her body so she wouldn't reopen it.

"You must be tired of fixing me up," she joked to Dr. Madder.

"I would prefer less of it, my dear," he replied. "Now you must rest. I will go back to Dr. Cochran and check on you later. Mary, please stay with her and make sure she doesn't get out of bed!"

Mary laughed, knowing she probably had the hardest job of all but replied that she would take good care of Sara.

Later that evening, Sara woke up to a knock at her door. "Who is it?" Mary asked, walking over to answer it.

"General Washington for one, ma'am," George answered back.

"Oh my," Mary whispered under her breath as she had not yet met General Washington. She opened the door and was surprised to not only see Washington but five other men with him. "Oh my." This time, she said it out loud.

"It is all right, Mary," Sara said as the men entered.

Besides Washington, there was Dr. Cochran, Dr. Madder, John Laurens, Lafayette, and to her surprise, Hamilton. Hamilton was the first to speak up. "We just can't keep you out of trouble, can we," he said. Sara laughed, then winced as she tried to sit up.

"Stay still, Sara, or you will remove your stitches, and we will have to sew you up again," Dr. Madder said.

George was just looking down at her when she said, "I wasn't doing anything wrong. I didn't even pick up a rifle. I was just…"

He raised his hand and stopped her. "I know what you were doing, yet I would still prefer you being away from the bullets. But alas, I am as good at keeping you under control as I am Hamilton here." Everyone except Hamilton and Sara laughed at that.

"Ay, now it is my turn to take care of you, madam," Lafayette said.

"Good luck with that," answered Hamilton.

"You have got to be the most stubborn and courageous woman I have ever met," Laurens added.

"I do try," Sara answered with a smile and continued with "What happened, did we hold them back?"

"Yes," Washington said. "They didn't engage in a full battle, though, I am sorry to say. I believe our position and the mood of the men would have taken this battle."

"I am glad to see you are doing well, Sara," Dr. Cochran said. "But I am afraid I will have to break up this little party as you need your rest."

They all bade farewell and left Mary and Sara alone. "I can't believe you know all those men," Mary said.

Tired, Sara said back, "They are all wonderful," then fell back to sleep.

Sara was supposed to remain in bed, much to her dismay. Even when the army moved to a different location she was not allowed to help. Washington's family helped Mary and made sure she didn't do anything. They did, however, visit with Sara every evening to talk about life after the war. This little family of Washington's was as close as any family of blood. Sara finally felt like she belonged somewhere. Every one of these men had a strong opinion that was against the norm, yet they were all accepted.

Laurens was always talking about abolishing slavery. To Washington, he was the bold young dreamer. Lafayette would talk about bringing this revolution to France and helping his people there. He was Washington's polished and noble one.

Then there was Hamilton; his dreams for the country almost mirrored Washington's. However, he was Washington's problem child. Someone who was headstrong and very knowledgeable but became arrogant and quick to anger whenever someone opposed him. His reaction was almost like they were dismissing him and not his ideas.

Finally, there was Sara. She was strong and courageous. She also refused to conform with what society told her she had to be. Above all things, she was true to herself. Washington cared for each one as if they were his own, even if sometimes the feelings were not mutual.

After a bit of time, the conversations would turn to more personal goals and ambitions beyond that of the country. It became so comfortable that the topic was wide open. There was no subject that was off-limits as it usually was around a lady.

"So what took you so long to return, Hamilton?" Sara asked one evening.

Hamilton challenged the line and said, "You all know that I enjoy my time with the ladies around here, but I did meet someone while I was away. If I could find her again, I may just give up this life and marry."

This made the others a little uncomfortable and worried about Sara's reaction. However, she said, "If this is the one to get you off the streets at night, go after her!"

"Oh, I thought you were totally against marriage, Sara?" questioned Hamilton.

"I am against it for me, but if it can help you, I say go for it," Sara answered.

Lafayette decided to test the line and asked, "Do you enjoy the company of other women?"

"No, monsieur, I wish for the company of men, but it is not worth the cost of my soul."

"So you do like men?" questioned Laurens.

"As much as I wish it wasn't so, I am female," she answered. "Sometimes, I believe it would be easier to be a male who enjoys the company of other men than a female," she said.

"Not if you're the male," Hamilton said, making everyone laugh.

Chapter 7

Valley Forge

Washington decided to have his winter encampment at Valley Forge and wrote to Martha to meet him there. Sara was still not allowed to help but was happy she was allowed to stay. She was able to watch the men cut down trees and make small huts to live in. They also built trenches and roadways, making this a small city. The Washingtons, Sara, and their small family stayed in a two-story house near Valley Forge creek. Dr. Madder was assigned to another unit within Washington's army, trying to get care for the sick as quickly as possible. Even though Sara and Dr. Madder brought blankets and shoes, it was nowhere near enough for the men. One morning Washington confided to Martha and Sara that he was expecting supplies for the men that would last months. The sad reality is it would only last a couple of weeks.

This was a low time for Sara because all she could do was go and sit with the ladies and read while they sewed and talked. "Some families got together and collected blankets for the men," Martha was saying.

"Are the merchants still not taking Confederate money for supplies?" Lucy asked.

"The value of Confederate money is not secured by any assets," Sara said, not turning from the book.

"Basically, it is an I owe you, and if the British win, there will be no one to pay what is owed, making the bills worthless. So the paper they are using to create the bill is worth more than the numeric amount printed on it," Sara finished, still reading her books.

All the ladies were looking at her like she was talking in a different language. As the room became silent, Sara finally looked up.

"What?" she questioned as the others were just staring at her. "I don't know where you dream up these ideas Sara," said Kitty, then turned to Martha. "How is George coping with this?"

"He walks the camp trying to help but can't provide any comfort. He said between malnourishment and freezing to death, we are losing ten men a day," Martha answered. "His heart is very heavy with the burden."

Since her arrival, Martha and George began sitting in on the evening meetings with the family. "A Prussian military officer named Friedrich Wilhelm Baron von Steuben will arrive at camp in about a week," Washington announced. "Hopefully, with his background of training Prussian armies, he can help us turn this militia into a fighting unit."

"I have heard about this Von Steuben, he is shall we say—" Lafayette began to say but was cut off by Washington.

"I have heard the rumors regarding this man, and I have also heard the facts of his military ability. I chose, for the benefit of this camp, to utilize his knowledge and help this group become an army."

"I was only going to say he is a very strict drill sergeant, but he cares very much for the men!" Lafayette answered.

"Choosing your words carefully, Lafayette?" Washington asked.

"Oui, very carefully, General." Both men started to laugh at a joke no one else understood.

The afternoon of Von Steuben's arrival, Washington arranged a meal so all officers and aides would be able to meet him. George was happy to have his cooks back with his wife, as a stew with bread was served. Von Steuben provided tales of where he had been and what he had done for other military operations. He was charged with evaluating the camp layout and making any sanitary changes he felt necessary. Second, he would be setting up drills and training exercises to turn the militia into a real army.

"Alexander and Laurens, please provide whatever aid Von Steuben needs to complete his operation," General Washington said.

The next day the camp was full of noise as latrines were being dug downhill and the kitchen areas were moved. The men who were not working on the structure of the fort were starting military drills. Sara would watch Von Steuben and remember her father's training drills. They would work on things like firing and reloading their weapons efficiently, charging with bayonets, and marching in columns instead of single-file lines. At meals, Sara would talk with Von Steuben regarding his training practices and compared them with her father's ideas. She found him to be very flamboyant and showy in his mannerisms but genuinely a gentleman.

Once the stitches came out of her arm, she tried to move it as much as possible. It was incredibly stiff and difficult to move, but the more she worked at it, the more movement it provided. She tried to go back to the hospital because typhus started running through the camp again.

Spring had arrived, and game was moving about, making it easier to obtain food. This also made the interactions between the men more frequent, allowing typhus to spread easily. This time both Dr. Cochran and Dr. Madder were using their tea and comparing notes on what was working. Neither doctor would allow her near the hospital, however, as they didn't want her to get sick while still recovering from the gunshot wound.

Sara's only option was to stay with Martha and the ladies who remained. She tried to sew when she could and would read when her shoulder hurt too much. When Martha had a pile of socks for the men, she and Sara would walk around the camp talking with the men and providing socks to as many as they could. They did what they could to uplift the spirit of the men and care for the sick who did not wish to go to the hospital.

One morning, Sara just watched Martha interact with the soldiers and care for them like they were her own. She became a mother figure of the camp, and the men began to call her Lady Washington.

This is one area of feminism that Sara felt lost to her. Her decision to never marry means she will never have children of her own. She will never know the tenderness this woman has to offer.

One afternoon the ladies were discussing a party that was held the evening before. Apparently, Von Steuben invited men to dine with him as long as their breeches were torn and tattered. However, most of the discussion was on what Von Steuben was or was not wearing. They even discussed the reason he was dismissed from the Prussian army. The rumor Lafayette and George knew about was that Von Steuben was interested in men.

"Do you really want to spread gossip about someone you don't know that much about?" Sara asked.

"You need to be cautious around someone like that," Kitty said. "Who knows what he is capable of."

"That is really not fair," Sara said, disgusted, and put down her book. "His methods and ideas on building a successful army camp are incredible, and he cares about the welfare of these men."

"Yeah, I bet he does. It doesn't bother you that he wants to be with men? That is just wrong," Kitty complained.

"Who has the right to say what is right and what is wrong? People create unjust laws to mistreat others, and that is considered right?" Sara complained.

"God looks down upon that relationship. I am not about to tell God he is wrong," Kitty replied.

"God said to love thy neighbor, and Jesus himself went to eat and talk with those deemed unacceptable. He never once damned someone for not being 'normal.' Why is it so hard to accept someone who is different?" Sara questioned.

"It is just not right," Kitty stated plainly.

"How can loving someone be wrong?" Sara said.

Martha made a noise wanting them to stop the argument. Sara just shook her head and left the room, fuming.

Sara stormed outside and almost walked right into Lafayette. "I am so sorry, Lafayette."

"Bonjour, Sara, What is wrong?" he asked her.

"People, I hate people," she said.

"Well, that is going to be a very big problem for you then," he said, and they both chuckled.

"Let's take a walk and see if Lafayette can help you with your problem or help you see where you are going at least."

"Why are we fighting in a war for freedom when what people really want is 'your allowed to be free and have your own views and opinions as long as your views and opinions agree with mine'?" Sara sounded off.

"Well, that is a big problem. Anyway, can we narrow it down a little?" Lafayette questioned.

"The 'ladies' are talking about, Von Steuben."

"Ah, and they are angry in his choice of company?" Lafayette answered right away.

"Yes, it shouldn't matter if he is or not. He should be allowed to love who he wants. As long as he is not hurting anyone and doing the job he was hired for, what is the problem?" she asked.

"You sound like someone who would do well in France. I shall like to invite you there when things calm down. However, to solve your problem, the issue, mademoiselle, is you," he said.

"Me?" she complained indignantly.

"Oui, you have a very forward-thinking mind when the world is in reverse. This country is fighting for freedom. The idea is revolutionary. However, when it is all over, the people will want to go back to what is normal," he said. "I believe Hamilton has the right idea, but I fear he has a difficult uphill battle to change the minds of the people to what freedom really is."

"Unfortunately, that makes a lot of sense," Sara said sadly.

"I recently met a man named James Monroe who is very fond of his slaves and will not let them go for any reason, yet he is here fighting for freedom. I see a very difficult road ahead long after this war is over," Lafayette said, looking around.

Chapter *8*

What happens at Monmouth...

One morning in early June, George, Martha, and Sara were eating breakfast in the dining room when Hamilton came in and handed a letter to George. After he finished reading it, George stood up and left the room without a word, followed by Hamilton. Sara noticed Frank and Billy talking just outside the door, then Billy followed Washington while Frank entered the room.

"Frank," Martha called, "is there news?" Sara smiled to herself as she thought Martha didn't like to wait for news either.

"Yessum, them British be movin' north, they done left Philadelphia be," Frank said as he cleared George's table setting.

"Well then, can you please tell Ona to start packing my things as we will be leaving shortly," Martha said, then returned to focus on her meal.

Sara always admired Martha's ability to pass something like "The British are on the move and left Philadelphia" off for "Would you like another cup of tea?" Sara could barely control her heartbeat and wanted to jump up and help pack the hospital.

"Please finish your hoecakes before they go cold," Martha told Sara.

"Aunt Martha, how is it you never seem to be bothered by anything?"

Martha gave a little laugh and said, "It took years to work at it, my dear."

After they were finished, Martha and Sara went their separate ways to pack. By the time Sara got to the hospital, Dr. Cochran and Dr. Madder had it taken care of. It wasn't too hard as they were severely lacking in supplies, so they were just waiting on orders and the wagon to put the boxes on.

"How is that arm doing, Sara?" questioned Dr. Madder.

"Good as new, sir, no trouble with it at all," Sara answered. "Have you heard from Margaret?" Sara questioned.

"Yes, they are holding the town together as best they can. You have people who will not go to her for medical issues, but she is really good at it. I wish they would trust her more sometimes," he said more, thinking out loud.

"They don't trust her. I thought they didn't like her bedside manner!" Hamilton said, entering the building. Sara tried not to laugh but couldn't help it. Even Dr. Madder laughed a little at the comment. "We will have a wagon here shortly for the men and supplies. As for you, Sara, the general will like to talk with you," Hamilton finished, and he left as quickly as he appeared.

"Let me go see what that's all about since you two are all right here," Sara said to both doctors.

Sara walked into General Washington's office and waited for an opportunity to talk. All the officers were there discussing ideas and strategies that caused some heated arguments between the men. An officer Sara had not met before but heard about was General Lee. He didn't want Washington to take the army anywhere and wanted to stay here at Valley Forge. The only other general who agreed with General Lee was General Knox. Everyone else was saying to hit a retreating army in New Jersey would be a tactical advantage, and the men can try out their new open field battle skills. General Washington looked up and saw Sara, who had entered the room, and gestured her over. The arguing men stopped quarreling and looked to see what took Washington's attention.

"I was told you needed to see me, sir?" Sara asked confidently.

"Yes, Sara, Martha has decided to stay with the army this summer, and I would like it if you would stay with her," he asked.

"I would be honored to, sir," Sara answered.

Washington did not need to call her into this busy room to ask this; he already knew the answer. Sara understood the further message behind this question that the rest of the officers may not know. He wanted Sara to personally take care of Martha and remove her if needed. There would be guards, sure, but they could not be with Martha like Sara could be, and besides, she still had the best shot.

Betty was ordered to help Sara pack her things so she didn't reinjure herself. Instead of this idea, Sara closed the door when Betty entered and had her take a seat while she packed her trunk.

"Did you hear anything new lately, Betty?" Sara asked.

"I heard that roughly five thousand men went out following General Lee to find the tail end of that British army," Betty answered.

"General Lee? What is he thinking?" Sara questioned Washington's decision. "I heard he was just released from capture a short time ago from his screw-up before Trenton. Why would he trust him with something so important?" Sara added.

"You know the general likes to give second chances," Betty said, smiling to have this chance to sit and rest.

"I just wish it was to people who deserved it. Well, Betty, I am sorry to say I am finished. I still don't have much to pack," Sara said.

"Thank you for the rest, miss," Betty said, then left the room. As Sara was about to open the door to leave the room herself, a knock came. It was Paris and Giles to take Sara's trunk downstairs. She thanked them and followed them down and outside. There was an excited noise around camp as the men lined up to march in the manner they were taught by Von Steuben.

"They actually look like an army now," Martha said as she walked up behind Sara.

"Yes, they do, it is a beautiful sight," Sara answered.

Sara tied Storm to the back of Martha's carriage and climbed inside. "I wonder why the British decided to leave Philadelphia?" Sara asked.

"There are a lot of things the British do that I don't understand," Martha said.

"Are the other ladies joining us during the summer?" Sara questioned.

"No, they will be returning to their homes," Martha said. "Besides, I believe you have had enough of their opinions lately," she added.

"I am so sorry, Aunt Martha. I try to be a proper young lady around your friends, but they just make me so angry," Sara said. "How do you stay so calm all the time?" She questioned.

"Well, dear, one has to learn how to survive with the life they have been given. I was born a Southern lady and even though I liked to climb trees when I was a young girl, it is not proper to continue that," Martha started, then continued. "The world will tell you how to behave so you can advance and be heard."

"That's not true. One of the reasons we are fighting this war is because we cannot change the station to which we were born. The colonies call for freedom to govern themselves and change the rules, but they don't want to change all the rules. They claim that if you work hard enough, you can adjust your status in this country, like Hamilton. However, I have been through the South, and no one works harder than the slaves, even yours. I don't see you just letting them go free if we win this war," Sara countered. "So it is not if you work hard enough, it's if you were born the right gender and color you have the chance to change your status."

Martha glared angrily at Sara for this comment. "First, you have to live with the way things are before you can consider changing them," she said. "Take a marriage, it is not ownership, it is partnership. I didn't know George was going to be selected as commander in chief, but I helped him decide to take the position."

"Do you really think he would have said no?" Sara asked, a bit sarcastic.

"There are ways a woman can talk to her husband and help him make a decision. However, there are also times when you need to take a step back and let him have what he wants," Martha tried to explain. "As much as he was honored to be offered the position, he wanted to know how I felt," she continued. "He was worried he wasn't the right man for the job. He also knew that I would have been perfectly happy living out the rest of our lives at Mt. Vernon. I suggested he agree to it because I believe he is the only man for the job. I also know he is constantly doubting himself, and even though I could go home like the other ladies, he needs me to be his silent support. As a wife, you must walk a fine line and give up some of your wishes to allow your husband to succeed. He, in turn, is supposed to do what he feels best for you and your family. But most men like a little help deciding what is best. Not all, mind you, and some can be a little slow to understand your needs, but they do try. It is not exactly a one-way street as you seem to think it is. That is why before marriage, ladies are kept wholesome and away from any gossip. It is why she dresses up to catch the eye of every man. Then she gets to pick the man she will be with, and if she picks right, he will be a partner. However, if she corrupts herself, no worthy man will even look at her," Martha finished.

"I don't see how it is a two-way street when a wife is supposed to submit to her husband," Sara complained.

"Don't forget a husband is supposed to love his wife as Jesus loves the church," Martha challenged back.

"That is precisely why I can't get married. I refuse to submit and hope for someone to love me back. If the promise was the same in both directions, maybe. I have too much of my father in me. I will not ask anyone to do something I will not or have not already done. I expect the same in return. If a man wants me to submit to him, then he will also need to submit to me," Sara said indignantly.

"Okay, so you refuse to get married, but that doesn't mean you should not conduct yourself as a proper young lady." Martha tried another direction.

"Why would I need to act like a lady if I don't need to catch a man?" Sara said, laughing.

"If you want to be part of society, you must do what society wants. If you get into high enough places, you may be able to talk with someone who can change the laws. That, my dear, is why you should do your best to be a lady," Martha said.

"Now that one makes sense, Aunt Martha," Sara said.

The ride and conversation took them into the evening. A part of the army crossed the Delaware River, but Sara and Martha stayed on the Pennsylvania side with the remainder of the army that would cross the following day. Sara suggested staying the evening with Martha Madder and fill her in on Sara's and Dr. Madder's condition. Martha, however, decided against it since it was already dark, and she would not want to impose on someone.

Dr. Madder was also on the Pennsylvania side and saw Washington's coach. He rode over and asked Martha personally, so she finally accepted the invitation. Paris followed Dr. Madder to his house about an hour away and let all his passengers out. Dr. Madder offered him a bed in the cooking house for the evening so he didn't have to travel back and forth. Margaret was excited to see every-one enter the house and called for June to make another meal for everyone.

"How are you, guys? What has been going on?" she said.

They discussed what they could until the subject turned on Sara. Margaret and Martha started to discuss how to get her married. At that point, Sara said, "You two keep plotting, I am going to bed."

The next morning, Sara awoke to a noise in the dining room. June already made eggs and coffee for everyone to eat before the jour-ney. Sara wasn't sure if Margaret and Martha were up all night talking about her because there were in the same spots laughing away.

"Still planning my life for me, ladies?" she questioned as she took her seat.

"We gave up on you last night. Now we're just telling stories," Margaret said.

"Oh, thank you, I am glad I am a lost cause," Sara said back.

"Well, you made it very clear that you don't want us to inter-fere," Martha agreed.

"Yeah, but I am not sure I like the two of you plotting with each other," Sara said, looking between them.

It didn't take long before they were ready to go since they were not sure when the army would be off. Martha climbed into the car-riage, but Sara decided to ride Storm this side of the river. Margaret said goodbye to Martha and gave Sara a hug and Jonathan a kiss, saying, "Please come back safe."

It was starting to rain as they headed out, making the road muddy. Martha, however, couldn't keep her eyes off the river as it picked up its intensity. She took a deep breath and tried to calm herself. She really didn't like rivers, and this one could be treacherous without rain. Sara could see her looking out her window and rode up next to her.

"It will be all right, Aunt Martha. I will sit with you on the way over."

"Thank you, dear," Martha said in a calm voice.

They got close to the rear of the army as the rain started coming down harder.

"Where were you, Lady Washington? We need to get you across before it gets worse," a captain Sara didn't recognize said.

When the barge came back across the river to pick up the next load, they escorted Martha's coach up and onto it. Sara walked Storm onto the barge behind the coach and climbed in with Martha.

"We will be fine, they got us," Sara said, holding Martha's hand.

Martha patted the back of Sara's hand and said, "You are a really good girl, I hope you know that."

The men on the barge started pulling on the rope, and they were on the river. Poor Martha started to turn a little green with all the rocking they were doing. The horses were sounding off their concerns with neighs and stomps.

"Don't let them break this thing, young man!" Martha called out the window.

"I got her under control, Lady Washington, there's nothing to worry about," a private said back.

Sara was looking at the young man and thought that his face said anything but that he had things under control. A particularly strong current pushed the barge down river tossing Martha from her seat. Sara was able to catch her before she fell and returned her to her seat.

"Thank you, my dear," Martha said, holding her hand to her heart. "I think this war is going to be the end of me."

"You're going to be fine, we will make it," Sara tried to comfort her.

It took the men a half hour to get the barge back on track again. This crossing seemed just as difficult as the one on Christmas Day. Finally, they were on the other side, and Sara said, "I am just gonna get Storm off and tied onto the carriage, then I will be back. All right?"

"Make it quick, my dear, please," Martha said.

It took another twenty minutes to get everyone off and ready to travel again, but once they were, Martha was back to her old self. "You certainly face your fears much better than I do," Sara told her.

"Well, Sara, my fear of not being with George when he needed me is greater than any other fear in my life."

"That is so sweet!" Sara said, smiling.

"That is what you're missing," Martha replied.

Sara's smile turned to a scowl. "What if I tell you I will think about it, Aunt Martha?" Sara said, trying to avoid this conversation again.

"That is all I ever wanted," Martha said, pleased with herself.

It felt like they were on the road for another hour when they heard gunfire and cannons. The pace of the soldiers picked up as Washington tried to catch up and support the men he sent earlier to pester the British. The two doctors, Martha's carriage, and the ladies of the camp were following the men at a distance. When the carriage stopped, you could hear General Washington shouting over the guns about something. Sara jumped out of the carriage and mounted her horse and rode to the doctors. Martha called out for her, but she just kept going.

The doctors were far enough back so they would not be in danger, but close enough, they could tell what was going on. "What happened?" Sara asked as she arrived.

"Lee retreated and left his men confused," Dr. Cochran shouted.

Looking back at the field, Sara could see General Washington riding in front of the army, trying to hold the lines. She could also see Lafayette's uniform taking charge of a unit behind Washington. This battle was different from the Battle of Princeton. The men were holding their lines and fighting the British move to move. They were definitely an army now. They could see the cannons moving to the right, cutting into the British. Sara also took notice of a skirt working on the cannon. There was a woman who picked up where a man had fallen. She picked up the sponge, placed it into a bucket of water, and cleaned the cannon after each shot.

"Look," she said to the two doctors, "a woman's manning the cannon."

"What did you start, Sara?" Dr. Madder asked.

The heat of the day seemed to be the complete opposite of Valley Forge. Sara couldn't remember a hotter afternoon. As the day lingered on, they were able to see men falling but were unable to safely retrieve them. The sun started to set and cool things off a bit. It seemed both sides decided to stop the battle until the next morning.

Campfires were set on both sides as the wounded were removed from the field and taken to tents for treatment. Dr. Madder was doing operations in one tent with Sara, while Dr. Cochran was doing operations in another tent with Elizabeth. Mary, Charlotte, Amiel, and John were moving patients in and out of surgeries. Privates were bringing the injured off the battlefield to the hospital. They told the doctors there were a lot of men who didn't have any wounds but were dead on the field anyway.

"With the temperature of the day, I believe they may have died from the heat," Dr. Cochran called out.

As Elizabeth and John brought in someone who was shot in the belly, Sara grabbed her and asked if she knew what woman was on the field today.

John spoke up. "That was Molly," he said.

"Molly? Who is that?" Sara asked.

"Molly Pitcher, she would bring the water out to the men on the cannons. Her husband is in the next tent with Dr. Cochran," John said.

"Sara, I need your attention here!" Dr. Madder said angrily. "You can find out about this Molly later."

They worked all night long trying to save as many as they could and didn't leave the tent until the sun was rising.

A rider was coming back into camp, shouting, "They're gone, left in the night!"

"When he finally gets to Washington, he is gonna get yelled at. Between the reds moving out in the night and that boy shouting the news, he is gonna be in a sour mood," Sara said.

They looked over the field at all the bodies that remained in the bloodstained grass.

"Too many," Dr. Madder said. "Well, I need to wash all this blood off and get some rest. Are you coming, Sara?"

She took a deep sigh, turning away from the field, and followed him.

Most of the people in camp were lying on the grass out in the open. The only tents that went up were for the doctors. Martha had her carriage placed under trees in the shade, trying to keep it cool, but she managed to find shelter in a nearby building. Sara decided to go find her and hopefully rest there if she could. When she entered the building, she could hear General Washington behind closed doors yelling profanities at General Lee for his behavior. She looked down the hall, saw Doll, and motioned for her.

"Can you please show me where Martha is?" Sara asked. Doll took her to the room and excused herself to leave.

"It wasn't you, was it?" questioned Martha. "I swear if it was you, you will be going back to Margaret," Martha said as she entered the room.

"What wasn't me, Aunt Martha?" a very confused Sara asked back.

"Firing the cannons, was that you?" Martha restated her question.

"No, I was on the hill with Dr. Cochran and Dr. Madder," Sara answered. "I never got close to the battle, I promise!"

Martha took a deep sigh of relief. "I am so happy to hear that!" she finally said. "After everything that has happened, I couldn't handle you being in battle again," she continued.

"What's happened? We don't get much news when operating," Sara asked.

"First, that fool Lee retreats off the field, then we get word that someone is trying to discredit George and have him removed as commander in chief," Martha said in what would be called a huff for her.

"Get Uncle George removed, but why?" Sara asked.

"I don't know, maybe they felt this war would be over by now. I guess they forgot the last one with the British lasted seven years!" Martha said. "Congress had to leave their comfy homes in Philadelphia to live in another town just as comfortable while these men were dying of starvation and frost." Martha still was controlling her emotions while talking, but this was the first time Sara ever saw her get close to angry.

"It will be all right, Aunt Martha. Uncle George will keep his status, and it will all be all right," Sara finally said.

"Oh, I know George will be fine, but it's the men I am worried about. What Congress is doing to the soldiers is nothing short of a crime," Marth said. "They refuse to send the necessary basic supplies for the men to fight and then get mad when they can't. This army should have dissolved a long time ago if it weren't for want of liberty. I wish there was something we can do away from Congress to show them we are behind them."

"That is a wonderful idea, but what is it that we can do?" Sara asked.

"We will figure it out, Sara. Somehow we will figure that out," Martha finished.

With the British moving, it changed what George had planned for the summer. He wanted to be close enough to keep an eye on the British but didn't want to stay in one spot to be easily attacked. He told Martha what his plans now were and suggested going back to Mt. Vernon for the Summer.

Sara stayed with the unit and found who Molly Pitcher actually was. Her name was Mary Hays McCauley. She volunteered to bring them water to clean the cannons, thus the nickname Pitcher. When Sara asked her about stepping in for her fallen husband, her response was remarkable. "I did what needed to be done, the cannons were saving the main army, and I could not stand by and let that falter."

Washington's family would try to get together every night, but there were times when Sara and Washington were alone. She found the times with the father figures in her life blessings sent from her father from heaven. One night, however, Washington seemed more upset than usual.

"I tried to let it go, but I just can't allow this," he huffed.

"What happened?" Sara asked.

"Lee, he pushed too far, and I need to go ahead with the court-martial," he answered.

The next day, General Lee was court-martialed for disobedience on the battlefield as well as for inappropriate letters he sent to General Washington began. Sara would sit outside the window or tent to hear what they were saying since she was not allowed inside. Hamilton and Lafayette both testified against Lee, causing a rift between the men. The trial took longer than normal because of the delays with constant travel.

When it was finally over, Sara was happy to hear that Lee was found guilty on all counts and suspended for a year from active military service. However, Congress wanted to go over the court-martial and decision before General Lee was removed. Lee decided to write to the newspapers to get backing and have the ruling overturned. He wrote about how General Washington was incompetent to lead the army. How Hamilton, Laurens, and Lafayette were Washington's puppets, and if they were not removed soon, the war will be lost. Washington tried to convince his family to ignore Lee, but the more he continued to discredit everyone's name, the more indignant they became.

Sara would talk with Lafayette and Hamilton about Lee's comments whenever they got a chance. They contacted Laurens by mail as he was sent to Rhode Island to help the French take back Newport. "I believe your Congress is plotting against the general. When they sent me to take Canada last year, I received word that Conway, Congress, and others were trying to remove the general from power. I believe they are still trying this but using Lee instead of Conway," Lafayette said.

"We need to keep a very close eye on our general from now on," Hamilton added. They all talked into the evening, and Hamilton came up with new plans to protect Washington.

A few more weeks had gone by when Sara was on her way to the hospital and found a newspaper that was tossed away. She gasped at what was written on her way inside. "What happened?" Dr. Madder asked.

"That pompous blowhard Lee started posting about General Washington's credentials again. He also called Hamilton and Laurens 'dirty earwigs' who will forever insinuate themselves near persons in high office. I don't believe this is going to end well."

At the beginning of December, Washington was summoned to Philadelphia and invited to stay at Henry Laurens's house. Sara overheard him telling Hamilton to leave Lee alone no matter what he said. She could tell Hamilton did everything he could not to blow up at this request. He stormed out of the office and almost pushed Sara out of his way without stopping. George then appeared and said Martha would meet him in Philadelphia, thus prolonging her return to camp, much to Sara's dismay. There was also a rumor that Lafayette would be heading back to France to help Franklin persuade the king for more supplies and men. It felt like her little family was being torn apart again, and there was nothing she could do about it.

Washington escorted the army to Middlebrook for the winter and divided the group into three brigades. Lafayette, Hamilton, Dr. Madder, and Sara were stationed in the middle unit together. She tried to talk with Hamilton, but he grew increasingly agitated with being told to leave Lee alone as well as being denied a command of his own.

The next day, Sara decided to go for a walk around the encampment when she was summoned to the hospital for an emergency. She ran as quickly as she could and found both doctors preparing for surgery. When she walked into the room, she saw Lee on the table with a bullet wound to the side. She picked up a strip of leather and asked Lee what happened.

"Cleaning my gun and it went off," Lee said.

"Yeah, like I am going to believe that," Sara said back and put the strap into his mouth.

The doctors came over and started operating to remove the bullet. Sara was holding Lee's shoulders down to keep him as still as possible. They were able to find the bullet and close him up without too much of a problem.

"Who was involved in this? How did he get here?" Sara asked.

"He was found right outside. I am not sure if he had help or not," Dr. Cochran said.

Later that evening, when Sara met up with Hamilton, she also found Laurens in the sitting room, and they seemed pretty happy.

"When did you get back?" Sara asked Laurens.

"Last night, I am just passing through as I am on my way to Charlotte. The reds are trying to take over the South now," Laurens said.

"Did anything exciting happen today?" Sara asked.

"Ah, nothing happened, it was a quiet day," they said, then laughed.

"Well, my day was full of adventure," she said.

"Really, was it a good adventure?" Laurens asked.

"It seems General Lee was shot and dropped off at the doorstep of the hospital," Sara answered, looking at both men, their glee seeming to wear off. "Do either of you know how Lee was shot today?" Sara question.

"Not a clue," said Hamilton.

"Why would I know?" claimed Laurens.

"He told me exactly what happened," Sara said, glaring at them.

"That coward. Look, a duel is a way for gentlemen to solve their issues, and with everything he was saying, he deserved it," Hamilton said. Sara just raised her eyebrows.

"Look, I wasn't even hit, he completely missed," Laurens said.

"But you didn't!" Hamilton chimed with a laugh.

Sara looked at them, just moving her eyes between them, and they quieted down.

"Sara, you saw what he was saying. Something had to be done to stop him," Laurens said.

Sara sat down and finally said, "Lee told me exactly how it happened—he was cleaning his gun, and it went off." Then she looked back up at the men. They both looked pretty embarrassed about what just took place. "I agree he needed to be stopped, but dueling is an old-fashioned, barbaric ritual that also needs to be done away with," Sara complained.

"It is the only way a man can prove his honor!" Hamilton said, a bit upset now.

"Dueling is not about honor, it is about who has a better shot. It doesn't solve anything," Sara complained.

"Most challenges don't come to this. The one who made false accusations usually backs down on his morals when his life is challenged. Also, you don't have to shoot at anyone. You can point to the sky and waste your shot," Hamilton tried to explain.

"That is supposed to make me feel better? Are you trying to tell me that because Lee missed it is due to some cosmic reason because he was wrong?" Sara stated. "You know how I feel about equality, so humor me a bit. What if he said something against me," she said, looking right at Hamilton, "and I challenged him to a duel for my honor."

"You know I would protect your honor, Sara," Hamilton said indignantly.

"And you know I wouldn't be satisfied unless I fought for my own honor," she said, a bit prideful.

"Calm down, guys. It's over with, and Lee is going to quiet down now," Laurens said, stepping between them.

"All I am saying is if gentlemen can solve their problems with a duel, then so could a lady. If you find that notion to be difficult to swallow, maybe dueling is not the best way to handle the situation. Especially for someone who has death chasing them," Sara provided. "Besides, I would be devastated if either of you fell that way."

"Fair enough," Hamilton agreed.

"Will both of you promise to never do anything that stupid again?" Sara asked.

They all gave each other a hug and were able to enjoy the remainder of the evening.

The next day, however, as Hamilton, Laurens, and Lafayette were all in the aides' office, she overheard them talking.

"Can you imagine ladies dueling?" Laurens said.

"Oui, I can see that lady dueling," Lafayette stated matter-of-factly.

"I know she is stubborn and hard-headed, but no one would ever take her seriously, would they, Ham?" Laurens asked.

She heard a mumble but not an answer.

"I believe Sara can hold her own in any situation. I would not like to see a man underestimate her," Lafayette added.

"Hey, look here." She finally heard Hamilton. "Congress upheld the decision to remove Lee from active duty. He is to leave the camp as soon as he is able to travel."

Heartbroken, she just walked away.

Sara tried to stay away from headquarters as much as possible after that. She didn't even say goodbye to Laurens before he left camp. Hamilton tried to say something to her, but she just walked away. Lafayette was the only one she would talk to, and even that wasn't much.

"I overheard the talk you guys had the other day about me. I thought I was worth something to you, but I guess I was wrong. I was just a joke," Sara said and walked away. She decided to go and check on Storm, but Lafayette followed her.

"You were never a joke, and you know you can't ignore him forever."

"I can try," Sara replied angrily.

"Sara, you need to discuss this matter with him," Lafayette protested.

"But he is part of the problem. No matter how intelligent we are, how strong we can be, how much better we can be, we will always be seen as inferior."

"Who's inferior?" said a voice she didn't want to hear.

They turned around to see Hamilton walking up behind them. "How are the two of you doing today?" he asked.

Sara didn't answer, so Lafayette did. "It is a wonderful day today, a nice day for a ride, oui?" He then turned and left them alone.

"Well then," Hamilton said, "I believe Lafayette to be correct. It is a lovely day for a ride, want to join me?" Hamilton asked.

"Fine," Sara answered indifferently, and she put her saddle on Storm.

As they distanced themselves from the army, Hamilton asked, "You seem really upset about something. Can I help?"

"That's your first question, really?" she snapped back.

"Come on, Sara, what's going on?" he asked.

"You can't help me. It's a ladies' problem, something you know absolutely nothing about," she yelled back.

Hamilton tried to make a joke and said exactly the wrong thing. "Well, if it is only a ladies' problem, I am sure I can fix it for you."

Something inside Sara snapped, and she turned on him. "Who the hell do you think you are? You can't fix me, you know nothing about me. You pretend to, but this is a joke, all this is a joke. A new better world, for who! Certainly not me, it doesn't matter who wins this war. I was born a nothing, and I will die a nothing. No one will care!" Sara patted her gun and looked at it. "I could shoot myself right here, and it wouldn't matter to anyone."

"Whoa, whoa, hold on now!" Hamilton said, holding up his hands. "I care, Lafayette and Laurens, we all care!" he said, trying to calm her down.

"Oh really, I thought you said no one would take me seriously," she yelled.

"Lafayette told me you heard that conversation, but I didn't say anything like that," he tried to explain.

"Exactly, Lafayette at least stood up for me, you didn't say anything! You don't understand, you can't. Just leave me alone." She kicked Storm into a run and rode off. She knew Hamilton followed at a distance. Part of her never wanted to see him again, and the other part wished he would hold her. She made it back to headquarters and went to her room.

She was so confused she couldn't quiet her mind. "You're just a stupid girl and will never matter to anyone," she would think one minute and the next. "Martha, Margarette, and yes, even Hamilton, Lafayette, and Laurens would miss you. They may not respect you, but they would miss you." This battle inside her head was more intense than any battle she ever saw on the field. Her heart felt like a knife was being pushed through it by every man she ever met. They betrayed her. They told her they cared, but in truth, how could they if they couldn't respect her? Who was she if no one would respect her? Maybe going to the mountains and living alone would be the best place for her. She never felt so alone and lost in her life and cried harder than she ever did. She could force death to catch up and take her life, but that was against her Christian beliefs. Then again, why would God care what she did if he created her to be a nothing female. Her thoughts were a jumbled mess swirling around and around, not quieting down no matter what she tried. It was the longest night of her life.

The next morning, Hamilton knocked on her door and asked if he could enter. She didn't answer. She couldn't say anything. "Sara, are you all right? I will kick the door in if you don't answer." He sounded really worried this time. She just sat there wiping away a fresh set of tears.

Bang! The door flew off the hinge as Hamilton kicked it in. Seeing Sara sitting there, he calmed down and said, "God, I thought you might have done something last night. You scared me," and hugged her. She just sat there, not moving, not pushing him away or hugging him back. She just stared at the floor. "Can we talk?" he asked. She just nodded but kept staring into the floor.

Hamilton sat down next to her and said, "Death has been chasing both of us for a long time now. You think I don't understand, but I told you before I do. Remember, bastard child?"

"Yeah, but you can improve your station, I can't," she snapped.

"Oh really. Do you really think no matter how hard I try or what I accomplish, people who would oppose me will not see me as just a bastard and call me so when angered? I am never going to outlive that," he said.

"You say you don't want to marry because you will lose your freedom. Well, I can't marry because of my birth," he continued. "Do you know how many times I wished death took me with my mother?" He shook his head and looked around. "Why do you think

I had no fear at Trenton or Princeton? I would welcome death with open arms. The men that are keeping you down are doing the same to me. Take George, he is promoting everyone around me to lead but will not promote me, even though I am more experienced and capable. He ignores my wishes to improve my station as much as I can in the military, so yeah, I am just as stuck in my birth as you are."

"I guess maybe you might understand a little bit at least, but then why didn't you defend me to Laurens?" Sara asked.

"My best friend was questioning something about my sister. I just felt stuck in the middle and didn't know what to say. It was wrong and I'm sorry," he added. He nudged his shoulder against hers and said, "Promise me one thing, though, if you want death to take you, don't let it be by your own hand. You want to be crazy and stupid and jump in front of a bullet fine, but not by you all right."

"I promise, only if you promise the same thing. You never answered the other day," she said.

After her conversation with Hamilton, Sara felt a little better knowing she wasn't the only one who felt alone. Somehow that didn't make her feel as lonely. Her emotions were still all over the place as she was trying to figure everything out and redefine herself. She was sad and angry and had times when she preferred to be alone. Then there were times when she was happy, excited, and hopeful.

Finally, she was able to talk with Hamilton about all of it, and he was able to compare stories. He seemed just as confused as she was because of that lady he met a while ago. He couldn't stop thinking about her and even stopped his nightly escapades. Apparently, she was from the world Sara used to live in. He felt she would never look twice at a bastard like him. Now above everything else he was trying to overcome, his lack of station in the military would not improve his chances with this general's daughter (he still has not told Sara her name) if she was even still available. Sara and Hamilton found they both had a personality that was bold and alive out in the world and another personality they tried very hard to hide.

One thing she was encouraged with was that the mountain scenery provided peace and comfort. When she started to feel the pressures of the world pushing in on her, she would ride to the cliffs and look out onto the horizon. Sometimes, Hamilton rode along, and they would talk about whatever was worrying them. Once Sara finally asked for the name of the young woman he was so smitten with.

"Her name is Elizabeth Schuyler," he finally admitted.

"General Phillip Schuyler's daughter?" Sara questioned.

"The very same," he replied, looking out into the world.

"Now I understand your issues more. With Angelica running off and eloping the way she did, he has been a bit more protective of Eliza and Peggy," she said. The fact that Sara could talk about this family with such familiarity did not ease Hamilton's anxiety. "Look," Sara said, seeing his face and understanding exactly what he was thinking, "if you want Eliza, do your thing!"

"*What?*" he said, thinking incorrectly. "I will not want to 'win' her that way," he said.

Sara started to laugh. "Not what I meant." She could barely control herself. "You need to charm her, entice her, intrigue her with your words."

"Do you think I couldn't?" he asked like she just spent the last five minutes insulting him. "It is her father I am concerned with," he added.

"Exactly," Sara said back. "Remember I had a general as a father as well. Turn her head the way I know you can. She will press her father, and Washington will vouch for you. I know he will. Finally, show her entire family you can be a complete gentleman, again which I know you can be, and they will not care for your current station."

"But as an aide, I can't provide for her the way she is used to," he complained.

"Listen, Eliza and I have some of the same notions. If you are honest with her, she will be able to look past it. Also, you were in college to be a lawyer before the war, and you are still planning on returning, am I correct?"

"Yes, but—"

She cut Hamilton off. "I know your heart will fight for justice, so you will be a great lawyer. You have been teaching yourself finances as well so you will be able to provide for your family financially. You can accomplish anything you put your mind to."

Hamilton then said, "I most likely will never see her again anyway, but why are you pushing this? You don't like marriage."

"I don't, but you do and so does Eliza." Sara grinned.

It was six weeks before the Washingtons returned and found the camp a bit melancholy. They were able to make use of the trees to create cabins and firewood. Food was a little more difficult, but the town was very patriotic, so they did everything they could to help the army out. Martha decided to have a small birthday party for George and Sara helped her plan it. The generals, their wives, doctors, Sara, and Hamilton were invited to go. Lafayette could not attend because he was already on his way back to France.

The meal consisted of ham and potatoes, followed by a cake George's cooks made for the occasion. It turned out to be a pleasant event that allowed everyone to forget their sorrows for a while. They stayed in the winter encampment until June of that year when Washington decided to head north with the army. Martha decided to head to Mt. Vernon again to be with her son, daughter-in-law, and grandchildren.

"Aunt Martha, may I join you this summer to work on some things?" Sara asked.

"Yes, my dear. We would be happy to have you at Mt. Vernon," Martha answered. They both packed up their things and waited for Jack to arrive for the ride home.

Sara found Hamilton and said, "I didn't want to leave you alone in camp, but there are some things that I need to address."

"Don't worry about me, just take care, and I will see you in the winter," he said and walked off.

Sara wasn't sure if something else was upsetting him or not but felt his salty mood was completely her fault. "I will stay in touch," she called after without acknowledgment.

Chapter 9

Virginia and the Offering of the Ladies

The ride to Virginia was long and treacherous. Martha wanted to stop to see friends and family for a day or two along the way. The first place they stopped was Philadelphia, even though Martha was just there. She took Sara shopping for more dresses that met Martha's standards. However, Martha appealed to Sara's "wild" side and picked up some riding skirts, breeches, and jackets.

"This way, you can enjoy some alone time while working on your skills," Martha told her as she shook her head, picking up the breeches. Sara just laughed and thanked her.

It took two and a half weeks to reach Mt. Vernon, and when they did, they were greeted with shrieks of joy as the girls ran up to their father. Jack introduced them to Sara. There was Eliza the oldest, the middle daughter was Patty, and the baby was Nelly. Suddenly Sara felt something on her leg and looked down.

"Well, hello, Hamilton," she said as she picked up the ginger cat. "I haven't seen you in a long time."

"He jumped into my carriage the first time in Middletown and has been here ever since," Margaret said.

As everyone else walked into the house, Sara started looking around. All she saw were fields full of slaves. It looked like there were at least 150 to 200 people working the fields. This made Sara cringed because she knew there were more for the house and other buildings around the plantation. It had been a long time since Sara was here. She forgot how upsetting it was to see.

"They will get your luggage and put Storm away. Come into the house," Martha called to her.

Her horse had a name, but these people did not. Sara took a deep breath and tried to keep herself under control as she walked toward the house. Before she entered, she heard someone cry out and turned toward the noise. A foreman had a woman tied to a post and tore her top off. Then to Sara's horror, he started beating her with a stick.

"That one tried to run away, but he caught her," Nelly said.

"If they are risking that to run away, how can you say they want to remain a slave?" Sara asked angrily.

"Well, we have a lot to work on when it comes to our manners, don't we," Martha said.

"I can't just ignore the disgusting practice of slavery," Sara said.

"And I won't listen to the disgusting tone of someone who enters my home and disrespects me!" Martha said back. "Maybe this was a bad idea. I will head back," Sara said.

"SIT DOWN!" Martha demanded.

Jake took his wife and children out back to leave Martha and Sara alone.

"Why did you come here?" Martha asked.

"I wanted to learn to be more 'ladylike' to help change the laws," Sara replied.

"And where else is going to challenge you more than here to keep your temper?" Martha asked.

"I have to admit this is very challenging," Sara said.

"Exactly, you think I don't know your feelings toward slavery by now, you think I didn't know this was going to be hard for you and you will fail before you can succeed? My goodness, Sara, the last time you were here, you screamed that George and I were monsters and never wanted to see us again," Martha continued. "You are still loved and welcome here, Sara. Besides, if you can learn to remain a lady in this setting, you can do it anywhere."

"I will try," Sara said. "I am sorry."

Sara was very familiar with the house slaves since they have been at camp all this time. After the meal, Sara asked if she could go for a walk to look around with Doll. As they walked away from the house, Sara wanted help to find the woman who was beaten before.

"You don't wanna go there, miss," Doll said.

"Actually I do," Sara insisted.

They walked to the servants' quarters, which were one-room cabins per family. However, some families were split up depending on their duties. Some had little farms or chickens they were raising to try and earn money when they were not working Washington's plantation. Doll knocked on the door and asked if she could enter. A small child opened the door and let them in. The woman from earlier was lying facedown on her bed, which was just a wood plank lifted off the floor by four woodblocks. Her back was bloody and bruised when she noticed Sara.

"What she want?" she said.

"I want to help you, I am a nurse," Sara answered.

"I don't want your help, get out my house!" she said.

Doll pushed Sara back out the door and started walking back to the estate. "I just wanted to help her. I am so sorry, Doll," Sara said.

"I know you different, miss, but folks here ain't used to different," Doll said.

"If there is anything I can do to help these people, please let me know," Sara tried again.

"Best thing is, leaves them be," Doll finished. It was quiet for the rest of the walk back.

Sara spent the next few weeks bringing back the lady she tried to hide away. They worked on conversations and when and when not to talk. How to act around gentlemen (this one was particularly hard for Sara) and when you're in the sewing circles. Martha also worked on how to discreetly change the minds of others while they believed it was their idea. Finally, they had dance lessons every weekend to get the rust off. She kept her promise to Hamilton and wrote him every week but never got a response.

Throughout this time, Sara struggled with the treatment of the slaves around her. She tried to talk with them, help them, ignore them, but nothing seemed to help. Finally, she sat down and watched them. By doing this, she realized these people were hardworking, dedicated family units who cared deeply about each other. They were strong and resilient and, to a point, lucky. From what little she was told, the Washingtons allowed and honored marriage among his slaves even if the state did not recognize it. Sometimes they lived in huts across his land, but he wouldn't sell a married couple or their children. They were allowed to earn money (on their own time, of course) and obtain personal possessions. On Sundays, she would see them come together and play sports and enjoy each other.

She admired the resolve of these people. They may not love being a slave, but they loved life and enjoyed it when they could. She made a promise to herself that as she tried to change the laws for women, she would not forget these people as well. She decided to write to Laurens and apologize for not saying goodbye. Then she added that she wanted to help him free the slaves in whatever way she could.

Sara became aware of another event that happened during this time when Martha called her for a private conversation. "Sara, I think my prayers have been answered!" Martha said excitedly, handing over a broadside page.

On this page, Esther Reed wrote a call to action of the American women to back their courageous men. It thanked each soldier for willingly giving up their lives for the families and for the country. It asked for mothers, wives, sisters, daughters, and sweethearts to remind the men that these women loved them, were proud of them, and were behind them. "They allowed us to sit at home with their children without fear. Now it was time for women to do more," she wrote. "Let us be engaged to offer the homage of our gratitude… and you, our brave deliverers…receive with a free hand our offering, the purest which can be presented to your virtue." She asked every woman to stand and give up unnecessary items like jewelry and new silk dresses while the men suffer. She believed giving this money back to the army will do a lot for the morale of the men.

"Sara, please do me a favor?" Martha asked. "Esther Reed is an acquaintance of mine. Please go to Philadelphia and find her for me. I want to know how I can help with this plan. This is her address and a note from me."

"I will leave right away," Sara answered.

"It is too far for anyone to go alone. Jack will go with you," Martha insisted, "but please go in disguise."

Sara got dressed in breeches, used cloth to compress her breasts under her shirt, covered that with a jacket, and tied her hair in a tail with a black bow tie and hat.

"Mother, I can deliver this for you alone," Jack said, a bit upset.

"This is a matter Sara needs to be a part of. I know I am asking a lot of both of you, but this is very important," Martha said. "And you may slow her down, but it won't be the other way," she added with a laugh.

Jack was not pleased by that comment but, when they got on their way, understood.

As they rode through the countryside, there were spurts of rain mixed with sunshine, but it was a pleasant ride. After a few hours, Jack said, "George's favorite pub is in the next town. We can stop there for dinner and rest for the night."

"Um, all right, I guess I will go by Sam," Sara said.

They entered the pub and were provided a table to sit. "Jack, it has been a long time, man, how are you doing?" a man said, walking up to them.

"I am good. We are running an errand for my mother," Jack said.

The man turned and looked at Sara and extended his hand. "Hi there, I'm Ben."

"Hello, I'm Sam," Sara replied, shaking his hand.

Ben sat down to join them and waved over two other gentlemen, Tom and Johnny. A waitress arrived and asked if they wanted food and or something to drink.

"How's your stepdad doing?" Tom asked Jack.

"He is holding things together up north," Jack said. "I heard he is walking his army into suicide missions and losses left and right."

"Where did you hear that from?" Sara jumped in.

"Some boys who came down after the battle at Germantown."

"So they fled from Valley Forge," Sara asked.

"What do you know about it, Sam?" Johnny asked.

"I was there that winter. I saw firsthand how Washington walked the camp and provided food from his personal funds since Congress wasn't providing anything. How he called in Von Steuben to train us to be a better unit capable of carrying out his plan. I was at Monmouth when we drove those redcoats back to New York," she said boldly.

"Really, if he was that great, why did you leave the army?" Tom asked.

"Who said I left? I am on leave and will return shortly," she said.

"Right," Tom scoffed.

"Are you questioning my honor?" Sara said, rising up.

"Slow down, no one is questioning you Sam. I will vouch for you," Jack said.

Tom was shocked at this. "Wait, really?"

Jack leaned into Tom and whispered, "He is one of George's aides."

"Sorry about that, Sam, I didn't know," Tom said.

Sara just nodded. They began to talk about politics and the hope for the country after the war. Tom, Johnny, Jack, and Ben spoke for the south and their beliefs while Sara spoke eloquently supporting the views of the north. She did this so well. They started buying her brandy and offering her cigars. Jack decided enough was enough and said they both needed to retire.

After they left the next morning, Jack asked, "How could you do that?"

"What did I do wrong?" she asked.

"Wanting to be a part of the conversation, then accepting brandy and a cigar?" he said indignantly.

"Well, I had to play the part, and they wouldn't have offered if they didn't believe the disguise."

"The disguise is really good, but please don't do that again," he stated. "Then buy a bedroll before we head back."

"I already have one," he said, tilting his head behind him.

"They also provided us with a bit of bread for breakfast," Jack said, handing her a piece.

From then on, they decided to stay away from towns and hunt for their evening meals. It took them a total of five days to make it to Philadelphia, and it was midafternoon when they rode in. Jack told Sara he would meet her in front of the Congress building by eight that evening to start home. She went to the address provided by Martha and knocked on the door. A young woman with long brown hair and a babe on her hip answered. Sara removed her hat as any man would and asked if this was Mrs. Reed's residence.

"Who wants to know?" called a voice from behind the woman.

Sara could see a few more ladies behind her. "Martha Washington, ma'am!" Sara said as she handed over the note included with the address.

The first woman with the babe took the letter and read it, smiled, and said, "Come in, please come in," letting Sara into the house. "I am Mrs. Reed," she finished.

"It is a pleasure to meet you, my name is Sara," Sara replied.

The other ladies were astonished.

"This is our first meeting to try and help those men," Esther said. Then she introduced Sara to the ten ladies in the room.

"This is such a wonderful thing you are doing. I have been with the men for the past two winters as matron, and these men could use a dose of patriotism," Sara said.

That afternoon they discussed what they wanted to try and do and just how to do it. They knew Congress was supposed to get supplies for the army but were not doing it. The ladies felt if they gave Congress supplies or money, they would take all the credit. It was important to them that the men, all the men, knew this "gift" was coming from the American women. They also know this would not sit well with even the most forward-thinking man, as women are now "trying to turn the tables and take care of the men." It seemed the men just didn't believe women could come together and be productive in politics, so the ladies just had to do it themselves.

They decided to recruit as many as they could to gather, beg, barter, and collect funds for the army. Sara said when she was at the winter encampments, Sara could ride back and forth to get messages passed between Martha and the Philadelphia Ladies Association. When they had a collection, she could bring it to Martha, who would take leadership of the funds within the army. She then had to excuse herself from the group to meet up with Jack for the ride back. They wished each other good luck, and she was on her way.

It took another five days to return to Mt. Vernon with the decisions.

"Come in, come in. I want to hear all about your journey," Martha said happily.

"Wow, Aunt Martha, I never knew you ladies could be so cunning and deceiving," Sara said, excited with the push for women's rights she found herself in.

"I keep trying to tell you there are ways, dear. You just need to out-think the men. Since you spent most of your time in the military with your father, you never really heard the schemes of the ladies," Martha said with a laugh. "Now, what happened?"

Sara explained the entire trip and the details of the meeting. "They are going to elect local treasures to keep track of the funds and a list of all donations. I will ride out from time to time and collect those funds and bring them to you for distribution."

"If that is the case, we are going to have to plan your travels carefully," Martha answered.

Martha and Sara would receive letters about what they were doing in Philadelphia. She was in awe of what these ladies accomplished. The group grew to about thirty-six women who would go out in pairs to collect funds. They would go door to door and tavern to tavern and stop people on the streets, asking for contributions. They were ambitious, intelligent, and bound to their goal. People would give them money just to get the ladies to leave. This was no longer a quiet society but a loud movement of ladies fighting for the same cause as the men. Martha then took a trip with Sara to visit

Martha Jefferson, who was not well enough to travel, and Eleanor Maddison to discuss starting this same type of group in the south.

Before they could start anything, however, they received word that George was informed about the collection happening in Philadelphia. Since he knew Mrs. Reed, conversations started between them about what she intended to do with the funds. At this point, these women managed to collect enough funds for each man to receive two dollars in hard cash. That is the equivalent to a year's pay for a private. Martha began getting letters from George and Esther complaining about the other.

"It seems George believes the men would waste the money on alcohol and wants the ladies to make shirts!" Martha read aloud.

"Congress is supposed to be providing the men with clothing, are they not?" Sara complained.

"Very true, but if Congress isn't providing clothing as we have seen firsthand, a loving tribute of warmth may still do them well," Martha concluded.

There was a second letter from Esther there that she hadn't opened yet, and she was not sure if she wanted to now. She was right to worry because the second letter made less sense than the first.

"A bank" is all Martha said.

Sara was upset now and said, "A bank, now he wants them to put the money in a bank? Sure, that way, Congress will get their filthy hands on it and spend it on whatever they want, and the men will not see a penny."

"No, George, that will never work," Martha added.

Sara picked up again. "Congress didn't provide the men with what they originally agreed to. Now we give them even more money to not apply it correctly? I just don't understand," Sara finished.

"I believe he is trying to force the ladies into making the shirts," Martha answered.

A few days into August, Sara entered the sitting room and noticed Martha looking at another letter. Sara closed the door and sat down to start sewing.

"It seems Mr. Reed decided to take matters regarding his wife's actions onto himself," Martha started saying.

"He wrote to George, saying they were having difficulty procuring fabric for the shirts and Europe was sending enough clothing for six thousand men."

"Well, that's a good thing, isn't it?" Sara questioned.

"Esther followed his letter with one of her own. This is what I am trying to teach you to avoid," Martha said, looking right at Sara.

"She is trying to tell George that she still believed the men would benefit from acquiring the money directly. What she wrote next is nothing short of insulting. She suggests that if he refused, she would give the shirts they had and the rest of the funds to other states for their armies."

"Nooo," Sara said, almost dropping her sewing.

"She is challenging George's decision openly. Now there is no way he can allow the men to have the money directly. Otherwise, he would look even weaker than the other men. Do you understand now?" Martha asked.

"I am beginning to, Aunt Martha," Sara said in return.

"He not only has Congress questioning his orders, making him look like a bad choice. Women are questioning them," Martha said indignantly. "Now I like Esther, but this was completely the wrong way to handle this situation."

"Because if he changes his opinion now, the other officers will wonder if they should still carry out his orders," Sara offered.

"Exactly! Even a man needs to be seen in a certain way by his peers to be heard. You destroy that, you destroy him." Martha ended the conversation, just shaking her head.

A few weeks later, they received a letter from Esther, saying they decided to go ahead and make the shirts for the men. Each lady will put her name on the shirt she made to try and make it personal. None of them were happy, but this was the only thing they could do. They were hoping they would be finished by late December, early January. However, in late September, Esther Reed passed away, and Sara Franklin Bache took over for her. Sara was deeply upset not only by her death but that she didn't live long enough to see the men receive at least the shirts she worked so hard for.

Washington decided to return to Morristown, New Jersey, for this winter camp and wrote for Martha and Sara to meet him there. It had already started snowing, which hindered their travel, and they didn't arrive till the end of December. Lucy, Kitty, and Gertrude returned this winter, and Sara tried to behave like a lady around them. However, most of the other thirty-five officers' wives were here as well. They did make the town a bit more lively and homelike. However, this site was a bit less welcoming for Sara. She liked to be able to walk among the army and see the men with their families.

Now that these ladies came into the camp, the regular army was elsewhere. Sara guessed these wives were much too delicate to see what an army camp in winter really looked like. She didn't like thinking about women that way, but these high society ladies and their self-righteousness left her uneasy. Most of the ladies went to their own homes during Valley Forge and Middlebrook. It was the enlisted men's wives that stayed for the devastation of those camps.

"*Those men and women would be the true heroes of this war if we won, and they are just tossed aside*, she thought.

The snowfall this winter was relentless and sometimes lasted multiple days. The drifts in places were higher than Sara, making things very difficult. The men could not pass most roads to obtain supplies, any game that could have helped feed the men froze or disappeared, so again, the camp went without eating for days at a time. When it did let up, Sara would spend most of her days at the hospital or walking the camp checking on everyone. She usually got back to the sitting circle later in the day because of the distance.

One afternoon, as Sara went to sit with Martha, Lucy, Kitty, and Gertrude, she heard excited chattering behind the door and wondered if they were discussing her future again. She entered the room and acknowledged everyone and took her seat.

"We have wonderful news, Sara! There is to be a ball!"

"Really," Sara said, trying to sound excited.

"The officers decided that they needed a pleasant distraction! Isn't that wonderful!" Lucy said.

"I have already written to my nieces to join us here," Gertrude added.

"Wow, that is so exciting," Sara said, trying really hard not to roll her eyes. The ladies continued to discuss dreams of the event until they decided it was time to return home, leaving Sara and Martha by themselves.

"Very good, Sara, you are doing really well," Martha said.

"Not really because I have a question I couldn't ask while everyone else was here," Sara replied.

"I figured, go ahead," Martha said, putting down her sewing.

"The officers are putting up the money for this event, correct?" Sara asked.

"Yes, they all agreed to help out with it," Martha answered.

"Wouldn't that money be better spent trying to get food for the army instead of one party?" Sara asked.

"Well, from what I heard, it is supposed to be three parties. I don't know the details, but I hope one of the parties is going to be for the enlisted men and their families as well. They could also use something to look forward to," Martha said.

Sara wanted to argue more, but she was tired, and it sounded like Martha truly didn't know much about the plans.

Sara again braved the elements during another storm to go see some of the patients in the hospital. She heard a familiar voice calling. "Sara, Sara Weinstein, is that you?" Angelica Schuyler said, getting out of her carriage.

"Angelica! How are you doing?" Sara called back and walked up and gave her a hug.

"Are you staying with the Cochrans?" Sara asked.

"Gertrude is our Aunt! Eliza and Peggy should arrive in a couple of days," she continued as they both walked to the house.

"I didn't know that," Sara said.

Gertrude opened the door and let Angelica and Sara in. Her slaves started gathering Angelica's belongings and brought them into the house. Gertrude walked Sara and Angelica into the sitting room and said, "So how was the journey?"

"If the coals could have stayed warm, it would have been an enjoyable ride, but they were worthless after an hour on the road," Angelica answered.

"So you're Phillip's sister?" Sara asked. "I never put that together."

Gertrude looked at Sara for a minute, then said, "Which means you were the little Sara that visited him all those summers ago. This is a small world. I did ask Eliza to bring an extra dress for you just in case you needed it."

"Why would you need someone to bring you a dress?" Angelica asked.

"My family was murdered by the British," Sara told her.

"Oh my, I am so sorry to hear that." Angelica gasped. "Are you all right, do you need anything?" she asked.

"No, thank you. Aunt Martha and Uncle George are seeing to my needs," Sara answered. "And they did provide a dress for this ball, but thank you for your generosity."

Whenever they were able to be alone, Sara and Angelica would reminisce about the times they were together. Sara could remember late-night outings with Angelica and Eliza, either running through their orchard or taking a midnight swim in the nearby lake.

"How did we ever get away with it?" They laughed together. "Well, I guess it was practice for your midnight runaway with Mr. What's His Name," Sara asked.

"John Carter," Angelica answered.

"And I am to believe you have children?" Sara questioned.

"Yes, my Philip is a year old, and Kitty was born in November," she said proudly.

"Like two months ago?" This question of Sara's had a bit of concern to it.

"Yes, my nanny just had a babe herself, so she is feeding Kitty while I am away?"

"Oh, okay," Sara said with a lot of questions running through her mind. Sara knew Angelica well enough by now that she knew there was a problem but didn't question it any further.

Another two days went by before Eliza and Peggy arrived. At this point, the ball was the talk of the town. Sara started to understand what Martha meant by needing something like this to look forward to. People just seemed happy even with the bitter cold blowing through. She still went to the hospital to help the men there but was unable to continue her walk through the camp. The snowfall made it nearly impossible to pass. You had to go a mile out of your way to get there, and Sara wasn't riding Storm in this weather. As she walked back to headquarters from the hospital, she finally met up with Hamilton.

"Hey, stranger, how are you doing?"

They gave each other a hug, and he said, "I'm all right, you know George keeps me busy."

"Are you looking forward to this ball?" Sara asked.

"Sure, I am always up for a party, but you?" he questioned.

"I am excited to see what happens there," she said.

"What does that mean?" he asked, looking at her inquisitively.

They started walking through the halls, and he looked up to see Gertrude and her nieces about to go into Martha Washington's sitting room. Sara giggled as he almost dropped his paperwork but managed to collect himself.

"Ah, this is Lieutenant Colonel Hamilton. Sir, these are my nieces, Angelica, Elizabeth, and Peggy."

The pleasantries went back and forth until Gertrude said, "Inside, ladies."

Sara turned and said "By Hamilton" with a smile.

"You could have warned me," he mouthed toward Sara as she entered the room.

"Well, he sure is a cute one," Angelica said in her nonchalant way.

"You, my dear, are married and need to not forget it," Gertrude said.

"Just because I am married doesn't mean I can't still have fun," Angelica said right back.

"Eliza, Peggy, how are you guys doing?" Sara said, disrupting the conversation and hugging them both.

"Sara, we are fine, how are you? Angelica told us about your family. We are so very sorry."

"Thank you, I am doing well under Aunt Martha and Uncle George's care," she said back.

Some of the ladies were surprised to hear Sara say it even though they were fully aware of the relationship. They all took their seats and spent the rest of the afternoon knitting and talking about the upcoming ball.

The day of the ball arrived, and so did another snowstorm. Lucy was sent to help Sara prepare for the event. Sara refused to wear the wigs or powder, which was fashionable for the day. She did pull her hair up with high bangs in the front and two long curls hanging down over her left shoulder. Her dress had crinoline underneath to help it puff out. The bodice and front of the skirt were gold with gold leaf embroidery. The rest of the dress and sleeves were blue with gold embroidery.

The storm did not let up as the day went on, and it was time to leave. Sara entered the sitting room where Martha was already waiting. "You look wonderful, Sara. That color blue really brings out your eyes," she said.

"Thank you, Aunt Martha, but you don't think it's a bit too much for me?"

"Not at all, now will you go tell my husband it is time we depart and to stop keeping those young ladies waiting for the young men in his family?"

Sara departed and knocked on George's office door. "Enter," she heard from behind it.

As she entered, every man in the room rose to their feet. "Aunt Martha's looking for you," Sara said.

George, however, just stared at her. "You look beautiful, young lady," he said, opening his arms and giving her a kiss. "Tell Martha I will be right there to make sure you don't have too much fun tonight."

Sara cocked her head a bit and looked at him with a glare. "I may be in a dress, but I can still kick the ass of anyone who would try." Then she turned and walked out the door.

A few minutes later, George arrived to escort Martha and Sara to the ball. As they walked past the aides' quarters, Sara saw Hamilton writing at his desk.

"Isn't Hamilton going?" she asked.

"I needed him to finish something before attending, but he should be along shortly," George replied.

"Uncle, I can't believe you would do that," she said and pulled away, heading back toward Hamilton.

"What are you doing?" George asked.

"Isn't it obvious? She is waiting with Hamilton because that wasn't right," Martha said. "Now let's go."

"Hamilton, I am so sorry about this, what is he making you do?" Sara asked as she entered the room.

Startled, Hamilton jumped a bit and looked up. "What are you doing here?" he asked.

"Well, I wasn't going to leave you behind," she replied.

"You should have gone ahead," he said, looking back at his letter.

"Absolutely not, it was wrong for him to ask you to do work tonight when everyone else is at the ball. It is not like you couldn't write that tomorrow." Hamilton started to laugh. "Well, I am glad I can make you happy," she said, questioning his laugh.

"It's just you standing there, in that dress, looking every bit the lady and still standing on your principles," he said.

"A piece of fabric will not change who I am," she stated.

"No, I guess not, so thank you for staying with me," he said and finished his letter.

By the time Hamilton and Sara arrived at the ball, it was in full swing. They decided to enter at alternate locations so they wouldn't draw any suspicion. It didn't take long for Sara to be noticed since there were only sixteen young ladies who braved the weather and went. The men outnumbered the ladies four to one, so there was basically a line waiting to dance. Sara could see the other young ladies dancing already, which included all three Schuyler sisters. She didn't get too far before someone asked her to join him on the dancefloor. They finished one waltz when another gentleman stepped up to do the next. The musicians stopped playing every now and then so the ladies could catch their breath and get a drink.

Angelica, as usual, had a large gathering of men around her. Peggy and some other girls that Sara wasn't familiar with all had smaller groups of men but were still surrounded. Sara wanted to know if Hamilton was able to talk with Eliza since he entered the room so late. She, however, was occupied by a small group of men vying for her attention. To her surprise, they were interested in her escape from the British and crossing the Delaware. They also heard that she picked up a rifle and saved a captain in Princeton. Finally, they wanted to thank her for helping the men in the hospital when they were wounded. Then the music would start up again, and the dancing would begin.

This went on for most of the evening, and by the time they retired from the event, Sara was so tired, she went right to bed. She didn't wake up until late in the afternoon when she got dressed and went to the sewing room. The only lady there today was Martha Washington.

"Well, I guess you had a pleasant evening," Martha said.

"I am not sure if it was more pleasant or exhausting," Sara admitted.

"You did have quite the group of young men surrounding you, I noticed," Martha said.

"And I was every bit the lady you wanted me to be, but I don't believe they are interested in me as much as they are interested in getting close to you," Sara said.

"Well, unfortunately, that happens, and since you have been closer to us with your father's passing, it is bound to happen," Martha added. "But don't sell yourself short, you were a beautiful young lady last night, and that got the attention of the men."

That evening Sara stayed up late reading in the sewing room, hoping to see Hamilton. He finally walked by and saw her sitting there and entered. "Sara, What are you doing up this late?" he said.

"I was hoping to see you. Did you have a good night last night?"

"Last night and tonight, yes!" Hamilton said with a smile.

"You went to the Cochrans' tonight?" Sara asked.

"Yes, and I hope to go again tomorrow night as well," Hamilton said back.

"I am so happy for you," Sara said with a smile.

"I am glad to be able to see Betsy, but we really can't talk," he said.

"Betsy," Sara said, giggling, and Hamilton turned red. "Wow, I made you blush," she continued to laugh. "How are you doing being a gentleman?" she added.

"I never had an issue talking my way through things," he boasted.

"Good, so does Betsy want you to come back?"

"Yes." He smiled back.

"Then you're good. I am sure John and Gertrude will allow more space until they tell Philip you are worthy of the prize," Sara said.

"The prize," Hamilton laughed.

"Again, we are property, a prize to be won, and you have to prove your worth to the family, not to her," Sara grumbled.

"I know, I know. It is just funny to hear you say it that way," Hamilton replied.

"Well, I am tired, and if I don't see you again for a while, good luck," Sara said.

The next few weeks, Sara saw more of Eliza, Peggy, and Angelica, then Hamilton. She didn't mind and enjoyed being a part of this group again. One day when she went to the Cochrans for a visit, Gertrude pulled her aside.

"About Hamilton, I know you spend a lot of time with him," she asked. "Are you trying to find out something specific?" Sara wanted to know.

"Elizabeth is very much smitten with him, and I want to make sure, well…" She paused.

"Well, what? I told you before, he is like a brother to me. Honestly, if anyone can work their magic with Hamilton, it is Eliza. I think they will be really good for each other. Not that my opinion matters on that account," Sara said.

"Not really, I just know he was a tomcat and wanted to know if he still is?" Gertrude asked again.

"No, he left that lifestyle when he met her two years ago. And I know that because he has been with me, Martha, and George every night," Sara said matter-of-factly.

"Thank you, he can be very charming, can't he!"

Sara just rolled her eyes and walked out of the room.

"How are things going?" Sara asked Eliza.

"It's all right," she said grumpily.

"Oh, it seems better than all right to me," Angelica said.

"Stop it, Angelica," Eliza scoffed.

"What's up?" Sara asked.

"Her new interest, young Alexander Hamilton, is what's up." Angelica giggled.

"Isn't that going well?" Sara asked. "I don't really know. It's not like I can talk with him to find out if I like him or not," Eliza said grumpily.

"You like him and you know it," Angelica said.

"You know, I know him very well, is there anything you're concerned about?" Sara said.

"How well?" Eliza asked with wide eyes.

"I am not going to give up the secrets I know about either of you, that is for you to do, but I can tell you about him," Sara said.

"Do you know what he is like when you're not around guardians?" Eliza asked.

"Well, sadly, he is like every other man, he is complicated. He can be very sweet and kind and passionate, but he can also be quick-tempered, challenging, and protective," Sara said, and Eliza just smiled. "Somehow, I believe you already know most of that by now. He is also incredibly intelligent and full of big ideas," Sara said.

"And how do you know him so well?" Angelica asked, smirking.

"I have been with this army for the past three years and mostly with the Washingtons and their family. I got to know Hamilton very well, and we became as close as you, Peggy, and Eliza are," Sara said. "We have a lot of the same issues, so we have become family."

They talked for another hour before Sara went back to headquarters.

A few days later, Eliza and Gertrude arrived at headquarters to sew with Martha. "Where is everyone else?" Sara asked, sitting next to Eliza.

"They went home, but Aunt Gertrude allowed me to stay. Papa will be stopping by on his way to Philadelphia," Eliza answered.

"Well, that's exciting," Sara said.

"And Aunt Gertrude allowed us to talk alone last night." Eliza's smile grew large.

"So what do you think about Hamilton?" Sara asked.

"He is so handsome and exciting, but I don't know if I am able to keep up with him," Eliza said, giggling.

"Once he gets started, I don't think anyone can." Sara laughed.

They talked and sewed for the remainder of the afternoon until Gertrude decided to head home. Sara and Eliza walked out the door side by side when an orange blur ran by looking at paperwork.

"Hello," Sara said, stopping Hamilton in his tracks, and he looked up.

"Umm, I am so sorry, ladies, I didn't even see you there," he said.

"That is no way to talk about Eliza here," Sara taunted him.

Hamilton looked at her with a hint of anger in his eyes and said, "I have to get this to the general right away, but I will try to stop by this evening if time allows," he said, then he rushed off.

"Oh, he is so smitten with you," Sara said.

"Do you really think so?" Eliza asked.

"I know so," Sara said and hugged Eliza as she left the headquarters.

Sara didn't see either Eliza or Hamilton over the next few days, nor did she try. She spent her time looking after anyone in the hospital as illness began to run through the camp again. She would also enjoy an afternoon knitting with the ladies in the sewing room. Finally, she was greeted by the news that General Philip Schuyler had arrived in camp and would be joining General Washington for an afternoon meal.

"Good day, General Schuyler," Sara said with a small curtsey.

"Well, well, this can't be the little Sara that played in the mud at my home all those summers ago?" General Schuyler said.

"The one and the same, sir," Sara answered.

"How are you doing?"

"Very well, I assure you, ma'am," he said with a bow. "However, when my Peggy returned home, she told me how you lost your family. If there is anything I can do, please let me know," he said.

"That is very kind, sir. Thank you," Sara replied.

General Washington walked up and cut in. "Hmm, excuse me, General Schuyler, but I wanted to introduce you to Lieutenant Colonel Hamilton. He is a very promising young man from my staff," George Washington stated.

"Yes, I do remember you stopping by the house a couple of years ago with a message while we were hosting a party," General Schuyler said, shaking his hand. The men exchanged pleasantries and took their seats, while Sara took her leave and went and sat down next to Eliza. Sara knew Hamilton must be a bundle of nerves, but it never showed.

"Don't worry, Eliza, that man knows how to charm the socks off a horse," Sara said. Eliza looked terribly worried and couldn't take her eyes off her father and Hamilton. "Look, they're laughing. It will be all right." Sara tried again.

"But he wants to ask father for my hand," Eliza stated.

"Oh, I am so happy for you, Eliza!" Sara said.

"He hasn't asked, and Father hasn't answered yet. Don't be too happy," Eliza stated.

"Honestly, I don't believe you have anything to worry about," Sara said.

"This is something you will never have to go through," Eliza said of Sara.

"Especially since I no longer have a father," Sara finished.

"Oh no, that's not what I meant." Finally, Eliza took her eyes off Hamilton and her father.

"It's all right, I just wanted to get your attention. When do you think he will ask?" Sara wanted to know.

"Well, Papa is looking to head to Philadelphia in a day or two, so I hope soon," Eliza wondered.

A few days later, as Sara was walking to the hospital, she saw General Schuyler and Eliza riding away in a carriage. She continued on her way, and upon entry, she asked Dr. Cochran why Eliza was leaving.

"Philip wanted to take her to Philadelphia for a while. Besides, Hamilton asked him for her hand in marriage."

"Did he give an answer?" Sara questioned.

"Not that it is any of your business, but he is writing to Catherine about it," he said.

Sara didn't say much more as she addressed the patients in the hospital and walked back to headquarters. That evening, Hamilton asked Sara if she could talk.

"Do you think that is appropriate, Sara?" Martha asked.

"Why wouldn't it be?" Sara replied.

Turning to Alexander, Martha continued, "I know you asked Philip for Eliza's hand, Hamilton, and to ask another lady to talk the very day she departs doesn't look good," Martha added.

"Hamilton and I have been very close friends for a long time now. Everyone in this camp knows it. Eliza understands our relationship and is all right with it. If anyone has a problem, it is their problem," Sara said. "I will not stop talking with my brother because he has found someone he wants to marry. Actually, I will talk with him all the more now," she finished as she left the room.

They went to the dining room to sit and talk without being disturbed. "Is everything all right?" Sara asked.

"I told you I would never be accepted by them," he said, so upset he was pacing, and he didn't even acknowledge how she talked to Martha.

"And why do you believe you are not accepted?" Sara calmly said.

"Are you kidding me? I asked, and he took her away the next day." His anger started to pour out now.

"Okay, first calm down," Sara tried.

"How can I calm down? I took the chance I swore I never would because of you, and now my worst nightmare has come true," he said, still pacing.

"Hamilton!" she said to get his attention.

"What?" he yelled back.

"Do you trust me?" she asked.

"What?" he said, more of a question.

"Look, I trusted you that night in Middlebrook, as much as I wanted out. So my question right now is, do you trust me?" Sara asked calmly again.

"I want to but…" he started. "I know you want an answer right away and you feel everything General Schuyler did was because of your birth."

She took over, and he looked at her. "I told you, Angelica ran away and eloped, causing him to hold onto Eliza and Peggy a bit closer. Also, they are a Dutch family, which means no child is given permission to marry without both parents' consent," she said. "Knowing the Schuylers, they will agree to the marriage but make you wait until this wretched war is over to see if you get yourself killed first." That at least got a smile from Hamilton.

"Do you really think he didn't just blow me off and take Betsy away?" Hamilton asked with a bit of longing in his eyes.

"Just between you and me, I know for a fact he wrote to his wife about you and your proposal. Please, before you jump off the deep end, let them return from Philadelphia and give you an answer all right!"

He closed his eyes and said, "Thank you, Sara, I really appreciate it."

Lafayette was still in France, and Laurens was fighting in South Carolina, leaving Hamilton by himself with Washington and his new aides. Sara was talking with Martha one afternoon, asking for advice on helping the two men in their lives. Hamilton was still being denied his own command and promotion in the army, which he attributed to the lack of a decision from the Schuylers no matter what Sara told him. Washington was constantly getting disrespected by Congress and news of desertion or losses, making him on edge and angry. They even split up the men in the evenings to keep the peace.

"Sometimes men are so stressed that nothing you do will help," Martha said. "All you can do is be a calming force and wait it out."

Sara was very excited when April brought some much-needed good news. Lafayette returned from France, saying six thousand infantry and six ships would be arriving from France soon. Also, Philip, Eliza, and Catherine Schuyler all arrived in Morristown to decide. Catherine met Hamilton and was taken by his charisma. Gertrude and Martha both vouched for the young man, as did Washington.

Late one evening, when George, Martha, Sara, and Lafayette were all sitting in the sewing room, Hamilton came in with a roar. "THEY AGREED! WE'RE GETTING MARRIED!" Everyone jumped up and congratulated him, and he continued, "They want us to get married in Albany, so it is going to take some time, but they agreed!" Sara didn't think she ever saw him so happy and almost started tearing up. He walked over to her and whispered, "Thank you!" and gave her a hug.

As the weather started to get warmer, Sara and Lafayette started going out for rides when time allowed. "Do you think both our countries can find peace after all of this?" Sara asked.

"I do not know, madam. But I believe both our countries have a hunger and resolve for freedom that we will fight longer than our oppressors," Lafayette said, looking out to the horizon. "I have always felt that if Congress would just work with General Washington, this war would already be over."

"Well, I am so glad you were able to persuade France to help us," Sara said.

"It is my honor and duty to ensure freedom for both our countries. I just hope your new country will support mine when it is called upon," he finished.

Chapter *10*

Betrayal, Weddings and Christmas

I n June, Martha decided to head back to Mt. Vernon again, and Eliza and Catherine went to Albany to prepare for the wedding. Sara, however, wanted to stay with the army this summer. As the ladies headed out of camp, Washington received a letter about the New Jersey militia.

"Our militia held off the British army a few days ago, saving our camp and sending them back to New York," he said at breakfast. "Sometimes those men can be disastrous, and sometimes they can be our greatest asset."

"They are the heart of the cause," Sara added.

Washington was on the move with his army around New Jersey when the British tried to attack again. Again Sara watched the British turn away and retreat to New York. The remainder of the summer passed by without another battle. Now at least Sara had Lafayette to try and keep Hamilton calm around Washington. He still couldn't get a command and stop being an aide. If Sara tried to talk with Washington about it, she was told to stay out of military matters. She then tried to talk with Hamilton, and he also refused to talk about the military. He did say, "I can't even get time off for my wedding.

It has been changed three times already." Lafayette and Sara both agreed that this was turning into a powder keg that was bound to explode.

"Sara," Washington called as he walked into the sitting room, "I need to take Hamilton and Lafayette north to meet up with General Rochambeau. I want you to stay with Dr. Cochran and Gertrude. We will be leaving in a couple of days," he stated then walked out.

"Umm, sure," Sara said to herself.

The rest of the staff stayed at headquarters when she left for the Cochrans'.

"Were happy to have you," Gertrude said, showing her to her room.

"Thank you so much for this," Sara said in return.

Without battles or illnesses, the Cochrans and Sara were able to just talk and relax. Dr. Cochran and Sara were able to go out to hunt and fish from time to time.

"Now this feels like home to me," Sara said. "Father would take me out every weekend. Most of the time, we just talked but being out in the woods and sitting with him was wonderful," she continued to reminisce.

"Must still be difficult, having a father who taught you this life-style and now that he is gone, most will not allow you to live it," Dr. Cochran said.

"It is. I am truly grateful that you invited me on these outings," Sara said graciously.

By mid-September, they met up with Washington again outside New York City, and Sara went back to headquarters.

"If you ever want to hunt again, please let me know!" Sara said as she left.

One evening, George entered the sitting room very angry, look-ing for Hamilton. "Hamilton, you're needed," he barked.

"What happened?" Sara asked without thinking.

George, however, was so upset, he said, "We just captured a British officer named Major John Andre, who was carrying proof that Benedict Arnold has been selling information to the British. He was about to just hand them West Point!"

"What?" Hamilton said, jumping up out of his seat. "What do you need from me, sir?"

"I need you to find that bastard and bring him back!" George yelled. Hamilton was gone in a flash, and George asked for forgiveness for his outburst.

Once Arnold heard Andre had been captured, he ran to the nearest British ship. Poor Andre was left to hang for Arnold's betrayal. Hamilton's mood did not improve since he missed Arnold and he had no wedding date and no command. Hamilton confided he felt the war would be over before he got his chance. Sara felt useless in this situation, not having any way to help. She could listen, but there were no answers to this problem.

"December 14," Hamilton said, walking up toward Sara as she was brushing Storm.

"Excuse me?" she asked.

"I just got approval. I'm leaving December 10 for Albany and we are getting married on December 14." His smile was bigger than ever. He picked Sara up and swung her around, hugging her. "Will you join me?" he asked.

"Is that a formal invitation?" Sara jokingly wanted to know.

"Yes, I want you there. You're the only family I have that can make it," he finished.

"Sure, I will accompany you there." She smiled.

"Well, I have a message from Washington to deliver. I will be back tomorrow."

"Have a safe ride!" Sara called back.

At the start of December, Sara started to feel sick and needed to remain in bed. Dr. Cochran came to look in on her.

"How is she?" Hamilton wanted to know.

"Her fever is really high. I don't believe it is camp fever, but it's bad, and she can't be moved," he said, worried.

"Can I see her?" Hamilton asked.

"You can talk with her, but please don't go near her. I don't want you to bring anything to Albany and jeopardize your wedding," Cochran said.

"Thank you," Hamilton said.

"I will go tell Washington," Cochran said and turned around.

"Come in," Sara called weakly when the knock came on her door.

Hamilton stepped inside and sat down next to Sara. "Are you ready to leave?" Sara said, trying to get out of bed.

"You stay put," Hamilton took hold of her shoulders and easily put her back in bed.

"I'm fine, I need to ride with you to Albany today!" Sara tried to say.

"You need to get better, Sara," he said in reply.

"No, I told you I will be with you, and I intend to be," Sara complained but didn't move.

"Please, Sara, I need you to be all right much more than I need you at the wedding. I know you want to go, but you need rest," he said. She tried to push herself up but fell right back down. "Sara, please stay put, Betsy and I will be back after the wedding, and we will celebrate here," Hamilton pleaded.

"I want to be there for you, for both of you, but as your family," Sara tried again.

"I know, and that means the world to me, but if you try to go, I will lose you on the way, and I am just not that important," he tried to joke.

"You know, when you're upset, your jokes stink!" Sara giggled.

"I know," he replied. "Please close your eyes," he asked.

"Well, perhaps for just a moment," Sara said and was asleep.

As Hamilton left the room, Washington was about to knock to come in. "She just fell asleep. She was fighting me to go to Albany. It was all I could do to keep her here. I need to depart before she wakes up again," Hamilton said to Washington.

"Our thoughts and prayers are with you, son," Washington said.

This time Hamilton wasn't upset that he was called son. "Just keep her alive till we return please!" Hamilton asked sadly.

"We will do our best to get her better soon," Washington replied with a tear in his eye. "Now you need to stop being sad. It is not a good look for a bridegroom," Washington said, shaking his hand.

Sara was asleep for three more days before she woke with Dr. Cochran placing a cold compress on her head. "Where's Hamilton? I need to ride with him," she asked desperately.

"Hamilton left four days ago. His wedding is today!" Dr. Cochran answered.

"No!" she said, starting to cry. "I was supposed to be there for him."

Washington entered the room upon hearing Sara and hugged her. "He knows that, Sara. He didn't want to risk your health. We will celebrate their wedding when they get back, but you need to rest." He turned to Dr. Cochran and asked, "How is she doing?"

"She still has a fever, and if she doesn't calm down, she is going to make things worse." Dr. Cochran then turned to Sara. "Please, Sara, drink this!" he said, handing her a glass of mead. "You need to calm down, Sara. Otherwise, Hamilton will be very angry when he returns." This at least got her to calm down a bit.

"But I promised him." She shuddered.

"So did I, Sara. I told him I would take care of you until he returned," George said. "Now please let me do that."

Sara took a sip of the mead and knew it had the herbs cooked into it. "Fever?" she questioned.

"Yeah, you have been down for a few days," Dr. Cochran said, laying her back down and putting cold water on her head with a rag. "You're better, but you're not out of the woods yet. Hamilton will be back around the New Year, and Martha will be here shortly. Just rest for now, all right?" he added.

She was still weak and dehydrated. She didn't resist.

A knock came on the door, and when it was opened, Martha entered the room. "How are you? How is she?" she asked quickly.

"She is improving, Mrs. Washington, and I think with your arrival, she will be just fine," Dr. Cochran said back.

"But she is still warm?" Martha questioned, placing her hand on Sara's head.

"Honestly, Martha, she *is* doing better," Washington said.

"Well then, I am glad I got here when I did. Now you men leave, and I will take care of her," Martha insisted, ushering them out the door. Martha began to change her sheets and clothes, whipped her down, and ordered broth. She sat next to Sara, feeding her, read to her, and took care of her.

It was another two days before Sara felt well enough to sit up on her own. She tried to persuade Martha to go rest herself, but it didn't help. So instead, she started asking questions.

"Where are we exactly?"

"New Windsor," Martha answered.

"New York, I don't remember leaving Morristown. I must have been really out of it," Sara wondered.

"From the sounds of George's letters, they were really worried about you and didn't think you would make it," Martha said. The fear in her voice was worrisome.

"I didn't mean to worry everyone. I am sorry," Sara stated.

"I don't want you in the hospital anymore," Martha said boldly.

"But, Aunty Martha, I—" Sara was cut off.

"No buts, I can't lose you too. Please just don't go back," Martha finished.

"What happened while you were home?" Sara asked.

"Nelly's twins only lasted three weeks," Martha said, choked up.

"I am so sorry! I had no idea," Sara said, crying.

"I couldn't upset George with that, it would be a distraction, and he is too close to the British," Martha said.

The two ladies hugged and cried together. "I will stay away, at least for now, all right," Sara offered.

She began walking to the new sitting room to sit with the ladies during the day. However, she was only there for about an hour or so before she needed to take her leave and return to bed. As the days continued, she started to regain her strength and could sit for longer periods.

"You really took a beating, Sara," Gertrude said.

"Well, it feels like a couple of horses stomped on me for a while," Sara replied with a smile.

"Do you think you will be up for some merriment? It's nearly Christmas," Martha added.

"It would be nice to celebrate Christmas."

"Good, then we will have a feast, and I will have George get a tree," Martha said.

"Can we sew popcorn?" Sara asked.

"You've got it, my dear. June," Martha shouted, "start popping some corn."

The ladies moved their sitting/sewing room into the dining hall to plan for the feast. Sara would sit and string popcorn as Martha and Gertrude would decorate the rest of the hall.

"What about the rest of the army, do they have plans?" Sara asked.

"I will make sure they get something special," George said.

"Wow, I must have been on my deathbed," Sara said.

"We thought we lost you twice!" George admitted. Sara finally realized how bad she really was.

"Thank you, Uncle, for everything," she said.

Martha and Gertrude attached candles to the shelving around the room with hot wax and draped the popcorn around it. Then they put up the garland and holly around the room to brighten things up a bit. As the decorating continued, Sara began to make personalized handkerchiefs for these people. She made a cross with the first initial of each couple around it and the family name underneath. There was one for the Washingtons, the Cochrans, the Madders, and the Hamiltons. The room looked festive, with green pines and red fabric on the walls and lining the table. The night of Christmas Eve, there was a roasted turkey, mushroom dressing, creamed celery, minced pie with rum butter sauce, and eggnog.

"How did you do this, Aunt Martha?" Sara asked.

"With everything that happened, we had to have a proper event," Martha said.

There were even some presents under the tree. They drank and ate and played games into the evening. They even heard the rest of the army enjoying themselves in the nearby barn where George had their event set up.

"Oh, to have this piece and be done with the war," Sara said.

The following week when they were celebrating New Year's Eve, the group at headquarters heard the army firing off guns. "Well, they're having a good night," Sara remembered hearing one aide saying.

However, the gunfire continued into the next morning, and the sound of the noise changed. It was no longer joyful shouts but screams of terror.

"Stay put," Sara heard George saying to Martha as she opened the door to her room. All the men in the building ran out the door with weapons in hand. Martha and Sara went to the window overlooking the army. They could see men and women running from the fields in all directions. There looked to be bodies lying in blood at the center of the commotion. Washington and the other officers were running toward the camp, but they arrived too late.

It was a couple of hours before Washington returned and explained what happened. "We lost General Wayne's Pennsylvania line. They yelled that their enlistment was over, killed three officers, and ran away. He is going after them." He sat down in his chair, looking defeated.

Sara decided to leave Martha and George alone and headed off to the hospital to see if they needed her help. There were three officers killed and other minor injuries. It didn't take long to treat everyone, but Sara and Dr. Cochran stayed at the hospital talking about what happened.

A few days later brought the arrival of Hamilton and Eliza. They were able to rent a little place by the Cochrans, and after they were settled, they went to visit Sara. She was in the sitting room with Martha when they arrived. Sara tried to get up, but they both stopped her.

"I am so sorry I missed your wedding!" Sara said.

"We are just glad you are doing better, Sara, you really scared us," Eliza said.

"Well, I have something for you. Call it a Christmas slash wedding present," Sara said, handing them each a small gift box.

"You really didn't have to do this, Sara," they said, and both gave her a hug.

"You're not due back until tomorrow, so please sit and tell us everything!" Martha asked.

They did as she asked and everyone talked and enjoyed the afternoon.

One evening, when Martha and Sara were busy, George entered in a huff. "What happened?" Martha asked.

"The Pennsylvania line killed three of my officers, and Congress decided to give them furlough and bonuses if they reenlist and head south! If word got out about this, we will lose half the camp to our own Congress!" he said. "They have been trying over and over again to remove me from this army, and this one is ingenious. Not paying these men for two years, they get upset and leave killing officers, they provide back pay and bonuses to rejoin under a different general. They are trying to steal my army right out from under me," he complained.

"That is just unthinkable," Martha said.

He did his best to keep the news from his army, but New Jersey heard about the deal and also tried to mutiny. "Congress is forcing George to be unmerciful against these men," Martha said, upset.

"What did he decide to do?" Sara asked.

"He sent General Howe after them with five hundred men to have them surrender and execute the ringleaders," Martha said.

"I know he doesn't like it, but it will be worse if he just lets them off. I mean, these guys would not have left if Congress didn't give Pennsylvania such a good deal for leaving," Sara said. As upsetting as it was, the plan worked and stopped the mass mutiny of the army.

If things were not hard enough, the battle between Hamilton and his position started up again. He still wanted to improve his station so he could provide a better life for his new wife. Sara could understand that and hoped George would see how useful he would be back in battle. However, the conflict took a turn for the worst. Sara and Martha were in the sitting room when they heard George yelling at Hamilton. Sara looked up at Martha, eyes wide open at what was said next.

"Colonel Hamilton, you have kept me waiting at the head of the stairs these ten minutes. I must tell you, sir, you treat me with disrespect," George grumbled.

"I am not conscious of it, sir, but since you have thought it necessary to tell me so, we part," Hamilton replied back.

"Very well, sir, if it be your choice," Washington said, ending the conversation and work relationship between the men.

"Well, the powder keg finally went off," Sara said.

"Well, I hope they can both move on now," Martha said.

"I don't believe that will happen, Aunt Martha. Hamilton will never return as his aide," Sara said, putting down her sewing.

"Where are you going?" Martha said.

"I need to take Storm out for a ride. I will ask Lafayette to join me," Sara said and walked out.

However, when she made it downstairs, Lafayette was busy, so she didn't stop to talk with him. She went to Storm, put on her bridle and saddle, and went out by herself. She was walking through the woods when she started to pray for the first time in a long time.

"Father, I could use your help a bit here. I love both these men so much, and all they can do right now is hurt each other." Tears started to fall with the snow. "I thank you for saving my life, but I would go home with you today if you can help calm these two. I don't see this getting fixed, it has been too long in the making. I also don't believe we can win this war without both these men being involved. Please help us!" The tears started freezing to her face when she heard Lafayette call from behind her.

"Sara, please wait up."

She stopped and turned around, waiting for Lafayette. "What do you think you are doing? Lady Washington was angry with me for not riding with you."

"I told her I would ask, but you were so busy, and I just couldn't stay in that building," Sara said, shivering.

Lafayette took off his cape and wrapped Sara up in it to warm her up. "We all heard the argument, it seems George lost his patients again, and Hamilton took it for the last time. But, my dear, everything will be all right, I promise you."

"But we need both men to fight this war. Hamilton has too much pride to accept an apology if George even offers one," Sara said.

"He already sent word to Hamilton, but I do agree. I do not think Hamilton will return for anything short of command. But first thing is first, mon amie, we need to get you someplace warm before you get sick again," Lafayette said, pulling on Storm's reins. "Don't worry about me, the reaper had his chance, and even he didn't want me." She laughed. It wasn't long for them to return to camp, and Lafayette escorted Sara back to her room where Martha was waiting.

"You said you were going with Lafayette!" she stated strongly.

"I know, but with everything else, I didn't want Uncle George upset at him as well," Sara replied.

"So it is better to have me angry with you?" Martha said, feeling Sara's head.

"And you're starting to get warm again, back to bed."

"I am fine," Sara tried to say, but Martha stepped in again. "I don't care what you think right now. Get back to bed before I put you in the grave."

The next morning, Sara didn't get a chance to prove she was still fine when a knock came on her door.

"Come in," she called as she was putting on her shoes. Eliza came in looking worried.

"I am so sorry, Eliza, is there anything I can do?" Sara questioned.

"No, not really. I heard about your adventure yesterday and wanted to make sure you didn't make yourself sick again. I don't need to worry about you as well," Eliza replied.

"I am fine, just upset with this entire situation," Sara said, giving Eliza a hug.

"Well, Martha summoned me here, so I better not keep her waiting." And she took her leave.

Sara didn't want to interrupt them, so she started for the hospital. Dr. Cochran was also on his way and stopped her before she got there.

"No more playing with the sick until I give you clearance. For now, do you mind staying with Gertrude for me? She is worried about everything with Hamilton and George," Dr. Cochran asked.

"Sure thing, but if you need me, please let me know," Sara said and walked toward the house.

When Gertrude answered the door, she looked a bit nervous, then relieved when she saw Sara. "Come in, please come in."

"Thank you, ma'am, how are you doing today?" Sara asked.

"Well, as good as can be expected in these situations. I told my brother he would be a good husband for Eliza, and in two months' time, he leaves his job," Gertrude said with tears in her eyes.

"Nothing about what happened makes him a bad husband. He will figure it out and take care of Eliza. Of that, I have no double," Sara offered, but it didn't seem to help, so she added, "He always wanted more, to be better for her. Now that they are married, he will not stop until he gets there. But he will not accept George's temper being taken out on him anymore. I don't disagree, and honestly, he lasted the longest," Sara said. Gertrude just looked up at her. "Remember that aide, what was his name, Burr, Aaron Burr, left after two months."

There was another knock at the door, and Eliza entered with the ladies. "Are you all right, my dear?" Gertrude asked and hugged her niece.

"Yes, Martha wanted me to know there were no hard feelings and gave me some advice," Eliza said.

"Where is Hamilton now, is he all right?" Sara asked.

"Oh, he is back to work like nothing happened. He still plans on leaving as soon as a replacement has been trained, but he is there now," Eliza said, looking worried and confused.

Martha decided to take matters into her own hands and told George she was taking Sara and going on a vacation. Sara packed up her belongings, said her goodbyes, and climbed into Martha's carriage.

"May I ask where we are going?" Sara wanted to know.

"I need to talk with my dear friends, the Schuylers, it has been too long since I have visited them," she said.

As much as Sara wanted to be in on this plot, she felt it much better to stay out of it. Upon arrival, they were welcomed into the Schuyler home and introduced to the remaining children.

"Please, Martha, have a seat," Philip said, pointing toward the sitting room. "To what do we owe this pleasure?" he asked as everyone sat down.

"I am sure you have already been made aware of my husband's momentary lack of composure," Martha stated.

"Yes, Hamilton wrote to us as soon as it happened," Philip said quietly.

"Well, I am here on both men's behalf. You know what George has been dealing with, thus leading to his remarks," she started.

"I have been in similar situations myself, yes," he replied.

"Well, I just want to restate what a fine young man Hamilton has become," Martha offered. "I also missed the two of you and wanted to offer my congratulations." That was the last Sara heard anyone talk about either Hamilton or Washington and the disagreement.

As April turned into May in New York, the smell of honeysuckles and roses began to take place. The sunshine brought warmth and, with it, Hamilton and Eliza. As they rode up to the house, Sara was outside playing with the younger children.

"Sara, what are you doing here?" she heard Hamilton call out.

"Eliza!" the children screamed, which caused people to exit the house.

"Well, hello, sir and madam," Sara said. "Apparently, I am here on vacation!" She laughed as Hamilton helped Eliza down from the wagon. She walked up and gave them each a hug as the remainder of the family came out to greet them. Sara could sense the tension Hamilton had as Philip Schuyler walked up to him. However, she also saw the relief her friend had when Philip extended his hand and warmly welcomed his new son-in-law.

The next couple days were relaxing and enjoyable for everyone. Sara and Hamilton, with some of the boys, went out to hunt some game for the family.

When Sara shot her first duck, one of the boys said, "I didn't know girls can shoot and hunt!"

"First of all, she is a lady! Second, Sara has one of the best shots I have seen!" Hamilton said to them.

"Thank you," she mouthed to him.

They were able to get a couple more birds and a few rabbits to dry the meat for upcoming meals. About midday, they packed up their belongings and returned home.

Upon arrival, Eliza ran out to get Sara and called, "Sara, come quick, it's Martha!"

"Go! I will take care of Storm," Hamilton said as she dismounted, handing him the reins.

"What happened, what's wrong?" Sara called back.

"She has been getting sick and her stomach is giving her a lot of pain," Eliza said as they ran into the house.

"Did someone call for a doctor?" Sara asked.

"Yes, Philip went for one when it started," Catherine said, placing a wet cloth on Martha's head.

Sara sat down on the bed as Martha moaned in pain. "Where does it hurt?" Sara asked.

Martha pointed toward the top of her stomach and became sick again. Sara wiped her up and helped her to relax back on the bed. Shortly after, Philip and the doctor showed up. The first thing Sara saw was a jar of leeches, and she pulled Philip aside.

"General, do you know where the army is camped now?" she asked.

"I believe the main army is still at New Windsor. Why?" he questioned.

"I will be back soon," she said and ran out of the house. She was still in her breeches and jacket for hunting, so she just grabbed a hat for a disguise.

"What's going on?" Hamilton asked.

"Martha's bad, and that doc wants to bleed her. I have to go get Cochran or Madder quickly," Sara said as she resaddled Storm.

"I will join you!" Hamilton said as he did the same. Then they both were on their way.

It took about three hours to return to the camp, and they went right to the hospital. Luckily both Dr. Madder and Dr. Cochran were there. "Please, something is wrong with Martha. I need one of you to come with us right away!" Sara called out. "Where is George?" she then asked.

"I will go," Dr. Cochran said, picking up his bag, and then said, "He went north to Connecticut."

As they started to leave, Hamilton saw an officer and told him someone needed to ride to the general and tell him about his wife and where she was. Then they were off.

By the time they arrived at the Schuylers, Martha was much worse. "Remove those leeches now!" Dr. Cochran demanded.

"Who do you think you are?" the other doctor said.

"I am her doctor and have been for years, now remove those leeches," Dr. Cochran demanded again.

"Well, I never!" the doctor began, but Sara stepped in. She took the jar and tweezer and started removing the creatures herself. Upset, the doc took his jar and left.

"Martha, Martha, can you tell me where it hurts?" Dr. Cochran asked. All she could do was moan.

"She said it was here!" Sara pointed.

Dr. Cochran felt her stomach and said, "Gallbladder, this is not good. Sara, stay with her while I mix up medicine for her to calm things down." He picked up his back and left the room with Catherine.

Sara was holding a bucket for Martha again when they returned.

"Martha, I know it hurts but please drink this, it will help," Dr. Cochran said. Martha took the cup and started drinking the contents. She sipped it slowly but did manage to drink it all and keep it down. "Now please rest, I will check in on you again in the morning," he said.

"I will remain with her," Sara said, patting Martha's head.

"I will have someone bring you dinner, Sara. Let me know if you need anything," Catherine said.

Over the next few weeks, Sara sat and took care of Martha the way Martha took care of her. Catherine, Eliza, and Peggy all forced Sara to rest as they would take a turn to help Martha, but as soon as she was awake, she returned. With the ginger root tea Dr. Cochran was giving Martha, she started to feel better, but it was a slow journey.

"You need to watch what you eat from now on," he said when she awoke.

"You will find different foods will trigger upsets. If you accidentally eat something, make this tea, then avoid that food," he said and handed Sara the directions. "I need to get back to camp, if anything worrisome happens, come get me. Otherwise, I will check in on you when I can."

A few days passed when a knock came on the door. One of the servants answered it and found George Washington asking about his wife.

"Come in, George!" Philip called out.

"Philip, how is she, where is she!" George asked.

"She's here, right this way!" Philip said, leading George to Martha.

"Martha, my darling, how are you feeling?" he began to say.

Everyone left the room to give the Washingtons some privacy. About a half hour later, he exited the room and said, "She just fell asleep again. Do you think Martha and Sara can inconvenience you a little longer while she regains her strength?" George asked.

"It is no inconvenience, George. They can stay as long as they need," Philip answered.

"I can't thank you enough for taking care of her. We are only two hours out, so I will be here as often as I can be," George said.

"You have an army to take care of. Don't worry about, Martha. She is in good hands with Sara here," Philip said, putting his arm around Sara.

"Don't worry, Uncle. If anything happens, we will get you right away, but she is going to be all right now," Sara said.

"What would we do without you!" George said to Sara.

As he started to mount his horse, Hamilton came back from hunting. "George," he said.

"Hamilton," George responded.

"When you find yourself in need of commanding office, I will come back," Hamilton said.

"Right now, please protect them," George said back and departed.

Hamilton walked into the house, handing over a couple of quails to the cook and shaking his head, and Sara followed. "He will see. He needs you before the war is over, Hamilton," Sara said. He turned on her angry but calmed down right away.

"Yeah, sure," he said sarcastically. "How is Martha doing?" he asked.

"She still can't eat, but the pain has subsided," Sara answered.

"I know you're a nurse and you care for her, but don't forget to take care of yourself. Get outside when you can. You will be no good to her if you don't," he said caringly.

She took his hand and said thank you, then walked back to Martha's room.

At the start of June, Hamilton announced that he found a home to rent for him and Eliza not far away. The Schuylers put on a small family party in which Martha had a servant lock Sara out of the room to attend. She sat at the dining table, talking and listening to the family enjoying the afternoon. Sara, however, didn't have much to say. As some of the family got up and moved around, she tried to step outside without being seen. Peggy, however, followed her out and sat on the porch swing next to her.

"Are you all right, Sara?" she questioned.

"I am not sure, Peggy. I am not really feeling anything, if that makes any sense," Sara tried to explain. "I'm not in the mood to party, but I'm not sad either."

"Well, that's all right, Sara. Sometimes I like to just be outside and enjoy peace when I can get it," Peggy said.

"Peace," Sara replied. "Maybe!" She turned and looked at Peggy. They hugged as Eliza came out to see if they were all right. "Eliza, I am going to miss you! It has been wonderful being with you again like this," Sara said, giving Eliza a hug.

"We will not be far, so if you need me or Alexander, just write, we will be there for you," Eliza said.

"Same for you," Sara said, then whispered, "I know he can be confusing."

Everyone started to come out of the house to bid the couple farewell. They climbed aboard the wagon and started off.

Martha's health was rocky for the next month. She would start to feel better, then try to eat something and get sick again. In time they started to realize what types of foods she needed to stay away from. They were able to write to Jack toward the end of June that she would be ready to head home. As promised, George stopped in at least two times a week to check in on her. As Martha improved, so did George's mood, and by the time Jack arrived to take her home, she was feeling herself again. Sara felt comfortable enough with her recovery to provide Jack the tonic direction and go back to the army camp with George.

She awoke the next morning in headquarters and went outside to look over the camp. There were next to a river and, to her surprise across, from Hamilton and Eliza. She waved at them when she saw them and just laughed. She continued onto the hospital and informed Dr. Cochran about Martha.

"So how is that going?" she asked, pointing toward Hamilton's house.

"It has been interesting!" Dr. Cochran said.

"When it is a nice day, he will spend all day outside just to aggravate him. But I think between that and the letters from Lafayette, it is starting to work."

"We don't have any patients today, so do you want to go for a ride?" Dr. Cochran asked.

"That sounds like a good idea," Sara replied.

They got their horses and headed out downstream. A few miles down, the river narrowed, so they were able to easily cross and then headed back up toward Hamilton.

"Hello there, sir!" Sara said as they came closer.

"Well, hello, Sara, how is everything going? Is Martha all right?" Hamilton asked.

"Martha is doing much better. She went back to Mt. Vernon to fully recover," Sara said. "So, this was your idea?"

"Hey, I found something I could afford to take care of my wife. The fact that it is right across from Washington's camp, well, that's a bonus," Hamilton said.

"I am sure it had nothing to do with your decision." Sara smirked.

"Absolutely not!" he said as he walked up and kissed her hello on the cheek.

"Is Eliza inside?" Sara asked.

"Yes, go right in," he said, then shook Dr. Cochran's hand as he walked up.

Sara knocked on the door and entered the house. The sitting room and dining room were together in the front with a fireplace. A secondary room in the back for the kitchen and a one bedroom upstairs. It wasn't close to what Eliza was used to but very cute for a couple just starting out.

"How are you doing, Eliza?" Sara asked.

"I'm all right," Eliza replied.

"Are you sure? You don't look right," Sara said, a little concerned.

"Well, I have been feeling poorly every morning!" Eliza said.

Sara's eyes became very big, and she asked a silent question. Eliza shook her head but put her finger to her lips to keep Sara quiet. Trying not to make any noise, Sara hopped over and hugged Eliza.

"Does anyone else know?" Sara asked.

"Not yet. I have to tell him first, but he is a bit distracted right now," Eliza said, staring out the window toward Hamilton. "He wants so much to rejoin the army and have his own command, but I am hoping that doesn't happen. I know how reckless he is, and he deserves to meet his child."

The two men walked in, and Dr. Madder asked, "How are you doing, Eliza? Hamilton here said he was worried you were having the same issues as Martha."

Sara tried not to giggle when Eliza told him she was fine. They all sat down and talked about the topics of the day. How Congress wasn't doing what they needed to do and how it needed to change if they wanted to have a surviving nation. He also went over his desire to help create the financial and democratic systems to hold this country together.

"Keep an eye out for me in the New York Packet," he said.

"Oh, Hamilton, you didn't write anything against Washington, did you?" questioned Sara.

"I thought you knew me better than that, Sara. As much as we may disagree, I would not disgrace Washington in public like Lee," Hamilton said.

"No, you will just annoy him by living across the river," Sara said back, smiling.

"This essay discusses our current political system that is in place for the war and how it needs to change after the war to ensure success," Eliza said proudly.

"Yes, my Betsy here helped me put it together," Alexander said, putting his arm around Eliza.

"It sounds like you should enter politics after this is over," Dr. Cochran said.

"Which is why I so desperately need to have my own command. I will never get there, otherwise," Hamilton said grumpily.

Seeing Eliza's face when he said that, Sara said, "You can get there by being a great lawyer, Hamilton."

"And how is that going to work? I need to finish my schooling, which if they refuse, the accelerated course will be three years followed by three to four more years of supposedly being an apprentice before I can begin my career. The country will be set up by then and incorrectly if the people I have heard from have anything to do with it," Hamilton said angrily. "No, I have to have command, so I can start advocating for this country earlier."

The reality of his statement was compelling, but Sara did have one piece of information Hamilton did now. As they were getting ready to leave, she whispered to Eliza, "You need to tell him soon so he can make an informed decision. If Uncle George offers him a command, a baby will either change or confirm his beliefs."

Chapter *11*

The road to Yorktown

L ate one evening, as Sara was reading in the sitting room, George came in, crossed the room, and looked out the window. "Is everything all right?" Sara asked.

"These are most troubling times, and I do wish Martha was with me," he said.

"Can I be of any help then?" she asked.

"Maybe, my dear, maybe," he answered and let his thought drift off.

Sara just waited for George to make the next move as she just looked at him. After a few minutes in thought, he turned around and looked at her before talking again. "I feel the need to provide advancement long overdue. However, I was just informed this subject will soon become a father." He started saying in codes, not knowing Sara already knew Eliza was with child. "I think the past behavior could pose costly to the mother and babe, but not accepting would prove costly to the cause," he said, sitting down, looking at a couple of letters.

"Well, Uncle, I may be wrong, but the choice *you* have to make is offering the position. The choice of accepting or declining is up to the young family," she questioned delicately.

"Yes, that is true," he mumbled.

"The unfortunate part of freedom is the number of widows left behind. It is a necessary evil that is understood. They do not have blame for it but pride," she said. She held her tongue after that letting him comprehend the discussion a bit more.

"Your aunt has taught you well," he finally said as he left the room.

As Sara walked the halls of headquarters, she overheard Washington talking to Tench Tillman. He asked for Tillman to deliver a message to Hamilton that if he retains his commission, he will be offered a command. Immediately, Sara went back to her room and wrote a letter to Eliza.

Eliza,

> *I have heard of your husband's possible command to this military and the knowledge of your confidence. I felt the need to address you expediently. If this appointment should reach fruition as expected, he will not be unnoticed, and your concerns will not go unheard daily. Please take care of yourself and the other joy, and I will care for what is yours here.*

> *With all my love,*
> *S. Weinstein*

She decided to take a walk through the camp and look around while she was thinking of the Hamiltons. She felt both worried and excited for this family and the possibilities for the future. Then she took note of the children running around playing. The thought of them losing their fathers over the next coming months was concerning. These children running around without a care in the world would not be here if there were other family members who could take them in. Unlike them, Eliza's family would make sure she and the babe would be taken care of. And though she was an orphan herself, she had a better outlook than these children. *This is something*

I must discuss with Hamilton when I see him again, she thought to herself.

She let a few days pass and mailed out her letter to Eliza, who returned to the Schuylers. She then took Storm out for a ride. Halfway down the river, she saw Hamilton riding on the other side. When she was able, she crossed over and said, "Well, how are you doing today, sir?"

"From the way you ask, I presume you already know Sara," he said, smiling back.

"Yes, I heard, congratulations," she said, then looked down. "Where did you get your mount?"

"He is a rental. I just felt like a ride today. Wish to join me?" he asked.

"If you don't mind, I would love to. Actually, I wanted to talk with you about something," she responded.

"Oh no, I know that voice," he said. "What happened?"

As they started walking down the river, she said, "When I heard about your promotion, I became worried and Eliza was at the center of the issue," she said.

"Not you too, I thought you would be happy for me! This is what I have been working for to be able to take care of her and our child," he added.

"Congratulations!" she said, pretending she had no idea.

"That is why I insisted on her return to the Schuylers," he said happily.

"And that brings me to my topic," she started. "We are both orphans, and I was thinking about how Eliza was able to return to the Schuylers. I also know if you should fall, they will take care of her and now the baby. I even have help from family friends, but what about the children in camp? If their fathers should fall, the families will be left with nothing. The wives or children will not get the promised pay the father would. Is there anything you may be able to do when you start trying to plan the government?" she asked.

"Well, that is something I can keep in the back of my mind, but it all really depends on how the financial system is created. I have been writing to Mr. Morris about it, but at this point, I have no control over that," he said. "However it is something worth discussion."

"From reading your books, I know there are several layers that need to be put into place to grow a strong foundation and economy. There need to be taxes placed on the public for the government to survive and help the states, so I do get that. I just hope as you continue to put your thoughts into the paper, you will remember not only the soldiers but their families," she explained.

"Your grasp of finances is better than most of the men I talk with." He laughed. "It will take time, but I will remember them," he added.

"Do you know anything about the command you are going to have?" Sara asked, changing the subject.

"Not yet, but I should hear something shortly," he answered proudly. "Will you be staying with the army when they travel?" he asked.

"Yes, I feel with Martha's illness, it is important to be close to George," she said.

Within a month, Hamilton was back in camp, taking over a light infantry battalion, which will be under the command of Lafayette.

"We will be starting out soon Sara and heading into battle in the South," George said one day. "When we travel this time, I want you to be in disguise as an aide." He handed her a uniform.

"Why is that?" Sara questioned.

"Let's just say I know you, and if you were to pick up a gun, I want you to look like everyone else and not such an easy target," George said. "I know you did this before, and this way, I can keep a closer eye on you."

"Well then, I guess you should call me Sam from now on," she said with a smile. Then they started to hear commotion outside and looked out the window.

"Drilling again," George said as Hamilton was working his men.

"If you would like my opinion, I think it is a good thing he drills like this. They need to be ready for whatever he would throw at them," Sara said.

He started drilling his group as soon as he returned and took great pride in making sure his men were battle-ready. Even as the army started moving south, he would keep up with the drills when possible.

"How are they doing?" Sara asked him one day.

He looked at her twice, not used to seeing her dressed as a man, then said, "They are a good bunch and pick up quickly," he said as they rode together to the next campsite. "I think they will be ready in time to fight. By the way, nice look," he added.

"George felt it would keep me a bit safer this trip," Sara said.

The journey south was, in Sara's words, interesting. It was long and tedious but had good moments as well. If the campsite did not have buildings, Sara would stay in the tent next to George again. One morning Sara saw three of the aides ride out of camp, most likely with messages to the different parts of the army.

"Sam, can you come here?" George called out for her. "I have sent my aides out and would like to ask you to take this to Rochambeau and wait for an answer." He handed her a letter, and she set out. Rochambeau's French army was about a mile and a half back when she found them.

"News from Washington, sir," she said, handing over the note.

He read the note, picked up a pen, and as he wrote, mumbled, "Very good, very good!" and returned the note.

She left the tent, remounted Storm, and started to ride back, thinking she could get used to being an aide. She knew George would not let her ride away from the army like the others, but this was exciting. Handing the note to George, he read it and said, "We will be stopping at Mt. Vernon to regroup before going after Cornwallis. I would like you to join us."

"Very well, General," she answered.

He looked up with a smile and said, "Dismissed."

That night she went to Hamilton's battalion to talk with him. "Have you heard from Eliza?" she asked.

"Not nearly as much as she has heard from me," he said grumpily, "but from what I received, she is doing well."

"Why so grumpy?" Sara asked.

"I want to hear about her and our child. Are they all right? Are they in need of anything? When days go by without word, I think something happened to them," he complained.

"The last thing she needs you to be is the nervous new father going out into battle. And no one can keep up with the way you write," she joked at him. "So what do you think about becoming a father?" she asked.

"I am excited and yet would rather face a hundred redcoats alone." He laughed. Then he became serious. "What if I can't do it? What if I mess up? After all, he will be the son of a bastard."

"He?" she questioned.

"Oh, I told Eliza this one had to be a boy, so there you have it," he said with a smile.

"You know she has no control over that." She laughed and hit him on the shoulder. "But seriously, you are going to be a great father. And if you have any questions, just ask Eliza! I am sure between the both of you, you will figure it out."

As they approached Mt. Vernon, George said, "I would like for you to keep the cover of Sam at Mt. Vernon. I have invited Rochambeau to join us there, and I want as little as possible to know about you."

"I know you don't want women as seen in the army, Uncle. I will keep this cover for you," she said. "But Aunt Martha and Jack saw me this way already."

"Don't worry, I already sent word to them regarding the situation. They will keep your cover," Geroge answered.

As they approached the house, they were greeted by Jack out front. "Welcome, everyone! Sam, nice to see you again. George, I would like to speak with you when you have a moment, sir," he said.

"Sure thing, son, let's step over here," George said, walking away as Sara led the officers inside.

Martha and Nully were there to greet everyone and lead them into the sitting room. Sara waited outside the room so she could serve refreshments that were prepared by the servants. George and Jack returned, and George entered the room with his officers. Every time Sara entered the room, she could tell they were discussing the attack on Yorktown. She would never stay too long, but with each visit, her excitement increased.

"We need to dig two trenches, one here and one here as quickly as possible, and take these two positions," Rochambeau offered, pointing at a map.

"Sam," Jack called the next time she exited the room, "a word please."

"Yes, sir, how may I help you?" she questioned.

"I will be joining you from now on, another set of eyes on you."

"As long as you cleared things with Washington," she said.

"Of course I did. What do you think we were talking about?" he answered.

"Then thank you for your service, sir." Sara provided a tip of the hat.

"So was our run the debut?" Jack asked.

"Yes, sir," she said with a smile. "And I must say it is upsetting and exhilarating at the same time. To be as free as a man but knowing I will never get the same respect as a woman."

"Well, maybe if there are enough as bold as you, it will happen," he replied.

They remained at Mt. Vernon for two days, with all levels of officers entering and departing the room. Sara would hold a vigil outside the room to make sure of those who enter were supposed to. There were another two armed guards at the front door keeping the building secure. Finally, the army set out east toward their destination and hopefully put an end to the war.

"Sam, a word," Hamilton called as Sara rode by.

"Yes, Lieutenant Colonel Hamilton," Sara said, riding up to him.

"I got it, I was able to convince them to allow me to lead," he whispered. "They weren't going to but in the end my rank forced it."

"I truly am happy for you, but please don't forget what you need to return to," she offered.

He turned to her and asked, "Did she put you up to this, reminding me about her every day? Don't you know I don't do anything but think about her?"

"No, I told her I would do it. Also, I see it in your eyes and don't want you to think of her and hesitate, which could cost you," Sara said.

When they arrived, the French, followed by Rochambeau, took hold of the area to the left of the city while Washington and his army took the right, making a semicircle surrounding Yorktown. The timing was perfect for the army as the French navy had arrived to remove any chance of retreat. On September 28, after the artillery was moved in, Sara would ride back and forth between generals, telling them it was their turn. By what she saw, each group was building some sort of structure between them and Yorktown.

Then one night, she saw men move forward to take attention of another group who started to dig behind the structure. By morning most of the men and artillery were moved into the trenches of the first parallel. Washington took it upon himself to fire the first cannon starting the battle. As the cannon fire continued, they began building a second structure even closer to the British this time. Again after they started digging, the parallel was filled with men and cannons by morning.

Now that the battle had begun and the cannons were none stop, Sara went up and down the first trench looking for wounded. She carried a small bag with bandages to help wherever she could. As the sun went down, she could occasionally tell two units were charging two fortresses lit up by signal fire. It looked like the one on the right was taken first and pretty quickly. The second one finally came under Continental control, and the British flag was replaced with the Continental and French flags, proving control. From then on, cannons from land and sea rang out until Cornwallis sent up a white flag of surrender.

The battle was over. However, there was one person down from illness that Sara was very concerned about. Jack had contracted camp fever during this fight and was not doing well. She received permission from Washington to retrieve Nelly and Martha and bring them to Jack. She arrived at Mt. Vernon as Sam and reported the surrender of Cornwallis.

"Martha, Nelly, your presence is required at camp please. I will call your drivers to get your carriage ready as you pack a few things."

Nelly was excited and took off upstairs while Martha remained with Sam. "That news is too good for you to look this concerned. What's wrong?" Martha asked.

Knowing she couldn't conceal the truth, Sara responded, "It's Jack, he is sick."

Martha's face went white as the words set in. She called for Ona and told her to pack her belongings as she felt too tired to do it. She stepped outside with Sara and tried to get more information.

Sara, however, just said, "I don't have information. I was just told to come get you while George and John Laurens discuss the surrender. The coward couldn't even hand over his sword and sent his second to do it," Sara said, trying to lighten the mood.

Leaving the younger children with the older girls, they were ready to travel. Sara rode next to the carriage but could talk with Martha and Nelly.

"I am so proud of Jack," Nelly said as they started out. "Following in his father's footsteps, he always worried he would never live up to father's expectations," she said.

"George was never disappointed with Jack's decisions, Nelly. He just wants the best for both of you," Martha said calmly.

"You can't be that far, we heard the cannons all month long from the house," Nelly said again, looking pleased.

"Just outside Yorktown," Sara said.

"What was it like to be right there? It must have been so exciting," Nelly asked.

"Well, after delivering messages, I was in the first trench looking for wounded. All I really have to say about it was it was loud," Sara replied.

"Loud, that's all? There has to be more," Nelly pushed.

"Nelly, if Sam here doesn't want to talk about don't push, it will be the same with Jack and George. I have found after being up close with the battles, they don't like to recall it," Martha said.

She was right. Sara didn't want to discuss pulling screaming or dying men from the trenches, standing talking with someone, and having his head shot off by cannons, not to mention the stench of rotting flesh left behind or urine smell from men not leaving the holes.

As they arrived, Sara instructed the carriage to go right to the hospital. They found Washington next to Jack, and Nelly's joy turned to concern upon seeing him. George stepped back to let Martha and Nelly come closer and talk with him. He was really weak and didn't say much, but he did seem to know they were there.

Sara started to back up when George said, "Sam, come here please. You are family, please stay." Sara nodded her head and gave him a hug.

"I am so sorry!" she said. "Is there anything I can do?"

"Not really. Dr. Cochran is giving him that drink, but he doesn't seem to be responding."

"Dad, Mom," Jack whispered, "please take care of Washy and Nelly! Patty and Eliza can take care of my wife!" He closed his eyes and didn't speak again.

She walked outside and around the camp to give the grieving family some space. Again she heard Alexander's name regarding the battle.

"What did he do this time?" she asked Laurens when she saw him.

"You didn't hear yet, he took down Redoubt 10 in ten minutes! He led the charge from the front as I led from the back. He was in his element, jumping over blockades, dodging bullets, narrowly avoided death again as we met up in the middle. Once both redoubts were down, the battle was all but over," he said.

"Reckless and heroic all wrapped up into one Hamilton, but where is he? I haven't seen him since the battle?" she asked.

"He took off for Albany right after the cease-fire. Poor guy couldn't stay away another minute." He laughed.

"All right, well, how about the surrender? I heard you took the lead in that," Sara wanted to know.

"Those dogs are going to get the same treatment they gave us when they took over," he provided proudly.

"Good work, sir, and look, I never got a chance—" Sara started but Laurens cut her off

"It's all good, actually after seeing you fight here, it is I who should apologize. You can definitely hold your own," he said.

On November 5, Sara went to the hospital to look in on Jack again. She found everyone around him crying. He was breathing very shallow and slow, and his face was pale; it was the look of death. A few moments passed by before he was finally at rest. George and Sara helped Martha and Nelly out of the hospital and to their residence. They all began to wear black and made final arrangements for Jack before the woman started for Mt. Vernon.

"I didn't think I could get through this one untouched but had you asked me if I thought it would be Jack, I would call you crazy," George said to Sara one evening with tears in his eyes. "I can't believe they are all gone. You are the only one from that time left," he said sadly.

"This world seems to take more than it gives. Your children, Jack and Patsy, along with grandchildren you never met. My parents and Dad's second family. I sometimes wonder if it is worth it, when will it be enough." A long pause took place between them as they were both lost in thought.

"Is Aunt Martha going to be all right?" Sara asked.

"I think the request to take the youngins was Jack's way of trying to help her through it. She is strong, but to lose every one of your children while you're still around is a bitter pill to swallow," he said, taking a sip of brandy.

"Was Nelly all right with that request?" Sara asked.

"I believe it did take some worry off her mind. It is difficult to remarry with young children," George said, looking into his empty cup.

"If there is anything I can do to help, please let me know," Sara provided.

"Thank you, my dear, Thank you!"

Days went along all connected together that Sara couldn't tell one from another. The army began marching north headed toward

Philadelphia. One morning, George handed Sara a letter as they were having breakfast.

"I haven't received a letter in forever, who could be writing to me?" Sara asked. She opened the letter and read it over a few times.

"What's wrong?" George asked.

"It seems like New Jersey has accepted that I am the only living heir. 'Since General George Washington has validated your biological status, we hereby appoint all rights of General George Weinstein's assets to be transferred to Sara Weinstein. The application of brother-in-law Jeffrey Thomas to inherit all property rights is hereby dismissed.' You wrote to them for me?" she asked.

"Of course I did, Sara. I was appointed executor to George's property in his will. We spoke often of how Donna's family wanted to remove you. I was not about to let that happen," he said.

"All this in the middle of the war. I don't know what to say. Thank you simply is not enough," Sara said, giving him a hug.

"Thank you is not necessary. Like Martha has been saying, you are our daughter now, and we will do anything for you," he said, hugging her back.

"Hello, my friends," Sara said, calling out to Lafayette and Laurens.

"Mon amie, we haven't seen you in a while, how are you doing?" Lafayette said.

"I am doing all right. I just got word that I will be inheriting my father's estate," Sara said.

"That's wonderful news, so you're not the pauper you would like all of us to believe," Laurens said.

"I should have been. My uncle was trying to steal it, saying I didn't survive the fire."

"How did you convince them of who you are?" Laurens asked.

"Actually, it was Uncle George who took care of everything," she muttered.

"So you will be able to stay in the class you have become accustomed to?" Lafayette asked.

"I don't care too much about the class, but with the new laws in New Jersey, I will be able to rebuild my home and turn it into a tavern to own and run myself. With what we have seen on the road, I know I can do better than that. Plus, having my own property, there is talk I will be able to vote!" Sara said excitedly.

"Vote, was that law overturned? How do you know?" Lafayette asked.

"Well, I am friends with Hamilton, so of course I keep up with the laws of my state as well as the rest of the states. New Jersey's politicians are debating that if a woman has property and is not married, she has the right to vote. Things may be starting to change, at least I hope so. Anyway, when I get it set up, you both have to come by, will you promise?" she asked.

"Sure, just let us know when you are ready," they agreed.

"Are you staying with Washington now, or are you going to be moved to a different unit again? Sara asked.

"Actually, I have just sent a request for leave of absence to return home since it doesn't look like there will be another battle for a while," Lafayette said.

Laurens then said, "I believe Washington is planning on returning to New York. When I get the chance, I will ask to return to Carolina and continue to work for a black battalion."

After a small pause, Sara added, "Splitting up the family again," with a half-hearted smile.

"Ahh, we are not gone yet, so let's enjoy the time we still have, oui!" Lafayette said as they walked back to headquarters.

At the evening meal, Lafayette, George, and Laurens were enjoying telling their tales, but Sara just sat quietly and tried to listen. She was thinking about all that happened in the last couple of years, what she lost and what she gained. When she decided to speak up, she looked right at George.

"What can I do to thank you, sir? You took me in when I was lost and helped me find a family again. You have stepped up and took over a fatherly role for me when I need it. You even stepped in when I didn't know you were doing it." She lost her words and shook her head.

"It was my pleasure, my dear, you are very welcome," he said, smiling.

"If I ever did decide to get married, I would want you to walk me down the aisle but don't hold your breath!" She laughed.

"I would be honored to!" he said back. "Who would be crazy enough to ask for your hand, then have the courage to ask Washington? Good luck with that idea!" Laurens said, getting everyone to laugh.

When Sara retired to her bedroom, she decided to write to Alexander and Eliza.

Dear Mr. and Mrs. Hamilton,

I do hope this letter finds you both well and happy. Sir, do understand your hast to return to your wife as soon as possible, but I am sorry I did not get a chance to say farewell before your departure. I have received word that my father's property will be given back to me upon my return to Princeton. Since you were George's aide, Hamilton, I guess you already knew that was in the works. Thank you for helping out in this situation. If you ever need anything, please let me know. Also, the next time you are traveling through Princeton, please stop by. I am excited to meet the new addition to your family.

With all my love,
S. Weinstein

The next morning, Sara handed the letter to the first clerk she saw and went to the dining room for breakfast. Washington was already there eating his hotcakes when she sat down.

"What are your plans today, Sara?" he asked.

"Well, I was thinking it was time to get back to the hospital," she answered.

"Actually, I have been thinking about that. I don't want you to go back there. I know you want to help, but I just can't allow that anymore," Washington said.

"Are you sending me back to Princeton?" Sara questioned.

"I just want you safe. Getting sick there is too easy, and I can't take the risk. You can remain here with me until I figure out another service," he said, staring into his breakfast.

"Are you sure I will not be a waste on your resources, Uncle?" She wanted to know.

"No, not at all, actually since Laurens, Lafayette, and Hamilton need furloughs, I do believe you again are the last of my little family."

"Hamilton asked for a furlough? I hadn't heard," Sara said.

"Well, he did get his moment in action leading a battalion, but I also think taking the chances he takes made him think about what he would lose now. He never had that issue before, and it just isn't worth it," George suggested.

"Maybe he saw death close enough this time to stop taunting it," Sara stated.

"Actually, I think everything caught up with him. I received a letter from Eliza that as soon as he arrived, he fell over and passed out. He has not been out of bed since arriving," George said, worried.

Sara just looked at him, not knowing how to express her feelings.

George pushed the remainder of his food around and decided he was finished. He started walking out of the room but gave Sara a small kiss to the head before he left. Sara was left alone, shocked and confused. She was worried about her aunt and uncle and now Hamilton, plus Eliza was about to have her baby. Her stomach started to roll with discomfort, and she couldn't finish her food, so she pushed it aside. When Lucy arrived, she apologized and offered to help collect the dirty dishes.

"No, thank ya, miss, is there somethings wrong? Can I helps you?" Lucy asked.

"No, thank you, Lucy, I don't want to complain, would be disrespectful," Sara said.

Lucy always knew Sara had a difference of opinion when it came to slavery, but she never talked about it.

"Did I upset you, Lucy?" Sara asked, looking up at her.

"No, miss." Lucy replied. "But may I speak truly, ma'am?" Lucy asked.

"With me, always, Lucy!" Sara replied.

"No one ever worried about respectins me," Lucy whispered.

"I am truly sorry about that, Lucy. The laws of the old country only support the white man, but I hope this new world will start to change that for both of us," Sara said. She stood up and gave Lucy a hug and said, "I just fear it will get worse before it gets better."

She left the dining room and started to walk around outside. She came upon Laurens packing his horse, preparing to return to the South. "Well, I guess you are off then," she said to him.

"Yes, I had said my farewells, and I am about to leave, but I wasn't going to do it without saying goodbye to you," he replied.

"I will miss you so much, but I love your cause. If there is anything a simple girl like me can do to help you, please let me know," she said.

"The last thing you are, Sara, is a simple girl. I am going to miss you as well," Laurens said.

They gave each other a hug, and Laurens mounted his horse and departed.

Lafayette walked up behind her as she watched Laurens ride off. "Ah, that man can not stay still for five minutes," he said.

"Speaking of that, when do you depart us?" Sara asked.

"I will board a ship when we get to Philadelphia," he said.

"I wanted this war to be over. I am just feeling the cost is too high," Sara said.

"Ah, oui, the price for freedom is steep, but even those who pass away for it believe the price is just. It is a very precious thing freedom, and we must never forget the cost to get it and to keep it," he said.

"And those who acquire it need to help others achieve it," Sara added.

"Oui, so very true," Lafayette replied. "Have you heard about Hamilton? Apparently, he became very ill getting home."

"George mentioned something, but I didn't get much information. I hope he can recover from whatever ails him." Lafayette said.

With no battles in sight, Lafayette and Sara decided to take a ride and take a look at the scenery. "It's nice to get away for a bit, isn't it?" Sara said.

"Oui, whenever I am dealing with things at home, I enjoy a ride through the country with my wife. However, she will never get onto the back of a horse, so we would use a carriage," Lafayette said.

"I don't believe I ever heard you talk about your wife before?" Sara questioned.

"My Adrienne," he said with stars in his eyes. "We were married in '74 at her family's hotel. It was arranged and took some time, but we did come around to each other," he said.

"Arranged. Oh my, that is worse than just losing your rights, but being forced to lose your rights," Sara complained.

"We are both from prominent families, and that is just how it is done. However, she very much enjoys high society, and I prefer to avoid it," he said.

"But when we both heard you're Benjamin Franklin talk about liberty, we believed in the lifestyle and hope for all classes. She felt so strongly that after the birth of our second child Anastasia, she was still behind me, joining your cause and fight. She even told me to stay in a letter when I found out our first child Henriette passed away shortly after. In that way, I see some of her in you."

"I am so sorry, Lafayette, I didn't know," Sara said.

"Merci beaucoup, now we also have a son, George Washington who will be turning two on the twenty-fourth," he said proudly.

"George Washington, nice name!" She giggled.

"Actually, George agreed to be his godfather," he told her.

"It sounds like you have a wonderful family back home. They should be very proud of you," Sara said.

"Oui, I am very anxious to return to them, but if I am needed to return, I will be back," he said.

"You will always be welcomed here, at least as far as I am concerned," she said.

They returned back to camp and took care of their horses. A chill came over the camp, and they saw campfires starting to be lit as they walked back to headquarters.

"I am so glad we met Lafayette, even if the reasons were not the greatest," Sara said.

"And I must say your presence has helped bring sunshine to a cold, dark war," he returned.

They both walked into the building, and Sara sighed. "I am excited about the future, but it also terrifies me. I wish I wasn't going into it alone," she confided.

"You, afraid, mademoiselle?" he questioned.

"I didn't believe that was something you could do." She smiled a little and took his hand in hers. "I always knew I would be alone someday. It is just now that it is here. I am not sure about it," she said honestly. "Then you just need to always remember that being by yourself is not that same as being alone. You will never lose that small family you made here, and we will always stand behind you, even from across the sea. Besides, if anyone can be reborn out of the ashes, male or female, it will be you, little phoenix."

She smiled and said, "Thank you for your words and the name of my new tavern, Little Phoenix."

"Where exactly are we, Uncle?" Sara asked at the evening meal. Tonight's meal had most of the remaining officers that did not stay in the south, so Sara dressed up for a special occasion. "With everything that has happened, I haven't taken notice."

"We are in Maryland, dear. Tomorrow we will start our journey straight to Philadelphia. I have already called for Martha to meet us there for the winter encampment," he answered. He then turned to Lafayette and said, "Son, I fear this is the last decent meal we will have together before your journey home. Eat well and safe passage until we meet again!" He raised his glass to Lafayette.

The rest of the table all stood up and did the same, calling out his name. "To Lafayette!" they cheered.

"Our victory would never have happened without you, good sir," George finished.

They all sat back down and started eating and talking, enjoying each other's company. Sara glanced up and down the table, looking at everyone having a good time. She had spent her entire life with the army and found leaving it troubling. She remembered what Lafayette had said earlier, but she had never really been a civilian, not like other people anyway. She looked upon George and Lafayette laughing at some joke that was just told, then she noticed Dr. Cochran and Gertrude talking with Dr. Madder, still looking overwhelmed but relieved. She had already realized that her evenings were becoming very quiet and internal. George also took notice of this and asked if she was all right.

"Yes, Uncle, you see, as much as I want change, taking the first step is difficult and scary and exciting, all wrapped up into one jumbled feeling. Remaining quiet helps me settle that feeling down and focus on what needs to happen next," she answered.

"Is that a new trick Martha taught you because all the time I have known you, quiet was never a characteristic," he said with a laugh. She glared at him, causing him to say, "Now there's my Sara."

Chapter *12*

A Winter in Philadelphia

After a three-day march, they arrived in Philadelphia to cheers and praise. "Seems like they like you now Washington," Sara said sarcastically as they rode in.

The night before, they decided she would arrive as Sam to calm any questions. The army was able to stay in and around the city with relatives or at abandoned Tory properties. Lafayette's boat was already in the harbor, so he took his leave as they entered the city. There were rambunctious parades and parties with fireworks the first few days after they arrived. When they began to slow down, Martha arrived in the city, so they started up again just so she could enjoy it. It was early December, so along with the celebrations, the city started to decorate for the holidays. Sara stayed with Martha most of the time, either in the house provided or shopping in the city. There weren't as many stores as there had been when Margaret took her into town but enough to keep them content. Every night another prominent household invited the general to a celebration dinner, which Martha and Sara would attend. Following the rules of high society, Sara dressed up and played her part very well.

"Donna would have given anything to see me wearing this to a dinner," she said one night to Martha.

"Well, you do look like a beautiful young lady now, Sara," Martha replied.

Sara played the part so well. She started to become well known around town as an eligible bachelorette, much to her dismay. The young men who did not take part in the army and fighting for their freedom, Sara didn't even want to talk with. Then there were the young men who did take part and knew of Sara well enough to not pursue her. She did, however, keep up with appearances which seemed to help Martha get through this difficult time.

One evening, Charles and Ann Thompsons hosted a dinner party for Washington and some of his coworkers in Congress.

On the ride over, Sara said, "Oh, I wish I was allowed to give them a piece of my mind for what they did to you, Uncle," as they were all in a carriage.

"You're not the only one, Sara, but diplomacy will prove our allies tonight," George said.

"Well, at least you have proven Congress wrong for thinking you were unfit to lead the army. It will be a bitter taste in their mouths," she said as Martha gave a small smile and turned to look out the window, hoping no one would see it.

"You will find Benjamin Franklin to be correct Sara, you catch more flies with honey than vinegar," Martha finally added.

When they arrived, Sara hung back a little behind the Washingtons even though she was supposed to be closer. She just loved seeing them enter a room with the elegance and majesty to challenge the dignity of any king and queen.

Like all the other parties, everyone wanted to be close to the honored guests, even though George kept telling them the war was not yet over. Sara also found a group of young men who wished to be close to her again.

"So how long have you been with the Washingtons?" one young man asked.

"I have known them my entire life," she replied.

"Really, I don't remember seeing you around Mt. Vernon," he questioned.

"I certainly don't remember you. What is your name, sir?"

"I am known by John Taylor," he said smugly.

"I have never even heard them talk about you, sir," she replied.

"You would have if you actually knew them, but you just snuck in behind them trying to get a status you do not have," he said, now talking arrogantly.

"Sir, I request you hush your accusations to a situation in which you obviously do not know," Sara said sternly.

Laughing, he answered, "You sound like you are trying to challenge me to a duel, which is outrageous."

"Well, I am definitely challenging your competence, sir," she sternly stated.

The men who knew her were hushed and worried about where this was going to go. Washington heard the voices rising and walked over and stood behind Sara, staring at the young man, startling him. She could feel her uncle behind her, so she added, "Since you have nothing to say to revoke or confirm your statements, I challenge you to a shooting match just to see how you would fare." Washington folded his arms and asked what the problem was. "This man is challenging my word that you are my uncle and that he has known you closely for a long time," Sara explained.

"Really, I don't even know your name, sir. As strange as it may sound, I do believe you owe her a target match," he said.

"I am truly sorry, sir, I misspoke." the man said.

"You insulted the word and honor of my niece. Either you take it up with her now or with me later," George stated firmly. Now the entire room was involved with the situation.

"I'll shoot at targets and even allow you to face them from the start," he said, smirking at Sara.

"Oh no, sir, to truly mess with your character, I will start turning around the same as you," she said firmly.

"Are you sure you want to do this?" Martha said to both Sara and George.

"It will be a great show before the meal," George said.

"You're not behaving like a Southern gentleman, George," Martha whispered one more time.

"He insulted her and us. I need to let her have this. Even though it is improper, it was the young man's decision," George stated.

Since there were very few open spaces in the city, everyone went outside and lined the street. Targets were set up in front of backdrops for guards, and George loaded and handed out the guns. Sara and the man, who went by John Taylor, stood next to each other with their backs facing the glass bottles. Charles, who also said he did not know the man, counted to ten. They both turned and fired. After the smoke cleared, Sara's bottle was gone, but John's was still there. Another man at the other end checked and saw a bullet hole in the backboard from John's shot.

He shouted, "Sara wins!"

Charles now addressed the man, saying, "You are a liar and a disgrace, sir, and I should have you arrested for insulting my guests."

"No, thank you, Mr. Thompson, I do believe losing a gunfight to me in front of all these people is enough satisfaction," Sara said.

The man was truly embarrassed and ran off. "Did anyone know who that really was?" George asked.

Someone in the crowd said he thought his name was Renalds. They all returned to the dining area and enjoyed the rest of the evening.

The next morning, when Sara arrived at breakfast, she was greeted with a letter.

My dearest Sara,

> *I apologize for not saying goodbye to you when I left Yorktown. All I could think about was getting to Betsy and our child. Unfortunately, the decision to not stop along the way was a very poor one as I have been confined to a bed ever since. The doctor said I was malnourished and exhausted, causing my collapse. Betsy appointed herself my care provider and has pushed herself too much, causing her to be on bed rest with the child. It is nice to be locked up with her, but we are both too tired to enjoy it. I hope to be well enough soon to return, but after this illness, I do believe my time in the army will be*

short. Sorry I was unable to discuss the legal matters with you, but I am happy to hear you will be receiving your father's property. Right now, we are staying with the Schuylers, but when we are both back on our feet and in our own place, you will always be welcomed. I have to keep this short as I am starting to get tired. I do hope to hear from you soon. In the meantime, be safe and well until we meet again.

Affectionately yours,
A. Ham.

"It's a letter from Hamilton. He is doing a little better but still on bed rest," Sara told George and Martha. "It looks like he is going to try to meet up with us somewhere but most likely to resign his position," Sara finished.

"I do believe that is a good option for him. With all his illnesses, especially this latest one, his soul is willing, but his body is not," George said.

The Washingtons allowed Sara to borrow some funds until she returned to Princeton to claim her inheritance. She was able to get supplies to make scented candles for gifts for her friends and family. She put a small note with Laurens and Lafayette's candle and shipped them out. The one for the Hamilton's had a reply message attached.

To the Hamiltons:

Please relax and enjoy your time together during this holiday season! I hope this gift brings warmth and calm to your recovery. My prayers go out to both of you during this time. Maybe life is trying to tell you to slow down, even just a little. I have heard about your ailments with your kidneys, sir, and I do believe leaving the army life now that you found your glory will be the best option for you. It may be a little easier on Eliza as well. She will never stop worrying about you but maybe worry a tiny bit less. Eliza, please take care of yourself and your child. There truly is nothing you can do about Hamilton; he is what he is. I do hope to see both of you soon.

Affectionately yours,
S. Weinstein

She mailed the gifts and letter the next day and tried to concentrate on Martha's emotions after that. There were times when it was just the two of them when Martha would allow herself to cry and Sara would just hold her. There really wasn't anything that could be said to comfort her. Sara also knew Martha was not the type of person to break down for any reason, even in front of her. With it being so close to Christmas, Sara would take Martha's mood into account as she planned the day.

"Would you like to decorate today?" Sara would ask cautiously.

Looking up at the tree, Martha said, "Well, I guess we have to, don't we? Could you go pick up some trinkets at the general store for it, though?"

Sara knew that meant Martha needed to be alone for a few minutes before they started. She walked to the store, picked up some hand-carved wooden figures, and went back to the house. By that time, Martha was well enough to work on the tree and was able to enjoy looking over the figures Sara bought.

After hanging a garland of holly and ivy plus a mistletoe, they were ready for Christmas Eve.

"Just in time!" Sara said as it was December 23. "Here, I created some candles for us this year for the fireplace," Sara added. Then she set four candles on the mantle—a green one with a mint scent for George, a purple one with bergamot and lemon oil for Martha, and a red one with peppermint for Sara.

"Who is the final candle for?" questioned Martha looking at the final white candle with lavender that was set in the center.

"For all those lost to us but not forgotten," Sara said. This made Martha start to cry again, and Sara joined in this time.

"Thank you for giving up your time and taking care of a silly old woman," Martha would say.

"Silly old woman, you give yourself way too little credit. You still have a lot of fire left in you, and being sad with the death of Jacky is not silly. I would be upset if it didn't bother you," Sara said as Martha wiped her eyes.

"There! All better now, thank you, dear," Martha said.

"However I wish to just rest in the sitting room looking at the tree and fireplace if you don't mind."

"Are you going to be all right if I leave you?" Sara questioned since this was the first time Martha basically told her she wanted to be alone.

"Oh yes, nothing to worry about," Martha replied. Sara got Martha all set up and asked if she needed anything else before leaving the room.

Then Sara got dressed for the elements and walked to the stables where Storm was being kept. It was a brisk winter afternoon when you could see the puff of air leaving your body as you breathed. Sara thought the city was a bit livelier than she figured it would be based on the temperature. One mother was walking her rambunctious children to the store for needed supplies. One of the children, who looked about three, would run up to the next snow pile trying to jump into it. Just before making the leap, his mother would make a noise, and he would stop almost midair. Sara watched this for a bit to see if the boy would get his way, but he never did touch a snow pile.

When she entered the stable, she heard Storm snort and neigh at her arrival. "Hello there, girl," she said as she rubbed her forehead. Sara gave Storm a carrot, then picked up a curry brush and started to remove dried mud and grime left on her belly and legs.

"I didn't think I would see you here today," George said behind her.

"Oh, hello, Aunt Martha needed some alone time, and I decided to check in on Storm," she said back.

"I need to thank you for taking care of her while I am still away. I don't think she would make it through this holiday without your help."

"No thank you is necessary, I am happy to help her with this as she helped me not too many winters ago." He walked up to the stall that held Blueskin, his stallion, and started to brush him as well. "Honestly, I don't think I would get through this without you either."

"With the win at Yorktown, we should be much happier but it is hard to find joy with so much loss," Sara said.

"Very true, and as much as I would like that to be the last battle, I know there will be more on the horizon. They may just be small skirmishes, but still, with every gunshot, there is going to be more loss of life," he said, slowing his brush strokes. "I have been thinking, maybe you should go to the Madders while your Princeton place is being built. Jonathan plans to ride with us until Morrisville after winter camp," he said quietly.

"I have been thinking about that myself," Sara said.

"For me to be able to vote, I need to establish residence for a year. I need to reclaim my father's land as soon as possible."

"Then we are agreed?" he asked, a bit worried.

"I believe we are, Uncle. However, if you need me to do anything, please write to me and let me know, all right?"

He just nodded and put down his brush. "Let's get back to Martha before it gets too late," he said.

When they arrived back at the house, they found Martha dabbing at her eyes again.

"Oh, you're back," she said as she got up from the chair.

George went over and held his wife as she relaxed in his arms. Sara did not wish to intrude on this moment and went to the dining room. As Sara walked away and into the dining room, she felt lost. She was in a whirlwind, and it seemed she wasn't even there anymore. It felt like she was looking into someone else's life that she was not a part of.

"Everything all right, dear?" Martha questioned, waking Sara out of her trance.

"Yes, um, yes, I just…I don't know what I was doing," Sara finally admitted.

"Well, maybe we will all feel better after we eat, sit down now."

The next morning, Sara came downstairs to find the sitting room alone. She lit the candles and sat on a chair, just looking around the room. Today was the start of a twelve-day celebration until the log burned out and should have been really festive. However, she just didn't feel joyful. There was no rhyme or reason for it, but her emotions were her emotions. She started to pray and stared at the white candle.

"Dear God, I thank you for allowing us to enjoy the birth of your son this day. With everything you have already provided through his life and death, you still show yourself to us in your grace. Please allow us to find joy in your promise and enjoy the thought of those we have lost to be celebrating with you today. Finally, I pray that you can see fit to allow the battle at Yorktown to be the last one this country needs to find peace. Amen!"

She turned around, hearing a shuffling noise as the Washingtons were standing quiet behind her.

"Merry Christmas," she said to them rising and giving them a hug.

"Merry Christmas, my dear," George said as they both hugged her back.

They all walked to the dining room and took their seats.

"You are looking well today, Aunt Martha," Sara said.

"Well, I just figured it was time to enjoy the celebrations," Martha said with a smile.

George gave a small grin and started to put the food that was on the table onto his plate. "Mr. Morris invited us to celebrate with him this evening, so please be ready for that, Sara."

"I will be ready," she answered.

"Mr. Robert Morris didn't he help get some funds for the army, dear?" Martha questioned.

"Yes, he was very instrumental in providing the funds needed to march to Yorktown. I believe he is working on starting a bank to stabilize the confederate funds," George answered.

"Oh, really, that's interesting," Sara said. "I wonder if Hamilton has been trying to influence how Mr. Morris will be creating that bank," Sara questioned.

"My guess is he has sent multiple letters every day." George laughed.

Chapter *13*

Charles

Later that evening, they arrived at the Morrises', where a Yule log was already burning in the fireplace. It was a very cheerful evening with smiles on the faces of all who gathered. There was a room with a table full of food and cider to pick from. A second room was cleared of furniture and had a small group of musicians around the piano for dancing. One young man noticed Sara walking around and walked up to her and introduced himself.

"Good evening, ma'am. My name is Charles Gutekunst."

"Sara Weinstein," she replied with a curtsey.

"Would you do me the honor of this dance?" he said, extending his hand.

She took it, and they walked onto the floor and started to waltz.

"How have you been getting through this war?" Charles asked.

"I have been a nurse in General Washington's camp. What about you?" Sara asked.

"A nurse? That is very impressive! I thank you for caring for the military men. I have been a captain in Germany. My service ended about six months ago, and I boarded the first ship to join General Washington's army but just missed the battle of Yorktown, I am sorry to say," Charles answered.

Sara began to be skeptical with his answer and decided to push the issue. "Well, the battle is not over yet, are you still planning on joining him?" she asked.

"I am planning on it as soon as I get the chance," he answered.

"My aunt in Bensalem knows Mr. Morris, and he invited me to this party. I was hoping to meet the general if it was possible."

"I think that can be possible if you truly wish it," she offered.

When the music ended, Sara asked Charles to follow her to the other room where the Washingtons were talking with Mr. Morris.

"Excuse me!" she said as the group turned toward them. "Mr. Morris, thank you for inviting me to your celebrations, sir," she said, bowing her head toward him. "General Washington, may I introduce you to Mr. Goo, Mr. Goo, umm?" She turned toward Charles.

"Gutekunst, sir," he finished with a bow. "It is an honor to meet you, sir, and, Mrs. Washington, thank you for allowing your husband leave of his duties to lead this great nation," he said honorable.

Maybe he is not making things up, Sara thought to herself. With his next comment, her doubts were answered.

"Good sir, I have been a captain in the German army and would be honored if you would have me join you in your cause?"

"Thank you, good sir, I would like to talk with you regarding this, but tonight, just enjoy dancing with my niece." With that, George gave Sara a wink while Charles gave her a confused look.

"Niece?" he questioned.

"Well, adopted, and I am tired of people seeking me out for our relationship," she said.

They both nodded to the group and walked back to the dance floor.

Over the next week, the Washingtons and Sara attended party after party. Charles always seemed to be in attendance. At this point, Martha started to hover around Sara, keeping her in check. One day Charles asked if it would be all right to call on Sara, and Martha approved. That evening, Sara found it difficult to fall asleep. She couldn't stop thinking about Charles and everything that has happened since their initial meeting. It seems now that she is always looking for him and disappointed if he is not to be found. When he finally does arrive, the butterflies in her stomach will not settle down. Now she is finding the sensation upon thinking about him. She never felt this way before and found she enjoyed the experience. If only she could calm it down now so she could fall asleep.

The next day, Martha and Sara were in the sitting room as they waited for his arrival. Martha decided to break the silence with "He is a handsome young fellow, so I have arranged for Margaret to join us this evening."

"I will be glad to see Margaret and John, but please don't read any more into this than there is," Sara said.

"I am only reading the book being provided to me, Sara. If the book's information is incorrect, maybe you should fully explain that to the young man before he feels something is happening that is not," Martha said sternly.

A few hours went by when Margaret and John arrived at the house. Warm greetings were given at least before the women started in on Sara.

"So I heard there is a handsome young man calling this evening?" Margaret said.

"A Mr. Charles Gutekunst," Sara said, finally able to pronounce his last name.

"German, interesting," Margaret said, a bit disgruntled.

"Please don't start with me now, Margaret. Martha is already upset, saying I am giving him false hopes," Sara said grumpily.

"Well, you are, dear, unless you really like him. And he may be German, but from what I hear, he is a decent man worth a chance," Margaret said.

"Worth a chance, really, worth a chance? Just being human makes him worth a chance no matter where he comes from!" Sara said angrily.

"Ohh, you're right, Martha, she really likes this one," Margaret said as they both laughed. Sara stormed out the back door and sat in the small garden in the cold. When she got cold enough to return to the house, everyone just looked up at her.

Finally, Martha said, "Well, Charles will be her shortly. You may as well go get changed. You certainly can't greet him like that." Sara started to get upset again but looked down at her dress. It was wet and dirty with ice hanging on the edges and agreed to change.

When she returned to the sitting room, she made her way to the ladies and pulled out her sewing from the basket on the floor. Placing the loom on her lap, she said quietly, "I am sorry for getting angry earlier. I have been thinking and do agree with both of you. I need to make sure he understands I am not interested in marriage," Sara said.

"Well, before you tell him to leave you alone, make sure it is what you really want. We both know you really like him," Martha said.

A knock came on the door, and Billy walked Mr. Gutekunst into the room. Washington introduced him to John, walked him over, and introduced Margaret. Sara was just able to look up at him when George walked Charles back to the other side of the room and sat down with John to discuss military strategies and politics.

Sara leaned over to Martha and asked, "How am I supposed to tell him I do not wish to marry if I can't talk with him?"

"If that is what you choose, just stand up and say it in front of everyone dear, that will scare him off," Martha responded.

Sara decided to stay quiet and sew her flowers. Every now and then, she would glance across the room and see Charles smile. This gave her a twinge in her stomach, and she would quickly look away so she wouldn't be noticed. There was no way for her to control her own smile, however. At the end of the evening, everyone rose up, and Charles started to say his goodbyes. When he stood in front of Sara, he asked if he could call on her again. Sara was not sure what to say to him, so Margaret spoke up. "Sir, your presence will be welcomed."

Sara looked over to Martha, looked back at Charles, and just smiled. He let out a small giggle. "Till we meet again then."

"Aunt Martha, can we talk please?" Sara said sadly the next day.

"Sure, dear, what seems to be the problem?" Martha asked.

"I don't know what to do. I really enjoy Charles's company, but I don't want to hurt him, and I still haven't changed my mind on marriage," Sara said timidly.

"Well, answer me this, how do you feel when he stops by?"

Sara couldn't help but smile as she thought about it. "I get butterflies in my belly, and I am just happy," she said.

"And you don't want to hurt him?" Martha asked.

"It is the last thing I want to do, but I don't want him to go away either," Sara said.

"Well, it sounds to me like you care for this man," Martha said, "so it seems to me that you need to decide if you care more about your so-called independence or him."

"I don't believe it to be so-called Aunt Martha. Why does it have to be that choice?" Sara said angrily.

When Charles entered the room that evening, Martha pulled George into the other room for what Sara knew would only be a short time. "Charles, I would like to talk to you for a moment if you do not mind," Sara said.

"Oh no, that doesn't sound good at all," Charles said.

"I don't mean to hurt you but..." She paused.

"I know where this is going," he said, and Sara gave him an inquisitive look. "I will not intrude on you anymore," he said, tipping his hat.

"Wait, what?" Sara said.

"You don't want to see me anymore, it is all right. I will not bother you again," he said.

"That's not it at all!" Sara complained. "I wanted to say I don't like the laws in this country when people get married, so I am opposed to it. But wait, you are willing to just walk away like that?" she said angrily.

"I didn't want to leave because I really like being with you, but I wasn't going to push you into anything," he said, followed by a pause. "So my question is, do you not like the institution of marriage or the laws of marriage?" he said.

"Aren't they both the same thing?" she questioned.

"Not really," he replied.

"I don't like the thought of giving away my rights," she said.

"Makes sense, that is everything your uncle and his army is fighting for," Charles said.

"Exactly!" she provided excitedly.

At that, the Washingtons entered the room. "We will discuss it later if you will like," Charles said.

"Yes, please," Sara answered, and they went to their chairs for the evening ritual.

Although the Washingtons would not leave Sara and Charles alone together, they were allowed more time to talk with each other. Sara and Charles would sit together on one side of the room while the Washingtons would sit on the other side.

"So may I inquire about your regards to marriage?" Charles asked.

"Well, we just spent seven years fighting and dying to declare independence from England. The men of this country want to be able to govern themselves, make decisions for themselves. They feel they know what is best for them and their families more than some-one across the sea. Well, I was raised to be able to take care of myself and make decisions for myself. I get to make my own decisions if I do not marry. If I do, I give all my rights as a human over to my husband. There are many women who agree with me and choose not to marry," Sara said matter-of-factly. "If laws were in place that I have a say over myself and my family, I would love to get married, but to give up my rights to decide is to give up my soul," she ended.

"You are a very strong, courageous woman, Sara. That is what attracted me to you in the first place," Charles said.

"Wow, not too many people would agree with you about that," she answered.

"As soon as you said you were a nurse for the army, I knew you were a very strong person. From what it sounds like, you do not con-test marriage but the laws here that strip your rights away," he said.

"Yes, even if the person I would marry would 'allow' me to have my voice, I would lose it among the people," she complained.

"Well, what if there was a place where the laws allow you to keep your voice, would you be open to marriage then?" he asked.

"And where would that be, sir?" she said a bit arrogantly.

"Well, for starters, there are no laws out west," he said, looking at her. "From the sounds of it, you can survive the wilderness just fine, and if you would have me, I would never try to take anything away from you," he asked.

Sara just looked at him, not knowing what to say. She then realized the room was very quiet as all eyes were on her. "I never considered getting married. I need to think about it," she finally said.

"Well, from the looks of it, once you decide, your uncle already knows what is on my mind," Charles said, looking over at George.

"I never thought I would find someone who isn't turned off by my character," Sara said to Martha a few days later.

"I will admit he is a special man with interesting thinking," Martha replied. "Actually, he reminds me of your father."

Sara looked up and smiled at Martha. "Really, do you think so?" she questioned.

"I do, and I believe that is why this one caught your eye," Martha provided, smiling at Sara.

"But if I want to run my tavern in Princeton, it makes the decision difficult," Sara said softly.

"If it were easy, It wouldn't be worth it," Martha said.

"At least he isn't pushing me for an answer right away. He also made a mention that George will be including him in the army when they leave winter camp?" Sara questioned more than stated.

"That seems to be the plan, so I am glad you will be leaving the army until you made up your mind," Martha stated very clearly.

Suddenly a knock came on the door, taking the ladies' attention. Martha barely had time to see the blur enter the room before Sara ran past and embraced it.

"Hamilton! How are you feeling? Are you all right? What are you doing here?" Sara squealed.

"Let him take a breath, dear," Martha said, coming over to say hello to Hamilton.

"Hello, ladies, I am doing much better than I was, thank you," he said to them, entering the room and sitting down.

"How about Eliza, how is she doing?" Martha asked.

"She is doing very well and presented me with a healthy son on January 22," he replied.

"Oh, congratulations! What is his name?" Sara asked.

"Philip!" he said proudly. "He has to be the most handsome babe there ever was," he finished.

Sara just looked at the pride beaming from Alexander. She had seen him proud before, but this had a different feel about it. "I do believe you finally found your family, your happiness!" Sara said.

"That I did." He smiled, looking down at his hands.

"So what brings you to Philadelphia?" Martha asked.

"Well, I was looking for the general and was told he was here," he said.

"I do expect him soon, but he is not here yet. You are welcome to stay until he arrives," Martha said.

"Are you planning on rejoining the army?" Sara questioned.

"That is a topic I will take up with the general," he said, and Sara didn't pursue.

They heard the door open and a lot of noise as George and Charles entered the room. Hamilton stood up, and when George noticed him, he smiled and extended his hand. "How are you feeling, my good man?" he asked.

"I am doing better, sir. Thank you for asking," Hamilton replied. "Ah, this here is Captain Gutekunst just arriving from Germany."

Small talk continued between the men, and Martha pulled Sara away out the room leaving them alone. Sara tried to protest, but Martha just waved her hand and said, "We will rejoin them when the time is right." At that, they heard the door close.

It was another cold rainy day in March, so they decided to stay in the dining area.

"I can't believe he is a father. I mean, I knew it was going to happen, but Hamilton, a father!" Sara began.

"I also wondered if he would settle down enough to have a family, kind of like what I wonder about you, my dear," Martha said.

"Well, I must admit I am as close to it as I am ever gonna be," Sara replied with a smile.

Martha returned the smile and said, "That is really nice to hear."

"I do believe if he truly is willing to acknowledge my quirks and allow me my voice, he is worth it. In the wilderness or in Princeton," Sara said.

A creak came from the other room acknowledging the ladies were allowed to return. Martha stood up to return to the men, but Sara did not. "Are you going to join us?" Martha asked.

"I don't think so, not just yet," Sara replied. "I am not fond of being summoned like a pup and expected to jump. I will be in when I am ready," Sara finished. She sat at the table looking out a window at the steady rain when she heard a noise behind her.

"So I heard you may be interested in this forbidden life after all," Hamilton started, making her jump.

"What?" she said, trying to sound ignorant.

"I was asked to retrieve you because you were still deciding marriage with this captain?" He smirked.

"Charles, and yes, he has shown interest." She tried to sound uninterested.

"Yet his head is still attached to his shoulders." He laughed.

"There is no reason it shouldn't be." Again, she tried to keep up pretenses, but Hamilton saw right through her.

"Look, I can tell you like this man, and to be honest from what I know, I like him as well," he said to her. "Just because you never thought you would go through with it, don't count it out, all right."

"I am keeping a very open mind." She smiled back.

"Now come back in the room please," he said, offering his hand.

"Ah, there she is," George said, and Charles's face lit up.

"I just needed to take a moment."

"I wouldn't expect anything different," Charles said.

"Neither would I," Hamilton added, giving her a kiss on the cheek.

Sara just glanced at him sideways, but Charles very much questioned the gesture. When Charles went to take a step toward him, Sara looked back and said, "Please don't read too much into that. Hamilton is like my brother and just trying to rile you up."

"And I like the fact that you get riled for her," Hamilton added.

They all sat down before Hamilton spoke up again. "Sara, I would like to invite you to meet my son Philip. It will be a while before you can properly break ground in Princeton and Betsy told me not to return without you." Realizing Hamilton had a family at this point, Charles's demeanor calmed down.

"Besides, it will give you an opportunity to think things over," he said, nodding in the direction of Charles.

That was the final blow. Sara wanted everyone to stop asking her to make up her mind about Charles. "I don't need any more time to think about it," she said, causing Charles to cough.

"Charles, I don't do anything properly, so this might as well be inappropriate as well. I accept your request for marriage, and since I do not have a father, you have no need to ask anyone else in this room for approval. The only approval you need is mine," Sara stated strongly.

Martha almost fell off her chair as she was both happy and appalled. George started to look a bit red, and Hamilton was trying not to laugh out loud, but it was Charles who spoke next.

"Sara, I am happy to hear that, but if you want me to accept you as you are, I need you to accept me as I am. I will not get married without permission from your family, who at this point is most certainly the people in this room." She took a deep breath and extended her hand toward George.

Charles turned around and said, "Mr. Washington, sir, I know this is most irregular, but may I—"

"You have my permission before she takes my life instead of this infernal war," George interrupted.

With that, the room erupted with joy as Sara and Charles hugged and accepted congratulations. When they sat back down again, Hamilton said, "Wait, you still haven't answered my question about meeting Philip."

The army was about to break up winter camp and move north back to New York, where the remainder of the British army was. Since they decided to hold the wedding off until Sara reclaimed her property and started building, Martha returned to Mt. Vernon and her grandchildren. Hamilton and Sara were going to ride with Charles and Washington until they reached Princeton. However, when they reached Bensalem, Charles and Sara took a small leave so she could meet his family. His uncle and aunt had a two-acre farm for livestock.

"Uncle John, Aunt Claria, I would like for you to meet my fiancée, Sara Weinstein," he said, smiling.

"I knew it wasn't just Washington's army you were traveling to Philadelphia for," Aunt Claria jested. "My dear, it is lovely to meet you!" She turned toward Sara and gave her a hug.

"It is wonderful to meet you as well," Sara replied.

Uncle John was shaking Charles's hand, congratulating him, waiting for a chance to say hi to Sara as well. Claria, however, linked her arm and walked Sara inside with the two men following. Upon entry, the only thing you could hear was whimpers and shrieks coming from behind a curtain in the corner.

"Ahh, it must be feeding time," Claria said with a smile. "They just passed eight weeks, and poor Peaches is tired of feeding them," she said as she pulled the curtain open to reveal eight Labrador puppies climbing over each other. John carried out a bowl and put it on the ground in front of the pups, and they fought their way toward the bowl. One yellow pup took a mouthful of food and stopped to look up. He cocked his head at Sara then went back to eating.

When the food was gone, most of the pups started to run the house, but the one who looked at Sara walked right up to her. After sniffing for a moment, he circled and sat down on her food. She picked him up, and he started licking her face in approval.

"Looks like someone else chose you," Claria said.

"You can have him with you would like, a wedding gift from us," John said.

"First of many," Claria added.

"I would love him, thank you so much," Sara said, petting her new pup.

After an afternoon meal and discussions, Sara and Charles started to get ready to return. "Here, this bag will be useful for this little guy until he can keep up with your horse," John said, holding a satchel with the pup inside and a bag full of puppy food. She mounted Storm, and John handed her the pup that she balanced in front of her.

"Please come back soon," they both said as Charles and Sara began to leave.

"I really like your family, Charles," Sara said.

"I believe they really like you as well," Charles replied.

"They felt I was going to be a forever bachelor as well." He laughed.

As they rode into Morristown before crossing into New Jersey, Sara and Charles stopped at the Madders and provided them with the news as well. When she dismounted, the pup couldn't wait to get out of the bag and run. As Margaret opened the door, he ran right past her into the house.

"What is that thing?" she yelled.

"That is my new puppy, Margaret, just give him a chance," Sara said.

"A chance to do what, destroy my house!" Margaret complained.

"He is just a pup, I haven't had any time to train him yet," Sara said, picking up the puppy.

Margaret looked at him and said, "Well, he does have sweet eyes. What are you going to call him?"

"I believe I will call him Chance," Sara said.

Later as Margaret and Sara sat in the dining room, Sara said, "I can't just get married after all this time not wanting to give away my freedoms. I am still very unsure about the rules of marriage, but I also know I care very deeply for Charles. It is not the thought of being with someone I care about but losing my identity to the situation. I don't want to be just his wife. I am still my own person," Sara complained.

"Are you having second thoughts then?" Margaret questioned.

"About the realities, yes, about the man, not at all," Sara answered. "That is why he agreed to allow me to have time to digest this situation. Besides, he is going with George to push the British all the way out of this country. That gives me time to set up my tavern and get over my insecurities," Sara said, trying to convince herself.

"Well, when you are ready to plan the wedding, please let me know!" Margaret asked.

"Well, I need you to help with the tavern so I will not have to go far," Sara finished.

The next day, Sara and Charles met up with Hamilton as they crossed the Delaware into New Jersey. It was a much calmer trip than any of the previous crossings. As they continued to march toward Princeton, Sara turned toward Charles and said, "Please take care of yourself and keep in touch?"

"I will return to you soon, my love," he replied.

She then took her leave and rode toward Washington, not realizing it would be so hard to say goodbye. "Uncle George, please take care of yourself and Charles for me?" Sara said, trying not to tear up.

"I will do my best, my dear, keep in touch," he replied. "Take care of her," he then said firmly to Hamilton.

"Nothing will harm her, you have my word," he answered.

They took their leave, riding off toward Princeton while the army went back to Somerset.

"Are you all right, Sara? You have been quiet for some time now. It is not like you," Hamilton asked.

"I don't think I am like me anymore. I have not been acting like myself since I met Charles," she replied.

"Do you remember me when I met back up with Betsy? I was a mess. I still am when I am away from her for too long," he encouraged.

"Maybe this time away will allow me to fully figure out what I want," she said hopefully.

"Are you still questioning marriage?" he asked.

"I will question that until the laws change," she offered.

As they approached the town, she stopped and looked toward the woods. "It seems like only yesterday I was running for my life in these woods." They turned toward the city and rode up to the burnt remains of her house. She dismounted, set Chance down, and walked up to what once was her front door. A charred piece of lumber smaller than her was the only thing left. Hamilton came up behind her and put his hands on her shoulders.

"I didn't get a chance to look at this during the battle," she said. "That was the end of my childhood and the beginning of my new life and family." She reached up and squeezed his hand.

"Let's find the lawyer's office and start the transfer," was the only thing he was able to suggest.

As she turned around, she noticed there were homes in all stages of reconstruction. Some were like hers and nothing had been done. A couple more had one or two rooms done where the family lived while they continued to fix the rest of the property. Finally, there were a couple of homes just about finished or completely new.

"It looks like it will be a good area for a home, but maybe not a place of business," Sara said.

"I think only time will tell on that one, Sara, if the rest of these properties were to become businesses like shops, general stores, black-smiths, and so on, it could be the perfect opportunity," he offered.

"Always the positive businessman you are." Sara smiled.

They rode off, with Chance following behind.

They turned the corner and found the representative of Capehart Scatchard law firm waiting for them.

"Good afternoon, sir, are you Richard Cunnings?" Hamilton asked.

"I am good, sir, and are you Hamilton and Mrs. Weinstein?" he asked.

"That we are," Hamilton said as they dismounted.

Mr. Cunnings escorted them into a one-room building to complete their paperwork. "We have permission from General Washington for you to act as his representative."

At this point, Sara started to get upset that nothing was directed toward her. "And do you verify the person sitting next to you is the daughter and only survivor of General Weinstein?"

"Yes, she is Sara Weinstein, and as far as we know, she is the only survivor," Hamilton answered.

"Do you have any written proof of that statement, or were you a witness of the deaths of the remaining family members?" Richard asked.

At this point, Sara couldn't keep silent anymore. "My written proof is in a pile of ashes down the street, and everyone who was there that night, including myself, could vouch that those bastards killed my entire family on the street. Now since I am the only remaining member of that family, I suggest you start to address me!"

Richard was taken aback, but Hamilton was furious. "I was sent here to take care of this for you, Sara, do not undermine me again."

"*And* you know very well I can take care of my own affairs. I am very well informed of what you can do, and I do not challenge that. But I will also not be disrespected and treated as I am not in the room."

At this point, Richard did not know what to do.

"And I will not be disrespected in this manner as well," Hamilton said.

"Well, it seems to me that Mr. Cunnings owes both of us an apology," Sara said angrily.

"Excuse me!" Richard finally spoke up. "Mrs. Weinstein, I am sorry if I made you feel disrespected by addressing your counsel. That is just the way legal disputes are handled."

"Then if I am not needed here, I will take my leave." And before anything else could be said Sara was gone.

She mounted her horse and rode out of town, not caring which direction she was heading in. As hard as he tried, Chance just couldn't keep up and was left behind whimpering. She stopped about three miles outside of town, giving Storm a break. Hamilton was about to catch up with her about an hour later.

"So did you finish everything?" she said, still angry.

"Actually, nothing got completed, your presence was required," Hamilton said. "How could you do that to me?" he asked.

"To you? I was the one being dismissed!" she shouted.

"And you completely disrespected me in front of someone I hope to be a colleague of as soon as possible. You know just how difficult it is for me to gain respect from others given my birth, and being dismissed by my own female client was embarrassing," he shouted.

"So if I was a male client, it would have been fine, right?" she huffed.

Now he was beyond angry. "Yes! Like it or not, Sara, most people don't care about the opinions of women, especially legal opinions. There is nothing either of us can do about it, it is just a fact of life.

And your arrogance could have just ruined my career. Sometimes you need to think about something besides yourself," he huffed and stormed off.

After about another hour, Sara decided to ride back to Princeton. She rode around town looking for Hamilton and Chance, but they were nowhere to be found. She decided to ride back to the law office and talk to Mr. Cunnings again. He was with another client but excused himself and walked over to her.

"Mr. Cunnings, I am sorry to interrupt your meeting here, but I wanted to extend my sincere apologies for my behavior earlier. I had just come from the burnt remains of my house and forgot myself in my emotions," she said.

"I accept your apologies. My sister gets caught up in her emotions and makes a complete full of herself as well. And after seeing your house burned to the ground like that, I guess it's expected to become completely unhinged," he said with a smirk.

"Well, I need to go find my counsel so I will leave you to your meeting," she said, trying to hold her tongue and leave without conflict.

"You may just want to find a different counsel, he can't seem to control things," he said.

"You have no idea what you are saying, sir. Once Hamilton gets started, he can debate you right under the table, and he doesn't need me to vouch for him. You will find out soon enough. Good day, sir!" she said as she turned around and left.

She started walking the town again looking for Hamilton when she heard a high-pitched bark and the pitter-patter of puppy paws running toward her. Chance jumped up on her knocking her over with Hamilton running behind him. "Bad boy, no jumping, Chance!" she said, trying not to laugh. She put him on the ground, made him sit down, and then said hello.

"He is as wild as you are," Hamilton provided as he walked up to the two of them, still a bit angry but giggling at the sight.

Sara stood up and said, "I am truly sorry about earlier. I let everything get to me, from leaving Charles and not knowing how I feel about that to seeing the house. I didn't think about you, and I was very selfish. Please forgive me?" she asked.

"It has been a trying day, and I had to reschedule our meeting for tomorrow. I found a couple of rooms for us over here," he said.

"Alexander!" she said sternly, catching him off guard.

"I can forgive you, I just need a little time," he answered.

The next morning, after walking Chance, they started toward the office. "Before we go in, I just want to let you know I forgive you, Sara," Hamilton said. "Sorry it took me so long to calm down about it," he added.

"This man is scum, and I understand where you were coming from, you had every right to be angry with me. Especially since I know how hard things are for you. Do me a favor and go get him," she said.

He opened the door and let her inside.

"Well, hello, nice to see you again," Richard said.

"Thank you for allowing us to reschedule," Hamilton said as Sara remained quiet.

"Please sit down." Richard pointed to the chairs in front of the desk.

Sara whispered to Hamilton, "He seems a bit smug today, I pity him."

They both took their seats and the meeting began. "Well, it seems there is a substantial inheritance here that we need to discuss," Richard began.

"What do you think we need to discuss about it?" Hamilton said.

"It is a very large amount for someone like Sara here to be in charge of. We feel it will be in her best interest to have her uncle take over the estate until she gets married," Richard said.

"Well, as George Washington already stated, Sara is more than qualified to take care of her own affairs. Plus given the laws of the State of New Jersey, she is entitled to the full sum of the inheritance since there are no other children who survived," Hamilton began.

"Well, since this establishment is in charge of the deliverance of the estate—" Richard began but was cut off.

"It is George Washington who is entrusted with who gets the estate, and he has provided me the power to make sure his wishes come to fruition," Hamilton began.

It was an hour later when Hamilton finally stopped his discussion about why the estate should just be handed over right now. Richard was a bit dumbfounded and appalled.

"Look, the uncle will not get anything from General Weinstein, and I will make sure of that, so you can choose to settle this here and now, or we will take it to the courts to settle there. We both know I will win there just as easily as I have won here," Hamilton stated.

"And that, sir, is why I don't need to adjust my counsel. He is the best around," Sara said with a smirk.

As they walked out of the office and back to where Chance was, she had the deed and signed paperwork for the full estate, including what George had in banks in France.

"You were wonderful," she said to Alexander as they walked.

"Well, I know the laws and I know how to debate," he replied happily. "If you want, when we reach Albany, we can arrange for the demolition of the remains of your house and the start of the new build," he said.

"I think that will be best!" she replied.

They were able to get something to eat, feed Chance, and pack up to get back on the road before too much of the day was lost.

"If you think you can handle it, we should be able to arrive by this evening," Hamilton said.

Looking down at Chance sleeping in his sack, she answered, "We may have to make a couple stops for him but I am up for the ride."

Then they were on their way. Sara was correct; they needed to stop a couple of times for Chance to run around, eat, and take care of things before restarting their journey. By the time they reached the Schuyler home, it was dark.

Most of the household had already turned in for the night. Fortunately, Mr. Schuyler was still finishing some paperwork and was able to answer the door when they arrived.

"Welcome, welcome!" he said joyfully, allowing them entrance. "We weren't sure when to expect you," he added as he took their coats. "Come warm up by the fire." They all sat down as Sara took out Chance and let him sniff around. "What a good-looking pup you have there," Mr. Schuyler said, giving the dog a rub on the head. Chance jumped around for a bit but ultimately lay down in front of the fire and fell asleep. "How is everything going?" he questioned.

"Really well, I have officially ended my time in the army, so I can restart my studies as a lawyer, having successfully mitigated my first debate," Hamilton said with pride.

"You should have seen him in action, that lawyer thought he would take my inheritance away and give it to my uncle, but Hamilton here made sure that didn't happen," Sara said, patting Alexander on the back.

"That is wonderful, my boy. And how about you now, Sara?" he asked.

"Well, I am trying to transfer to civilian life, and I need to plan my wedding," she said with a smile.

"You married, congratulations. That is cause for a toast," Mr. Schuyler said.

"Can we do that tomorrow when everyone is awake please? I am too tired right now. It was a bit of a long journey," Sara said, trying to hold back a yawn.

"Sure, dear, you can stay in the room Martha was in when she was here. It is all ready for you and Chance," he said, pointing in that direction.

"Well then, good night," Sara said, picking up a very sleepy puppy and walking to her room.

"What about you, son?" she heard him ask Hamilton.

"Sure, I could use one before retiring," was the reply.

The next morning, Sara woke up to a whimpering puppy scratching at the door. She took him outside and let him run and take care of things as she did a dance to keep warm. She praised him when he ran back to her, and they both went back into the house to warm up. Sara got dressed and gave Chance the last of the meat she had for him, saying, "Well, boy, I guess it is time to go hunting for you." When she left her room again, she saw Eliza walking the floor of the sitting room with a small bundle in her hand. "Oh, that can't be little Philip?" Sara asked, and Eliza jumped and turned around.

"Sara, welcome. Yes, this is my little Philip," she said, lifting the baby so Sara could get a better look.

"He is beautiful, Eliza. So precious," Sara said with a huge smile.

"Would you like to hold him?" Eliza asked.

"Can I?" Sara asked.

"Sure, here," Eliza said, handing over her precious bundle.

Sara took the baby and started rocking him in her arms while a feisty pup nipped at her heels, not liking losing the attention.

"And who do we have here?" Eliza asked, calling the pup over.

"This is Chance. My fiancé's family gave him to us," Sara said.

"Wait did you just say what I think you said?" Eliza asked.

"Yes, I met someone who asked, and believe it or not, I said yes."

"Oh, we are definitely going to win the war soon, Alexander Hamilton has a son, and Sara Weinstein is engaged. The moon is going to about-face." Eliza laughed.

Taking the baby back, they both walked over to the sitting room and sat down. Chance ran around and found different items to play with and hunt as the rest of the house started to wake up. The remaining Schuylers welcomed their guest and started their day. The men got dressed for hunting, so Sara asked if they could get an extra bird for Chance.

"We will take care of it, dear, you and Eliza just rest today, all right?" Mr. Schuyler told her.

"Is everything all right, Eliza? Why did your father tell you to rest?"

"This little boy caused some issues, and even though I feel all right now, they still insist on coddling me. But honestly, with how much this one eats, I am happy to be able to rest," she said.

As the hustle and bustle of the morning routines started to die down, Sara and Eliza made their way out to the garden. It was a bit cool still, but the warmth of spring was showing up all around.

"So you must tell me about this fellow who captured your heart?" Eliza asked.

"I don't know what to say. I guess when we first met, I took him for another gentleman trying to get to Uncle George through me. However, it became obvious that he didn't know of the connection between us. Then as we danced and talked, I don't know, I just felt some sort of, well, I don't know how to describe it. We have the same feelings on politics and human rights, his kindness and compassion were apparent, and most of all, he understood I didn't want to marry, and that didn't frighten him away. He understood why I felt the way I did and wanted my happiness regarding it," Sara said with a smile. Then it began to fade away.

"He sounds like a wonderful man," Eliza said.

"He is, he really is, but sometimes I don't feel like I am the right person for him. He deserves so much better than me," Sara said.

"I have known you most of my life, Sara, you are a wonderful person yourself, and you deserve to be happy," Eliza said. Philip started to fuss as a cool breeze came by, and Eliza wrapped his blanket around him even more.

"I just don't know if I want this, though," Sara said, looking at Philip. "He is beautiful, but I can't imagine giving up even more of myself for this lifestyle," Sara said.

"Well, to have a child is to give up yourself, but it is the best thing you can do, even someone who is as strong and independent as you are can find joy in giving yourself to your child," Eliza said.

"Besides, you don't have to have this lifestyle. It sounds like this young man is willing to create a new lifestyle with you," Eliza continued.

Sara smiled at the thought of creating her own rules and life but quickly thought of the issue she had with Hamilton and the other lawyer. *This world will never allow me to be anything else*, she thought and became very quiet.

"Sara, what's wrong?" Eliza asked.

"I don't know, sometimes I am just sad and angry, and then I feel guilty about being sad and angry. Sometimes I don't even know where it is coming from."

"You're allowed to have feelings Sara. That is part of being human. It is what you do with them that matters. Try your best not to let them take control, and if they begin to get overwhelming, write to me. I will be here for you, and when I need to write to you because I am upset, I will let you know, all right?" Eliza said, trying to help.

"Yeah, but you live with Hamilton." Sara laughed. "You will have many more letters."

"Sara, you are the Hamilton of young ladies!" Eliza chuckled.

"Hey, I don't know how to feel about that," Sara said.

"You are your own free spirit. When you want something done, it has to be done now. You create your own rules and live full out by them no matter what anyone else thinks about it," Eliza stated.

"Well, when you put it that way, I guess I am," Sara said as the man himself walked up to them.

"How are my ladies and my little man?" He quickly handed Eliza the goose he killed and took Philip tickling his tummy.

"Hey, we just got him to sleep," Eliza snapped.

"Well then, I arrived just in time," Hamilton said back.

"He is yours then, even if he is hungry." Eliza took the goose into the house.

"Well, that will be an interesting trick," Sara said.

"You're telling me." He chuckled as he sat down next to Sara. "This has to be the best feeling of my life. Are you sure you don't want this?" he questioned.

"I want my independence. If that can include a child in my life, I would love that, but with the way things still are, I am not sure that will ever happen. You heard those men back in Princeton. 'She'll never be able to keep a place like that by herself' and 'Don't worry, a husband will be in her life before she can try to vote.'"

"You have got to let people like that roll off your back," Hamilton tried to say.

"Oh, like you do? Damn, Eliza was right," Sara began.

"About what?" he asked.

"I am the female Hamilton." She laughed.

"Ugh, sorry about that," he said, "but at least they just don't pay attention to you. They completely disrespect me and my birth, telling me I don't belong in this country," he added.

"Hey, I was born here, and I am still basically an immigrant to the people here," Sara complained.

"Are you two trying to see whose life is worse again?" Eliza said, returning from the house.

"Well, I guess we are," they chuckled.

"Well, if nothing else, I can play with your little ones whenever you are around," Sara said.

"Give me Philip, Hamilton. It is time for his nap." Eliza pushed.

He reluctantly handed the little one over and watched Eliza bring the babe back to the house. "I think I can be happy now," he said, smiling.

"I don't know about that, Ham. Will you ever be satisfied?" she asked.

"Only the Lord knows," he said. "I am gonna go get cleaned up from the hunt. I will see you inside." He walked into the house, leaving Sara on the swing by herself.

As she looked around at the grounds, she wondered if she could ever be happy. *Is this what I really want?* she thought to herself. *I can see myself enjoying this for a little while but not forever. But he doesn't want this lifestyle either. Can we really make it work? This is a new day and a new country. Why can't we make it work? It may take a while for everyone else to catch up, but it is worth the fight,* she told herself. After a few more moments of sitting in the sun, she decided to return to the house, where the news of her engagement started to spread.

"We must have a celebration dinner tonight. I never thought this would happen," Catherine said.

"Please do not make a fuss over me," Sara asked.

"But you were even less likely to get married than Eliza here." Peggy laughed.

"If I am not mistaken, you are still not engaged yourself," Sara said back.

"True, but I am younger than you and already have someone…" She let the remainder of her tale fade off, but it was still heard.

"You will not be marrying Van Rensselaer until he has graduated college, and I will not hear any more of it," Mr. Schuyler said sternly. Peggy just rolled her eyes at her father's statement and turned toward Sara.

"We will have to discuss that later," Sara whispered.

As promised, a large feast was held in honor of Sara's engagement. "How did you ever acquire musicians in such short notice?" Sara asked Mr. Schuyler.

"I do what I can for my girls," he said.

"For an orphan, you sure do have a large family." Hamilton chuckled.

"I can say the same for you, good sir," Sara replied. They both looked around at everyone smiling and having a good time.

"This is what I always wanted," he said.

"And I still question is this what I want!" Sara said.

"Charles is a good man, you will be very good for each other," he said.

"That is the one thing I hold on to. I know he is a good man," she offered. "Well, to the lady of the evening, may I have this dance?" Hamilton questioned, extending his hand.

"I would be delighted, good sir," Sara replied, and they took to the dance floor.

The evening went by in a blur, and Sara was awoken the next morning by the noise coming from the front hall. She got dressed and started to walk toward the commotion. A soldier was there talking with Hamilton, and although he looked delighted, Hamilton did not.

"You should have seen it, sir, this Hessian thought he could come in and tell us what to do, but we showed him. During drills, a private shot him right between the eyes." He began to laugh at this thought.

"DO YOU HAVE THE LETTER, GOOD MAN, OR NOT!" Hamilton shouted.

The man looked stunned and handed over two letters, then noticed Sara. "Good morning, Miss Sara, here is a letter for you as well," he said.

"Give me that and get out," Hamilton said sternly yet quietly.

"What happened?" Sara asked. Hamilton didn't answer. He only looked down at the letter he had just received. "ALEXANDER, WHAT HAPPENED?" she shouted.

He finally looked up and quietly said, "'It is with my deepest regret to inform you that Charles Gutekunst was killed while in General Washington's army.'"

Sara dropped to her knees. There wasn't much else she could feel to do. He ran over to her and tried to help her up, but she refused. "They killed him because he was German? They didn't even give him a chance to prove himself a Patriot," she said, staring off into nothing.

Soon the rest of the house was upon them, and Eliza, with the help of her mother, took Sara to her room. Chance jumped up on the bed and lay down next to Sara. This time, she allowed it.

"They called him a Hessian," she said. "They just heard he was from Germany and killed him for it," she kept saying over and over.

"It will be all right, Sara," Catherine and Eliza tried to tell her, but Sara seemed lost to them. She was just talking to herself over and over again, saying the same thing. She couldn't even find the strength to cry. She just stared into space repeating herself.

She must have fallen asleep because when she woke up, it was just her and Chance in the room. "At least I have you," she said as she finally began to cry. Chance sat up and started licking the tears running down her face. "He was barley mine, and now he is gone forever," she said. "God, I am sorry for thinking about marrying. I know now that I am not supposed to now, but why did you have to take him?" she questioned.

Eliza heard the noise and entered the room, running to Sara and holding her. "It's my fault, he wouldn't have been with George if I didn't introduce them," she cried.

"Why do we always blame ourselves? He was going to join up with Washington no matter if you introduced them or not. The man who took his life has been taken into custody, and charges will be filed. That would have happened with or without your involvement.

Don't put this on yourself. It is hard enough without that haunting you," Eliza said.

Just then, Philip started to cry, calling his mother to cure his hunger. Hamilton entered the room to switch places with Eliza so she could take care of Philip. "I am so sorry, Sara. I didn't know you were in the room when he was here," he said.

"It doesn't matter. Actually, I rather prefer to know how he was killed and not given some excuse to save my feelings," she offered.

He then gave her a hug, and she cried herself to sleep once again.

The next morning, Sara woke up before anyone else in the house. She was numb and had a difficult time thinking about anything really. She started packing her belongings and took Chance out to the barn. After saddling Storm and preparing a return trip to Princeton, she heard the barn door open.

"Leaving without saying goodbye, do you think that is appropriate?" Eliza asked.

"It's time to go home. I intruded on your house for too long," Sara said without feeling.

"You have not overstayed your welcome, and right now, we want you here," Eliza offered.

"Why, it is time for me to start my tavern. If I stay away too long, who knows what will happen," Sara said bluntly.

The barn door opened again, and Hamilton entered this time. "Where do you think you are going?" he asked.

"Home, where I am needed," Sara said, turning toward Storm and took the reins to lead her outside.

"Please don't go, Sara," Eliza said. Hamilton walked over and took the reins from Sara and looked her right in the eyes. "You don't have to do this, Sara. You can feel around us, we are your family," he said sternly.

"What are you talking about? I feel fine, I just have to get started on—" she started.

"Stop it, Sara." He began to become angry.

"Stop what? There are things I need to do," she said.

"Sara, I really need your help with Philip. I am still having problems with the difficult delivery and require your assistance. Besides, Father knows some people in Princeton who can start demolishing the old site and get a small area started so you can live while the rest of the building is being completed," Eliza said.

Hamilton gave her a confusing look, but the look from Sara was worse. She looked confused and unable to decide what to do. "Okay," she finally said, "I can stay for a couple more days to help you, but I do need to get back."

Sara walked back toward the house with her bag but left Storm tacked up and Chance crying. The last thing she heard was Eliza saying she will call for the doctor. Sara put her bag back in her room and walked outside to sit on the swing. Chance bounded out of the barn and over to her, jumping up on her. Sara, however, didn't even notice.

"Sara, would you like a glass of lemonade?"

Sara turned toward Eliza and looked at her like this was the first time she saw her today. "I am sorry, Eliza, I was lost in my thoughts. What did you ask?"

"Would you like a glass of lemonade?" Eliza repeated.

"I would love a glass, thank you so much," Sara said with a smile.

"I will get some for the two of you," Hamilton offered, looking very concerned.

"I love the spring, don't you?" Sara said, looking around the garden. "It is a time for new beginnings and hope for the future."

"Yes, it is," Eliza said, taking her hand.

"I wasted so much time Eliza, my stupid need for my independence caused me to put off marrying him. I never questioned loving him, so why did I question being with him?" Sara said as she started to tear up again.

"You have had a horrible loss, and nobody can explain why, but please stop blaming yourself," Eliza said. "Hamilton and I waited for about a year before we were able to get married. You know him very well. I could have lost him at any time. We have to trust that God can help us get through what we do not understand."

Hamilton came back out and handed over two glasses.

"I don't know if I can trust him anymore. He took Charles from me. How can I have faith that it was what he wanted?"

"You are a good Christian woman, Sara, so you also know it is not what God wanted, but he can heal and do good with it," Eliza said.

"I just don't know. I think he is mad at me for even thinking about marriage," Sara said again.

"Sara, just look at me," Hamilton said as she looked up at him.

"You know where I started. You know I should have died many times by now. Yet I was taken from that darkness and put here with Eliza. Please don't lose hope," he tried.

Then Sara seemed to tune out of reality again. "I need to get my hunting things on to get a rabbit for Chance. He looks hungry."

"I will take care of the hunt for you," Hamilton said.

"Oh, all right, then how about a swim, Eliza? That will be fun," she said.

"It may be spring, but it is still a bit too cold for that right now," Eliza said.

"I'm not cold, I like the sun," Sara said, looking up toward the sky. "I think I will write Charles and tell him I would like to marry in June. That would be lovely, wouldn't it, Eliza?" Sara asked. "Oh look, a carriage, I wonder if that is him," Sara said, pointing.

"I believe that is the doctor, Sara," Eliza said.

"Is someone not feeling well? That's too bad," Sara said, then just started humming and looking around.

Hamilton walked the doctor over to Sara and introduced them. "Sara, this is Dr. Rush. Do you remember him?" The name from the past seemed to clarify things for Sara.

"Dr. Rush, how are you doing, you were starting that new hospital, am I correct?" she asked.

"Yes, Sara, it has been a while. How are you doing?" he asked.

"Well, I could be better, but I guess I could also be worse," she offered.

"Really, what is going on?" Dr. Rush asked.

"This lousy war is taking too long. I tried to leave it, but it followed me here," she said.

"What do you mean by that?" he questioned.

"My fiancé, can you believe it I was going to get married? He was killed, and there wasn't even a battle for him to fight in. Just ignorance. Sometimes I hate people," she said as she looked off toward the distance.

"Do you mind if I ask what happened?" Dr. Rush pushed.

"It was camp fever, Doctor. Twenty-two men in all died on Christmas Day because we couldn't stop it. Two more men died on the way to Trenton, frozen to death. Doesn't Congress know we need more supplies? How can they expect Uncle George to win when his men are dying due to the elements as well as the battles?" she argued.

"I know what happened then, but what I want to know is what happened to Charles, Sara, can you tell me that?" Dr. Rush asked.

Again, she looked at him like she just woke up and said, "They killed him because he was German. He didn't hurt anyone or do anything wrong. He didn't even talk down about anyone, but they killed him anyway," she said.

"Okay, Sara, can you please take these, and Eliza will take you to your room, all right?" He handed her some pills that made her very tired

. She remembered walking to her bed and Chance laying down across her legs. She could hear the doctor talking with the people outside her room.

"You have not lost her yet. She seems to be going in and out of reality, though. Whenever she seems to be out of touch with things, ask questions to bring her back. The longer we can keep her mind in reality and deal with this death, the better for her," he said.

The next few days, Sara stayed in bed, not wanting to get up, move, think, or do just about anything. Eliza, Catherine, and Peggy would regularly sit with her, and they tried to keep her thoughts on reality. However, Sara seemed to just shut down and not talk anymore.

One night, Hamilton came into the room with her. "Sara, we have been in the trenches together, you can tell me anything. You know that, right?" he asked. She didn't respond with words, but she did nod. "Can you explain to me how you know this man for a matter of weeks and are more upset than when you lost your father?" he asked.

"You didn't see me when I lost my father," she snapped.

"Ah, words, that's a start," he said sarcastically. "Now for real, I have seen you take the world on your shoulders and not break down this badly," he stated.

"I am just so tired of fighting this war. It took everything from me. I should have known it would take him like it took everyone else," she said.

"It didn't take me, it brought us together," Hamilton said. She just looked down at the floor and started to pet Chance. "You're not thinking un-Christian thoughts again, are you?" he questioned.

"I am not thinking about anything, it's too hard," she said.

"Look, I don't know what I would do if something would happen to Betsy, especially something as cruel and vicious as what happened to Charles. I do know it came close, though," he said.

"What?" she questioned.

"One night, when we were headed to Yorktown, the reds and Indians came here to take Philip. They got as far as downstairs and someone tossed a tomahawk at Peggy, just missing her running up the stairs with the baby," he explained.

"I never knew," Sara said.

"I didn't know until I returned, but the point is, I could have lost everything that night myself. I don't know what I would have done if that were the case. I do know that sometimes you just need to stand up and move forward. When the hurricane wrecked the island, all was lost. I did the only thing I could—I started to write. It kept me sane, and that is what got me on a boat here. I didn't give up, I kept going, and that is what you need to do," he said.

"Ah, but men don't always have the best ideas when it comes to the woman's heart," Eliza said from the door.

"And with that, I take my leave," he said, kissing Sara on the forehead before exiting the room.

"However, he is not totally wrong either," Eliza said to Sara.

"I know, and I will get past this, but right now, I just need to hurt, you know?" Sara said.

"I understand completely, and it will get better," Eliza said. "I just can't seem to get over the guilt of questioning marriage?" Sara said.

"You always knew you would not get married because of the laws, but he was special enough to make you think giving into those laws even for a little bit would be worth being with him. That makes him a very incredible person. Besides, you were willing to marry him no matter what doubts came into play. Just remember there are always doubts when it comes to marriage. Instead of dwelling on those thoughts, think of how much you loved him and he loved you," Eliza offered.

"Did you doubt marrying Hamilton?" Sara questioned.

"Oh my goodness, yes. I know what people were saying about him and what he told me himself. I was worried, but then I just saw him, I saw his heart, and I knew it was right," Eliza said.

"Yes, Charles had an amazing heart and love for a country he just entered. He had such high hopes for this land and all its possibilities. It's talk of inclusion for the outsiders and to be able to rule by the people and not by the monarch," Sara said, smiling.

"Then take his wishes with you and push for their reality," Eliza said. "Sometimes that is all we can do for the men we love."

The next morning, Sara reentered the world sad but functional. She had a purpose again, to take the dreams and wishes she and Charles had together and make them true for others.

"Sara, how are you doing today?" Mr. Schuyler questioned.

"I am doing better, thanks to everyone here," she answered.

"Do you think you are ready to discuss some business matters?" he asked.

"Philip, give her some time and space please!" Mrs. Schuyler said.

"It is all right and very much past time, Mrs. Schuyler," Sara said.

Philip and Sara entered his study and took seats around his desk.

"I have been in communication with some men in Princeton about the rebuilding of your home. The gentleman in question is a German builder and works in stone as you have requested. They have already started demolition on the property, but we need to discuss how you would like to restart the building process," he said. He rolled out three different designs they had come up with and wanted her opinion on it.

"Thank you for caring about the details!" Sara said. She looked over the plans but didn't seem to like anything they had arranged. She picked up a pen and started reworking the first layout.

"First, in the basement, I would like a room over here for barrel and wine storage. Next, this area needs to be as open as possible to hold the remainder of the products. A few more rooms would be all right if they need to do it that way. The first floor should have plenty of open space for tables to dine and drink. Back in this area, I would like a few rooms and off this side of the house the kitchen area. Up on the second floor, I would like two privies at either end of the hall but facing this direction, away from the kitchen. Then I need six rooms, three on either side. Finally, the third floor will have a bedroom, privy, and living room as my quarters," she said, drawing everything out.

"That is going to be very expensive. Do you know what you are getting into?" he asked.

"With New York and Philadelphia being key cities for the new government and ports for goods, people will be traveling back and forth. Princeton is right in the middle and a good spot to need something to eat or rest for the night. I believe it will pay for itself," she said. "Besides, it is what we both envisioned."

"Well, I will send these plans out and see what they come back with, all right?" Philip asked.

"Thank you," Sara answered.

Sara went outside to sit in the sun. The younger children were playing with the chickens while the older children were doing their daily chores. After feeding her son, Eliza came out to sit with Sara and see how she was doing.

"Good afternoon, Eliza!" Sara said.

"Good afternoon, Sara. How are you doing today?" Eliza asked.

"I am all right, thank you for helping me come to terms with Charles's death. I know I added a great burden to your family, and I am so sorry for that," Sara said.

"You are family Sara, and I am just glad you were here when you got the news and not alone in Princeton," Eliza said.

"Yeah, that would not have been pretty." Sara smiled. "I am truly blessed to have people who care about me willing to put up with my circumstances."

"And please know you are welcome to stay a few more months until the basement and first floor of your tavern are built," Eliza offered.

"Thank you for your kindness," Sara said.

"Oh, it is not kindness, it is a busy time around here, and we could really use the extra pair of hands. It is me being selfish." They were both laughing when Hamilton rode up quickly from the road. "Oh no, what happened this time?" Eliza said under her breath.

"New York decided to allow those of us who were studying law before the war and fought in it to be allowed to take the bar and not spend yet another two years in college," he shouted, running over to Eliza and picked her up, swinging her around. "Here it is, I passed, I can practice law in New York!" He smiled.

"That is wonderful news, Hamilton. I am so happy for you both," Sara said as he just realized she was there.

"How are you doing today, Sara?" he asked, trying to hide his enthusiasm from his news.

"I am doing much better. Mr. Schuyler and I planned out the tavern, so building on that will start shortly," she provided.

"That is wonderful news as well," he said.

"Betsy, I do need to see you please," he said, looking at her and pulling on her hand slightly.

"Sure. Excuse me, Sara," she said.

"Take all the time you need!" Sara said.

Later that evening, Hamilton addressed the room of adults to which Sara thought he would divulge news of passing the bar.

"Betsy and I have some news to provide to all of you. We have found a property in New York and will be moving there in a few days so I can start my law practice," he said, shocking everyone.

"So soon. Well, congratulations to the both of you," Mr. Schuyler said, standing up shaking Hamilton's hand.

Mrs. Schuyler hugged Betsy and started to cry. "You better visit often, you know your sister doesn't stop by nearly enough for me to enjoy my grandchildren."

That evening, Eliza walked up to Sara and asked, "Are you going to be all right?"

"I am going to be fine. I wish you both the best of luck in New York," Sara said with a smile.

"I didn't want to leave you in such a critical state," Eliza said.

"Critical would have been last week. I am doing much better now, and I can feel a difference even if I can't explain it," Sara tried to explain. "Your family has been wonderful with me and allowed me the time to work through my issues. I still have moments of sadness and would be worried if I didn't, but I can deal with them now," she said after seeing the look on Eliza's face. "That being said doesn't mean I will not miss you so please keep in touch all right!" she ended.

"Okay, fine, but you're welcome at our home anytime, understand?" Eliza asked.

"I will take you up on that, I promise," Sara said.

"Well, I have to go and start to pack. You sure you're all right?"

"Will you get going!" Sara laughed and pushed Eliza toward the stairs.

The Hamiltons were gone by that weekend, so when Sara heard a ruckus in the house, she figured they forgot something. However, when she appeared, she found out that Peggy was missing with a letter explaining she was going to marry Steven Van Rensselaer against her father's wishes. The Schuylers were arguing with each other regarding what they should do.

"It's too late, Philip. There is nothing else to be done about it now," Mrs. Schuyler said.

"I can stop it. One way or another, I can stop it!" he shouted back.

At the end of it, they fell to their knees together in a tight embrace crying and praying about their daughters.

Sara did not want to cause any more issues, so she slipped out the back with Chance and started to walk toward the garden. The servants were out gathering vegetables for the day's meals and talking about the second Schuyler daughter's betrayal. Sara didn't know how to feel about it. She knew the proper thing to do would be to wait like Mr. Schuyler had advised.

"I mean, it is not like he said no," she said out loud, startling everyone. She smiled and walked toward the river to continue her thoughts with Chance alone. "But it is not like I ever did anything proper, and given the chance and what I know now, I should have done it myself. Then again, that would have taken the honor of the day away from Uncle George. I just don't know what is right and what is wrong anymore, Chance. Maybe all the rules will change now that we all get to make them." The pair slowly walked down the river and sat in the grass by the bend.

"Sara, where are you?" she heard Mr. Schuyler calling.

"I'm here!" she answered.

"Thank goodness I thought you had run away as well," he said.

"No, Mr. Schuyler, I just wanted to give you space," she said.

"I don't need space, I need everyone to stop running away," he said angrily.

"I didn't run anywhere. I took Chance for a walk," she argued.

After taking a deep sigh, he said, "I just didn't know where you went off to and thought…Well, I am glad you are still here." He turned around and started to go back home.

"Mr. Schuyler, what can I do to help?" she questioned.

He stopped, started to look over his shoulder, then just walked away. Sara looked down at Chance and said, "Come on, boy, now it is our turn to save them."

Over the next few weeks, Sara helped with the household chores, was a shoulder to cry on for Mrs. Schuyler, and took care of the younger children's schooling.

"What did we do wrong to have two of our daughters elope like that?" Mrs. Schuyler said one evening while sitting with Sara.

Mr. Schuyler tried to deal with things by ignoring them and going about business as usual. He was a member of the New York Senate, which kept him busy as well as away from home for long periods at a time. This left the only person for Catherine to talk with was Sara.

"But Eliza waited a year to marry, so your children were given the proper instructions. They were just also raised to be strong, independent, and capable women to make up their own minds and deal with the known consequences," Sara told her.

"Make up their own minds, yes, but not challenge social etiquette." Mrs. Schuyler said.

"The rules for society worked prior to this war, but all the rules are about to change. People will not even care how others were married, just that they were. That still leaves poor Hamilton as a no-good bastard." She tried to make a joke; however, it backfired that all the older girls have married irresponsibly.

"See, even my Eliza gives us grief. She married the way we wished, and Hamilton is a fine young man but still against society!" Mrs. Schuyler offered.

"What I am trying to say is, your daughters will be fine, your sons-in-law are good men, and history will show their true value and do away with the temporary looks of indignancy," Sara provided again, making Mrs. Schuyler cry at the thought. "I am just not good at this!" she said, finally getting a chuckle.

Then Mrs. Schuyler said, "You are doing fine, my child, and just like you, this is too new and raw to just get over. I need to be angry and sad about it first."

On the afternoon of Mr. Schuyler's return, he brought an unexpected guest. "Uncle George!" Sara yelled as he dismounted his white horse.

"Sara, how are you doing, my child? I am so sorry I couldn't get to you sooner. Business matters, you know," he said, giving her a hug this time.

"I am doing much better now," she replied.

"I can assure you, the man responsible was dealt with accordingly. Charles Gutekunst has been honored," he said.

Sara could only look down to the ground and say, "Thank you, that means a lot to me." She was finally able to look back at his face and asked, "So why have we been honored with your presence at this time?"

"Well, we were maneuvering the area keeping the British in New York while Congress discussed an end to this in France. I figured we were close enough to finally be able to pay you a visit and provide my respects," he replied.

"Have the reds been giving you trouble?" she asked.

"There are a few skirmishes here and there but nothing my men can't handle," he said, then added, "However, there have been no large battles since Yorktown. I think they have given up!"

"That is wonderful news in this time of sadness, sir," Mrs. Schuyler said after greeting her husband. Washington just moved the corners of his mouth and looked at Sara, but she said, "No, not just me. Peggy ran away to get married."

"Philip, Catherine, I am so sorry to hear that. I do hope everything will turn out all right in the end," Washington said.

After the evening meal, Sara moved her belongings up to Eliza's old room, giving Washington the downstairs guest room for the evening.

"Chance is growing up into a fine dog, Sara, you are doing well with him," George said to her while she picked up the last few things.

"Thank you, he has been a comfort through all of this," she said.

George then took her hand and looked into her eyes, "I will never be able to ask for forgiveness regarding what happened. I can only say how truly sorry I was when it did. I ignored the warnings thinking they would just disappear if Charles just led them. I couldn't have been more wrong!"

"For the longest time, I blamed myself for what happened. Then I came to realize no matter what I did, Charles would have done exactly the same thing, and the man who shot him would have also. That is not your fault any more than it was mine. If you could have somehow stopped it from happening during training, he would have taken his shot during one of the battles. Trying to change some-

245

one's hate is like trying to move a mountain. It might be done if it is God's will, but it is still very difficult and will take years. During that time a lot of harm can still be done," she said to him.

"When did you become so wise, my child?" he questioned.

"When you see the things I have seen and done what I have done, you tend to grow up quickly or jump off this world," she told him.

Washington's visit only lasted a couple of days, but during that time, Sara received a message the basement and small room for her lodgings were completed in Princeton. She wished to return to see the foundation and be there for the remainder of the build.

On the day Washington returned to his army, Sara and Mr. Schuyler set off toward Princeton. He would see her safely there, then continue onto Philadelphia. During this trip, Chance was old enough to run beside the horses without getting trampled on, so Sara did not need to carry him.

"The world seems to run on ebbs and flows. Do you think it was meant to be that way?" Sara asked Mr. Schuyler.

"I am not sure, what do you mean?" he asked.

"Well, there are years when things are going really good and you think nothing bad can ever happen to me, then the next several years, it is like all went wrong and you feel nothing can ever make me smile again," she tried to explain.

"Well, I am not sure if it is meant that way or if we humans create it to be that way. I do think, however, without the hurts and pains of life, how can one truly enjoy the blessings that are provided?" he responded.

"How can you be sure blessings will still come?" she asked

"Well, God tells us that in his book. Right now, I am still angry with Peggy for doing what she did. However, when she shows up happy and with a child of her own, all that hurt will go away for the blessing," he pondered a bit more to himself than to her.

"Then I guess the best thing to do in the sad moments is to wait until the good ones return, like riding out a storm," she questioned.

"Are these questions for your benefit or for mine?" he asked.

"Oh, I don't know, just talking, I guess." Sara smiled.

Chapter 14

Rise of Little Phoenix

"So once this place is built, how do you plan on running it all by yourself?" he asked.

"I am going to have to get support staff as soon as I can, I guess," she replied.

"Well, there is something we can do for you," he stated.

"If you are offering what I think you are offering, no, thank you," Sara said boldly.

"It will only be a loan of a couple of our servants, just to get you started," he offered again.

"I would not want a business started that way, thank you," she said.

"So be it, but I still don't see how you are going to do it alone," he said.

"That is my problem and, I will take care of it in time," Sara provided, wanting to get off the topic. The truth is, without Charles, she wasn't exactly sure how she was going to run things herself.

They rode into town while the sun was still up. "Ah, I love the summer sun and its longevity," Sara said. "Look, there it is," she said, pointing down the street. "It is a lot different than when we were here a couple of months ago. I like it so much more like this. It is providing a feeling of hope and not despair," she said. All of the burnt timbers and remains were taken away, and the hole was now a

247

complete foundation for a building to stand on. It looked to be just a concrete floor with a small hole that led to stairs.

Philip found the man who was working on the building named Jack Bunting. He walked them down the stairs and showed them around the basement area. It was wide-open apart from the beams, with a small room toward the back end. "Just like I wanted!" Sara said, walking around, looking at everything. There were parts of the building aboveground that Jack added windows to for light and ventilation.

"It is a suitable room, miss, but I would recommend staying down at Mrs. Stockton's until it is completed. See, we start early, and the noise could be an issue right above your head," he stated.

"When are you planning on starting the cookhouse?" she asked.

"We are on schedule to start that building and the first floor next week," he said.

"Well then, I will stay with Mrs. Stockton until that is complete," Sara stated. She was too focused on the plans that she just realized the name she said. "Wait, are you talking about Annis Boudinot Stockton?" she asked.

"Yes, do you know her?" he asked.

"Yes, I didn't know what happened to anyone after the war. Is she still at Morven?" she asked, looking down the street.

"Well, what is left of it," he said.

"Oh no, we must go see her," she said.

"Sounds like a very good idea," Philip agreed.

Even with the sun remaining, the day was late and drawing to a close, so Philip decided to stay the night as well. They knocked on the door and were allowed into the estate. "I will be right with you," called a voice from the other room.

"Well, you always kept me waiting, so why not continue the tradition?" Sara called back.

"No, that can't be, is it..." Annis said, hurrying into the room. "Sara, I thought you died that night," she said, crying and hugging Sara. "Are you the one fixing up the place?" she asked.

"Yes, I want to turn it into a tavern," Sara said. "And how are you and Richard doing since that night?" she questioned.

"I am afraid the toll of singing the Declaration of Independence took its toll on poor Richard, and he passed away," Annis told them.

"I am so sorry to hear that, Annis, are you all right?" Sara asked.

"I am holding my own right now, but that is something we can discuss later. I am guessing you need a place to stay until your tavern is up and running?" she asked.

"If that is all right with you," Sara asked.

"That is what I have been doing to help my town get back on its feet," Annis said.

"Well, thank you for that," Sara said.

Once they got settled in the rooms, they had a late meal and went to bed.

By the time Sara woke up, Philip had already had breakfast and left for Philadelphia. "So you are the one doing all the building down the end of the street?" Annis asked Sara. "I thought your uncle was trying to do something with it."

"He tried, but I had some help getting all that belongs to me," Sara said.

Annis asked Sara about what she had been doing and how she got away from the British that night. After Sara told her story, she asked Annis the same question.

"Richard returned right before they arrived and got us out to Monmouth. It was there in the middle of the night he was arrested. They broke his body and his spirit while in prison. I was able to take the children back to Morven since Washington relieved us quickly, but the British had enough time to completely destroy our property, took anything of value, and drove off our prized stock. When Richard was released in '77 he was allowed to practice law but unfit to do so. By the time cancer showed up in '78, he was already so depressed and lost the will to live. Now I am taking in people who are trying to rebuild their homes so I can adequately run this place," Annis said.

"And what about your poems? Are you still writing?" Sara asked.

"When I get the chance to. I have to start over basically. Most of my writings were destroyed by the reds," Annis said.

"I truly hope this new world offers as much as it has taken," Sara said.

"I hope the 'freedom' the new government creates is worth the sacrifice," Annis said.

Sara wanted to go see exactly where the kitchen was going to be built, so the two women walked to the site.

"You said you wanted to create a tavern?" Annis asked.

"Yes, I found it was more comfortable to be out in the open than in one of the taverns on the roads. I believe I can do much better. I just wasn't expecting an old friend as competition," Sara said.

"I don't plan on being in competition for long. I am just trying to reclaim some of what I lost," Annis said.

"Really, I think we may be able to help each other," Sara offered.

"How do you suppose?" Annis asked.

"I have starting funds for my business but limited grazing land in town. You have plenty of land but no stock. What if I supply the stock, you supply the land, and we work together. I get enough beef per week for my food supply, and you can have the rest. What do you think?" Sara offered.

"That may be all right to start, but my son will come of age in a few years and take control of everything. I will have no say into what happens then," Annis said.

"Well then, I will need to make sure I have my own place set up before then," Sara said.

They arrived at the tavern location as the men started putting up the frame. "Looks like they are off to a nice start," Annis said.

"Sorry, ladies, but you can't come in here. Oh, hi, Mrs. Weinstein, I didn't realize it was you," Jack said.

"Good morning, Mr. Bunting, you should know Mrs. Stockton," Sara said.

"Yes, good morning, Mrs. Stockton." They gave each other a nod before he continued. "Is this location we staked out for the cookhouse all right?"

Sara looked things over, then said, "I think the location is fine, but it needs to be a bit larger. I would like a second fireplace. Plus I would like some land for a stable and run. Do you know a piece of land here that may be for sale?"

"I believe the Johnsons were Tories, so they are not coming back. That should be available at a low price," Annis said.

"Tories, I never would have guessed." She sighed. "They were always so nice when Papa and I were home," Sara said.

"You don't have to be Patriots to be a nice person, Sara. Just because someone has a different opinion than you doesn't make them a bad person," Annis said.

"I don't know about that, Mrs. Stockton. Most of the Tories that left with the reds would have tossed all of us in that prison with your husband just to obtain our belongings and increase their personal wealth," Jack said.

Sara was uncomfortable with where the conversation was starting to go and decided to change it. "Do you think I can have a large fireplace right here at the center of the tavern?" she asked.

"Well, I can, miss, but you sure are doing things quickly. Are you sure you can handle this?" he asked.

"I know I am pushing things, but I feel if I start this correctly, I will have a place where people and even families would like to stop between Philadelphia and New York," Sara said.

Annis pulled Sara aside and said, "Look around, Sara, people in this town are still hurting. You haven't been here since that night. What's it going to look like for a young lady to come in here buying up the place and throwing money around like a king?" Annis said, worried. "Most people will take you as a Tory yourself, coming in to take over. You must be careful," she pleaded.

"Well, once I raise our flag, no one will question my loyalties," Sara said.

"Raise the flag, are you trying to get yourself killed? Tensions are still very high here, and there are some Loyalists left. If you bluntly call them out with a flag, who says they will not try to burn you down again?" Annis stated.

"I was in the bunker Hamilton led his battalion from to take Yorktown. I have been shot sickened and saw my family die. I am not afraid anymore. Let them come and see what happens this time," Sara said sternly.

Annis just shook her head and said, "I have always admired your grit, Sara, but I still think you push things a bit too far."

"You know me, living with my beliefs on my sleeves. However, I can't do anything until I settle up with this property. Who is taking care of the sale of this property?" Sara asked.

"I believe it is the same lawyer that was handling your property," Jack said.

"Oh, wonderful." Sara sighed.

"Come in," Mr. Cunnings said from the other side of the door.

"Well, hello again, Mr. Cunnings, how are you doing today?" Sara questioned.

"Mrs. Weinstein, I am doing well. I see you have started on your property. How have things been going?" he replied.

"I am doing all right, but I do have some more business to go over with you," Sara said.

"Well, I see you are without Mr. Hamilton this time, so what is it I can do to help?" he questioned.

"The property right next to mine that is now vacant. I wish to put in an offer for that location," she stated.

"Oh, well, that is a wonderful piece of property, an acre of open space right at the entrance of Princeton. So what is it you were thinking of offering?" he asked.

"I would prefer to know what the state is asking for that property?" Sara asked.

"Well, like I said, it is a great property, and we have plenty of interest in it, but I think I can let it go for $5.00," he said.

"You are out of your mind if you think I am that stupid. I know for a fact no one is interested in the property as no one is buying right now. I will not pay more than the going rate of $1.50," she snapped.

"One dollar and fifty cents? Do you want me to give my job away? I will take it down to $3.00, but that is it," he offered.

"You will lose your job if the governors find out you had a buyer for property who offered a fair price of $1.75 and let me walk out the door, especially since they can't give the land away," she said.

He sat quietly for a while, then said, "The next time I see you, I hope it is as a client. I should be able to do $1.75, but I have to get it confirmed."

"I am doing so much better without you, so why would I do that?" she questioned. He filled out the paperwork to start the sale and had her sign. "Thank you for your business, my good man!" she said, then left him as grumpy as ever.

She returned to the sight so quickly that Jack and Annis thought the lawyer was not there. "The sale of the land has been started. I am just waiting for everything to be finalized now, but the property is mine," Sara said. She looked around at the property and almost started to get sad.

"What's wrong, Sara?" Annis asked.

"Charles told me once he would be able to build me a house and furniture. That was one thing I never learned how to do," Sara said. "Jonathan and Margaret!" she squealed. "They can help me build what I need," she said. "How could I have forgotten?" She laughed. "It is going to be a few more months before you get the first floor completed, correct?" she asked.

"Yes, we are working on getting the stones and material in, but the first floor should be done by September," Jack said.

"All right, I will return to the Madders and work on the furniture in the meantime. We will be stopping in to check on things from time to time if that is all right," she said. He agreed, and Sara and Annis returned to Morven.

As they walked back, they Sara and Annis talked about the town before the war. She was always among the social elite and educated prior to the war. It was where her love for poetry and writing began. She had published works regarding the American cause, including odes to General Washington.

"I kept the article from the *New York Mercury* that published the poem I wrote as Richard was dying," she told Sara.

"And Richard was never bothered by your writings?" Sara asked, a bit surprised.

"No, he encouraged me to continue writing, even after the children were born," Annis said proudly.

"I guess I have been a bit sheltered. I didn't realize more men were allowing their wives to explore their talents," Sara said.

The next thing that happened was the most surprising to Sara. The townspeople all greeted Annis with the respect and propriety of someone with the high social standing she had prior to the war. Some of them even remembered Sara and greeted her as well.

"You have grown up so much since we last saw you and your family," they said.

"Are you going to return to Princeton?" others asked.

The people seemed genuinely pleased to hear of her rebuilding and return to the town.

"There are still battles we need to fight for and win as women, but at least in this town, they do not fear a strong woman," Annis explained as they continued.

That evening Sara had a difficult time falling asleep. She was thinking about Charles and what he would think about the tavern and the town. Then her thoughts turned to the townspeople.

"They would have allowed us to be us, darling!" she said out loud to Charles, causing Chance to look up at her. She gave him a rub on the head, and he went back to sleep.

"That is probably a good idea, but I have so much to think about," Sara said out loud again.

More thoughts came crashing in like where was she going to purchase livestock, how and when was she going to hire help, who was going to cook, how was all this going to happen. Sometimes she would drift off to sleep then snap back awake when another thought entered her mind.

"Damn you, Charles, I was confident running this thing alone until you, and now I don't know if I can!" she almost yelled. This time Chance jumped up, growling, thinking something was wrong. "I am sorry again, boy, come here," she called him. He whimpered a little bit but curled up into a ball next to her. This tiny bit of pressure was enough to relax Sara and allow her rest.

She struggled in the morning, trying to wake from the challenges of the night before, but Chance finally got her out of bed. "All right, I will let you out. Let me just get a gown to put on," she said.

He couldn't get outside soon enough and went toward the nearest tree.

"Rough night?" Sara heard behind her as Annis was preparing books for Abigail's lessons. Her youngest of six children.

"I just like to take on challenges, that is all," Sara said as Chance ran back into the house.

"Do you need any help?" Sara asked.

"No, thank you, and besides, don't you have a long ride today?" Annis replied.

"I have had worse. Besides, I wanted to help if I could," Sara offered.

"If you can find stock and keep your bargain, that will be help enough," Annis finished. Annis allowed Sara to keep some of her belongings in the room as she would be in and out until her tavern was finished.

Sara and Chance set out a little later for Morrisville on a sunny warm August afternoon. This time she went as a woman in her riding skirt, but she still had her gun at her side. She didn't need it, however, as the ride was very uneventful. Before long, she was at the river waiting to cross on the barge.

"Good day, miss, just you crossing today?" the man working the barge asked.

"Well, me and my dog, yes." Sara replied.

They all boarded and rode across the bumpy river. Chance didn't seem to like this idea as he cowered in the center, but as they got close, he jumped off and swam the rest of the way.

"I am glad he is a water dog," the man said. He was still shaking water off when Sara exited with Storm.

"You better dry quickly, or the Madders will not let you near their house," she said as she mounted her horse.

As they turned the corner toward the Madders, Sara could hear Margaret shouting with joy. She must have been outside enjoying this weather when she saw Sara approaching. June ran out to see what was going on, and they both were ecstatic with her arrival.

"I am sorry I didn't write that I was coming, but I just decided yesterday. I figured I would arrive before the letter," Sara said as she dismounted, hugging both ladies.

"You don't have to write, just stop by whenever you want," Margaret said. "How is everything going? Are you still needing to make wedding plans?" she questioned.

"I didn't tell you. I was so upset, I just didn't write," Sara said, choking up a bit.

"What happened?" Margaret questioned.

"Charles was killed in a gunfight," Sara provided with tears in her eyes.

"Oh no, my poor dear, I am so sorry. When did this happen? How did it happen?" Margaret questioned.

June took Storm to the stable, allowing Margaret and Sara to talk, joining up with them afterward. Sara explained everything that happened since she left. By the time she was finished, Jonathan had arrived back home from his rounds.

"Sara, my dear, how wonderful to see you," he said. Then he noticed all three had been crying. "What happened?" he asked.

"I will explain later, dear," Margaret said. "For now, why don't you go to your old room and wash up for evening meal."

After Sara gave everyone a hug and went into her room, Margaret told Jonathan about what happened.

When they were seated for the meal, everyone was quiet, and it was a bit awkward.

"Really, everyone," Sara finally said, breaking the silence, "I am sad but all right. I came home to ask for your help."

"What is it we can do, dear?" Jonathan asked.

"It is in regards to the tavern. I am in need of furniture and will eventually need a stable built. I remembered what you did here and was hoping you could help me out please?" she asked.

"A stable for two is one thing, but you are asking for fine wood-working. I am afraid my skills are not that good in that area. I do know someone who can help if you would like, though," Jonathan offered.

"I was hoping to work with you so it wouldn't cost too much," Sara said, a bit sad.

"Some mills have been started up north of here so that can help with the material cost. Plus, I am sure I can work something out with Tyler to help keep the building cost down as well. I will see if he can come over on Friday to talk things over, all right?"

"Well, I guess that will have to do," Sara said.

"What he is trying not to say is he has been traveling further to patients and may not have the time to build things," Margaret said.

"How about you Margaret, do you think you can help me with quilts and pillows for the beds?"

"I would be happy to, and we can go into Philadelphia to provide you with washbowls and things like that," Margaret offered.

"I am not asking you to pay for anything, I wouldn't have come," Sara protested.

"We said we would help you, so let us do it," Jonathan said.

"Besides, it was going to be your wedding present," Margaret said.

The next morning Sara and Margaret set off toward Philadelphia to get fabric for quilting and anything else Sara may need for the rooms to start. They needed to place orders for some items like the washing bowls since she needed so many. They also ordered dishes and silverware, glasses, and linens. Finally, they picked up as many colored squares for quilting as they could get.

"This will be a good start for you don't you think?" Margaret asked.

"It will be the best start ever, thank you so much!" Sara said.

"You are worth it," Margaret finished, and they hugged again. As they continued shopping, one thing got Sara's attention, a new flag. "That is a must!" she said as she picked up the flag, gazing at it. "A time for beginnings."

When they returned that evening, Sara asked for some time to herself as she wanted to write to the Washingtons. She sat down with pen and paper, but the words just did not come.

To George and Martha,

I am staying at the Madders. They are helping with supplies for the tavern. I am doing all right with things. I will be here for a while, so if you need me, you know where to find me.

Love,
Sara

She really couldn't find the right words to say what she really wanted to say. She figured George let Martha know about what happened with Charles, but she wasn't sure. He was still in danger with the war, and now she was taking care of her grandchildren. Though they accepted her as one of their own, she was an adult, and their attention needed to be on their own situations. Besides, the Madders were helping her out as promised. He did not run a tavern, but Jonathan did know how to run his medical business and helped Sara put together a plan to be financially stable.

"You are trying to do way too much, too fast, dear. You're going to need to slow down and build this business slowly. You can keep the tavern at two stories right now and take one of the rooms until you know what your client flow will be," Jonathan said. "Plus a smaller stable and run can always be expanded when that need increases," he continued. They also went to taverns in the city to talk about business strategies and what they were doing to get some perspective.

As promised, that Friday, Tyler, Jonathan, and Sara sat around the dining table to talk about what was needed. She wanted one bed, a chest, and a small table in every guest bedroom. The main area was to have a large bar for eating and drinking, so stools were needed there. Finally, she wanted to start with four tables, each with four chairs for more proper dining. They went over the types of woods that could be used and haggled over the final pricing. Once everything was decided, Sara wrote up a contract and signed it. Tyler seemed a bit taken aback, thinking a handshake would do. Even though he was upset by it, he signed the papers and departed.

"Did you have to embarrass him like that?" Jonathan asked.

"How did I do that?" Sara asked.

"We have done everything with a handshake. He is an honor-able man, you can trust him," Jonathan said.

"It is not about honor or trust. It will take him a while to make everything, and this way, neither one of us will question what was ordered. It protects him as well as myself," she said.

"Well, still sometimes I think you have been around Hamilton a little too much," he said.

Chapter *15*

Saying Goodbye

The ladies spent the next few weeks sewing quilts and filling pillows with feathers Sara got from hunting. One day Sara received a few letters and put down her sewing to start reading over everything.

"We are going to have to ride to Princeton soon. Jack has questions regarding the fireplace," she said, putting down the first letter. After reading the next letter, she squealed a little bit as her washbowls were in. Finally, she started reading the final letter and the world seemed to stop. She wasn't even sure if she was still breathing.

"What happened, dear?" Margaret questioned.

"A battle took place in Combahee, South Carolina, where the British ambushed a small regiment of soldiers led by Lieutenant Colonel John Laurens, who was shot and killed," Sara said, stumbling over the words. She dropped the letter and walked out of the room to go to her bedroom. Margaret followed her and stopped her at the door.

"Where are you going?" she questioned.

"Hamilton, I need to know if he is all right," Sara said.

"First thing is first, are you all right?" Margaret asked.

"What?" Sara questioned.

"Laurens was your friend as well!" Margaret said.

At that, Sara started crying. "This damn war just won't stop taking!" she screamed.

Margaret just held her upright and walked her to the nearest chair. Jonathan came in to see what happened and Margaret handed him the letter. "Sara, I am so sorry, he was a wonderful man!" Jonathan said.

"I really need to see Hamilton," Sara said. "Can you ride with me to go to him?" she asked.

"Sure, let me get some things together, but I will ride with you," he replied.

"Margaret, will you be able to take care of Chance for me while we are in New York?" Sara asked.

"Sure, dear, whatever you need," Margaret answered though the sound was much more cautious than the words.

As Jonathan put a small bag of food together, Sara was saddling the horses. She could hear Margaret ask if he thought this was a good idea.

"They were all very good friends. She will be taking this trip with or without me. This way, I can keep my eyes on her to make sure she is all right," he said.

He met up with Sara in the stable, and they mounted the horses and started off. After several hours, they reached the outskirts of New York.

"Now the reds still control most of this area, so we need to be very careful," Sara said.

Jonathan was well aware of this but let her do what she felt she needed to do. They were able to carefully make their way to the address Eliza provided Sara and knocked on their door.

Eliza opened the door holding a tired Philip in her hands. "Oh, Sara, I am so glad to see you. Please come in!"

"Thank you, Eliza. I thought I would take you up on your offer of stopping by at any time," Sara said.

"I am so glad you did. Alex could be a bit better, and I am hoping your presence will help," Eliza said.

"He knows about Laurens then?" Sara questioned.

"Yes, and he hasn't been the same since. He was nominated to the Congress of the Confederation for New York and will not take his nose out of a book for anything," she said.

"Let me try to go get him, will you hold Philip for me?" Eliza handed Philip over and quickly went toward the study. Within a few moments, Eliza and Hamilton emerged to greet their guests.

"Sara, what are you doing here? We weren't expecting you," Hamilton said.

She walked up and gave Hamilton a hug and a small kiss on the cheek. "I decided I would take Eliza up on her offer. I have never been in New York and thought I should come before it gets too cold," Sara said.

"Well, I am glad you did. I have some exciting news!" he provided. "I have been chosen to represent New York in Congress. It looks like I will be spending some time in your tavern as I travel between cities," he said.

"Well, you are gonna just have to wait until it is built like everybody else," Sara said. Then there was a small silence. "Hamilton, are you all right? I know about Laurens and just had to see you," she said.

"I am fine, I took the liberty to write the news to Lafayette and some others as well," he said.

"Did you hear he was promoted to brigadier general?"

"I have not heard that yet, that is wonderful news," Sara said.

Eliza offered something to drink to Jonathan, leaving her husband with Sara.

"Alexander, I know how close you were with Laurens. You can't ignore it, remember. I tried, it didn't go over so well," Sara said.

"I am not trying to ignore it. He is dead and there is nothing that can be done, so we just move on like I have done with everyone else," he snapped. She just stared at him, letting him brew for a bit. Finally, he said, "You wanted and needed time to yourself to get past Charles. That is what I need right now. Time to deal with it myself," he said.

"We can give you that time. Just know we are here when you are ready and need us, all right?" she asked.

"I can do that, thank you," he answered.

"So Mr. Small Time is now involved in Congress!" she jested as Jonathan and Eliza returned to the room.

"Finally, we get to start creating the world that we always wanted," Hamilton said.

"But Congress is made up of many different members. What if everyone else has a different opinion than you on what is right?" Jonathan questioned.

"Well, that is the exciting part. Not everything regarding the monarchy was bad, so we have a place to start. Then we add in some parts of Roman democracy, Greek philosophy, Egyptian architecture, and some of our own pride and strength. We can create something spectacular that is beholding to its other parts. One section cannot be more or less than the next section to rid ourselves of the worst parts of the world: greed and hypocrisy," Hamilton said.

The men spent the afternoon discussing politics while Sara and Eliza entertained themselves with Philip. When they discussed anything about Laurens, they spoke quietly so they would not be heard.

"He will not talk with me about this. I just can't get a feel on how he is doing, and I am so very worried," Eliza said. "He has never kept anything like this from me before." She almost started to cry.

"Laurens's death hits him on so many levels. He did not wish to discuss it with me either, just to let you know, but it is very similar to what happened with Charles," Sara said. They were very good about making it look like they were just talking about Philip. "The governments are trying to find peace and declare an end to this war. This was a 'battle' that should have never happened," Sara said.

Philip was sitting up and trying to scooch across the floor to his mother, taking their attention. She held her hands out to her son as he reached back. "It is so amazing how quickly they develop!" Sara said.

"He is the greatest joy of my life, next to Hamilton, of course." Eliza smiled.

"Of course," Sara laughed. "Just looking at him," Sara continued, "this war has taken so much more than it has given. I do believe Hamilton will be all right. He is just going to need time. However, he is not going to want help," Sara said, a bit scared.

"I know, that is what worries me the most," Eliza said. Now Philip started to scooch over to Sara, laughing at his accomplishments. "I don't remember a time when he just shut me out and ignored a situation like this," she continued while smiling at Philip. "With everything that has happened, I didn't think he was capable of it."

Philip used Sara's hands to pull himself up to a standing position and started bouncing up and down. This action got Jonathan's attention. "Look at the little man go. He will be running around here in no time at all." Then Philip flopped down on his bottom and started giggling, making everyone in the room laugh with joy.

"He is such a happy child, Alexander. How on earth could you have possibly done it?" Sara jested.

"It is all the work of my wife, Betsy!" he boasted. "She could make the loneliest snake smile with joy," he said as the men walked over the two ladies on the floor.

But now, Philip was quite literally the center of attention and took it for all it was worth. He would stand up, bounce a few times, sit back down, and clap at what he had done. Then he would giggle at the cheers of adults that surrounded him.

"I do say I think he is going to be an even greater challenge than you." Sara laughed.

"Oh, Betsy, I do feel sorry for you if that is true!" Hamilton said.

Despite the requests for Jonathan and Sara to stay the evening, the accommodations were small, and they knew it would be a great inconvenience. "I will be traveling to Philadelphia soon, so I will stop by to say hello on my way through," Hamilton said as he hugged Sara goodbye.

"You better, or I will have Chance bring you back by the seat of your pants," Sara jested. When Sara gave Eliza a hug goodbye, she whispered, "If you need anything, please let me know, and I will come to you."

Eliza nodded, and the two were off.

As they made their way out of the city, Jonathan said, "I hope for peace in that man's life."

"Why do you say it like that?" Sara questioned.

"I don't know him as well as you do, dear, but no matter how much he tried to hide it. I could see the painful struggle he was going through as well," he answered.

"He will be all right. He just needs a bit of time," Sara said.

"Don't we all when we are grieving? I know he will be all right. I just think he is so bold a man to attract more hardships than peace," Jonathan argued. He saw the upset look on Sara's face and continued. "Don't get me wrong. His policies and beliefs are intriguing. I do believe a great many of them will be very helpful to this country, but he doesn't have a gentle way of expressing them. I think some men will dislike his policies just based on how they are presented. Then after a while, they will dislike them just because they are his."

"Leading to more hardships than peace," Sara mumbled in agreement.

"However, if Eliza can continue her teachings with Philip, I see that boy being their pride and joy!" Jonathan said.

They stopped that evening at Annis so they could look over the building the next morning. They also needed to explain the changes they had decided on to cut costs down.

"If you have a different man with you every time you enter the city, Sara, people are going to start to talk," Annis said when she saw Jonathan.

Sara said, "I can't help it. I have three fathers taking care of me now! This one is named Dr. Jonathan Madder. He and his wife saved me after the invasion."

"You did most of the saving, if I recall correctly," Jonathan said. "It is a pleasure to meet you, Mrs. Stockton," he said.

"It is a pleasure to meet you, sir," she replied. "I have a room you can stay in for the evening if you like. That will give you both a chance to see the tavern tomorrow!" she said.

"That would be wonderful, miss, if it is not an inconvenience to you," he replied.

"Enough of the niceties, I am tired and we can discuss everything in the morning," Sara said, cutting the two of them off. "I remember where my room is, so good evening!" she said, a bit impatient, then took off, leaving Jonathan and Annis staring at her retreating back.

"She hasn't changed after all this time," Annis said grumpily. "When she would return with her father on their short visits, she would snap off on anyone who didn't agree with her. As we got older and men started showing interest, her mouth would always embarrass me, then she would storm off just like that," she explained.

"It is not easy for a young lady to be brought up within the military the way she was. She is trying to change," Jonathan said.

"But a tiger cannot change its stripes, can it, Doctor?" Annis said back.

"Let me show you to your room, sir," she finished before they both went to bed.

The following morning, Sara woke up rested and a bit more social than the night before.

"My apologies for last evening," she said to Annis and Jonathan.

"I am not sure why I was so rude. I didn't even feel angry or upset. I was just so tired all of a sudden," she tried to explain.

"Are you feeling all right this morning? Do you think you may be coming down with something?" Dr. Madder questioned.

"No, I am feeling all right now," she said.

"Well, it was a long day with a longer ride yesterday. Besides, we discussed some serious issues so we can forgive you this time," Jonathan said.

Annis really didn't say much about it and just started her day.

Sara walked up to her and said, "I really am sorry, Annis."

"Well, you were never one to care about propriety and such," Annis replied.

"I never meant to disrespect you," Sara tried.

"You never did, but that also never stopped you," Annis snapped back.

Sara looked at her for a few minutes then walked out of the house.

She was walking down the road slowly when Jonathan met up with her. "Now what is going on?" he inquired.

"I don't know, I was trying to apologize, but it didn't seem to go that well," Sara complained.

"Well, it is like the story about the boy who cried wolf. If you don't control your temper when you are stressed out and just lash out first, sorry starts to lose its meaning," he began. "And Annis has known you for a while. It seems she has been around more sorrys than others," he tried to explain.

Instead of listening, however, Sara started to get angry.

"I am just trying to help you, Sara. Even when we are pushed to our limits, we need to keep civil, especially in this new environment," he said. They both remained quiet for the rest of the walk.

The quiet walk in the cool air seemed to help Sara calm down and think about things.

"Martha was trying to teach me those same rules. I guess I haven't learned the lesson very well," she finally said.

"Some lessons are harder than others," Jonathan replied, "especially when our own emotions are involved," he finished.

When they reached the tavern, the first-floor walls were completed, and they were planning out the inside.

"Mrs. Weinstein, it is a pleasure to see you again," Jack said.

"Jack, so nice to see you. How are things going?" she asked.

"Well, as you can see, we have gotten a lot done, but I am glad you are here. We can go over some placements, if you don't mind," he said.

"Sure, and this is Dr. Jonathan Madder. He is like another father to me, so he will be helping as well," she said, introducing them.

"It is nice to meet you, Doctor. Right this way please," Jack said, taking them inside.

Chapter 16

A Changing Mind

They finalized the location of the bar and two downstairs rooms based on the size of the fireplace in the center of the room. They also discussed where tables could be placed around the support beams throughout.

"We should have this area up and running for dining in two months. Then we can start working on the upstairs bedrooms," Jack told them.

"Looks like you are going to need help soon, Sara," Jonathan added.

"Thank you so much for everything, Jack. It looks amazing," Sara said.

They started walking back toward Morven and decided to ride back to Morrisville to check on the tables. As Sara was packing some of her things, Annis called upon her.

"I have packed up some bread and dried meat for your journey. Is there anything else you need?" she asked.

"Yes, actually. I am very set in my ways, but I am also trying to gain more control of my temper. I would really like it if you would be able to assist me in that endeavor?" Sara asked.

"I can certainly try, but I do believe this war was easier than that particular battle," she said in jest.

"I agree, probably a lost cause but worth the try, right?" She giggled back.

As Sara and Dr. Madder headed out that afternoon, the day was bright and crisp. It was September '82, and the leaves were changing as quickly as the feel of the nation. Whenever they passed someone, there was happiness and optimism that Sara hadn't seen in a very long time. It became very contagious and had Jonathan, saying, "The colors God places on the earth this time of year are just majestic." They were surrounded by dots of red, gold, yellow, and orange, and even some green remained.

"There is also that sweet smell in the air signifying the change of seasons!" Sara said, smelling the wind.

"Yes, it is a time of harvest, the end of a long hard growing season and a time to rejoice and settle into the winter," he said.

"I just wonder what types of seeds this government will create this winter to plant new for our spring," Sara offered. As they got closer to the river, they saw V-shaped patterns of the Canadian geese flying south. "I think I will go for a hunt when we get back as Martha and June don't know when to expect us," Sara offered.

"That is a good idea. Thank you, Sara," Jonathan said. "That will allow me to catch up on the patients."

While Sara was hunting, a different scent caught her and Chance's attention. Someone was cooking something wonderful nearby, so they followed the trail. What they came upon was a family of colored folks cooking dinner.

"Hello there," she said, startling and scaring everyone.

The father jumped up in front of his family (wife and two children, a son around six and a daughter around four) and cautiously said hi. Sara could tell nerves were running through this family much more than she felt normal.

"Is everything all right?" she asked, worried about the answer.

"Yes, ma'am, just making dinner for my family, that's all," he said.

"Hi there," Sara said to the children cowering behind their scared mother.

The father took a small step toward his family, causing more concern for Sara. She looked around to make sure no one else was close enough to hear her and asked if they were running.

"No, ma'am, we just stoppin' before we continues north to my brother's place," he said.

"I know you have no reason to believe me, but I am not going to hurt your or your family," Sara tried to say. They all just stared at her. "Some advice, it looks like you are trying to keep to yourselves, and I will not bother that, but if you continue to make food like this, people will be able to smell for miles and come running." She smiled.

Just then, they heard a rustling noise in the distance. "I think it's coming from over here," one man called to another. Soon enough, two men got closer to the camp, not expecting what they saw.

"Well, what do we have here?" the first man questioned, taking his shotgun off his shoulder.

Sara recognized them as two brothers she and Jonathan helped when they got smallpox.

"Timothy Jordan, is that you?" Sara called out.

"Yeah, Sara, is that you?" he called back.

"Yes, what are you doing out here?" she asked.

At this point, the family was even more scared.

"We are looking for some game and smelled vittles. The question is, what are you doing out here with them?" he asked.

"Well, put down your gun and come over here. I will introduce you," she said.

When they finally made their way to the camp, Sara said, "Tim and James Jordan, this is Mr. Jones and his family. My father knew his family when he was stationed in Connecticut, so I wrote to him and asked if he might be interested in working for me as a cook at the tavern, as long as he passed my test, of course," she said.

"Working for you, are you planning on paying him?" they asked.

"This is a free family from the North, so yes," she said, then whispered, "but I can pay them less than someone else 'cause I don't have a lot to offer for starters."

"Where's your papers?" James said grumpily.

"I have them back at the house. You don't think I would have tried his food if he was lying to me?' she said.

"But why are you way out here?" Tim asked.

"You were able to smell that food from way over there in a forest. How many people do you think would have come running if he cooked this in town? I would have had to pay extra!" she said.

"Do you mind if we try some, ya know, to give you our opinion? Tim asked.

"Yes, I mind, this is my interview, and I will go with my judgment," she snapped.

"Well then, if you're all right we will be leaving you to your interview," James said.

"I am fine, thank you," she replied, and the men left.

When she turned around, the father looked pissed and rightfully so. "What did you do that for? I am not gonna be a slave to anyone!" he said angrily.

"I just wanted to help," she said, a little confused.

"Well, we don't need your help. Come on, we got to go," he said to his family.

"Look, I know I came up with that on the spur of the moment, but the part about a job was for real," she said.

"Ohh, so you can pay men less than another man, like I am worth less than another man," he growled back.

"I would not do that. I said it for those two idiots. I didn't mean it like that," she tried to say.

"You all are alike, none of you ever mean it like that. Let's get outta here before they come back."

The family started to walk away without eating, and Sara tried one more time. "I was just trying to help. That's why I said it was an interview, and you were from up North so you could continue on your way."

They stopped with the father turning around and marching back toward her. "So now what, if I wanted to stay, I just take up another name some white person decided to brand me with?" he said, almost yelling, but didn't want to bring the hunters back.

"I didn't think they would believe me if I didn't know you," she apologized softly again.

"Exactly, you didn't think. You just believed you knew what was best for someone else without even knowing their names." With that, the family walked away.

Sara just stood there looking in the woods as their silhouettes disappeared. She tried to figure out what just happened. *I could have just saved that man's family with my story, and he is angry with me? What is his problem?* she thought. After thinking about it for a while, she did realize she didn't know anything about that family. For all she knew, they could have been a free family trying to start their own business here, as other black families have done, and she just ruined it for them. "Dr. Madder was right," she started saying to herself out loud. "I really need to stop acting on impulse and get some facts before I open my big mouth." She looked down at the rabbit that was left behind and thought, *Now those children are going to go hungry because of me. But I don't want this rabbit's death to go unneeded. I will take this home with me.'*

She walked Storm back to town as she continued to think about the situation. After handing June the rabbit, she found Jonathan putting Shadow away and asked, "Can we talk please?"

"Sure, what is on your mind today?" he asked.

"Not here. Let's put Storm away and go to the river," she said.

As they walked, they crossed paths with Tim and James. Tim called out to them.

"Did you get your cook?" he questioned.

"It smelled better than it tasted," she replied quietly, then walked away.

"What was that all about?" Jonathan asked.

"Well, that is what I want to talk with you about. When I was out hunting, I came across a black family in the woods cooking dinner. They looked like they were runaways, so when Tim and James walked up on us, I said they were interviewing for a job trying to help them out," she said.

"Let me guess, the family wasn't pleased with what you did," Jonathan said.

"We never really talked about this issue, have we? Well, besides the fight between you and Martha, of course?" he asked.

"No, not really," she said back with a small smirk.

"It is a very difficult and uncomfortable issue to discuss between people. Even members of the same family have a difficult time discussing the atrocities that happen between humans," he said.

"Most people have a firm feeling regarding slavery but turn mute when discussing the matter," he finished.

"I know I never agreed with what I saw when my father and I first traveled the South," she said definitely.

"And did you discuss it with your father?" he questioned.

She tried to answer but couldn't really remember a true conversation about it. "I knew he didn't like the practice, but I can only remember him, saying, 'Well, that's just the way it is, dear. That is an issue for a later war,'" she finally said.

"See what I mean?" Jonathan asked. "When you first spoke of that night in Princeton, you told us your father saw what happened to women and children in the Seven Years' War, so he taught you how to fight to defend yourself, am I correct?" he asked.

"Yes," she questioned.

"Did you ever ask yourself what happened to the people who lived on this land before we got here?" he wanted to know.

"Well no, but how did this go from black slavery to Indian warfare?" she asked.

He laughed and said, "It is exactly the same thing if you look at it from a certain view, and that, my dear, is the point." He saw the confusion on her face, so he continued. "Every human being is limited to their upbringing for knowledge and acceptance within their society. Even children within the same house can have different experiences creating different beliefs," he said.

"I do understand that, like girls get some schooling only if their mother provides it, but boys get to go to school if their family can afford it," Sara stated.

"Right, you have never been quiet about not being treated fairly based on your gender," he said.

"Yes?" she questioned, waiting to see where this was going.

"But will you also agree that there are girls and young ladies who are content and even enjoy the state they were born into?" he asked.

"I can agree with that," she said.

"So would you agree those ladies are confined to the education they were provided and ignorant to the abilities they are not using?" he asked.

"Exactly!" She started to get a bit of excitement with this line of questioning.

"And you want independence, but what about the others who don't even know or understand what you are asking for?" he said. "Should they get that same independence even if they don't know what it is and possibly may not want it?" he questioned.

"Definitely, if they like their life, they can stay, but if they don't, they improve themselves," she said.

"Well, how would they know if they want to 'improve' if they don't know what is available? They are under their own limited education, and if they do not seek answers or differences, why change?" he stated. "You have been taught and educated and privileged. However, you did not seek beyond the education provided to you. You didn't question what you were taught and tried to learn about what happened when we arrived here. How entire families and villages were killed in many different ways so you can call a piece of land yours," he pointed out.

After a pause, he continued. "I was involved in the Seven Years' War just like your father. I don't put down his memory, but he has you believing negatively about a group of people who were fighting for their land and families. It is only after a war and a winner has been decided that good and evil are designated. If we had lost that war, we would be the savages trying to take over this land. Do you see the difference now?" he asked. "I mean, if I am not mistaken, you are now friends with a Frenchman, are you not?" he added prior to her answer.

"I never saw it that way before, and yes, I consider Lafayette one of my best friends," she said with tears in her eyes.

"Good, because you were not able to change your mind before you looked at this from a different point of view. You are allowed to be ignorant once because you don't know what you don't know. What is important is what you do with the information now," he said.

"But if I try to increase my education and overcome my own ignorance, won't I just put my foot in my mouth once again?" she asked.

"Sure, you will, but try to learn something from your mistakes," he answered. "Now let's take this conversation even further," he said. "Slavery. If you go back in time, slavery started when someone sold themselves to someone who was better off," he started to say.

"*What?*" she jumped, a bit startled.

"Someone who couldn't take care of themselves would sell themselves to someone else who could teach them a skill or service. The servant was indentured to the master for a specific period of time. They would work for that 'owner' until the debt or the cost of the sale for the person was paid off. It allowed the 'owner' a chance to put funds upfront and get help for a designated point of time. The 'slave' had a chance to learn a trade, and when he was no longer an apprentice, he was able to get a job or start his own. However, sometimes hardships fell upon the 'owner,' and they couldn't take care of the 'slave' anymore and needed to have the funds back. Now we are getting into people being bought and sold, and oh, what a lucrative proposition that became. However, it was limited to the number of people one had on hand." He took a small pause again before continuing. "Wars were happening all over for the gain of land, which also included the acquisition of humans who were sellable. People started to realize that they didn't have to wait for someone to give themselves up. They could just take someone and sell them. Once money changed hands, that person became property and not human."

He knew this was a lot to process and took yet another small break. "Do you want me to continue?" he asked.

"Yes, please," she said.

275

"Now just remember, the information I have come from books and stories, so I am also as ignorant as my information all right?" he questioned before proceeding. She nodded back, and he went on talking. "Every man, woman, and child who came to this country in shackles and sold as soon as they arrived were stolen and did not enter that life willingly. So when people try to defend slavery by telling me about stories in the Bible that discuss owners and slaves, I discredit that information right away. If I am not forgetting my readings, even though some parts talk about slavery being a good thing for both parties, the biggest story was about an entire nation of people being led out of slavery by a man with a staff who talked to God as a fire in a bush!"

Sara giggled and said, "Moses."

"That's right, but even they didn't get freedom right away. It took time for them to be lead out of Egypt and while Moses tried to remove the people from the hands of Pharaoh, they were punished for it and turned on him. Then it took forty years to cross a desert that should have only taken a couple of months at the longest," he said.

"Wait, are you saying people are supposed to wait years to gain their freedom?" she asked.

"No, I am saying that the slave and non-slave needs to fight for the freedom we all deserve even if the non-slave is hated for it. Sometimes it is with a gun, other times with a pen, and still others with discussion. It takes time to change the minds of people who do not wish to change. You're how old, and you're just now changing your minds on the natives. Take into consideration you want to improve things and change things. You wouldn't even ask the question, let alone allow us to have this conversation if you wanted the realities to remain the same," he said.

"There are children who were born here that do not remember, living free themselves, but I believe they are hearing stories about what life was like before," he said. "So they are also confined to their own ignorance as well. Some people never saw a white person caring about anything but themselves. Some have had very difficult and painful experiences. They have seen things and had things done to them that would make even your skin crawl. Remember, each person has a different experience and a different belief. The family you tried to help today got angry with you but someone you try to help tomorrow may be grateful." he said.

"So if I want to help, how do I do it without causing pain to someone?" she asked.

"Now that is an interesting question. Sometimes, it can't be helped. No matter what we do or how we do it, someone will be upset. Even if you help someone escape, they may only see you as a white person to be hated, but it is still better to help, then turn from the situation," he explained.

"So I guess June wasn't mad at you and Margaret, and so she stayed when you freed her?" she asked.

"Now please don't be angry when I explain this, but June isn't as free as Margaret would have you believe," he said.

"What do you mean? You pay her, don't you?" she questioned.

"You see, the law states any property brought to the marriage by the wife cannot be sold unless she agrees to it, even though it is considered her husband's property. Since slaves are considered property, I was unable to free her. I would not allow her to come with Margaret unless she was paid and treated by my rules. I do everything I can to give her a voice and a say about what happens, and yes, she is paid very well. However, if she leaves one day for any reason, she would still be a runaway like those under much harsher conditions. Unfortunately, it is the best I can do for her right now while trying to talk with as many people as I can to get the laws changed," he said. He looked up toward the setting sun and suggested they start for home.

Chapter *17*

Meeting the Johnsons

When they sat down for dinner, Sara had a difficult time eating the rabbit. She just kept looking at June and wishing there was something she could do.

"June, this has got to be the best rabbit you have ever made!" Margaret exclaimed.

"Well, if truth be told, I didn't cook the rabbit. Sara brought it home already cooked."

"Already cooked?" Margaret asked.

"Yeah, I came upon a small family in the woods who ran when they saw me. I didn't want it to go to waste, so I took it," she answered.

"I am surprised at you, Sara. That family could have come back for dinner after you scared them off, didn't you think about that? Now they have to start over, if they can find another rabbit, that is," she said in a bit of a huff but taking another bite.

Later that evening, when the Madders went to bed, Sara looked for June. Off the dining room, there was another downstairs room that Sara never took notice of before and knocked. June answered in her nightgown and robe, looking exhausted.

"How can I help you, miss?" June said, weary.

"I am so sorry if I woke you up. I just wanted to say…Umm, thank you for everything and good night," Sara said, trying to break the conversation and let June go back to bed. "

"Well, you're welcome and good night, miss," June said, then closed the door.

Sara was able to look into the room enough to see that June had much more personal items than any other person considered a slave she had ever meant. The difference between this room and the one she saw the beaten slave at Mt. Vernon was night and day. June had a regular wooden bed with a mattress and feather topping, blankets, and pillows. A table with a wash bin and what looked like a closet with clothes and shoes. There was also a shelf with books, flowers, and a small rug on the floor. As she walked back to her room, she wondered how to change her ignorance and better help the people in her world.

The next morning, Sara made sure she woke up early to meet June in the kitchen. She knocked before she entered and found June making some hoecakes at the stove.

"Why, Miss Sara, what are you doing up so early?" June asked.

"I wanted to talk with you, if you don't mind?" Sara replied.

"Why sure, miss, what can I do for you?" she asked.

"What would you do if you were freed?" Sara asked. This question shocked June and she dropped her spatula. "Maybe that was too fast into the conversation. Let me try again. Are you willing to discuss your relationship with the Madders with me?" she asked.

"I work here, there's nothing else to discuss!" June said, then went back to the hoecakes.

"I am sorry, I do not wish to upset you or ask the incorrect question. I know this subject is upsetting—" Sara tried to start but was cut off by June.

"What is it that you want, Miss Sara? I am trying to get breakfast on the table. I do not wish to discuss the situation here with you." She was doing her best to keep her composure.

"I stuck my foot into my mouth again. Honestly, Miss June, I feel you are a part of my family now, and I thought you were free and just worked for the Madders. I just found out that was not so and didn't know if I could help in any way," she tried to explain. "I will leave you to your chores. Please know I never meant to hurt you," she said as she left the kitchen. On her way back to the house, she was able to hear June crying in the kitchen.

When Sara returned to the house, she told Jonathan what she was trying to do. She suggested he go and talk with June if it would help.

"You are the bold one just as Washington said so long ago," Jonathan said. He then sat down at the table and started to read a paper he received. Sara slowly sat down staring at him, so he said, "Looks like Washington has been traveling the outskirts of New York keeping the reds centrally located."

Margaret then walked into the room and sat down, asking where the coffee was and holding her own conversation, not realizing no one was listening. June then came in and set down the hoecakes and coffee in the center of the table. She still had tears in her eyes and would not look at Sara.

"Thank you, June. Oh, do we have any butter left?" Margaret asked, not paying attention.

"I'll get it now," June said quietly and walked out the door.

Sara almost said something to Margaret, but Jonathan stopped her. "I will need your help today Sara. We need to look in on the Sanders children. The baby died last week, and the other children seem to be feeling poorly," Jonathan said, shaking his head no as he talked to her.

She looked down into her food and just responded, "Yes, sir."

Nothing else was said until they saddled Storm and Shadow and began to ride out of town. "You already upset June, then you wanted to start a fight with Margaret. Are you trying to upset all the ladies in my life?" he asked.

"No, I was just trying to get a better understanding like you were saying," Sara stated.

"By asking someone basically how they enjoy being a slave?" Dr. Madder questioned sarcastically.

"I guess that was basically what I asked her wasn't it?" Sara said, upset by what she had done again.

"Listen, most people of color that I have talked with do not wish to discuss matters with white folks. From now on, just try to be friendly and stop pushing the slavery issue. This is a subject that has to be dealt with over time," Jonathan said as they rode into the Sanders farm.

Mr. Sanders was waiting for the doctor while Mrs. Sanders was running from child to child. There were three boys and two girls who were all in bed with fever and a rash. Dr. Jonathan started looking at some children while Sara looked at some others.

"What do you think this could be, Sara?" Dr. Jonathan asked.

She was looking at one of the girls and noticed a swollen tongue and neck as well. "I haven't seen this type of rash before. I am not sure what this is?" Sara questioned.

"That is because you basically treated adults. This is a child's disease called scarlet fever."

He turned to Mrs. Sander's and said, "They are going to need tea made with these herbs every three hours." He was feeling the head and neck of one of the boys and continued, "Keep them in bed and continue the cool rags on their heads." He then walked over to Mrs. Sanders and took her hands. "I am so sorry to hear about your baby. If there is anything else I can do for you, please let me know."

Mrs. Sanders had tears in her eyes but didn't say a word. She just nodded in agreement taking the bag of herbs from Dr. Madder. Sara also came over and expressed her condolences. They took their leave after explaining things and provided condolences to Mr. Sanders as well.

A few weeks later, after drinking the tea, all the children started to get better. Sara and Dr. Jonathan would ride out every other day to check on things and look in on other patients. June and Sara started getting back to normal, and Sara refused to bring the matter up again. Margaret was just enjoying her everyday life having Sara back again. One morning a letter arrived for Sara from Hamilton.

My dearest Sara,

Thank you for taking the time to come and see me when I needed you. I know I wasn't very open regarding the reason you traveled, but I appreciate the gesture all the same. My law firm is doing very well, and I am getting new clients every day. I really enjoy helping people who have been wronged and make it right. Some lawyers are in this for the prestige or money like Aaron Burr, but I can't and won't overprice my services. It is not in my best interest financially, but I really enjoy the nuances and matching legal witts with someone to make sure the right outcome happens for my clients. I actually feel like I am making a difference in someone's life. I just can't wait until I can make a difference in everyone's life in Congress. Betsy was pleased with your arrival as well and just loves to share our little Philip with everyone. We have been talking about providing a sibling for him, but as of right now, we are just enjoying watching him grow. I have been called to Philadelphia in November for the Constitutional Convention, so I will stop by and see how you are doing.

Best regards,
A. Ham.

"How is he doing?" Jonathan asked Sara when she entered the room. She looked up from her letter and came swiftly back to reality.

"Excuse me?" she questioned, not really hearing what Jonathan asked.

"Hamilton, how is he doing?" Jonathan asked again.

"He is doing wonderful. I think he finally found his calling," Sara said happily.

"I hope you're right, he does deserve it," Jonathan said, going back to his paper.

They were both startled when a knock came upon the door. Jonathan answered the door and called for Sara while walking into the medical room she once occupied. She ran into the room, followed by a small family crying behind her. A large man with a wide frame, curly black hair, brown eyes, and a very deep voice said, "He was climbing a tree at the edge of town when the branch gave way. They said you are a doctor! Please help him."

Margaret heard what was going on and entered the room shortly after. "Margaret, please escort this family out to the sitting room while Sara and I set his arm!" Jonathan said. He looked down at the boy; he was probably eight years old, in tattered clothes and mussed hair. The most notable was he was not saying anything or moving. "He is in shock, we need to do this quickly," Dr. Madder said.

The bone on the upper part of his left arm was sticking out of the skin. Sara tied the boy's upper body to the bed frame while Jonathan got a splint ready. Jonathan took hold of the lower part of the arm, and Sara wrapped her arms around the boy's shoulders. Jonathan counted to three, and both pulled until they felt the pop of the bone going back into place. He then said, "I got it, get the splint." Sara released her grip, allowing the boy to be held by the sheets, and started applying the splint to his arm. Now Jonathan was able to make sure the wound was clean and stitched up. They set his arm across his body and put it in a sling to keep it still. He then picked up a paste that smelled horrible and put it under the boy's nose. It didn't take long for the boy to cough and start to cry, feeling the pain in his arm. Jonathan took a deep sigh when the door flung open.

The boy's father had rushed in when he heard his son. "He is going to be all right now. You can all sit with him for a while if you want to." The father wasn't too pleased when he saw Sara unstrapping his son from the bed. "Don't be alarmed. That was for traction so we could set the arm," Jonathan said, seeing the concern on his face. The mother, a little taller than Sara with long black hair in a braid and green eyes, ran past the men and hugged and kissed her son.

The father put his hand out and said, "I can't thank you enough. My name is Tom Johnson. That is my wife Amber and my son Tommy." Tommy was older and larger but could have been a twin to the child they worked on. "And you were working on Samuel."

Jonathan returned the handshake and introduced his family back. "We have some food in the dining room when you are ready.

We will leave you alone now, but if anything happens, just let us know."

Margaret and June went to the dining room to set the table while Sara and Jonathan went outback to wash the blood off. When they returned to the dining room, the Johnsons were entering from the other side. "He is resting now. Thank you so very much, sir," Tom said.

"Please take a seat," Jonathan said, pointing around the table. There was cheese and dried meat on the table with a pitcher of mead.

"How do I repay you for what you have done? I don't have much money as we were passing through looking for a job," Tom asked.

"Don't worry about repayment, your boy needed help," Jonathan said. "You can stay here with Samuel while he recovers. Do you have anything we need to go get?" he asked.

"We just have what we are carrying," Tom replied.

"What is it that you can do?" Sara asked.

"Well, I am very good with my hands, and my wife can keep house," he said.

"Any chance either of you can cook?" Sara asked.

Tom seemed a bit confused that she was the one asking questions but answered them anyway.

"Amber is a mighty fine house cook, and I can create a mean barbecue," he provided, puffing up a bit.

"I am opening a tavern in Princeton. Would you be interested in trying it out for a couple of weeks? If what I see is satisfactory, we will discuss payment. Room and board will be included. Does that sound all right?" Sara asked.

"Excuse me, did you say you're opening a tavern?" Amber said.

"Yes, I am opening a tavern, and right now, it is just me. I really could use the help," she explained.

"I never heard of no woman tavern owner," Tommy said.

"Well, this new world has a place for things that no one has ever heard of before, so why not?" Sara smiled back at him.

"We'd be happy to, miss, once Samuel is ready to travel," Tom agreed.

Over the next few days, the Johnsons took over some of the meals allowing June a couple of nights off. The few samples they each created were exceptional.

"Have you ever worked on a farm, Tom?" Sara asked. He seemed a little hesitant but told her he did work on a farm in central Pennsylvania, where they came from. "So if I get cows and sheep will you be able to help with the slaughter?" she questioned.

"That is something I have done in the past, yes! But you want to run a tavern and a farm?" he asked her.

"No, just the tavern. The farm animals will be on a friend's farm, but if you can help with the slaughter, then I will not need to hire a butcher," she explained.

Every day Tommy would take Chance out toward the river, and the two would just run back and forth. "Oh, to have a child's energy," Sara said to Amber one afternoon.

"It is good to see him playing and enjoying the day," Amber said, smiling at her son.

"Hopefully, there will be many more enjoyable days ahead," Sara said.

Margaret walked up to them as they watched Tommy and Chance and told Sara the supplies they had ordered in Philadelphia had arrived. After another few days, Samuel started running around the house against his mother's threats.

"I do believe he is just about ready to travel," Sara said jokingly.

"Looks that way to me," Jonathan said, joining in the laughter.

"Oh, Jonathan, this afternoon I would like to go to Tyler's and see how things are going with the furniture. Would that be all right?" Sara asked.

"That will be fine. We can also stop by the Sanders farm and see how everything is going there," he replied.

As Sara and Jonathan got their horses, Samuel, Tommy, and Chance went out for a much-needed run. It had rained the day before, so the area still had the earthy smell, and the road was muddy.

"I wanted to talk with you about hiring the Johnsons," Jonathan said once they were far enough away.

"Go ahead," Sara said, "but you will not change my mind."

"I didn't think I could, but you must be very careful. I noticed a brand on the back of Tom's neck," Jonathan said.

"Oh my God, a brand! What barbarians!" she yelled.

"Now he may be free and he may not, but anyone who sees that will believe he has run away," Jonathan explained. "I would like for the four of us to talk this evening about it, all right?" he asked.

"What is there to talk about? If they are runaways, I want to hire them all the more," Sara questioned.

"I know, Sara, but if I was able to see it, someone else is bound to. I have an idea of how to help, but I would like everyone's okay before trying it," Jonathan said sadly.

They remained quiet for the rest of the trip, looking at the river and trees.

When they rode onto the Sanders farm, they were delighted to see the children outside playing. Mr. Sanders was in the field when he noticed the company and started to walk toward them.

"Hello, friend!" he called from a distance.

This caused Mrs. Sanders to come out of the house. "Oh, Dr. Madder…Sara, thank you so much for everything!"

"How is everyone feeling today?" Dr. Madder asked while they both dismounted.

"They are doing so much better, sir," she said as the younger children chased the chickens around the yard.

"That's wonderful news, and how about you, my dear, how are you holding up?" he questioned.

Mr. Sanders made it over to the group and shook Jonathan's hand. After hearing the question as he got close, he decided to answer. "Every day is a bit better, thank you." Mrs. Sanders decided not to say anything.

"Well, if you need anything, please let me know, all right?" Jonathan said directly to Mrs. Sanders.

"Sir, do you still have that wagon you were trying to sell a couple of months back?" Jonathan asked.

"It's behind the barn. Why do you know someone who might be interested?" Mr. Sanders questioned hopefully.

"Well, Sara here is going to need a wagon to get her supplies to Princeton," he answered.

"Well, come on, Sara, let me show it to you," Mr. Sanders said as he directed Sara to the back of the barn. Jonathan stayed back to talk with Mrs. Sanders a bit more just to make sure she was all right.

It was a typical wagon large enough to carry a lot of items but too large to keep at the Madders' house. Sara and Mr. Sanders agreed on a price, and he allowed the wagon to stay on property until she was ready to travel back to Princeton. They all said their goodbyes to each other, and Sara and Dr. Madder traveled toward Tyler's farm.

"Have you heard how things are going with the tables and chairs yet?" Sara asked.

"Nothing yet, but I didn't really expect to either," he replied.

Some more birds and geese were flying south, and Sara suggested catching one before heading home. However, her thoughts were still on what Dr. Madder had in mind for Tom.

Sara hadn't seen Tyler's farm before. It was a beautiful location near the river covering about two acres. The house was a two-story British colonial made of wood with eight front-facing windows surrounding the door and a chimney directly in the center for the fireplaces. The barn, however, where Tyler did his building, was twice the size. That was where they found Tyler working on some chairs.

"Good day, sir," Jonathan called, making Tyler jump a bit.

"Good day, I was so involved with this that I didn't hear you ride up. How is everything going?" Tyler asked.

"Who could complain on this fine day." Jonathan chuckled.

"Well, I guess you are here to look into your order, am I correct, Sara?" Tyler asked.

"Yes, sir, if you don't mind. The tavern is almost complete but looks so bare," she answered.

He walked them over to where most of her items were. The craftsmanship on each piece was elegant. The time and dedication it took that went into the tables and chairs were evident. She asked for this but never requested or dreamed of the curves, lines, and carved florals on each piece. Sara stood there for a moment without being able to say anything. Then when she found her words, she said,

"My good sir, this is more beautiful than anything I could have ever imagined. I was expecting something so much more basic with the description I provided."

"Well, I do hope it is to your liking?" he questioned.

"I do believe it is too grand for a basic tavern, but then again, that is why I like it so much," she provided as she looked over and touched each piece.

"You have outdone yourself again, Tyler," Jonathan said.

At this point, there were only three beds for guest rooms done. However, she noticed a four-poster bed to the side and gave Tyler a questioning look. "That one is for you, my dear. Compliments of Dr. and Mrs. Madder."

Joy overwhelmed her as she choked. "You shouldn't' have, you've done so much already." That, however, didn't keep her from admiring the spirals of the posts and carvings on the headboard.

"The remainder of the project should take me about another month to complete," Tyler said as he glowed with pride.

"No rush, it will take that long to complete the next two levels anyway," Sara said, still admiring the furniture.

"The mattresses are being completed by a friend of mine and should arrive in a day or two," he finished.

"Tyler, I have another request if you don't mind," Sara said.

"What else can I help you with, Sara?" he replied.

"I need lumber sent to Princeton for the barn and fencing. Are you able to order that for me please?" she asked.

"Consider it done," Tyler replied.

When they were finished, they all shook hands and parted ways.

"I can't believe you did that," she said again to Jonathan.

"Like we said, we consider you our daughter. You are worth it. Now we just need to get you two more horses for the wagon, and you should be set," he replied.

"That is so funny. When I first met you, you wanted nothing to do with getting a horse. Now it seems you can't stop getting them." She laughed.

Chapter 18

A Plan gone wrong

When they sat down that evening, Jonathan started the conversation. "I wanted to let you know, for starters, you are safe here. Second, I saw the brand on the back of your neck, so that being said, I have two questions." Tom and Amber almost became white as ghosts and were terrified when they were looking at each other. "I don't care if you were given your freedom or if you ran away. I don't even want to know that answer. What I would like to know, however, is are you the only one with a mark Tom and would you like it to be covered up so you don't have to worry about it anymore?" Jonathan asked.

A few moments went by without a word from anyone until Sara spoke up. "Just so you know, I hired you and that employment is still offered. No one is going to hurt you or your children here."

June just so happened to be walking by when she heard the conversation and entered the room. "Mr. and Mrs. Johnson, you don't need to fear these two, they good people. They want to see the end of slavery," June said as everyone's eyes were on her.

"But you ain't free," Amber said, holding her husband's hands.

"That ain't no fault of these here. The missus, well, she just can't seem to come to that same answer," June said, choking a bit on the words. "If you in need of help, they will help you, don't worry none 'bout that," she finished with and sat down.

A few more moments went by when Tom finally said, "I am the only one with the mark. My wife and children, they free. But how do you suppose to get rid of it, Dr. Madder?" he asked.

"Well, that sir is the bad part of this conversation. We are going to have to burn you again to cover up the symbols. Make it look like you were in a fire, not branded," he said. "I will not do it without your consent, and it will hurt like hell, but it may just be enough to get anyone off your tracks," he finished.

Amber started crying and telling Tom not to go through with it and that they would find a different way.

"I feel if there was a different way, Dr. Madder would have suggested it," Tom responded.

"If there was another way, I would gladly suggest it. If I tried surgery, it would leave a scar, but you would still be able to tell where the brand was," Jonathan said.

"Do we have to do anything at all? It is bad enough he was branded once but to purposely burn him again? Why can't he just keep it covered and work for me?" Sara asked.

"Because if someone came looking for me and pulled off my shirt, they would attack you as well," Tom admitted.

"What's to say you burn him and someone doesn't take him anyway?" Amber asked.

"Unfortunately, that is still possible. It would be easier if it was just Tom as a family of four on the run is harder to convince you are not who people are looking for. It may still be best for your family to travel to Canada, but the choice is yours," Jonathan said.

"You don't need to decide right now, it is a big decision. We can discuss it further later, all right!" he finished.

The next morning, Jonathan and Tom were outside by the stables as Sara approached them. "I need you to fully understand what this means. I would need to create third-degree burns to basically peel off your skin. I can help with the pain, but I can't take it away," she heard Jonathan say.

"First, it was your idea, sir, and second, if there is a way to get this bastard's mark off my neck, I am willing to do it," Tom replied.

"Well if we are going to go forward with this, we need to get ready," Jonathan said.

"More than that, we need a full plan that doesn't look like one," Sara chimed in.

"What do you mean?" Jonathan questioned.

"If we can get Princeton to back me up with a story regarding the burn, it would be easier to protect them," Sara said.

"That means we need a fire!" Tom said.

"And how do we control that?" questioned Jonathan.

"Well, the barn is away from anything. We can give that up," Sara said.

"Give up, you mean burn it down?" Tom questioned.

"Yes, that will work!" Jonathan stated.

"That is asking too much!" Tom stated.

"It's nothing compared to what has happened and what is going to happen to you." Sara and Jonathan both agreed.

They decided the way to make it look like an accident was to have the horses and tack in the stable at the time. Jonathan started a fire in some dry hay next to the barn, and they all went into the house to let it grow. When it was large enough to produce smoke that was seen from the street, they heard someone yelling fire. That is when the plan went into action. Tom and Jonathan ran out to the barn and removed the horses.

As Jonathan took the horses to the front of the house, Tom went back in to get as much tact as he could. That is when the building started to collapse while Tom was inside. Sara took the horses from Jonathan so he could pull Tom from the wreckage. Margaret, Amber, and June were on the side crying and yelling at the sight.

Finally, the fire brigade arrived along with the town and started a bucket line from the river to extinguish the building. A few men helped Jonathan bring Tom into the patient room and put him on the bed stomach down. Tommy ran out to where Sara was, and she asked him to hold the horses while she checked on his dad. When she arrived, she noticed that the doctor was holding his hands in the air and not really assessing Tom.

"Oh no!" she said. "Get Martha, I will explain what to do," Jonathan added.

Margaret removed herself from the sight of the burning barn and entered the patient's room. Seeing her husband's hands, she started crying all the more. "Stop now, I need you to be the nurse for Sara, all right!" he said to her. She started to get her tears under control, and Dr. Madder instructed Sara to cut the shirt off of Tom to reveal his back. The burning beam that had landed on Tom's shoulders (she never found out if it was placed or just happened to fall there) removed most of the skin. "Okay, you need to take the scalpel and cut away the dead and burning tissue. Margaret, get some cloth and my burn jar and start applying that to his back as she removed the rest of the skin." The two ladies did as he asked and finished by putting bandages across his back. Then they turned to the doctor and looked at his hands. They were burned but not as badly as Tom. He didn't need any skin cut away, just the solution and wraps put on his hands.

The fire did exactly what they wanted it to do. Not only were there witnesses to the fire, but it was in the newspapers.

Fire in Morrisville, PA!

Late yesterday evening, the fire brigade was alerted to a barn fire at Dr. Jonathan Madder's house in Morrisville, PA.

Dr. Madder was injured when he tried to removed someone from the burning building. The doctor could have lost everything, including his life, if it were not for the actions of a free black man who saved him.

It took days for Tom to fully wake up from the incident, but when he did, he was in incredible pain. The wound on his back was infected, and Sara cut away more dead flesh every day. She continued putting the paste Jonathan made for burns on his back which helped a little. Now that he was awake, she was able to provide some tea and herbs to help with the infection. Jonathan had to have the paste put on his hands daily as well. Margaret became his full-time nurse even as he still checked in on Tom.

The townspeople all came to their aid and donated supplies and time for a new stable. They also received some new tack that needed to be replaced. June and Amber would prepare meals every day for all the people trying to help. To her bewilderment, they always asked how Tom was doing and wishing him well. They even called him a hero for trying to save the doctor and his animals. Sara also received a letter from Hamilton and the Washingtons. The newspapers only said someone with the Madders was hurt, not who got hurt. She wrote back to them, letting them know she was all right and what happened, mostly.

Jonathan wanted to seek the advice of a friend and surgeon at the hospital in Philadelphia. To do so, he would need to obtain a letter of license and to bring funds to cover his burial or transfer home cost. When Jonathan Potts (a friend and doctor at the hospital) received his request, he suggested the Madders just come to his home for a few days instead. The skin on his fingers healed too tight around his knuckles and did not allow him full motion. Jonathan was hoping Dr. Potts would be able to repair them with surgery. Sara wished them good luck and hugged them both. She is the one who suggested the fire, but the damage wasn't supposed to be as bad as it was.

"It could have been much worse, Sara, and now look around. Tom is healing and safer now," Jonathan said.

Sara hitched Shadow to a new buggy, and they were on their way.

Sara walked into Tom's room and found him awake. "So how are you feeling today?" she asked.

"I could be better, that is for sure," Tom answered.

"Well, let's see what it looks like today. Boys, please take Chance outside for me, thank you," Sara said.

When the boys were out of the room, she removed the bandages carefully. The wound was still open and angry, but the infection had passed. "Well, it looks like you are out of danger, and you just need to rest and heal," Sara told him. "You know, when we talked about the fire, you were not supposed to have the entire barn fall on you. Don't you think that was pushing things a bit far?" she questioned.

"I wanted to make sure it was convincing," he said back with a laugh, followed by a moan from the pain. "And what about the doctor? Are his hands better?" he asked.

"He went to Philadelphia to get them looked at by a surgeon. I was hoping to travel there tomorrow if Amber was all right with you," she said.

"That will be fine, Sara, and please give him our best," he said.

She helped him drink some more tea when Amber came in. "There is someone at the door for you Sara, I take over here," she said. She went to the door and found Hamilton standing there.

"Oh, thank God, you are not hurt!" he said.

"I guess you missed my letter letting you know I was doing fine," Sara replied and let him in.

They went into the sitting room to continue their conversation. "You can't blame me. It is not hard to see you, running into a burning building for someone," he said with a bit of a smirk. "Where is Dr. Madder, is he all right?" he asked.

"He went to Philadelphia. I don't know if he will ever regain use of his hands, to be honest," she explained.

"I am so sorry to hear that," Hamilton said. "He is a very good doctor. I hope he can continue his career," he added.

"So do I, to be honest. I am a bit worried about him," Sara said. "And what about you? Are you on your way to serve in Congress?" she asked.

"Yes, I need to be there by next week, so I decided to give myself time to see if you were all right and get someplace to stay," he replied.

"Would you mind if I rode with you into Philadelphia to see what is going on with Dr. Madder?" she asked.

"Are you sure you're all right, Sara? It is not like you to ask for a companion rider," he questioned.

She told him she was doing fine, but he could tell there was something she was hiding from him.

It was cold and rainy the next morning as they rode toward Philadelphia. Sara didn't mind the weather as it matched her mood and worry. When they were far enough out of town, Hamilton tried again.

"So why are you so upset, and what really happened?" he questioned.

"We know each other all too well," she said.

After explaining the events and the reason for the fire, Hamilton just looked somber.

"It is my fault Dr. Madder is hurt as badly as he is," she finished.

"Well, it sounds to me like you all had an equal share in responsibility. However, I understand the reasoning. All that can be done now is to wait and see if he heals," Hamilton said.

By the time they got to the city, the rain was so hard they could barely see.

"You better not get sick again or Dr. Madder will have my head, hands or not," Hamilton said to her as they arrived at Dr. Potts's home.

They were putting Storm in the closest stable when he explained that he was going to look for housing and would be back for her later that day. She said goodbye as he rode away and knocked on the door. When a servant named Ruth answered, Sara explained who she was and was shown into a room with Margaret.

"How is everything going?" she asked.

Margaret ran up and gave her a hug. "He is with Dr. Potts now, but it doesn't sound good," Margaret answered.

They sat in silence for a few hours before the men returned. After introductions and hugs, Dr. Potts told the ladies that he could try a procedure where he would cut small slivers in the underside of each knuckle and stretch the fingers to try to regain movement, but it was risky, and he wasn't sure it would work. Jonathan wanted to try, though, so they decided to have it done later that evening when Dr. Potts returned.

"John, let's talk about this please," Margaret asked after Dr. Potts left.

"No! I don't have use of my hands now. Things can't get any worse," he said sternly. He walked out of the room, leaving the ladies alone.

"I am just so worried about him. He is trying to act like this doesn't bother him, but not being a doctor will destroy him," Margaret said.

"Well then, we need to make sure that will not happen," Sara offered more assuredly, then she felt.

"I wish I had your confidence, Sara," Margaret said, holding her hands.

Dr. Potts came home with two trowels and fabric that he purchased. He began to remove the trowel handles and modify their shape. He then padded the trowels and covered them with fabric so they didn't have any sharp edges. Sara was asked to help Dr. Potts with the surgery, and she was more than happy to be doing something to help out. Dr. Potts unwrapped Jonathan's hands, revealing the tightly stretched skin underneath. "Ready?" he said as Jonathan took the leather strap in his mouth from Sara and nodded. With the slightest touch of a scalpel, the skin split open, relieving some of the tension. "Sara, I am going to need you to straighten the fingers and splint them for me. That way, he will have the best chance of movement," he said as he split open another section. "The splints I made will hold his fingers comfortably while the skin grows back."

As they were starting to clean up, a knock came on the door. Sara recognized the voice as Hamilton and excused herself from the room. "My name is Alexander Hamilton, miss. May I please address Miss Sara Weinstein?" she heard him say to Ruth when she answered the door.

"I will see him please, Ruth," Sara said behind her, and the door opened wider, revealing a very drenched Hamilton. Ruth took his coat and hat away, and Sara walked him into the sitting room to sit beside the fire.

"How is Dr. Madder doing?" he asked, looking very tired.

"We just finished operating on his fingers. I am hopeful it will work. How about you? Did you find somewhere to reside?" she asked.

"I am glad to hear that. And yes, I have lodging on the other side of town. That is how I got to look this way." He laughed.

"Are you hungry? Do you need me to get you anything?" Sara asked.

He declined, but she could tell he needed something. "Well, either you're being stubborn, or your kidney is acting up again," she questioned.

"I am feeling fine, just still chilled from the cold," he answered.

She decided not to listen to him and went to the dining room and poured a bowl of soup and got a piece of bread and a cup of tea that was there for the evening meal. As she returned, Margaret was just leaving Dr. Madder's side, saying he fell asleep. They both returned to the sitting room as lightning started to flash through the windows, followed by thunder shaking the house. It seemed to Sara, even for just a moment, she was the only one not bothered by the noise. Hamilton graciously took the food, and while he was eating, they talked about the operation and plans for Congress. As the storm raged outside, Sara felt a storm brewing in the room. Even though he was pleasant, the attitude and tone from Hamilton seemed off to Sara. She knew his feelings toward Margaret were not warm, but they were never harsh. She hoped it was because he was tired, but she had seen him tired before. In the war, she saw him on the verge of passing out but never acted like this.

After about an hour, Margaret excused herself to get some soup and return to her husband. "Did something happen today?" Sara asked.

"Why do you ask?" Hamilton said, sounding a little better.

"Well, because the man that sat before me just a moment ago was not the same man who was talking with me last night and on the ride to Philadelphia," she questioned.

"Nothing is wrong or new. I am just a bit tired, and you know how I feel about the Articles of Confederation. We, as a new nation, are on the verge of crumbling, and we have not been declared free yet. We need to sure up our laws and our finances, or this dream will turn into a nightmare," he explained.

This was a good excuse but not the true answer. Sara decided not to push the issue any further.

"Are you staying in town, or will you be returning to Morrisville soon?" Hamilton asked, changing the subject.

"I will be taking Dr. Madder home tomorrow, but we should return in a few weeks for Dr. Potts to check on him," Sara said.

"Well then, I hope you stop by, here is where I will be staying. Now I better return home before I am not allowed to. It sounds like the Presbyterians and Baptists have this town quiet by eleven. I don't want to be out on the streets tempting rumors of my fidelity," he said. Ruth returned a dry coat and hat to Hamilton and went to bed.

"I will make sure to stop by upon our return," Sara said, walking him to the door. She gave him a small kiss on the cheek and reminded him she would be there for him if needed as he left.

The next morning, Sara hitched Shadow to the buggy and tied Storm to the back. The rain had passed in the night and brought a new sunny day. "Every storm brings new hope," Jonathan said, looking down at his hands as he walked out of the house. He thanked Dr. Potts and was helped into the buggy. Dr. Potts gave Sara some suggestions about treatment. He wanted her to wait a few days then have him move his hands every day. She agreed to work with him and remembered the stiffness in her shoulder after she was shot. She knew it would not be easy, but it could happen. They also stopped by the store that had the items she ordered for the tavern. Once everything was loaded, they had a quiet ride home as everyone was weighed down by their own thoughts.

Upon arrival, Jonathan finally spoke to Margaret. "There is a very good chance I will not be able to use my hands again. I have allowed you time to come to terms with the fire and my injuries. However, now I need you to step up and be my hands," he told her. She made a small noise, and he continued. "If I didn't believe you could do it, I wouldn't ask. I know you have this in you," he finished. Sara felt like she was intruding on a private conversation and started to climb down off the buggy. She stopped when Jonathan addressed her, however. "I wish to thank you for allowing Margaret the time to recover herself, Sara. I am really glad you were here to help out," he said. Sara also only made a small noise to acknowledge Jonathan. She was still worried he blamed her for what happened to his hands, and this conversation did not help.

Margaret helped Jonathan down and into the house while Sara put away the horses and buggy. There wasn't much room in the house now for her tavern belongings, so she left them where they were. She decided to allow the Madders to have more time and started across the road to the river. The boys were playing with Chance when she walked up to them and got a happy greeting.

"Thank you for taking such good care of Chance for me. I need to take a walk and would like him to join me, all right?" she asked. They nodded and ran back to the river with Chance starting to follow, then returned. "Let's go, boy," she said, looking down and petting him on the head.

As they walked, she recalled the events that happened on this riverbank five years prior. "So much has happened in this short time, Chance. It is almost like two lifetimes went by in the blink of an eye. I lost my family and got a new one. And now, Jonathan may never be a doctor again. Something's not right with Hamilton even though he tries to say he is okay. I have never seen Margaret so helpless and quiet." She paused for a moment and sat down on the bank watching the river. Chance sat next to her and pressed in on her side. He could tell she was upset and tried his best to comfort her. She put her arm around him and restarted her conversation. "You and a dream are the only things I have left of Charles, and I haven't seen Aunt Martha or Uncle George in such a long time." Chance gave her a sniff in her ear, making her giggle which caused his tail to wag. "You're a good boy," she said, petting his head again. "I wish I could help, but I don't know how. It must be nice to be a dog, just being there is helpful." She smiled at him. The two of them sat there for about an hour before she decided to return home.

"Where have you been? I turned around to talk with you, and you were gone," Jonathan complained.

"I thought we both needed some time," she said as she entered the house. "It sounded like you and Margaret needed to talk things over," she finished.

"Why would that mean I wanted you to go away, Sara?" he asked. Again, she just made a small noise and shrugged.

"You don't think I am kicking you out or replacing you as my help, do you?" he questioned.

"I figured you didn't want my help anymore because I caused…" Her voice trailed off as he tried to reach out for her and moaned.

"I am not angry with you, and what happened to me was not your fault. However, I need to be very cautious with Margaret. I never told you about her brother, did I?" he asked. Sara shook her head, and he began to explain, "When Margaret was about ten years old, she had a younger brother, Jonny, whom she just adored. He was seven and always getting into mischief as little boys tend to do. Well, one day, lightning struck their house and started a fire. Margaret made sure Jonny got out of the house and told him to stay by the tree while she tried to find their parents. When she returned with her parents, Jonny was gone. He ran back into the house for some reason. No one ever found out why but he didn't make it back out. She was devastated, and no matter what anyone did to console her, it wasn't enough. About two months later, a seven-year-old June and her mother ended up with Margaret's family. It turned out June's older brother was sold down south. He was about ten. It took a while, but they just sort of helped each other through it. When the fire happened here, it just took Margaret to a very dark place. I am hoping to get her back," he explained.

"I am so sorry, I never knew," Sara said.

"I know, I just don't want you to feel we are upset at you in any way. But we may need you around here for a bit longer if you are all right with that," he asked.

"I will be happy to help any way I can," Sara offered.

"Well, with winter coming, I could use a good set of hands." he laughed.

Over the next few weeks, Sara would unwrap Jonathan's hands and have him more his fingers as much as he could on his own. Then she would carefully manipulate them, trying to get them to have a larger range of motion. She made sure she did not reopen the cuts in the skin, causing more damage. Slowly he started to regain some movement and freedom in his fingers. During this time, Tom started sitting up and getting some movement himself. His skin was regrowing and revealing the scars from the fire, but there was no trace of the brand. Finally, the people of the town would call upon the Madders for medical questions. Jonathan would be able to diagnose, and Margaret would treat. It became a wonderful partnership, and the townspeople started to trust Margaret much more.

Whenever they went into Philadelphia to see Dr. Potts, Sara made sure to look in upon Hamilton. He was usually extremely busy writing or discussing political matters with someone, but on the rare occasion he had time, they were able to talk for a little bit. She found he was able to relax in her presence, but he still seemed a bit distant at times. One day she decided to press the issue a little bit more.

"Hamilton, is everything all right with you? I am concerned," she asked.

He began to ask why she would question him but knew he couldn't hide who he was from her. "I am struggling to get Congress to understand just how weak the Articles of Confederation really is. We don't have the power a government needs to survive. Some people realize we need more to stabilize our situation, but they are still falling short. If only Lau—" he cut himself off.

"Laurence was with you. You were a great team getting things done with Washington," Sara finished.

"We had the same views. Did you know I invited him to join me here?" he finally said sadly.

"I just feel like I am doing this with my right arm cut off. Plus I need to do it right for him. I owe him that." His mood totally changed and got harder after that comment. He did not wish to discuss this topic anymore, and Sara heard his body language loud and clear.

"Well, it seems like Dr. Madder will still be able to practice at least with Margaret's help," she said to change the subject. It worked as Hamilton's body and tone calmed down as they continued talking.

"I am happy to hear that, and what about his hands, are they any better?" he asked.

"Yes, he is getting more movement in his fingers every day. I tried to help him, but sometimes you just need your partner," she said, slipping in the hint.

"You know, I have been thinking of writing Betsy to join me here with Philip as it looks like I will be here for some time. It would do her well to have you stop by from time to time," he said.

"I would enjoy that very much," Sara offered as a knock came upon his door.

"For now, I will excuse myself and allow you to have your meeting," Sara said, gathering her things and walking to the door.

"Just remember, I am here for you anytime you need me, all right?" she offered.

"Thank you for your understanding and compassion," he said, opening the door revealing James Monroe.

The looks he gave Sara as she stood there felt very uncomfortable and she guessed rumors would be starting. Seeing the looks on both faces, Hamilton introduced them to each other.

"I believe you to have met at least in passing," he said with a smile on his face.

"Mr. Monroe, this is Sara Weinstein, General Washington's niece, who accompanied us during the war. Sara, this is James Monroe. He was wounded at the Battle of Trenton, so I believe you saw him in the hospital," he suggested.

"Not likely, that is when I was sick and with the Madders," she said, reminding him.

"Oh yes, and then you took off for Princeton," Hamilton replied.

"So you are the woman who fought at Princeton. I heard about that," Mr. Monroe said, extending his hand. "And that also means you were the one who fought off those men in Trenton before crossing the river."

"That would be me," she said, laughing with a smile toward Hamilton.

"Well, I will leave you to your business. It was a pleasure meeting you, sir," she said as she took her leave.

As the holiday seasons came and passed, the bodies and soles of the Madder household were showing the healing power humans have. Tom was able to move about the house and participate with his family. Jonathan and Margaret were working seamlessly together with his hands and the medical needs of the town. Sara did what she could to help keep the house in order with June. She did not want to tell June she heard about her brother and bring up another argument. She decided to just keep the conversations general, and if June wanted to talk about anything, she could take the lead. June, however, was much more appreciative of the extra help with the large number of people in the house. Sara took over the laundry, cleaned the sitting room, and helped with cooking. June needed to teach her how to do everything correctly for this house, and Sara was happy with the instruction.

During this time, Sara exchanged letters with the Washingtons, the Hamiltons, and Lafayette. Margaret explained she received notice that Charles had passed away and asked if there was anything she could do. She also explained how much she was enjoying Mt. Vernon with her grandchildren during the holidays but desperately missed George. George still wouldn't provide specific locations but hinted at possibly going through Philadelphia in the spring. He was also doing well and hadn't seen any major battles since her departure. Eliza accepted Hamilton's invitation to join him and would be traveling to Philadelphia shortly. Finally, Lafayette, as he put it, was promoted to maréchal de camp. He was still trying to get the freedom for his country that was so close to this one now. He told her of an American delegate named Thomas Jefferson, who helped him write a declaration for France the way he did for his own country. Most of his letter regarded Hamilton, though. He also received word that Laurens had died in battle and was worried about his friend. Since he was so far away, he was hoping Sara (being the closest left to Hamilton from their small family) could guide him through it.

Later in January, Eliza stopped by the Madders' house before continuing to Philadelphia. Chance took one look at Philip and got excited seeing the small child. He laid down and crawled up to Philip providing a small kiss. When the boy started to giggle, Chance got scared and looked at Sara for direction. Seeing the smile on Sara and Eliza's faces, his tail started wagging faster, and he continued to kiss Philip causing belly laughs.

When they pulled themselves away from the two on the floor, Eliza asked, "Have you been in to see Alexander lately?"

"I try to go see him whenever I get the chance," Sara said.

"His letter requesting me to join him sounded, well, is he all right?" Eliza asked cautiously.

"He is struggling, that is true. I do believe with your arrival, you can help him work through his thoughts. And little Philip here will help him forget for a time," Sara offered.

They spent the rest of the afternoon talking and letting Philip exude his energy as they still had a long ride ahead. It was only after Philip fell asleep on Chance's stomach that Eliza decided to continue on.

"Please come out to see us whenever you can?" she offered. "I will come out as much as my time allows," Sara said as the carriage started off.

"And if you want, bring Chance, he is a wonderful babysitter." They laughed.

During the next few days, snow began to fall and just didn't let up. "This reminds me of Morristown in '78," Sara said, looking out the window. June and Sara would gather eggs and spend much of their time in the cookhouse.

"I remember that winter, not much better here," June answered.

Sara started taking inventory of what supplies they had left as June cooked a soup. "We are going to need some wheat soon," she said out loud.

"Don't worry, we will make it work," June stated.

"I just don't know how you do it? We don't have supplies, yet you still create enough food to feed everyone," Sara stated, turning toward June.

"Just gotta know what you can replace something with," June said, still not giving up her secrets.

"I remember once Mama used crushed straw for grain and didn't tell no one." She laughed. "They all ate it up, though," she continued with a smile.

"I never heard you talk about your Mama before. What was she like?" Sara asked.

"She was the strongest woman I knew. Was up before four, started in the kitchen, helping Joe the cook get things going. Then she would scrub the floors before anyone could mess it up further. She would bring the rugs outback, and she and I would beat those rugs clean. I would help her set the table and bring out the food before the family came down. Only then would we go out to the kitchen and have some porridge before cleaning up the dishes from breakfast. Jimmy would go and gather the firewood so we could wash the clothes and linens. Before you knew it, it was lunch, and things started over again. After the lunch dishes, we would mend what needed mendin'. Jimmy would chase the chickens and gather the eggs. She would then take care of dinner and put us to bed as she washed those dishes herself. She might show up two or three hours later before she got to clean our cabin and take care of her own mendin'."

"I don't know how she took care of it all. By the time I was old enough to help her out more, they got more help, so she wasn't weighed down so much. However, she always made sure Jimmy and I were happy and taken care of. That was until…" Her voice trailed off. Her face that was happy dreaming about the past turned agonizing, remembering the events of her life.

"I'm sorry, I didn't mean to upset you," Sara said.

June seemed to come back to the present and saw Sara there. "Not your fault, but may I ask you a favor?" June questioned.

"Sure, anything!" Sara replied.

"If you take that family in, please don't split them up," June said with tears in her eyes.

"I don't plan to own them, June. They will remain free," Sara said.

"That's good, Miss Real Good," June said, then went quiet.

"What are you two doing in here?" Amber said from behind them.

"There is not much room left in the house, and this is the warmest place around." Sara laughed.

"Well then, do you mind if I help?" Amber asked, looking for relief.

"Sure, as long as you tell us how you and Tom met," Sara asked. Sara figured she went too far again as the look on Amber's face went down. "I am sorry, I just meant to start a conversation, not cause an issue," Sara said, feeling even more guilty than she did a moment before.

"Tom and I were both free when we met. We were born in a small town out west, so we knew each other from the start. When we grew up, he was working as a blacksmith, and I was helping my Momma with laundry in our town. We would walk by his work every day to get water, and he would hand me a flower when Momma wasn't looking. Six months later, we got married," she said.

"That's so sweet!" June said. "Would you mind if I ask what happened?" June questioned.

"Well, Samuel was about a year old when the war started, and everyone in our town either joined the fight or moved away. We were traveling when we were picked up by some men. They didn't believe we was free and was going to kill us. Tom pleaded with them and agreed to enslave himself if we could remain free," she said sadly. "As the war raged on, those men left to join, and we were able to make a run for it, this time going north," she finished.

Sara didn't know how to respond to this story, so she remained quiet. June, however, spoke up. "Damn folks thinking they can do anything they want."

Sara finally tried to add her own opinion. "I agree. This needs to be stopped. I hope Hamilton can do something about it in Congress," she said.

"I won't hold my breath. I heard people talk about it, but they never actually take action," Amber said.

"I would agree with that when it comes to most people. However, it was something that was very important to Hamilton,

Laurens, and myself. We discussed the issue often, and he doesn't care about saving face. He cares about what is right." Sara offered. They discussed the matter for a while until Tommy came out and told his mother he was hungry. They realized they talked right through mealtime and almost burnt the food.

Over the next few months, Jonathan and Tom's healing was going very well, and they both started getting a better range of motion. Sara put ads in the newspapers requesting beef and lamb stock from around New Jersey to be delivered in early spring. Some farms responded to her, and she was able to order a hundred head of beef and fifty head of lamb to be sent to Morven. She also made arrangements for two more horses to pull the wagon she purchased. Sara would occasionally ride to Philadelphia to see Eliza and try to stay long enough to say hi to Hamilton. All too often, he would not return for meals and stay until well late in the evening. Eliza was doing well and able to regain friendships she started when her father took her here after Hamilton asked for her hand. Then there was Philip; he seemed to be growing in leaps and bounds every time Sara saw him.

One day when she entered, he stood up and said, "Chance?"

"No, sorry, he stayed home today," Sara answered, shocked she was having a conversation with him.

The winter started to change to spring and become warmer. It was then that Sara decided to head back to Princeton and her tavern. On her way out to Tyler's farm, she picked up the two horses she purchased and decided to name one George and the other Washington. This time, Tyler had the tables and chairs, bar stools, and beds finished. He also created a sign for her to hang: *The Little Phoenix Tavern*. She thanked him for everything he had done so far. He then told her he would bring the end tables to her when they were completed. They put everything in the wagon, hitched up the horses, and tied Storm to the back.

On the ride back to the Madders' house, she found herself getting excited about finally opening her tavern and taking full control of her life. The spring season started entering her senses on a much higher lever. The warmth of the sun was hugging her, and the fragrance of the blooming flowers was sweeter than she ever noticed before. She was on the verge of a new chapter in her life, and the joy of the moment was bubbling out of her with giggles. She couldn't help it, nor did she want to stop it. This was one of the happiest moments in her life, just short of running around the military camp as a child.

Chapter *19*

Little Phoenix Opens

W hen they pulled into Princeton, she could see the second floor of the tavern had been finished. There was also a pile of lumber on the side for the barn and fencing. She pulled the wagon up to the front door and stepped down. Tom, Amber, and the boys were admiring the building before getting down. Jack walked up, greeting Sara, and invited them inside. She introduced Jack to the Johnsons, causing Jack to remember the paper.

"You're that free black who pulled the doctor out of the house, aren't you?" he asked.

"Yes, he is the one who went into the stable," Sara answered as Tom was quiet.

"Well, Dr. Madder has done this town a wonderful service over the years," Jack said.

"It was my pleasure. He saved my son's arm as well," Tom replied.

Upon stepping in through the door, the first thing they noticed was the large river stone fireplace greeting them. To the right was the bar bending around to the stairs and to the left the open space for the tables. Next to the fireplace were two doors; one led to the basement, and the other led to the bedrooms and outback. The dark mahogany of the bar was in clear contrast to the white and blue walls throughout. Jack then took them upstairs and showed them the bedrooms and privies on that floor. There was just enough space for the beds and end tables per room. Jack showed her where the next stairway would be to go up to her quarters. Seeing everything in reality, she became fearful of the situation.

"What is wrong, miss? Isn't this what you wanted?" Jack asked.

"Yes, it is what I asked for, but this is the floor I was on when our home was set on fire. I was able to get out through the window and off the first-floor roof. If this goes up another level, there is no way I can get down should that happen again," she said.

He started looking around and took notice of her concern. "I am not sure how to fix that right now, but I will think about it," he told Sara.

They went back downstairs and entered the back room, where two more bedrooms were located. These were larger than the ones upstairs. "You can decide who gets which room," Sara said.

"You mean Samuel and I get our own room!" Tommy asked.

"Yes, and it also means so does your mom and dad, so you can't bother them, all right?" Sara said.

The boys started jumping up and down, running between the rooms trying to choose. The adults walked out back and across to the kitchen.

"I am so impressed with everything you have accomplished, Jack," Sara said.

This was a one-story building with two fireplaces for cooking and a long table across for food preparation. He also added iron hooks from the ceiling for drying herbs and anything they needed to hang. As they walked back toward the house, Sara pointed to the left of the kitchen and asked Amber if she thought that would be a good spot for a garden.

"I think that will do just nicely, and maybe a chicken coop over here," she said, pointing next to the kitchen.

"That sounds like a good idea," Sara said.

They walked back into the tavern and heard there a knock at the door. Annis walked in, calling for Sara, asking if she was there.

"Annis, hello. How are you doing?" Sara asked, walking back into the main room.

"I saw your wagon out front and thought it might be you," Annis said, giving Sara a hug.

"Is everything all right?" Sara questioned.

"Yes, it is wonderful. The beef and lambs you purchased arrived the other day. I can't thank you enough," she answered.

"It is my pleasure," Sara said.

"This is the Johnsons. They will be helping me here," Sara introduced everyone.

"Come, boys, help me unload the cart," Tom said to his sons.

"I don't want to interrupt you, so I will let you get things set up. If you wish to join me for dinner, I would love to talk with you."

They began to unload the furniture and other items from the wagon. Sara's take-charge attitude kicked in as she told them where each item belonged. When she went back into the tavern, it began to come alive. If possible, it looked much more inviting than it did before. The tables and chairs were set up in the open area. The stools were set in front of the bar. Tom was putting some of the mugs on the shelves behind the bar. Amber was upstairs setting up the beds with the straw pads, goose feather toppings, and quilts that Sara and Margaret made. Some of the items they could not use right away were taken to the basement for storage, like the silver and Sara's bed.

"Where are you planning on sleeping, Miss Sara?" Samuel asked.

"I will have to figure that out. I am not sure yet," she answered.

"You can have our room, Miss Sara. We can stay with Mom and Dad until your room is ready," Tommy suggested.

"Well, that is very thoughtful of you, thank you." Sara smiled at the boys. "Jack, tomorrow I would like to start on fencing and a barn for the horses," Sara suggested. "I would prefer Tom not do that until his strength is back completely. Do you know someone who may be able to do that for me?"

"There is a bulletin board up by the church. You can post something there. You should be fine asking for a basic fence and barn from the boys around here," Jack suggested.

Sara decided to take the first room up on the second floor allowing the boys to have their room. As she was dressing for dinner, a knock came on her door.

Amber requested entry and said, "I can't thank you enough for what you are doing for us, Sara. However, I want to ask you to be careful, for our sake. I saw enough coming into this town to know they are still very happy with slavery. I am worried someone will start asking questions and find out about Tom," she said.

"We all know how you feel about us, but Tom's safety is most important to me," Amber said.

"I care about his safety as well, but I thought that is why we burned down the barn?" Sara said. "Besides, when I introduced him to Jack, he knew Tom as the free man who saved Dr. Madder," Sara stated.

"Yes, but free black people are also treated very differently than everyone else. They are even kidnaped and sold down south even though they are free," Amber said.

"Well, if anyone tried to take any one of you, they would have to go through me first. Then through this town. They may still believe in slavery here, but they will fight for their own," Sara said.

On the way to dinner, she stopped at the church to post the advertisement for help. Upon arrival, Annis walked Sara into the sitting, where she saw a couple sitting on the couch.

"Do you know Aaron and Theodosia Burr?" Annis asked.

"I recognize the names, but I don't believe we ever formally met," Sara said, offering her hand and providing her name.

"Theodosia and I became very acquainted when I traveled into Philadelphia," Annis told Sara.

"They were married last summer!" she continued.

"Well, congratulations to the both of you. I hope you will be very happy, and by the looks of things, I would say so," Sara said as Theodosia held onto her belly.

As small conversation continued before dinner, Sara felt they were a pleasant young couple who were very entertaining. This was the type of people Annis usually associates with. She did, however, notice Mr. Burr was very shady about any opinions and usually just let his wife answer.

"Sara, I wanted to talk with you about the tavern. Even though Princeton is starting to get back to normal without the British occupation, the feeling around town has not been as successful. When you are ready to open, why don't we have a ball?" Annis asked.

"That sounds like a good idea. I think I will want to do that, thank you," Sara said.

"A ball, I haven't been to a ball in ages. Would you mind if I helped plan the event?" Theodosia offered. "That would be wonderful, thank you," Annis said.

The remainder of the evening was dedicated to planning the ball between Theodosia and Annis. Sara's eyes just bounced back and forth between the two ladies listening to their planning.

"I guess I should be glad I don't have to plan this thing. That is not an area I excel," Sara said to Aaron.

"I am sure you would have been fine." He smiled back.

The next afternoon, several college-age boys arrived regarding the ad she posted. They settled on a price for completed work and began the job. She had Tom start cooking for the workers while Amber helped her go through the kitchenware and put that away. While they were busy unpacking, a knock came on the door. A gentleman handed Sara a letter and asked where he should put his delivery. She looked out the door and saw a wagon full of barrels.

"What the—" she stuttered and began to read the letter.

My dearest Sara,

Here is a supply of the south's best bear and whisky for you to start your tavern.
We wish you well with your endeavor and hope to see you soon.

Love,
Uncle George and Aunt Martha

She stared at the wagon for a while before looking at the gentleman again. It looked to contain ten barrels of each drink for her to start with. "I guess just bring them downstairs and put them in the cellar," she said. When Tom was finished cooking the meal, Sara rang a triangle bell calling the men to eat. The boys would run the food from the kitchen to the tavern while Amber and Sara dished out the food to the men. Most of them came around again for more saying how much they enjoyed the food. When everyone went back to work, Amber and Sara started to clean everything.

"That was a wonderful trial run for us," Sara said.

"Yes, I feel that went smoothly," Amber said. "Now for the evening meal." Amber laughed.

When the dishes were done and put away, Sara walked around to where the boys were building the barn. Two of the boys have made it halfway around the paddock while the other two boys had the stable almost finished. Jack walked up behind her, looking out to what the boys had done.

"Looking good," he said, startling her.

"Yes, but I still want you to build the main stable once we have the revenue."

"Sure, but I wanted to talk to you about your other situation," he said.

"I don't think going up will rid your safety concern so how about we build out. Start at the hallway and pull around over here for your rooms," he said as he pointed out the plan to Sara.

"I think I will feel a lot better on the ground," she said, a bit ashamed of her worry.

"No problem, and with keeping things on the ground, it will shorten the amount of time needed to build," he said.

After a week of supplying the meals for the workers, she started selling meals at half price. She was worried that the men would be upset with her, but they were more than willing to by the food. The boys had finished the barn and fence, giving Storm, George, and Washington room to run and play. However, there was a nice pile of leftover wood Tom and Sara used to build a chicken coop.

"Now, all we need is wire and chickens," Sara said, looking at what they built.

"Things are going really well here. When do you think we will open for overnight guests?" Tom asked.

"I am hoping soon, I have to start recovering from all my expenses," Sara said.

"Did you start off too aggressive?" Tom asked.

"I started off right, but now I want to see it grow," she answered. "Since your food is already drawing a crowd, I am anticipating good things." She smiled at him. "I am glad we are this close to the college. It allows for that crowd that I never thought about."

Annis had asked if they could meet again at the tavern to discuss the ball and set a date. After agreeing with this, Sara also wrote to Eliza to join them so she might have someone to talk with. A buggy rode up to the tavern as they started back inside. To her surprise, Eliza, Philip, and Alexander exited the buggy.

"Well, hello, is everything all right," she asked, welcoming them into the tavern. Chance heard the voices and ran over to Philip to say hello.

"Everything is fine. I hope you are all right with my arrival. I needed to get step away," Hamilton told her.

"Well, sir, you are always welcome here. You have an open invitation," she said, giving them hugs. "Annis and the Burrs will be along shortly," she said.

"The Burrs, do you mean Aaron and Theodosia?" Eliza said.

"Yes, are you acquainted with them?" Sara asked.

"Yes, he is working as a lawyer in New York as well," Hamilton said.

Amber walked into the room with her boys. "Oh, I am sorry I interrupted you," she said as she started escorting the boys back out.

"No, please don't leave Amber. I want to introduce you to my friends. This is Alexander, Eliza, and Philip Hamilton. And this is Amber, Tommy, and Samuel Johnson," Sara said. Sara guided everyone to the nearest table and sat down to talk. She also pulled the other tables close so they could all be together once the other guests arrived.

"Do you plan on staying a few days?" Sara asked.

"If you don't mind, I think Alexander would do well with a weekend away from Congress," Eliza stated.

"That is fine with me, are your things in the buggy?" Sara asked.

"I hid a bag in the back, so Alexander didn't know we were going to stay." Eliza smiled.

Hamilton grumbled as he stood up to go get the bag when Sara told him to sit and relax. She would take care of everything.

She went outside and unhitched the horse, letting them run in the paddock. When she got back, Hamilton was there at the back of the wagon.

"I didn't know she was going to stay, but I guess she is right. I could use a small break," he said.

"What is going on?" Sara asked.

"I just thought we would be doing important work and not voting on how to vote," Hamilton said.

"Oh, that…sounds…horrible. I am sorry, there is no other way to put it," Sara said.

"It is. There is so much work we need to do to secure the future of this country and these men have no clue how to do it. Worse yet, they are not willing to listen to anyone with ideas," he grumbled. "Then when I try to say anything, they complain that I want to start another monarch!" He almost shouted.

"Okay, well, you are away for the moment. It sounds like you don't have to worry about them making any important decisions until your return so just relax and enjoy your family," Sara offered.

They gave each other a hug and heard "I don't believe that one is your wife Hamilton" from behind them.

"Aaron Burr, how are things going in New York while I toil away in Philadelphia?" Hamilton said.

"Well, you do realize they elected you for Congress because they knew I would be able to take care of the legal situations without you," Burr said, laughing as they shook hands.

"Mrs. Burr, I do pity your decision in a husband, but I enjoy your company," Hamilton said.

"Sara, you better watch out for this one. He may give you a bad reputation," Burr said to Sara.

"I know Hamilton's reputation and past history very well," Sara provided.

Burr gave her a questionable look when she finally revealed her relationship with the Washingtons and how she spent time with Hamilton, Laurens, and Lafayette during the war.

"Look who I found!" Sara said as they entered the tavern.

As everyone was greeting each other, Sara took the Hamiltons' belongings up to a bedroom. When she returned downstairs, everyone was looking around admiring the tavern.

"This looks amazing, Sara. I wish you the best of luck with it," Annis said.

"Thank you, I am really excited about how it turned out," Sara said, stepping behind the bar. "Is anyone thirsty?" she asked.

As she was pouring the drinks, Theodosia asked Sara if she had anyone special in her life. "Well, I did. I was engaged, and this tavern was our dream. That is why it means so much to me," Sara told her.

"I am sorry to hear that, but you know, if you outlive your husband, it is all right to find another. I did," she said.

"Well, thank you for the advice, but I am not looking right now. We will see where life takes me," Sara said back.

Tom started to bring the food into the room, and the aroma that filled the air made your mouth water. "Do you need any help bringing in more food, Tom?" Sara asked.

"No, thank you, I just have two loaves of bread that I will get in a moment," he replied.

"All right, I will get the dishes then. Everyone, start taking your seats please," she said.

When she put the bowls down for the stew, the Johnsons were surprised she set the table to include them. "Are you sure you want us there, Sara?" Amber asked.

"I am positive. We will be discussing the opening of the tavern, which you are very much a part of," Sara said.

When everyone was seated, Sara blessed the food and thanked Tom for making it. The feeling and conversation started out awkward. Hamilton decided to ask Tom about the fire in Morrisville, Pennsylvania, and how he was doing now. This began a long conversation of heroism and running into the line of fire for the men and Ball details for the ladies. By the end of the evening, they decided to keep the tavern open for dining but have the grand opening ball in three weeks.

The day of the ball arrived, and Annis, Eliza, and Theodosia came early in the day to help decorate and set up. Since summer had arrived, it was warm enough to have more tables set up outside, giving plenty of room for the entire town. Tom was already preparing a full barbecue that you could smell from the other side of town. He had already smoked most of the meats days before, so as they were cooking, he also prepared the side items like potatoes, carrots, onions, beets, and breads. Annis brought five of her servants to help with the party so Sara could properly host instead of serving during it. The Schuylers had sent down a gift of rum, tea, and brandy from the north. Sara had invited them, the Washingtons and the Madders, but wasn't sure if anyone would be able to make it. When the entertainment started to arrive, the ladies went off to get dressed for the event. Amber went to help Sara put on the dress Martha got for her years before.

"I am beginning to think this was a bad idea. I am not comfortable with these arrangements," Sara said as Amber was cinching her corset. "Are you and Tom all right with this?" Sara asked.

"We feel the more we lay low right now, the better for Tom. The news of the fire spread the way we wanted, but there is reason to be concerned about someone hunting for us," Amber said.

The evening went better than Sara expected. The people from the town were impressed with the facility and food that was being served. They were all having a good time dancing and talking among themselves. The Madders were able to make it and show Sara just how well Jonathan was doing. He almost had full range of motion back in both hands. Hamilton even took Sara around the floor a few times when he wasn't dancing with Eliza.

"We never got a chance to do this before," he said during their first dance.

"No, you were busy that night keeping everyone else off Eliza." Sara laughed.

By the time the night started to quiet down, Sara's feet hurt worse than any day she had spent with the army. When everyone else went to bed, she kicked her shoes off and helped Amber clean up.

The serving of food and drink allowed Sara to see some profit. Occasionally there would be someone riding through who would need a place to sleep, but that area of her business started out very slowly. One day as they were preparing for the afternoon meal, Sara received a letter from Washington.

Dear Sara,

I received your invitation for the ball that would open your tavern. I wish I could be there as I love a good ball as you very well know. However, keeping the British contained in New York has me detained too far away to join you. I did receive a notification the other day from General Patterson. He informed me that one of his light infantryman was shot in the shoulder and developed a fever. It was only then that Robert Shurtiff was found to be Deborah Sampson. It seems like your little stunt in Princeton has caused others to take up arms. You know I care about you, but would you please keep your crazy ideals to yourself and out of my army!

G. Washington

After she read the letter, all she could do was laugh. When Amber asked what was going on, Sara told her that more women have decided to fight for freedom themselves. I think we started a woman's movement to get out of the shadow of men. They were both laughing and talking about it when patrons started entering the tavern for the meal.

The next few months went along with business starting to pick up from word of mouth. As members of Congress started traveling more, the rooms were starting to be used. Sara and Amber worked together on creating an efficient flow for the tavern chores. They split up the rooms so they would each take care of three. They were both needed to serve the food drinks during mealtimes as well as clean the dishes afterward. Finally, Amber took over the laundry while Sara calculated the inventory and purchased more supplies. The boys would take care of the garden they created, fill a well with water, and take care of the animals. It quickly became a seamless routine that ran efficiently.

One evening James Monroe came into the tavern looking for Sara. "Well, hello there, how can I help you, Mr. Monroe?" Sara said, walking out from the back.

"Hamilton said you may be able to put me up for the evening before I continue onto New York," he said.

"Sure, I have a room you may use. Are you also in need of a meal?" she asked. "

That would be wonderful, thank you," he replied. There were a few other men sitting at the bar drinking, so James asked for Sara to meet him at a table.

"Here is a bowl of stew and a beer," she said, walking over to him.

"Can you sit for a moment?" he asked.

"Sure, is something wrong?" she asked.

"No, but I can't have anyone else overhearing," he said with his eyes looking all around. She looked around just like he did and asked if he could talk yet.

"How well do you know Hamilton?" he asked. To this, Sara became cautious.

"Let's just say I know him," she responded.

"Well, be careful around him," he said.

"Why do you say that?" she questioned.

"He has some decent ideas regarding finances. However, he wants to take away your slaves," he stated.

"He does, how do you know this?" she asked.

"He was pushing for that young Laurens's idea of a black battalion. Just be careful," he said.

"Well, thank you for warning me," she answered.

He took a spoonful of stew and quickly changed the subject. "This is really good. The food at the taverns in Philadelphia don't taste like this."

"Well, thank you, I am very proud of our cook," she answered.

"You should be proud of everything you created here," James said.

"Well, I have to get back to work, but I will be back to talk with you some more, all right?" she asked. She figured she should keep a close eye on James for Hamilton's sake.

Once the final three men departed, and it was just James Monroe, Sara sat back down with him. "Hamilton said you were injured at Trenton? Do you mind if I ask what happened?" she questioned.

"Musket ball to the shoulder," he told her.

"Really, I was hit in the shoulder in White Marsh," she said.

"That was you? I heard about that, which means you were the one who picked up the gun at Princeton!" This started a long conversation regarding the war, the people, and their travels.

"The worst part for me was the fever. I don't think I have ever been so tired before or since," she said.

"Speaking of tired, I need to depart early tomorrow for New York, so I should retire," he said.

"Well, you get a breakfast when you stay overnight, so please, if you cannot wait for a hot meal, get some dried meat, cheese, and bread before you leave," she told him.

Sara started overhearing conversations in the bar about meetings that were taking place in Paris. Our representatives were very close to bringing an end of the war. Finally, in late September, the news came.

FREEDOM!

Franklin, Adams, and Jay, along with France, get Britain to recognize American independence and agree to end the war! The remaining British forces in New York must depart by November 25, taking any Tory sympathizer back to England with them!

There was a full range of emotions with this news. Some people were excited that the fight was finally over, and they were free. Others were scared, not knowing what was going to happen next. Then there were some that had lost so much in the war. It really didn't matter to them. Sara decided to ride to Philadelphia and talk with Eliza and Hamilton. There was no shock to find when she arrived, Hamilton was still at Congress. Eliza and Sara were able to rejoice in the news and discuss the hope for the future.

"I always believed in our cause and have tremendous hope for our future. And next weekend, I will be giving my vote for Congress representatives in New Jersey," Sara said.

"You're going to be allowed to vote? I heard rumors but didn't think it was true," Eliza said.

"It is true, and I am not the only one. If you are a single lady with property and fifty pounds, you have the right to vote," Sara said proudly.

"The direction this country is going in is very encouraging indeed," Eliza said.

"How is Hamilton doing with everything?" Sara asked. "He is helping to ratify the peace treaty, then we will be going back to New York when he will go back to being a lawyer. He just doesn't feel he is getting anywhere with this Congress," Eliza said.

"Well, I guess we know why they were so bad at helping the army during the war," Sara said.

Hamilton stormed in and walked right past the two ladies and went upstairs. Eliza and Sara just stared at each other for a minute, and Hamilton came back down.

"Betsy, I need to take a moment and head back to Congress in about two hours. Please…oh, Sara, how long have you been here?" he asked.

"I arrived a few hours ago. I wanted to celebrate the end of the war with you," Sara said as they hugged each other.

"Yes, that is wonderful news. Did James stop by your tavern? I suggested it," he said. "Thank you so very much. Yes, he was able to stop by," she said.

"It does seem, however, he doesn't like the fact that you wish to include the slaves in this freedom," she told him.

"James and so many others. That is going to be a difficult mountain to climb," he said.

"We have come so far and still have a long way to go," Sara offered.

"If only I could talk with you about just how far, but I took an oath," Hamilton grumbled.

Sara didn't even think he meant to say that much. "Is there anything I can do to help you?" she asked.

"No, I'm fine. I just came home to eat before going back," he said.

"Well, I will go get you something," Eliza said, looking woebegone.

"It seems like you don't normally come home in the afternoon for a meal," Sara prodded.

However, when he looked at her and just said "*Sara*," she knew to let it go.

"Eliza said you are going back to New York and to your practice, that must make you happy," she tried. Again he just looked at her. "Okay, what topic can I discuss with you?"

"I wasn't expecting you to be here," he said.

"Do you wish me to leave?" she said a bit angrily.

"*No*, no, that is not what I meant. I was just expecting to spend some time with my wife. You know I am always happy to see you."

"Well, maybe, I should go if that is what you were expecting," Sara said.

"Honestly, Sara, your presence helps me calm down as well. I just can't talk with you about everything I would like to." He smiled.

Eliza came back out with some dried meat, bread, and cheese. Hamilton just looked at it and sighed.

"I wasn't expecting you home so soon, dear," she said, trying to smile. They all sat down and talked a bit longer before Sara and Hamilton needed to return.

That weekend Sara rose out of bed, got dressed, and went downstairs like it was any other day. However, it was a very important day for her. Amber gave her a shawl and wished her good luck. She walked out into the sunshine and took a deep breath. It was getting colder, but she couldn't feel more warmth inside. She walked halfway up the street and found Annis waiting for her.

"Are you ready?" Annis said.

"I have my paperwork right here. Let's go," Sara said back.

With that, they walked to the church where they were going to cast their vote for a representative to Congress. They took their place in line surrounded by men and waited patiently. When it was her turn, Sara stepped up to a table where she showed the paperwork of her ownership of the tavern. She was handed a piece of paper, wrote down the name of William Huston, the person she felt best to represent what she believed in, folded the paper, and put it into a small wooden box. When she stepped out of line and waited for Annis, she could see there were other women in line about to do the same thing. Annis finished with her vote, took Sara by the arm, and they both walked back to the tavern for a celebratory meal.

"I finally feel like I am home. A place that accepts me for me," she said emotionally. A few days passed before getting the results of the election. *Hopefully, these men will be able to move us forward*, Sara thought to herself.

Now that New York and Philadelphia became two major areas for the government, there were more people moving about the country. Sara's tavern became a very popular place for people seeking rest and food as they traveled. She would go to Annis's and used the excuse that she was there to make sure the herds were doing well. Her main objective, however, was to talk with Annis and step away for a bit. They found they had more in common now than when they were younger. Since Annis was still writing poetry and crossing those boundaries, it created a bond between the ladies. They really enjoyed each other's company since they each lost their significant other. They also encouraged and supported each other to go after whatever they wanted.

News that the British departed New York finally arrived, bringing a visual end to the war. Sara received a letter from Hamilton telling her about possible new laws in New York allowing Patriots to collect damages from Loyalists who took over their property. He wrote, "I think I am going to be very busy if this happens. We need to come together as a nation and not take out anger on these people. They are our brothers and sisters, and the world is watching us. We must show compassion for them." She was always so impressed with his ability to take on multiple intense projects at one time.

The days were beginning to move much faster now, and one day started to run into the next. Everything became so repetitive that she would get excited about receiving mail. Anything to break up the monotony. One day she received a letter from George that caught her off guard.

My dearest Sara,

I am writing to you believing you already heard the war is over. We have finally won our freedom from Britain and can move on. With that, I have also decided to move on. I wish to return to Mt. Vernon and spend the rest of my days quietly with Martha. That being said, I wanted to let you know I will be resigning as commander in chief upon my arrival in Philadelphia. It seems forever ago that I took this position, and I regretfully have lost too many people because of it. I stayed in the position because many more people would have died if I didn't. Now that the realities of tyranny are over, it is my duty to relinquish the power of this great

nation back to Congress. I was honored to accept
this great responsibility, and I am relieved to relin-
quish it. I just wanted you to hear it from me. I pray
you are doing well and will see you soon.

G. Washington

Sara didn't know how to take this news. She was happy for her uncle to return to Mr. Vernon but knew Congress was not able to run itself, let alone the country. As she discussed her concerns with Annis, she said, "Well, I hope the men we voted in are smart enough to lead or at least smart enough to listen to others who can lead."

"Better yet, I hope the ladies behind these men are smart enough to direct them." Annis laughed.

Over the next few months, Sara realized she needed to hire a few more people to help with the tavern. One evening a young couple who fought in the war and lost their home to the same entered. James and Donna Fisher were hoping to get some scraps, but Sara took them in and offered them jobs. She found out they were from Rhode Island and came down to Princeton after the army disbanded looking for work. Beyond that, they really didn't say too much and kept to themselves. Arrangements were made with Annis for the Fishers to stay with her as there was limited room at the tavern. Sara divided up the daily chores so that Donna would help Amber with the bedrooms, laundry, and serving. James would take over the slaughter of animals, make repairs, and take care of the horses and tack. Sara still kept track of the books and served at the bar where she could keep her eyes and ears open.

Again, with help from Annis, they decided to celebrate the holidays at the tavern with more parties.

As they were celebrating, Sara received a newspaper saying General Washington resigned power to Congress in Philadelphia on December 23, which caused a lot of confusion around town. Most people felt safe with Washington in charge and felt anyone could attack now that he resigned. Sara tried to tell people he would return if he was needed, but they didn't believe her. Most still didn't know of her relationship with the Washingtons, and she didn't push the issue. She just tried to keep people calm and have them trust the process.

Hamilton kept to his word and stopped by the tavern on their way home in January after the treaty was signed by Congress. He told Sara about Washington walking into Congress one day and resigning his command, shocking the entire group. Hamilton, however, knew him well enough not to be shocked by his decision.

"I have found, however, not to resent him anymore. I have a much greater place for him in my heart now. I realized it after Yorktown when I almost lost my chance to meet Philip. Since we have been apart, it has developed into greater respect," Hamilton told Sara.

"So you finally know what it means to be part of his family," Sara said back. He looked at her wanting to say something but couldn't find the words.

"Wow, I shut up the great speaker Hamilton for a second time," she chastised him. "Then again, now you are looking after others yourself so you may understand where he is coming from a bit more," she suggested. You could see the thoughts processing through his mind, but again, he stayed quiet.

"So do you have a lot of clients waiting for you back in New York?" she asked to change the subject.

"I have people asking me questions, so I am hoping to get right back to work when I return," he said. "I am most excited to see the city without the British occupancy," he said with a smile. "And to be honest, I am glad to be stepping away from Congress and getting to be a father, husband, and provider," he said.

"You will be happy with that for a small time, but you will not be satisfied with that forever," Sara said. "You need variety way too much!" she joked.

The Hamiltons finished their meal and continued onto New York. "Please let me know where you end up so I can stop by and surprise you," Sara called after them.

A few weeks later, she received letters from both the Hamiltons and the Washingtons. It seemed that the Hamilton's found a place on Wall Street to live. This allowed him close access to the Burrs and the rest of his colleagues. It also allowed Eliza to further her friendship with Theodosia. It seemed they were doing really well in this stage of their life. As for George, he was very happy being back home with Martha and their children. His primary goal at this point was to remain this way for the rest of his life.

As the military began to disband, the single men who went through Princeton stopped at the tavern hoping for a meal and possibly a place to sleep even if it was outside. Sara, however, would allow anyone who fought in the war and was traveling home to get breakfast and supper and a bed to sleep in without payment. At the beginning, men would get upset for the acts of charity that felt more like a handout. She then posted a sign stating she would accept the military funds (that had no real value) in exchange for the food and bed. This created a feeling of honor within these men to pay for this service even though no one else would accept the notes.

One afternoon as she was talking with Amber and washing laundry, Amber asked, "What are you going to do with all the military notes?"

"Well, I am just going to keep them safe for now. They will remind me about the men I helped trying to go home after the war and of the men who didn't make it," Sara said.

"The only downfall I see from it is everyone trying to court me." She laughed.

"Isn't there anyone that may look good to you?" Amber asked.

"This tavern was a dream of mine, and when Charles and I decided to marry, it became a hope for our future. I will not give that away to anyone," Sara said.

"Well, that's a shame, some soap and water and some of these boys could be right handsome." Amber laughed.

They returned to the tavern to get ready for the afternoon meal when they heard a rowdy noise outside. They both ran out to find a mob of people carrying around a man on a board who was stripped of his clothing, they had boiling hot tar poured over him, and the crowd was tossing feathers and dirt at him. Sara, who always had her gun on her, fired into the air, causing the shouting and chaos to stop.

"What do you think you are doing to this poor man?" she shouted.

"He is a Tory who is trying to return to Princeton. We are just giving an example to those traitors who think they can return," one man shouted back.

Sara then pointed her gun at the crowd. "You will let this man down at once. You have made your point," she called.

"No, I think one more ride around town is needed," another man called out. She took aim and fired at the ropes binding the man cutting him loose.

"Let him down now!" she commanded.

As the men carrying him set him down, another man called, "She's a Tory lover!"

When the crowd started to get noisy again, she fired into the air one more time. Amber ran into the tavern to get another gun and more ammunition as Sara was now running low. "Each and every one of you knows who my father was and what happened right there," Sara said, pointing at the ground where they stood. "You also know I fought with the men who recaptured this town when those redcoats took it. I have no love loss for the king or anyone who fights against our freedom. However, from what you have told me, this man's only crime was siding with the British and wanting to live. If he committed a war crime and aided the enemy, hand him over to Congress. If not, hand him over to me," she said firmly.

The crowd started to murmur that they had their fun and would just let this man go. They also agreed Sara was not someone not to mess with, and if this man had anything to do with killing her family or people within this town, she would be the first in line to shoot him. Once the crowd dispersed, Sara and Amber carefully walked the man to the back of the tavern and sat him on the grass. The Fishers did not want anything to do with the mob and decided to return to Annis's and keep away from the tavern for a while. Sara had the boys hang a closed sign out front on the door. Then they had Tom bring them buckets of cool water from the well to cool the tar so they could try to remove it. The man was in so much pain, for the hot tar he was in shock and could not say anything.

"Tommy, go to my bedroom, under my bed you will find a black bag. Bring it to me please," Sara said, not looking at the boy. What he came out with was a medical bag Dr. Madder gave her with some supplies. He knew she could be a good doctor if there was ever a need, and this truly was.

Once the tar cooled down enough to start, cracking she took a scalpel and started pulling the tar off the skin. Some of the tar was taking skin and hair with it, and Sara would try to cut those areas to help remove the tar and leave as much of the man as possible. After several hours, they had finally removed most of the substance, leaving plenty of large holes in the man's skin. In the bag was the substance for the salve they used on Tom's back along with directions on how to make more. She started to apply the mixture, and Amber wrapped the wounds, like they did with Tom. Once the man was fully bandaged, Tom carried him into the boys' bedroom and placed him on one of the beds. The boys picked up their belongings and brought them into their parents' room while Amber tried to comfort the man. Sara and Tom went out to the kitchen and mixed up as much of the salve and herb tea as they could.

"I can't believe they did such a thing," Sara said as she was stirring some of the herbs.

"When folks are angry, they can do just about anything," Tom said. "It makes the mind wonder where such hateful thoughts come from to want someone else to hurt that much," he said.

"And what is worse is they feel justified in what they are doing," Sara added.

Sara was returning to the injured man when she heard a knock at the door. "We are closed!" she shouted.

"Sara, it's me, Annis," came the voice from the other side. Sara unlocked the door and let her in. "I just found out what happened, is there anything I can do?" Annis asked.

"I'm not sure, his injuries are bad. If he staves off infection, he will recover," Sara said.

They walked into the room, and Annis screamed at the sight of the man. The wrappings, which were already turning bloody, covered most of the man's head and torso. There was enough of the face showing that Annis was able to identify him.

"Why, that's Adam Wells. He moved in a few months after you left with your father. Never harmed a fly. He was a bit quiet but helped anyone in need," Annis said.

"Why did everyone take him as a Tory?" Sara asked.

"My guess is because he did help the injured men when Princeton was invaded, they just decided that is where his allegiance is," Annis stated.

Sara kept the tavern closed as they cared for Adam. Tom would still prepare and cook food for anyone who needed it, but the bar and beds were not available. The three ladies took turns changing the bandages and helping Adam drink the tea. Once the shock wore off, Adam was able to thank them for helping him.

"What did they do with my family?" he asked.

"I don't know. We will try to find them," Sara said.

Annis went to his farm and found his house and stock was taken over and his family forced off. She was not sure where they were at this point but did her best to find them without letting anyone know she was looking. When he found out they were missing, he tried to get up to look for them.

"We will find them, I promise. But you will not do them any good if you don't let your skin heal," Sara told him.

That evening there was a small knock at the back door. When Tom opened the door, a woman and a child were huddled outside.

"Please, sir, I believe my husband was taken here?" she questioned.

"Your name!" Tom requested.

"Beverly Wells," she provided, backing up.

"Your husband is here, please come in." Tom opened the door wider for her. She was taken to Adam and ran to his bedside in tears.

"I can't thank you enough for taking care of him," Beverly said.

Sara walked up behind her and gently rubbed her back. "And who do we have here," Sara said, talking to the little girl hugging her mother.

"This is Darlene," Beverly answered.

"Tommy, why don't you take Darlene here to a table and get her something to eat please?" Sara told him.

When they left the room, she continued, "He will be fine. He still has wounds from the tar removal, but they are starting to heal," Sara said.

"I'm fine now, dear, I just needed to see you and Darlene," Adam said.

Amber went to get some food for Beverly and Adam. When she returned, they left the couple alone.

By the next day, Adam was sitting up and moving gingerly. Overnight they decided to leave the following evening and head to Beverly's family down south. Sara tried to convince them to stay even just a bit longer, but they did not want her to jeopardize her tavern any more than she had. After some discussion, she decided to give up on convincing them and changed the questions.

"So what happened?" she asked.

"I don't know," Adam said. "I was working on the farm when a mob came and attacked me. They stripped me down and painted the tar on me. They were yelling to take it back. I am not sure why or what they felt I took."

"Darlene and I were in the woods picking berries. When we heard the mob, it was too late to help him. They already had him on a board and were lifting him into—" She cut off and started crying again. When she regained her composure, she started up again. "We hid in the woods and hoped for his return. When that didn't happen, I thought they might have killed him. Then I saw Annis running here and hoped," she said.

The rest of the day, they collected items for the Wells to take with them. Some blankets, eggs, dried meat, and bread. As they were preparing to depart, Sara said, "No one deserves this, I am so sorry."

"Sorry for what? You saved my life, I am forever grateful," Adam said. They all walked out, and Sara pointed them in the direction she traveled to cross the Delaware.

They waited another two days before reopening the tavern. She didn't want anyone to try and track them down. She figured it would be slow to rebuild the reputation of the tavern, but the want for food and drink was greater than the anger about a possible Tory. Besides, since some days had passed, most of the anger disappeared. However, Sara would not allow anyone inside the bar to discuss the incident. After a while, other topics around the country became more important. There were some major changes happening in New York that Sara attributed to the fact that Hamilton was there. New York passed a law called the Trespass Act. This allowed the Patriots who returned home to New York to demand back payment from the Tories that took over their property during the war.

"This has got to be why I haven't heard from Hamilton lately," Sara mumbled as she read a newspaper. There was also talk about a new bank being built that would acquire and pay for the loans from overseas. They also published the exchange rate based on each form of currency being used in each state. "This is going to help me out a lot."

"I knew it would get worse before it gets better, but this is ridiculous," Sara said to Amber one afternoon following the meal. "I am so glad he posted these exchanges, but this is still out of control," she said, looking at four different types of currency. "Not to mention the laws that are completely different from one colony to the next. Heaven forbid, I shoot the wrong animal at the wrong time in Pennsylvania," she complained.

"What's that, dear?" Amber questioned.

"Oh, nothing, Amber, I am just angry with the state of things again," Sara said. "Do you think it was better under British law? I mean, at least there was law even though it was not right," Amber asked.

"Absolutely not! I just wish our Congress would actually accomplish something instead of just acting like they are trying." Sara stated.

Chapter 20

A Safe Place

The year pressed on but did not improve much with the colonies. They were still divided on how they wanted to run things. The bank started to default on the loans with no real way to collect funds. If each town did not have their own laws, Sara believed the colonies would start fighting each other. Finally, in late January, Sara received a very encrypted letter from Hamilton.

My dearest Sara,

I cannot explain, but I am in need of your presence. Please join me as soon as you as you are able.

A. Ham.

This letter scared Sara into action. She told Amber she wasn't sure how long she would be away and to take care of things for her. She packed a small bag and was on her way north. She rode Storm a bit harder than she normally would but was worried about what she would find at the end of her ride. When she came upon New York, the city looked completely different. With no redcoats, it could have been peaceful. However, most of the buildings were still destroyed from cannonballs and wartime destruction. She found Hamilton's home on Wall Street and knocked on the door.

"Sara, how wonderful to see you. How is everything going?" Eliza asked.

"I was going to ask you the same thing. Hamilton wrote to me to come here," Sara said, a bit confused.

"We are going well. I am not sure what he wanted. But please come in," Eliza said.

They talked all afternoon until Hamilton returned. "Good evening, dear, how was your day?" he asked Eliza before noticing Sara.

"Well, hello there, how are you doing?" he asked.

"Did you send for me or do I have to worry about my tavern?" Sara asked, handing him the letter.

"Yes, I did. There is a meeting next week that I would like you to attend," he asked.

"A meeting, this is all about a meeting? You terrified me with this letter," Sara yelled.

Hamilton laughed. "I didn't mean to worry you, but the fact that there is a meeting is not known," he said.

"Well, I am here now. I might as well stay for this meeting," Sara grumbled.

"Good, then let's eat," he said, then walked away.

Sara just looked at Eliza, hoping for help, but there was none coming.

Sara and Eliza spent the next week enjoying each other's company. Philip, now two, was a big brother to little Angelica, born in September '84.

"I am sorry I didn't write about her. I just got caught up in the days," Eliza said.

"I didn't write to you either, so please don't worry about it," Sara told her. They would take the children on short walks as it was the beginning of February and enjoyed the interaction between the children. You could tell just how much Philip doted on his little sister. He would get her toys and blankets to help calm her when she cried.

"He is such a wonderful child, Eliza," Sara said.

"He is my pride, that is for sure," Eliza said.

"If he is going to have all the looks and charisma of his father, you need to give him the Schuyler obedience." Sara laughed.

Occasionally Theodosia would join them for a sewing circle and let the children play. Sara would even cook some meals Tom taught her so they could enjoy an afternoon with their kids. She wasn't as good as Tom, but it still came out good enough for everyone to compliment her. One evening after work Hamilton came in and told Sara to get her coat, he kissed Eliza, and the two were off, telling her they would be late.

"Am I finally going to find out what all the secrecy is?" she asked as they left the house.

"Shh, we still need to be quiet right now," he said, walking her down the road.

They finally arrived at a house that was lit up and didn't seem to have the precautions that Hamilton was pushing. When they entered, there was a large group of people talking and looking around at everyone else.

"If this is a party, why didn't you take your wife?" she questioned Hamilton.

"It is not a party, it is a meeting regarding slavery and how to end it," he finally told her.

She looked again and noticed there were a number of colored people around the room. She also started to recognize some people like John Jay.

The people gave her questioning looks, and Hamilton assured them that she had the same intentions. Sara was a bit overwhelmed with this meeting and what everyone was saying. The strange part to Sara was there were slave owners among the group who wanted to see slaves get their freedom, just not theirs, at least not now. They decided to work on getting the laws changed so the sale of any person would be unlawful, and anyone who was a slave would gain their freedom when they turned a certain age. That age had yet to be determined. They also started a collection to provide financial and legal help to any person seeking manumissions to get the help they needed. There was talk about how to enforce a law making it illegal for someone from the south to take any person from the north and bring back as a slave. This would protect any free man as well as any slave who made their way north.

Finally, they started to discuss how to help people escape the South. Some people talked about how former slaves were able to escape using safe locations to hide and rest. They found some volunteers who were preparing to return to the south and guide runaway slaves to the North.

"We are going to need some more people to help guide folks, and we also need safe houses along the way. This was a way to do something now, and Sara offered her tavern as help. I knew you would want to help but being a stop along this line is extremely dangerous," Hamilton whispered to her.

"If these people are willing to get beaten, tarred, or even worse to have a chance at freedom, I am willing to take the chance and help them get through," she said. She showed them where the tavern was located and just how to navigate the woods to get there. There was a plan put into place that a note would be delivered to Sara with encrypted details of an expected date of arrival, how many are expected, and who was leading. She would put one lamp up at night when it was safe to enter and two lamps when it was not.

When they arrived back at the house, Hamilton asked Sara if she really wanted to put herself and her tavern in the line of fire like this. He thought she would want to help, which is why he invited her but didn't expect her to offer what she did.

"After seeing a man branded because he was black, a woman beaten trying to be free, and finally someone tarred trying to help other people and he was saved from hanging because he was white. I can't just sit by and let my country do this. I am so glad you invited me to this meeting," Sara said.

"Is everything all right?" Eliza asked, coming downstairs hearing them enter.

"Yes, dear," Hamilton said. "Tonight was a meeting discussing how to abolish slavery," he said. "It is going to be a challenge and take time. It is also going to be dangerous. We all have family who accept and enjoy the business of slavery. Until it is abolished, we need to be careful, *all* of us," he said, looking at Sara when he did.

When she returned to Princeton, Sara pulled Tom and Amber down into the basement and told them what happened. She decided on the ride home to have him build a fake wall where the barrel room was. That way, if anyone came looking, even those who built the tavern, they would not know there was a secret room hiding people. Sara also decided to keep this endeavor to themselves and not include the Fishers after what happened with Adam. She said they would move people in and out after the Fishers retired for the evenings. Tom and Amber were in agreement with Sara trying to help people escape, but they would be putting their own family in danger. Sara wanted them to take time to decide what they wanted to do, and if they decided to move on, she would fully understand. They, however, decided to stay put and help her out. They ordered stone and mortar to build the wall, but Sara would start with a small wall in front to explain the materials. It took them three months to fully build the wall and secret entrance into the room. Sara and Amber quilted blankets to lay on the floor for people to try to get comfortable. Once they were ready, she sent a letter to Hamilton.

Dear Hamilton,

> *I went for a ride today and found a cave I never saw before. You know me, I couldn't help but enter and found it large enough to hold a few bears and cubs. I wouldn't be surprised if this fall a few families would take refuge there. If you would like to go hunting with me, I will show you where it is.*

> *Your friend,*
> *S. Weinstein*

She sent this letter out the next day so the group would know she will be ready in the fall. Then they just went about their daily lives waiting for the first request. She received the first letter in September of that year.

Dear Sara,

I just had to write to you today. I saw two couples walking down the street today enjoying the weather. I overheard them saying their special delivery was due in late September. I guess they are having a baby.

It reminded me of when you tried to hide the fact you knew about Eliza. That day we went for a ride and did not have a care in the world. Do you remember that time in the middle of the war? Jason would accuse us of taking advantage of Washington's good graces, but we didn't care.

Your friend,
A. Ham.

"What is the secret of the letter? How do you know it is telling you something about a runaway?" Amber asked.

"Well, there is a part of the letter that tells me there are clues within the letter. Once I notice that, I know to look. This letter is telling me there are five people coming in late September. The person leading them is Sampson," Sara said.

"All that is in this letter?" Amber questioned.

"It is based on the encryptions my father would send me as a child. If you don't know what you are looking for, it looks like a regular letter," she said.

During the last two weeks in September, Sara would put either one or two candles in her window. Finally, they received a knock on the back door, and Sara answered it. "Who is there?" she called.

"Sampson," called a deep voice from behind the door.

She opened the door and ushered in the six people she had been expecting. She led them down to the cellar quietly and moved the barrels leading to the hiding place. Once everyone was inside, she told them she would be right back with food. Tom and Amber had already started on bowls of stew and bread for everyone and headed down to the cellar.

"I'll get the mead and be right with you," Sara said, passing them in the hallway.

When she returned, the group was already discussing their journey. "They almost found us in Delaware, but we made it," one person was saying.

"Thank you for this," someone else offered.

Sampson just sat in the corner, looking weary. "Is everything all right?" Sara asked him.

"We had a few close calls, and getting across the river was harder than I figured," he said.

"Well, you rest here as long as you need before starting again," she offered.

When they said good night, Sara and Tom replaced the barrels so you couldn't see the door.

The very next day, they were introduced with the dangers of this endeavor. Three men with rifles stormed into the tavern, yelling, "WHERE ARE THEY?" Sara marched over, demanding to know who these people were and why they were barging into her facility.

"The runaways, I know they came this direction. Where are they?" he demanded again.

"There are no runaways here, so you can just show yourself out," Sara demanded back.

"You think you can toss me out?" he said in a huff.

Before he could finish his sentence, Sara had her gun cocked and on his forehead. "Now I just cleaned these floors, but I will do it again if you don't simmer down," she said urgently. The other two men stood completely, still not wanting their friend shot.

"Hold on, miss, my property is missing and we tracked them here. Now I want to see if they are here. No need to get hasty," he said, holding up his hands.

"Well, this is my property, and I am not the one barging through the doors hollering like a banshee. And now you're calling me hasty?" she questioned, forcing the gun into his head pushing him backward.

"I guess we came in a bit loud and I am sorry about that," he began to say as one of the other men started to move behind Sara. Before he could place his second step, she had the second gun up, cocked, and pointed at that man's head. "And I got one on you, sir," Tom said from behind her holding the shotgun.

"Who's he?" one of the men asked.

"That is my cook and bodyguard," Sara replied.

"You need a bodyguard?" another man questioned.

"Curious, isn't it?" she said, just staring at the first man.

"Can we start over please?" the first man asked.

"Let's try," she stated.

"Hello, ma'am, I am looking for some runaway property of mine and wanted to know if you saw anything?" he asked.

"Well, why didn't you say so," she stated, lowering her guns. "I haven't seen anyone. How about you, Tom? Did you see anyone?" she asked.

"No one, ma'am," Tom answered.

"Now I can't say anything about the woods, can't see two yards into them even on a bright day," she stated.

"Would you mind if I take a look around?" the first man asked.

"Sure, I will take you anywhere you want to go," Sara offered.

They walked into every bedroom upstairs and behind the bar. They went out in the kitchen area and barn. Then he asked if they had a basement in the tavern. "Yes, we do," Sara said and walked them down there. As they looked around, they wanted to know what was in the room in the back. She opened the door revealing the barrels of whisky, rum, and beer. Able to keep calm while he looked around, they did not see the door to the hidden room.

"I am so sorry I intruded that way, miss. I thought you might be hiding them," the man said.

"Well, maybe if you remember that the next time you try to assume what is going on, you will enter with a smile," Sara said, walking the men upstairs and out of their tavern. They did not even look into the secret room all day just in case they were still around somewhere watching. When darkness took over the area, Sara finally went to the room to check on everyone. They were worried but safe, and she let them out. They were each handed a bag with dried meat, bread, cheeses, and a wineskin of rum. Sara walked the perimeter of her property to make sure no one was there before the group ran toward the woods. "Good luck and Godspeed," she said. Then they disappeared into the darkness.

"I don't know how you did that. I was so scared when those men showed up. And you walked them right next to those folks," Amber said.

"Well, that was nothing compared to being in the trenches with cannon fire all around. Besides, if you don't act worried, the enemy will not assume you have anything to hide," Sara said.

As the search for runaway slaves continued, there were more inspections of the tavern, but no one noticed the shortened wall in the basement. They were able to pass four to five people through every couple months, and after a while, no one looked for the run-aways in the tavern anymore. Even the Fishers never questioned if they were hiding anyone. Though to be honest, Sara wasn't sure if that was because they tried to stay out of things or they really didn't know. She made sure they were careful with every new life traveling along the path.

Chapter 21

Rumours, Congress and the Trial

As the town continued to grow, Sara began to feel eyes on her back. She heard whispers in the distance only to have silence when she turned to locate the intruding noise. It seemed the new young ladies of the town have decided a woman owning a tavern was not acceptable and would soil her reputation. At first, she did her best to just ignore the criticism surrounding her, but then it took on a very different tone. The talk went from her being improper for not having a husband to her tavern being a brothel. This drove some customers away and unfortunately others to her tavern, which she promptly turned away. Even the Fishers, who knew there was nothing improper or immoral going on within the tavern, decided to continue south for a new life.

"How do you fight a rumor?" Sara complained to Annis one evening. "There is nothing there that would allude to it being a brothel, but no one cares about proof. Just because some self-centered old bitty decided to make a comment, I lose my livelihood," she said.

"They just can't let a woman be successful," Annis said. "I think they see you as a threat."

"Who am I a threat to?" Sara said, getting angrier.

"You are a threat to their way of life, you are different, and people do not like different," Annis stated.

"Why did we spend all the time fighting for our freedom if we were not going to change anything? That doesn't make any sense," Sara said as she got up and started pacing.

"We will figure something out, I promise," Annis told her and gave her a hug.

Sara went about her daily business as she tried to decide what to do next. However, it seemed some of her more prominent allies decided to help out. The men from Congress started to utilize her rooms as they traveled through. They even had their families with them at times. Men like John Adams, John Jay, James Maddison, and even George and Martha Washington finally made it to the tavern. It seemed they heard about the rumors and wanted to set things straight. Thankfully it provided the credibility she so desperately needed to move past the tales. Typically, these men and women would not even look at this location with the type of rumors floating around about it. Since they stayed there, any noise of misconduct was whipped away. Some talk was still out there and talked about, but less and less people believed them now. That being said, this caused a stain between Sara and the ladies of Princeton from then on. She would not be able to forgive them for trying to sabotage her home.

She would limit her travels in the town to the general store and Annis home. She felt truly betrayed and wanted nothing else to do with the town. At this point, she didn't even try to be nice to anyone. She just went about her business without a word. She began to take afternoon rides with Storm through the woods to escape the town. She relished this time to be quiet and alone, so much so that her rides began to get longer and longer. After one such lengthy ride, when she returned to the tavern, she was greeted by a familiar voice.

"Ah, there she is. I have been waiting for you," Hamilton called out.

"What are you doing here?" she questioned, giving him a hug.

"Haven't you heard? I am back in politics and heading to Maryland," he said. "I have been elected to the New York Legislature," he explained.

"You just can't keep away, can you?" She laughed.

"No, I guess not," he said and continued, "Well, since I started the bank in New York, I guess they felt I would be able to negotiate interstate trade."

"Don't they already know you can negotiate a pig to give himself up to slaughter?" she said.

He just shook his head and asked, "So how are things here? Are they any better?"

"Are you the reason the men from Congress started showing up?" she asked.

"Well, I did mention this nice place to stop between Philadelphia and New York to a few people," he suggested.

"Thank you so much. I truly didn't know what I would have done without you helping like that," she said.

"Hey, I just said for them to stop by, you are the one creating the atmosphere and enjoyment they found," he told her.

She decided to walk him back to her apartment sitting room so they could talk without private topics being overheard. "I can't stay in Maryland too long this trip, though," he said with a smile.

"Eliza is expecting our third next month!" he told her.

"Congratulations!" she said, hugging him. "You two just can't stay away from each other, can you?" she commented.

"What can I say, she is like a sweet poison to me that I can't ignore for too long." He chuckled. "So how is everything going with you?" he asked.

They talked about the way Sara was removing herself from the town, his possibilities in this new political arena, as well as many other topics. It reminded both of them of their time in George's family and of what they gained and lost. Their conversations took them well into the evening before they decided to retire for the night. Instead of sending Hamilton through the tavern at this late hour, she had him remain on her couch while she went to her room.

He decided to remain there a few days before continuing to Maryland. Every day they would take a ride together and enjoy the land now that the bloodstains have washed away.

"Aren't you afraid the town will start talking again?" he asked.

"I don't care what the town thinks of me anymore. I am done with them," Sara stated boldly.

"You can't cut yourself off like that, Sara, it is not good for you to do that," he said, worried.

"And that from someone who will not allow himself to be truly seen since Laurens died," she said back.

That comment made him angry. "What could you possibly mean by that?" he yelled.

"When you are with your family or me, I see the man that I met walking into the hospital to see how his friend was doing. But when anyone else is there, it is like you become this different person altogether. Don't tell me I am not allowed to protect myself from these insignificant people when you are doing the same thing," she said. He remained quiet for a few minutes before she continued. "It is all right that you are doing it. I understand where you are coming from. Just don't judge me for doing the same thing," she said.

When it was time for Hamilton to move on, there was a sadness that surrounded Sara she could not explain. It was not like she wasn't expecting him to continue on like he had done so many times before. She figured this time was different because of how closed off to the world she had become. He knew the sting of doing what is right and getting falsely accused all too well. He was a breath of fresh air, and she felt some peace and joy for the first time since the accusations. She was in her sitting area and began to feel truly alone. From here, she could hear the chatter happening in the tavern but had no desire to be included with the sounds. "

I've been here before," she told herself quietly.

"I can't allow myself to become depressed again. I don't want that." She picked up the blanket Hamilton had used the night before and wrapped herself in it. She lay down on the couch and told herself she would pick herself up tomorrow, but for tonight, she will just be.

The following morning, Sara finally emerged from her apartment. "Could you use a coffee?" Amber asked.

"That would be wonderful, thank you so much," Sara said, then asked, "Did everything go all right last night?"

"It was a typical evening here. Did you get the rest you needed?" Amber asked.

"I didn't rest much, but I did start to recover. I can't thank you enough for allowing me to have that time," Sara said.

"I decided something last night that involves you and Tom. Is he around?" she asked.

"He is outside, I will get him," Amber said.

They returned, looking very nervous, and sat down with Sara.

"Don't look so worried. What I want to tell you is good news. I have decided to give you the tavern after I am gone," she said.

"What do you mean gone, Sara?" Amber asked, worried about her.

"When I die, which I hope is none too soon," Sara said. "You helped me get it up and running and take care of it when I am unable to. It belongs to you as much as to me," she said.

Tom and Amber just looked at each other, confused yet happy.

"I do hope you will accept," Sara said.

"Before we can accept, I need to know if you are all right. I know it has been rough, and you needed time, but we are very worried about you," Tom said. "Then spending time alone with Mr. Hamilton like you did right after the accusations, well, you are just encouraging the whispers," he added.

"My relationship with Hamilton is my business," she shouted angrily.

"I know your relationship with him is your business, and I also know how you both feel about each other. If anyone questioned your honor, he would be the first to come to your aid. I am not questioning that. I just witnessed the hurt you took on from those rumors and want to help," he pushed.

"I have been down this road many times before, and this will not be the last time. I can pick myself up, dust myself off, and move forward. But I do thank you for wanting to help. If there is anything I need from either of you, I will ask," She stated.

"As long as you allow us that, we accept," Amber said.

Sara noticed as she worked the bar over the next few days that she was able to communicate with everyone, but she also kept herself distant. This made her conversations seem cold and uncaring. She started to understand a bit more of her friend. When Hamilton lost Laurens, he lost a part of himself as well. That friendship and trust allowed him to show sides of his personality to others without being afraid of getting hurt. Even if other people despised who he was, Laurens would always be there for him. Now that part of him was totally exposed and vulnerable. For Sara, when they attacked her tavern and tarnished it because she was not married, they were attacking Charles. If he had survived, no one would have suggested anything because it would have been his tavern, not hers. She was also feeling exposed and vulnerable and did everything she could to protect that part of her. She decided she would never question Hamilton about it again.

As politicians and families started moving between the colonies more, the tavern started to regain the popularity it had prior to the comments. One afternoon, a gentleman came in with his wife and two young daughters. Sara asked if they were there to dine with or without a room for the evening.

"It is still a few hours to get to Philadelphia, and I do believe my wife could use a break from the buggy for the night," he said.

"Sure, we have a wonderful cook and can make you comfortable for the evening so you can be ready to restart your journey," Sara said as she took the family to a table. "Where are you coming from?" she asked.

"Boston," the older child replied.

"What have I told you about intruding on a grown-up conversation," the father snapped.

"Well, that was a long ride, wasn't it," Sara replied, smiling at her.

"Yes, it was, I'm Julie," the child said, extending her hand.

"Well, hello, Julie, I am Sara. It is very nice to meet you," she answered.

"Julie, hush up now. I am sorry she is a bit chatty and forgets herself sometimes," the mother said.

"It is all right. I don't mind talking with her if you don't," Sara said.

Julie took that opportunity to jump back into the conversation. "I saw the sign outside. What is a Pon...Pon..."

"Phoenix!" Sara provided.

"Yes, what is that?" Julie asked.

"Well, a phoenix is an ancient mythical bird that would burst into flames when it was time for it to die, then it would be reborn from the ashes," Sara said.

Julie's eyes got as big as pounds and all she could say was "Wow!"

"I will be right back with some food," Sara said as she started to walk away.

She returned with some meat, potatoes, and bread for everyone. "Miss Sara, why is this place named after a bird?" Julie asked.

"Well, when I was little, I lived in a house that was right where this tavern is. One night it caught on fire and burnt down to the ground. When I decided to rebuild and created this tavern," Sara said but was cut off.

"It was born from the ashes like the bird," Julie said. "So this place belongs to you?" she asked.

"Yes, this is all mine," Sara said.

"Where is your husband?" she questioned.

"Julie, mind your manners," her mother squealed.

"I was never married. My fiancé was killed in the war before we could get married," Sara said.

"I am so sorry to hear that," the mother said.

"Thank you, ma'am," Sara replied.

"And you take care of this all by yourself?" the father asked.

"Well, the Johnsons help me take care of everything," Sara said, pointing out Amber.

"You mean your slaves?" Julie asked with a frown.

"They are not my slaves. They are a free family that helped me start this place," Sara said boldly, changing Julie's frown into a smile.

"Tom, the one who cooked this meal for you, was the man who pulled Dr. Madder out of a burning barn and was injured. But I don't know if that news made it all the way to Boston," Sara added.

"So everyone from here was reborn from the ashes." Julie smiled.

"Very much so, Julie. Very much so," Sara said.

When everyone was in their rooms or left for the evening, Amber asked Sara about the family she met. "That is the first time in a long time I have seen you open up to someone. It was a little girl, and it was nice to see," she said.

"The little girl spoke out of turn, was interested in things that were different and seemed very much like I was at that age." Sara giggled. "It was like talking to my younger self."

"Well, did you warn her that when she grows up, she will turn into a stick in the mud." Amber laughed.

"I didn't want to ruin the surprise." Sara laughed back.

The next day that family rode out, and another came in their place. It got to the point where the families passing through all seemed the same. Little Julie was the last stand-out that Sara could remember. The congressmen, however, were much more recognizable. They would ride through every other week or so to go home to their families, then back to whatever political matter that was taking place that day. That basically explained the next few months. Eventually, Sara started to reengage herself with what was going on in the land.

As the men came through from Congress and were talking among themselves, she would hear bits and pieces of what was taking place. Sometimes she got information regarding plans like the discussion of turning the colonies into states. Other times she would just hear about this one man from up north that would talk for hours trying to create his own vision of what the country should be. She could only assume they were talking about Hamilton and just laugh. Sometimes they would be so despondent with his propositions they would come right out and talk about him without holding anything, including his name, back. The next time he passed through town, she would have to tell him to allow others to talk every now and then.

That time came soon after as he was bringing a friend to New York to discuss some things. He introduced her to James Maddison. A Southern gentleman with a certain amount of charm behind his eyes. He was small, soft-spoken, and very charismatic, reminding her a bit of Washington.

"What part of the South do you typically reside in?" Sara asked.

"These days, I enjoy removing my hat in Orange County, Virginia," he told her. "However, when I was a youth, I used to take up my studies just down the road here," he added.

"You went to the College of New Jersey?" she asked, a bit intrigued.

"Why yes, right up until the war that is when I became a colonel in the Orange County militia."

"That is why you are so familiar to me, sir," she said.

"Why, what do you mean by that, miss?" he asked.

"My father was commissioned to help recruit and train the Orange County militia along with the other militia in Virginia," she said.

"May I ask your name again?" he questioned.

"Sara Weinstein, daughter of General George Weinstein," she provided proudly.

"Why yes, I do recall hearing about your father. I am sorry we lost him the way we did. He was a good man," he offered.

"Thank you for that," she replied. "Did you see many battles during the war?" she questioned.

"Unfortunately, my constitution is not good for military life, and so I represented Virginia at the constitutional convention," he said. "For that endeavor I worked with my good friend Thomas Jefferson."

"Oh yes, he is now in France with Lafayette, isn't he?" she asked, looking at Hamilton.

"Yes, I do believe I received a letter telling me that as well," Hamilton answered.

"And now the two of you are working together to provide our experiment a solid base to stand on," she said.

"Why yes, we are, miss. The two of us have found common ground where that situation resides," he said.

"Well, I hope the two of you can do as well with setting up our government as Mr. Jefferson did with the Declaration of Independence. We are all depending on you," she said.

Hamilton was getting excited as this conversation began to grow, and Sara became a bit worried about it. She also took notice that Mr. Madison was looking weary and asked if he needed to rest. "I am starting to feel a bit weary and would like to retire," he said. She showed him to his room and returned to Hamilton, knowing he is going to want to talk for a few hours more.

As she predicted, he went right into plans for the government just like they did while in the army. "I want to caution you about this, Hamilton," she said softly.

"This is no time for caution, we need to move forward," he replied.

"Just give me a moment. Please. I have heard a lot of talk about you trying to bully your ideals around. You are the new face to politics, and they don't want to deal with it. Now if you have someone on your side like Madison, who is soft-spoken and has been around politics for a while, he may be able to get your ideas passed a bit smoother," she said.

"So you think I should stop talking and just let him take over?" he asked.

"That is impossible for you to do, so I would never ask that of you. So what I am proposing is for you to take some points from him on how to get things done without angering everyone. I am glad you found someone to work with again," she said with a smile. He looked up and smiled back, then went right back into discussing his ideas.

As he usually does when he is this excited about a topic, Hamilton talked all evening until the sun began to rise. When Maddison joined them, he gave one look to Sara and chuckled. "You allowed him to have your ear all evening, didn't you?" he questioned.

"It's nothing I haven't done before or will do again if he needs," Sara said.

"Excuse me, but do you mind?" Hamilton stated like they were interrupting him. "I was thinking last night and wanted to know what you felt about this proposition. It seems very wrong that we are holding these meetings, creating our country in Maryland. They should be somewhere significant. Now since Yorktown was destroyed and Virginia and New York are still coming back from the British takeover, it should be Philadelphia, am I right?" he stated. Hamilton rarely asked anything or anyone's opinion.

"There is something to be said by that good sir. I will think about it a bit longer," Madison said.

"The problem with Congress, always thinking, never doing," Hamilton interrupted.

"Alexander!" Sara said abruptly. He just looked at her and nodded.

The two men were on their way within the hour after a warm breakfast. "You look absolutely fatigued," Amber said, looking at Sara.

"It was a very long evening, but I cherish those nights the most," Sara said, wiping down the bar. "It warms my heart to see and hear him that optimistic about our future. It gives me strength to endure the day and all the challenges it brings."

Luckily for Sara, the day was typical and uneventful. She was able to go about her daily activities with a bit of a spring in her step. Even her interactions with her customers were more cheerful. By the end of the evening, Amber just had to ask her if Hamilton could stop by more often to help keep her happy. Sara just laughed and said she would be moving away from her anger and just worry about the tavern.

She was only able to keep half of that promise, however. One morning she was going over some articles in a paper with Tom and Amber.

"Oh my, someone made a balloon large enough to carry them into the air!" Sara exclaimed.

"You're trying to mess with me." Tom laughed.

"No, it's right here. They were flying above the English Channel," she said.

"If God had wanted people to fly, he would have given them wings," Amber said. "They are going to upset the order of things by doing that," she finished.

Sara continued to look through the paper and found a small finance section. This area was mostly used to update the rate of exchange that day or place ads for selling goods. "It seemed that our government is hiring people to survey land they acquired from England with the Treaty of Paris," Sara said. "Now why is something like that in the finance section?" she questioned. She decided to keep an eye out for any news regarding this information.

As news came in from gossip and papers, Sara could see the work of her friends everywhere. First, to stabilize the economy, Congress agreed on one type of currency for all of the states, the dollar.

"This will make things so much easier when travelers come through here. I don't have to fumble with exchanges anymore," Sara said. There was also anger in the military of men who still had not been paid for their time fighting the British. Some had gone nine years with only broken promises to live one. Congress was trying to come up with ways to pay these men, as well as France for helping during the war, but they still had no way to raise funds. Each state was worried about taking care of itself and rebuilding after the war to collect and send funds to the government. Congress was helpless without the authority to collect taxes to support itself and the nation.

"Why would you want to start paying taxes? I thought that was why we fought the war," one man asked as Sara said her thoughts out loud.

"We did not fight so we could get rid of taxes. We fought so we had a say in our laws and government for those taxes," Sara told him. He just laughed and blamed her opinion on a foolish woman's perspective. "Really, well, how do you think we are going to defend ourselves as a nation if nobody will fight to save it because they are not going to be compensated for their time? Or how are we to take our place in the world if we cannot pay our debts back?" she argued. He had no reply to her objections, so he just scoffed and walked out the door.

Later that night, three men stormed into the tavern with their face covered and yelling at Sara to hand over her money. She refused to do so, and when one of the men came at her, she pulled out her gun and shot him between the eyes, dropping him at once. Other members of the town heard the commotion and ran to the tavern to see what was going on. At that point, Sara and another man were fighting each other hand to hand while the last man was fighting Tom. The townspeople were able to break up the fight and started to ask Sara what happened. She was still a bit angry but able to explain the events of the evening. When they removed the mask from the man on the floor, she recognized him as the one from earlier that didn't appreciate her answer. The other two men were taken into custody, and in a short time, the town quieted down from the events.

The next morning, she started to write to Hamilton when Mr. Cunnings entered the room. "Sara, I was just asked to prosecute the case against last night's robbery," he said.

"I greatly appreciate that, sir," she replied.

They discussed the full events of the evening, and Mr. Cunnings gathered his belongings to depart. "I will head to the jail and see what is happening with the men," he said as he departed.

"Sir, I shouldn't have to worry about being charged, do I?" she asked.

"Well, I do have to talk with a few more witnesses, but I don't think you have to worry about anything," he said and walked out.

Amber was bringing in a plate of food as Mr. Cunnings was leaving. "Is that man going to help you?" she asked.

"He said he can, I just hope he will," Sara said.

"You don't trust him?" Amber asked, handing over the eggs.

"Let's just say I would feel so much better if Hamilton was here," Sara stated as she started to eat.

The next morning, Mr. Cunnings arrived with more news. The two defendants were brothers named Paul and John Jacob. The man that was killed was their older brother, Abrim. "And what about me being charged with his murder?" Sara asked.

"No, everyone could see they were trying to harm you and your tavern. The killing was justified." Mr. Cunnings said. "They are being brought up on aggravated assault and theft charges."

Only a few days passed before the trial began. Sara was asked to be there as a witness and arrived early in one of the dresses Martha picked out for her. It seemed like everyone in town showed up to see this trial and hear what happened. The only seat in the entire building was for the judge; the accused would stand in a small area boxed off, and the townspeople were to stand behind a rail. The lawyers were able to walk freely in the open space before the judge. When the room was called to order, the people became quiet, and the defendants were brought into the room.

The judge entered the room, gaveled the trial into session, and asked Mr. Cunnings to start his case. Both Mr. Cunnings and the judge were wearing black robes and white powdered wigs, signifying their status in the room.

"Thank you, Your Honor. This case should not take up too much of your time. Everyone in this room already knows that Sara Weinstein is the rightful owner of the Phoenix Tavern and would protect it with her life. I am going to prove that the dead man along with these two gentlemen entered the tavern for the sole purpose to rob Mrs. Weinstein believed she was an easy target and had to deal with the wrath of her superior skills," Mr. Cunnings said, entering his opening statement.

Then the two men had their chance to give their statement since no one would defend them. "We were just riding through town with our brother and stopped into the tavern for a drink. Abrim asked the slave for a kiss when she picked up a gun from behind the bar and shot him. This woman is trying to get the bitch off by saying she shot my brother," they said. A rumble came over the crowd, and Sara could tell they were wondering if that was true.

"Well, if that is all you have to say, Mr. Cunnings, you may begin," the judge said.

"I call my first witness, Mrs. Sara Weinstein," he asked.

Sara promised to tell the truth and stood in the center of the room. Mr. Cunnings had her recount the events of the evening, starting with the arrival of Abrim earlier that evening. Then Paul Jacob walked over toward Sara and began asking her questions.

"Was there anyone else in the tavern to prove my brother was there earlier that evening?" he asked.

"Amber and Tom saw him," Sara said.

"So your only defense is the word of slaves, who cannot be trusted against me and my brother?" he stated and started to walk back to the defense box.

"IT IS THE WORD OF MYSELF AND TWO FREE ADULTS WHO WORK IN THE TAVERN. MOST EVERYONE IN THIS TOWN KNOW US TO BE

TRUTHFUL, UNLIKE TWO STRANGERS WHO TRIED TO ROB ME," Sara said aggressively. The crowd became loud and angry, some agreeing with Sara and others against.

"I will have order in the court." the judge said, hammering his gavel.

Once everyone calmed down again, Mr. Cunnings walked up to Sara, saying he wanted to ask more questions. "When was the first time you held and fired a gun?" he asked.

"Since I was three years old. My father made sure I understood how to manage all sorts of weapons," Sara said.

"And how many times have you seen Amber hold a gun and fire it?" he questioned.

Sara's face contorted a bit as she thought back. "I don't recall ever seeing Amber with any weapon," she answered.

Mr. Jacob then shouted, "ISN'T IT TRUE YOU ARE JUST TRYING TO PROTECT YOUR PROPERTY?"

"No, sir, first she is not my property, and all the words I am speaking are the truth," she said, glaring at him.

"Judge, I would like to call Mr. Samuel Stanhope Smith to the stand," he asked, trying to stop the conversation between Sara and Paul.

"You may step down, Sara, and Mr. Samuel Stanhope Smith is now called as a witness," the judge said.

Mr. Smith was a slender man with white hair. He was wearing a well-pressed black jacket, a white collar tucked into his jacket, and dark trousers. He looked very well off and was well known around town. After he agreed to tell the truth, Mr. Cunnings asked why he was well known.

"Well, I am a clergyman and a teacher at the College of New Jersey right down the street," he said.

"What is your primary field of study, sir?" Mr. Cunnings asked.

"Well, I am very proficient in mathematics, natural sciences, and theology," Mr. Smith responded.

"And would those fields of study along with your own experience allow you to explain the challenges of using a firearm?" Mr. Cunnings asked.

"Why, yes. There are a lot of outside influences that dictate the ability to accurately fire a weapon such as distance, if the target is moving, if they have a weapon pointed at you, weather factors, along with the weapon itself," Mr. Smith said.

"Then in your opinion, would someone who never used a weapon before be able to pick one up, shoot, and accurately hit a target?" Mr. Cunnings asked.

"Well, someone may be able to pick one and shoot, but accurately hitting a target is unheard of. You need years of practice to understand weaponry," Mr. Smith said. "Even if the target is right in front of you with no outside conditions, you may hit the side of the target," he finished.

Mr. Cunnings turned to talk with the judge when Mr. Jacob interrupted again. "I would like to ask a question."

"Go ahead, Mr. Jacob," the judge said.

"Isn't it true you are trying to free slaves and say these blacks are equal to us?" he asked.

"It is true that science has shown that human beings were profoundly shaped by the environment—natural and social—in which they lived," Mr. Smith said.

Mr. Jacob then turned to the people and said, "See, he is trying to say your blacks are equal, and therefore, he cannot be trusted!"

Mr. Smith remained calm and tried to explain himself. "Although I do believe we were all created equal, we were not brought up equal, and those of different backgrounds like Mr. and Mrs. Johnson and the natives need to be educated to successfully adapt to our society," he said. "In fact, I wrote an essay explaining this, and George Morgan White Eyes will be admitted to our university as a freshman this fall to prove my theory," he finished.

"Your Honor, the question that came up for this case is about who was able to accurately fire a gun to shoot Mr. Jacob between the eyes as he was charging them. It is not about Mr. Smith's essay and belief in human evolution. I recommend we have a small challenge outside as to which lady can hit the mark correctly five times," Mr. Cunnings asked.

"Yes, I do believe we are far off topic, and a target test would help us see who has a better shot," the judge answered. "Court will be adjourned for fifteen minutes until a shooting range can be set up."

As they walked out of the courthouse, Sara walked up to Mr. Smith and asked to talk with him. "Sir, I have a question if I may?" she asked.

"Sure, dear, how can I help you?" he replied.

"If I heard you correctly inside, you believe everyone is created equal, but you also believe certain people are inferior? How can that be?" she asked.

"Well, God created Adam and Eve, which created all human life after that. Where people live had changes they needed to survive their circumstances. Now some of us developed faster than others, and it is our job to bring the others up to the same level. It is not their fault they didn't learn as fast as we did," he said.

"But the natives that were here prior to our arrival and the people of color from other countries all had thriving societies, that is until we stole from them, kidnaped, tortured, and enslaved them. How could that possibly mean our society's ethics is better and more advanced than theirs. Shouldn't that mean we are more violent and self-centered than others?" she questioned.

"We get our laws from God and the Bible, now that should be enough," he replied. "Excuse me, but I do need to return to the university," he said as he left.

"Typical, you get an objection, drop everything on religion, and run away," she said.

The crowd reemerged in an open area where there were two targets and a table with firearms on the other. Sara's gun was present along with handguns donated from others around the town. It was a calm sunny afternoon, so they didn't have any wind to attest with. Finally, Amber was called to the location to take part of the test.

"Amber, I am so sorry you have to be involved with doing this," Sara said to her.

"I don't want to do this. I don't like seeing guns and don't want to touch one," Amber said, almost crying.

"It will be all right, Amber, just do your best, and it will be all right," Sara said, trying to help her calm down.

Sara then picked up her gun, made sure it was loaded, and provided it to Amber. Terrified with the weight of the weapon in her hand, Amber lifted the gun, trembling. She took a shot and missed the target. She tried again and, this time, hit the outside edge of the target. She took one more shot hitting the other edge before she dropped the gun and covered her face crying.

Sara hugged her and said, "You did good, Amber. Don't worry, you will not have to shoot it again."

Sara picked up the gun off the ground and quickly fired the next two shots hitting her target on center and just to the right of center. Then she picked up the rest of the guns and created a little circle around the center.

"Well, I think that settles who shot the gun. You are very good with weapons, Miss Weinstein," the judge said.

"Thank you, sir. My father would be happy to hear you say that," she answered.

"I have seen all I need to see here. Let's go back to the courtroom," he said.

When they returned, the judge called the room to order again and said, "Well, given the demonstration of the two ladies in question, it is clear to me that Sara was the one who took the shot that killed Mr. Jacob. This shows that the statement by the defendants of Amber Johnson firing the guns was a complete lie, so the rest of their testimony is also in question. Finally, Sara was very deliberate in saying she was the one who fired the gun. That is not something one just admits, given the risk of murder charges. I believe her testimony was truthful and believe she fired in self-defense, as these men tried to rob her. I, therefore, sentence them to five years in prison each. Court's adjourned," he said, hammering his gavel and causing a roar in the crowd.

Sara wasn't sure if the noise was positive or negative, but she didn't care. She felt vindicated but a bit frustrated. She was trying to figure out why the trial went from these men trying to rob her to find out if it were she or Amber who shot the gun. What if Amber was a better shot? Would she be put on trial for murder?

That evening, when the tavern quieted down Sara, Amber and Tom sat down and took in the events of the day.

"Well, that was a very interesting day," Sara said.

"I never want to hold a gun again," Amber pushed.

"I am so proud of you, dear," Tom said, hugging Amber.

"Can I ask both of you something?" Sara started. They both just looked at her, wondering where this conversation would be going. "I was talking with Mr. Smith, and I just don't agree with him. I mean, I believe all people are created equal, but how can a group of people who use physical force to destroy another human still claim they are following God's will? I thought God wanted man to extend a hand to their fellow man and turn the other cheek. Where does it say beat them down until they do what you say?" Sara asked.

"Well, you need to remember there is a difference between policy and religion. People will always find and twist words from their religion to empower their political beliefs. If they can convince others that their religion is guiding their political beliefs, they can obtain power. They want to say 'it is our job to cleanse the world of...' well, fill in the blanks. Most people can see past the rhetoric and understand that the Bible wasn't pushing those beliefs at all. However, there will be others who are looking for any excuse to give themselves a reason to justify immoral behavior," Tom said.

"It is sad when someone uses God's name to inflict harm on someone else," Amber said.

"I never heard you talk like this before. It is nice to hear," Sara said.

"Most people don't want to hear us talk like this. Take your professor who believes we need to be better educated to join a proper society," Tom said. "He may try to say we deserve to be treated like everyone else, but he doesn't want to believe we have anything to say that would be useful to his lifestyle," Tom continued.

"We can be educated to help his society grow, but we must stay in our place as his education would describe. I could go to that university and get an education to practice law, but I would only be privileged enough to take notes for some white lawyer. I would never be seen as intelligent enough to practice law or contribute to Congress," he said as Amber took his hand.

"Is there anything we can do to combat that type of thinking?" Sara asked.

"I don't know, but I think those who use bits and pieces of religion to push their own personal opinions will boil up and over, causing a break in society and start another war," Tom answered.

"That is scary to think about, and what is worse is I agree with you," Sara said.

Chapter 22

A Hope for change

A short time later, as Sara walked past the church headed toward Annis's, she stopped to look at the bulletin board. Some people were looking for help. Others wanted to sell something. Still, others were looking for runaways to be returned. Then she noticed a small note stating LAND FOR SALE. She began to read the note and found the US Continental Congress was auctioning off lots of land. Pennsylvania had newly created townships that were acquired from the Treaty of Paris and purchased from the Indians. *Acquiring some land from this would be an interesting investment as our country continues to grow*, she thought, taking the paper with her. When she arrived at Annis's, she began to discuss the possibility of buying some land. Annis didn't become interested in the possibility and just wanted to focus on her property. She did, however, show Sara some new poems she wrote and sent to newspapers to publish.

It started to rain on her way back to the tavern, but she couldn't stop thinking about buying some of this land. She decided to write a letter to Dr. Madder and ask him to help her. She wanted him to find out when and where the auction would take place, and she would send him the funds for the purchase. When she finished sealing the letter, a loud bang came to the back door, causing her to jump. Tom was the first to arrive and found a very wet small woman pleading for help. Tom let her in, and she explained a group of men was hunting her and close behind. Tom took her directly down to the secret room and closed her in.

Amber turned to Sara and asked, "I didn't know we were to expect anyone tonight."

"Neither did I. Just do me a favor and mop the tavern floor," Sara said, stunned as another knock came to the back door. "I will handle this," Sara stated as Amber took off. Sara opened the door holding her gun and saw seven men with rifles and ropes standing outside.

The leader put up his hands and said, "Sorry to scare you, but we are looking for a runaway. Have you seen anything?" he questioned. Sara remained quiet, just looking at him, so he continued. "I know we look rough, we have been riding for five days now, and we saw some tracks coming to your door."

"The only tracks back here belong to my hired help and myself. I should warn you, the last person who tried to rob me was shot, and he came through the front door," Sara said angrily.

"My intention is not to hurt you at all, just to find my property and get out of the rain. Would it be all right if we came to the front door?" he asked.

Sara nodded and closed the back door. She started walking through the tavern just as Amber was finishing the floors. She directed Amber to the back to get some dried meat and bread ready. The man was just short of the door when Sara opened it.

"I sent some of my men to look around town for a bit before coming back here. By the looks of the tracks out front here, you get a lot of traffic," he said.

"That we sure do," Sara said, letting him in and getting a glass of beer.

"Do you run this place all by yourself?" he asked.

"No, I have a family who helps me out. Like I said, it was most likely their footprints you saw outback," Sara said. He just looked up at her with a questioning expression on his face. "I will be right back with something for you to eat," she said, leaving the room.

She met up with Amber in the back and asked her to take off her shoes. "This man is a tracker. If he finds any footprints in here, I want him to believe they belong to you or your sons," she explained.

When she returned, other men were starting to arrive, saying they lost their quarry. Amber started bringing in bowls of dried meat and bread and went the extra length of stepping outside in the mud to track some into the tavern. The first man's eyes became very shifty, looking at everything in the area.

"So is there anyone else here?" he asked.

"We have a few guests sleeping upstairs," Sara said.

Just then, Tommy opened the door and started to call for his mother, not realizing there were people in the tavern. "I am sorry, he thought we were closed for the evening," Sara said.

She, however, noticed the man looking past the boy at the footprints behind him.

"Would you mind if I took a look around just to make sure our runaway hasn't intruded onto your property without your knowledge?" he asked.

"I don't believe anyone entered without my knowledge, but a second set of eyes is not a bad idea. Let's go," Sara said, talking the man to the back. Amber was walking Tommy back to their room, applying more footprints on the ground.

"Where would you like to start?" she asked.

He looked out back again, and the rain and mud washed away any possibility of tracking to or from the tavern. He then turned to Sara and asked what was behind the door to the left.

"That is my living area, let's go check it out," she said. After they looked around and the man felt no one was hiding inside they returned to the main room.

"Since the rain took any hopes of tracks away, do you have any rooms for us for the evening?" he asked.

"I only have two left, so you will have to share if you don't mind," she said.

"Thank you, that would be wonderful."

"Would you like to move your horses into the barn for the evening then?" she asked.

He pointed to two men having them go and take care of all the horses, then returned his focus on Sara.

One by one, the other six men retired to an upstairs room and went to bed. The only two left in the bar area now were Sara and this lead fellow.

"I didn't get your name," she questioned.

"Benjamin," he replied as she poured him another beer. His speech was starting to slur, and his eyes were glazed over from what he consumed, but he barely took his eyes off Sara. "Ya know, I believe you are hiding that bitch somewhere. I just can't figure out where," he said.

"Really, well, when you sober up, maybe you can explain to me just how I am doing that," Sara said.

"I am…gonna…find…umm, I've never seen blue eyes like yours before. They remind me of water," he said.

The next thing Sara knew was he dropped his head onto the bar and started snoring. "Well, I guess you are going to sleep there tonight," Sara said.

The next morning Benjamin lifted his head and looked around, trying to get his bearings.

"Good morning, I would ask if you slept well, but really, our beds are more comfortable than our bar," Sara said, bringing out some coffee.

He tried to look around but found he was so stiff he couldn't move very much. Then he heard the sounds and believed it to be the woman he was chasing. "Where is she? I know she is here!" he started to shout. Some of his men were beginning to come down the stairs and told him to calm down.

"It is just a couple boys out back. It is not our runaway," they said.

"Would you like some eggs before you leave?" Sara asked with a smirk on her face.

"She already has too much of a head start. We need to be on our way. I am sorry we bothered you," Benjamin said.

Sara, Tom, or Amber didn't dare to check in on the woman until late that evening. "That was the closest encounter we have had yet," Tom stated on their way down.

"Very true, we are going to need to find a way to keep trackers away from here, or something very bad is going to happen," Sara agreed.

The woman was terrified when the door reopened but happy to see Tom smiling. "We were not told you would be traveling through. How did you find us?" Sara asked.

"There are codes to all the doors along the way," she said.

Sara moved closer to talk but then took notice of the woman's feet. They were badly cut up and almost unrecognizable. Remembering her own feet, Sara went to get the salve and bandages to wrap this woman's cuts.

"What's your name?" Sara asked as she was taking care of the woman.

"I'm Patsy," she said.

"Well, Patsy, it may be quiet for long periods in here as we keep everyone away, but you can stay as long as you need for your feet to heal, all right?" Sara offered, leaving the wrappings and ointment with Patsy.

During her stay, they gathered yarn, needles, candles, blankets, and anything Patsy may have needed to keep her occupied as she healed. A few weeks went by before she was able to stand, but when she was ready, Alexander was taking his family to the North so Betsy, Philip, and Angelica could visit with her family. Sara would have the Hamiltons stay with here in here quarters whenever they stopped by. This made any and all communications easier for them to have in private.

"I am sorry to have to ask, but we have someone hiding downstairs that could use some help getting north. She injured her feet getting here, and you just may save her life taking her with you, if you don't mind," Sara asked. They were more than willing to help and decided the sooner to head out, the better.

Throughout the evening, they discussed their favorite topic—politics. There were a lot of details Hamilton would not go into for security reasons, but he told Sara what he could. More people were agreeing to move Congress to Philadelphia to better serve the nation. Slavery was still a heated topic the South would not even discuss, let alone rid themselves of. New Jersey's politics, however, brought to the attention of Congress that women were capable of owning property and voting. This topic was still a problem area with more than just the South, but at least they were willing to talk about, even if the discussions were short. They also started to develop the areas of government and what was needed. Here Hamilton was able to push more of his ideas, but Sara found they again came across incorrectly. It seemed that most of Congress believed he wanted a monarchy instead of a complete governing body. He was trying to push the idea of a solo family representative for one section of government with another by being run by the scholars and lawyers of the day, followed by yet another group run for the uneducated group of people and finally a judicial group of just judges making sure everyone else is doing their job. As much as the details were up in the air, the general hope within the room was that of optimism for their future. In the infancy of their new nation, they finally had the hope to wonder what the future would bring for all of them.

First chapter next book

1787 began with the feeling of spring. Buildings were being repaired, the government, if you can call it that, moved to Philadelphia, and the feeling among the people was of hope. Throughout this year the delegates from each state were finally updating the article of confederation. They found the need to be able to support the states as a union instead of individual provinces. They named this new document the Constitution of the United States. It was a very transparent document that allowed the people to fully understand how their new government was to be set up, how the officiants were to be elected, what positions they held, and what laws they were entitled to enforce. This document also created the need for the monarchy-type seat Hamilton had wanted. Someone outside of the core unit of government that can also make amendments, laws, and checks and balances between the remainder of government. As monumental as this document was, it would take a lot of convincing to adopt it for the nation. Soon after its finalization in the fall of 1787, newspapers started publishing the reasons the Constitution was needed and why every state needed to back it. These anonymous articles were dubbed *The Federalists Papers*, and even though there was no true name involved, Sara Weinstein recognized the tone and structure of one of the authors as Alexander Hamilton!

CPSIA information can be obtained
at www.ICGtesting.com
Printed in the USA
LVHW030445301121
704812LV00001B/39